Watch Me

Owen Keehnen

RATTLING GOOD YARNS
PRESS

Rattling Good Yarns Press
33490 Date Palm Drive 3065
Cathedral City CA 92235
USA
www.rattlinggoodyarns.com

Cover Design: Rattling Good Yarns Press

Library of Congress Control Number: 2022945465
ISBN: 978-1-955826-24-2

First Edition

Dedication

To the gay pulp fiction authors of the 1960s and 1970s—Thank you for the hours of pleasure and tawdry delight.

Thank you, Gordon Merrick.

A big thanks to the gay men of porn—I wanted to give your world a Jacqueline Susann and Harold Robbins spin.

Thanks to my mentor, John Preston, who suggested the key to a good sex scene was to write it naked or in special underwear.

As always, thank you to my husband, Carl, for your love and support.

"Everyone has an identity. One of their own, and one for show."
—**Jacqueline Susann**

1

Vincent loved the feel of being pinned to his seat as the earth moved beneath, below, and away. Looking through the ghost of himself reflected in the window, he found it hard to believe any of this was happening. Plenty of guys would kill for this chance, but the opportunity had been given to him!

Sure, there were things to consider, but he would be a fool to turn down a free trip to L.A. That was all this was so far. He hadn't done anything yet, but the more he considered it, the more he liked the idea of being desired not by one man, or two men, or even twenty, but by thousands of men.

Five years ago, or even five months ago, Vincent would not have had the nerve to board this plane or even admit the appeal of being desired by strangers. The old Vincent would have never posed for nudes. But four months ago, everything changed. Four months ago, Glenn dumped him after cheating on him with Robert for weeks.

Vincent was the last to know. He and Glenn had even attended a birthday party at Robert's place for a mutual friend. Everyone at the party had known Glenn and Robert were having an affair, yet no one had said a word. Vincent had considered several of those in attendance to be his friends. His obliviousness had undoubtedly been a great source of amusement for many of the guests.

The betrayal and humiliation had changed him. The day Glenn told him it was over, Vincent vowed never again to be anyone's fool. There were two kinds of people in the world, those who took what they wanted, and those who took what was left. Vincent was through being second best. He was going to get what he wanted. Being on this flight was proof that he had changed.

He leaned back into the headrest. A moment later, Chicago disappeared in the haze of a cloud.

2

Glenn broke up with him the week they were supposed to move in together. Vincent had suggested getting a place together on their six-month anniversary. Glenn had agreed. Vincent was excited. He thought Glenn was excited as well. Their friends thought they were rushing into things, but Vincent was confident.

He'd been disappointed before, only this time he had been so sure that he had finally found the right guy. He and Glenn had taken two vacations together and were recognized as an established couple. Supposedly they wanted the same things.

Even a storefront psychic said they would be together a long time.

We are soul mates. Vincent had actually told people that on several occasions. How long had his friends known about Glenn's philandering? When did the affair become common knowledge? Had they been secretly snickering every time they called him the lucky one?

Maybe he had been lucky, but in a way they never imagined. He'd been hurt, but he would survive, and he had learned a lot about people in the process.

Four days before the move, Glenn still hadn't started packing. Vincent had teased him a bit for procrastinating, but he thought things were fine. Vincent was right. Things were fine, only he didn't realize that "fine" was the problem. For people like Glenn, fine was not enough. Like most failed actors, a part of

Glenn was chasing an absent spotlight, wanting to be noticed, wanting to be seen. Vincent thought love would be enough, but he was wrong. Love was not adoration.

On the day they broke up, Glenn texted Vincent in the middle of his server shift at the Amethyst and asked if they could meet for coffee after work. "We need to talk."

Although the request was unusual, Vincent ignored the cryptic wording. He didn't give the text much thought aside from thinking a late-night coffee date sounded fun. Vincent replied, "Sure," and added a couple of heart emojis. Glenn did not respond to the text, but Vincent thought nothing of it. Things were fine. They were fine. There was no cause for concern.

After his last table left, Vincent tipped out, grabbed his coat, and headed to the coffee shop. He sensed something was wrong the moment he sat down. Glenn's eyes were red. His gaze was elusive. Vincent thought someone had died or Glenn had been laid off. A lot of people were being let go lately. Those things happened. They would get through it. They had each other. Vincent had ordered his coffee and was half turned to hang his coat on the back of his chair when Glenn blurted, "This isn't working."

At first, Vincent didn't understand, then suddenly, he did. He no longer felt present. He was watching himself listen to Glenn as he attempted to explain.

Glenn began to cry. Shake. He was turning this into an actor's moment.

"It's not you, it's me. I'm not ready. Moving in together and having a nice home, all that stuff. Those are things you want. Not me. I love you, but I'm not in love with you."

Vincent tried to remain calm. Glenn had cold feet. That was natural before taking a big step like moving in together. Vincent tried to level his voice. "If you're not ready we can each keep our own places for a few more months. We have options."

Glenn looked out the front window of the coffee shop. He didn't want a solution. This scene had already been scripted. "I don't want you to compromise what you want and end up resenting me. I couldn't stand that. You need someone who is looking for the same things." Glenn just wanted out.

Vincent had trouble thinking, much less speaking. When the words eventually emerged, he sounded weak and desperate. "But I need you. You're what I'm looking for."

"It will never be right between us. It's not wrong; it's just not the right choice for me. It's not part of my life plan." Glenn's inability to react in the moment explained why he had failed as an actor.

Read your audience, for fuck's sake.

Glenn continued with his reasons. Explanation became justification. Vincent's world was crashing, and all else Glenn had to say was swallowed by the shatter.

Days later, Vincent discovered that Glenn's "different life paths" excuse had been bullshit. Glenn didn't have the balls to admit there was someone else.

Coward.

Scumbag.

Vincent's despair had turned to anger.

3

The following week, Vincent stopped by the Barracks for a cocktail on his way home from work. Leaning against the bar, waiting for his drink, he ran into Ted, one of Glenn's buddies. After saying he was sorry, Ted slapped Vincent on the shoulder and, in under thirty seconds, let it "slip" that Glenn was seeing someone.

When Vincent didn't immediately respond, Ted, not satisfied, added that for the past three months, Glenn had been screwing a mutual friend, Robert. The surprise must have shown on Vincent's face. A moment later, Ted added, "I thought you knew."

Vincent lied and said he did know.

Vincent had worked with Robert at Amethyst. He had a sexiness that was just this side of trashy. Guys were always pursuing him. Robert had lots of stories. Vincent was sure that Robert was probably going around now telling the story about how he rescued Glenn from the ex who didn't understand him.

Ted was being messy. "Well, if I said something I shouldn't have I figured you ought to know." Ted's voice was void of compassion. He wanted a reaction. "They can't keep their hands off of one another." Ted was another failed actor who thrived on drama.

Vincent had heard enough. "Excuse me, I thought I saw someone I wanted to talk to." His shady exit comment made him smile for the first time that day.

So, Glenn was fucking Robert. That made sense. Glenn couldn't stand to be alone. Of course, he left him for someone else. He and Robert probably considered the secrecy and sneaking around as sexy. Vincent imagined that was how it began. He recalled the evenings Glenn came by the restaurant after work. Usually, Robert was there. Sometimes he'd chat with Glenn while Vincent finished up. He thought Robert was being friendly, but he should have known. When he started at Amethyst, Robert had been sneaking around with someone else's partner. Vincent never imagined the same thing might happen to him.

Ted was talking too loudly on his phone when Vincent left the Barracks. He overheard him say, "I thought he knew."

Fueled by a couple of cocktails, Vincent took a cab to Glenn's place. The scene in the hallway of his building was ugly. He knew a moment after he knocked that he should not have come. Glenn answered the door in the middle of a call. Seeing it was Vincent, he told the person on the line he would call them back.

"How could you?" Vincent hated how pathetic he sounded. Weak.

Glenn looked him square in the eye, "Okay, you want to know? You really want to know? I wanted to spare your feelings, but can you blame me for finding someone else?"

Vincent wanted to say, *Yes, I can blame you.*

"Things between Robert and I just happened. We didn't mean to hurt you, but I couldn't help myself. We connected on a really deep level."

Vincent tried to hide the tears welling in his eyes. This had been a mistake. He had already heard enough, but Glenn clearly wasn't finished.

"… I was bored with our life, but mostly I was bored with you. Robert is exciting. He wants to do more than settle down and grow old. Robert likes to keep things fresh. Do things. Experiment. It's sexy. And he has an awesome body."

Glenn felt entirely justified in what he did. He was right. Vincent had wanted them to grow old together. Maybe it wasn't exciting, but Vincent saw it as beautiful. He walked away without saying another word.

None of his friends shared their doubts about Glenn until *after* all this happened. Instead, his friends had said all the things that supportive friends were expected to say. *We are so excited for you two!*

Now they shared that they knew things with Glenn were doomed from the start.

We didn't think it was our place.

We didn't think you would listen.

His friend Ty looked him dead in the eye and said he never thought Glenn treated him right.

Randy mentioned that Glenn always had a roving eye. "Not a keeper."

Both Ty and Randy said he was better off.

"Glenn was never good enough for you."

"Not by half."

Vincent didn't want to hear it. If he was so much better than Glenn, why was he the one getting dumped? Vincent didn't need their consolation. He didn't need to be coddled. Being coddled was part of the problem.

Randy confessed that he had heard talk about Glenn hooking up with Robert, "I never saw them, but I heard about them. We all did."

They all had known but said nothing. They loved him, but not enough to want to get involved. They were concerned, but not enough to be truthful. He and Glenn were moving in together, but they remained silent. He had gone on about Glenn only last week, talking with them about what to get Glenn for his birthday. *What color do you think will go best with his eyes?* He had discussed plans for a housewarming party.

Another humiliating memory.

By telling him all this, Vincent wondered if Ty and Randy were gloating as much as consoling.

We told you so ....

But they hadn't told him. Instead, they knew and had watched his relationship fall apart, and when it did, Ty and Randy were waiting to welcome him back to the sad and single club. *Welcome home.* Randy and Ty weren't friends so much as fellow journeymen bound more by what they lacked than what they shared.

4

Despite invitations from Ty and Randy to hang out, Vincent chose to fly solo. For a few weeks after the breakup, he did a good amount of clubbing and hooking up. Proving that he was desirable was necessary. Proving that he wasn't dull was important as well.

Hitting the gym became essential. Whenever he felt like cutting a workout short or feasting on carbs, he remembered Glenn's words—*Robert has a great body*. After a few weeks, Vincent hired Frank, a gorgeous gay personal trainer with a chiseled body and a dirty-blonde man-bun.

The night after his first session, Vincent lay in bed thinking how sorry Glenn would be the next time he saw him. By then, Vincent didn't want Glenn back as much as he wanted him lousy with regret. Vincent's bruised ego still had a score to settle.

With consistent and rigorous training sessions, combined with a dietary overhaul, Vincent's physique went from good to amazing in three months. He thought of Glenn less every week. Vincent was in the middle of a new relationship—one with himself and his body. He began to notice men watching him, wanting him. His number of admirers increased every week. Initially, the attention made him self-conscious, but he quickly came to expect it. By then it was something he needed. And if those hungry looks didn't come naturally, Vincent encouraged them. It didn't matter if a guy was taken. Most times, Vincent wasn't after sex, just desire.

He was proving something to himself. Men became conquests. That was what happened with Frank.

Ripe and coated with sweat after an intense workout, Vincent and Frank headed for the showers. The two available stalls were opposite one another at the end of the row. Lacking curtains, the cubicles offered the illusion of privacy and little more.

Vincent knew he looked great and suspected Frank might be interested. He had been waiting for an opportunity like this. He closed his eyes and let his hands explore his body, feeling the gratifying ache that meant his muscles had been pushed once again. The feeling always made him horny.

When Vincent opened his eyes, Frank quickly looked away. His ass was perfection. The way the water ran down his back and between the crack of those lovely mounds. When he reached up to remove the band from his man-bun, Vincent thought he saw a bit of hard cock. But Frank was being shy, turning away, hiding his desire.

Trying to maintain professional boundaries.

Good luck with that.

Just ten feet of tile separated them.

Frank turned. His dick was no longer hard, but was floating heavy. Frank hid his gaze beneath a curtain of water and hair.

Vincent smiled. *Showtime.* He got a palm of liquid soap from the dispenser and reached down. He began to stroke himself. Frank was watching. His head tilted higher. His stance was a bit wider, and his cock was a little fuller. Vincent gave himself a few smooth strokes. Slowly Frank reached down and began to echo his movements. After a few strokes, his fat tool was flush to his belly.

A loudspeaker crackled through the high-energy mix of the club. "Attention members and guests, the shower and sauna area will be closing in ten minutes."

Frank washed the soap from his body and grabbed his towel from the hook. After a quick wipe-down, he wrapped the towel around his waist and headed to the lockers. Vincent followed him a moment later.

As they were getting dressed, Frank asked Vincent if he wanted to come over "for a drink." His place was two blocks away. No drinks were poured. They headed straight for the bedroom.

"Working out always makes me horny," mumbled Frank. No wonder he was a trainer. They ran admiring hands over one another's bodies. Their tongues explored. "I don't usually do this with my clients," said Frank.

Vincent pushed him back on the bed. "I'm glad you made me an exception."

Both men were hungry for one another. Sex was short, frantic, and fevered. Vincent left his shoes and socks on. Frank didn't even undo his man-bun. As they wiped themselves clean, Frank asked Vincent if he wanted to go and grab a bite sometime. Vincent said, "Sure," but he didn't mean it. There was no point. This had been fun, but Vincent wasn't looking for anything. He had already gotten what he wanted from Frank.

5

One evening after a couple of glasses of wine, Vincent retrieved a shoebox of old photos. He kept his pictures loose. Photos from high school, the day he taught himself to ride a bike, downtown Chicago, a stiff pairing with Mother, another with Father, his hand on his shoulder.

He fished out a picture from his first real date with Glenn.

They had actually "met" the week before at the bathhouse, Steamworks.

In the photo, they crouched on either side of a goat. They had biked along the lakefront and made fools of themselves at miniature golf. After pizza, they went to pet some of the animals in the Farm in the Zoo in Lincoln Park. The picture was taken there. A moment before, Vincent had told Glenn it was the best first date he had ever been on.

The day had been absolute perfection. Vincent knew by the end of the day that he and Glenn were destined to be together.

After another glass of wine, he phoned Glenn.

It was almost midnight. He had no idea what he was going to say. He was dialing with his heart and not his head. Maybe he just wanted to remind Glenn how good they had been together. He needed to tell him things were different now. He was different now. Someone had probably already told Glenn about Vincent's transformation. News about an ex travels fast in the gay network. *Telephone, telegraph, tell-a-queen.*

Maybe Glenn was having a change of heart. Maybe life with Robert had soured. Couples reconciled and relationships reconfigured all the time. Vincent was fine with living apart, fine with an open relationship. He was willing to negotiate.

Glenn's "Hello" shook Vincent from his merlot stupor. Even though he dialed the phone, he didn't expect Glenn to actually answer.

Vincent tried to sound sober. "I was just sitting here looking through pictures and found the one from the petting zoo." But, even before finishing the sentence, Vincent knew that he sounded pathetic. His desperation was apparent.

"The what?"

Vincent cleared his throat. "The petting zoo, our first date."

"Oh yeah."

Glenn sounded distracted ... or maybe disinterested ... or maybe just half-asleep. Vincent had to tell him what he called to say. "Glenn, I still love you."

Silence.

A pause so long it was unbearable.

"Vincent, I ..." Glenn was polite and passionless. His courteous distance hurt Vincent more than anger or rudeness would have. Glenn was disengaged. If Vincent were sober, he would have realized that all Glenn wanted was to get off the phone. Vincent heard Robert whispering in the background.

When Vincent said he missed him, Glenn said he had to get going. "I have something in the oven."

He hung up before Vincent had the chance to ask what the fuck he was baking at midnight.

6

The next evening Vincent ran into Ty, a buddy of his, at the gym. Ty was the first friend he made in Chicago. They used to hang out all the time before Vincent and Glenn became a couple. Vincent invited Ty over for drinks. As he poured them a second glass of wine, Vincent told Ty what he had done the night before.

Ty winced. "You called Glenn and said you were thinking about your first date?"

Vincent nodded. "And I told him I still loved him."

"What did he say?"

"He said he had something in the oven."

Ty's exhalation spoke volumes. "I am only saying this because I care. This stuff with Glenn has gone on long enough. You look superb, but once you start talking about Glenn you sound pathetic."

Vincent knew it was the truth. "I just feel like we were destined …"

"Just because something is destined to happen doesn't mean it's destined to last. Glenn is not coming back and even if he does, you shouldn't take him back. He's trash and he always will be. Vincent, you're a beautiful man, and you're a nice guy as well, which makes you even hotter."

"Shut up." Vincent knew it was true, but accepting compliments embarrassed him. False humility had become a prison. He even kept his spa visits a secret. He felt compelled to make his looks appear effortless. *God-given.*

For some in his circle, any show of pride was ample reason to tear a fellow down. *Vincent is so self-involved. That guy thinks he's so hot. He's not all that!*

"I'll prove to you what a good-looking guy you are." Ty grabbed his phone.

From the way Ty started to move it was clear he was taking Vincent's picture.

"Come on, Ty."

Ty stopped taking pictures for a moment. "No, you come on. A picture is worth a thousand words. I'll prove how hot you are. If I'm right, I don't want to hear any more about Glenn aside from an overdue good riddance. I want you to admit that almost any guy, any gay guy, would be lucky to have you."

Ty resumed taking pictures. "Come on Vincent, have fun with it. Give me something."

He was tipsy from the wine, and the thought of being photographed excited him. Vincent wanted evidence of how desirable he had become. He wanted his beauty documented, celebrated, and added to his box of memories. He wanted it shared on social media. He wanted *Likes*. He wanted *STUD!* He wanted *HOT! WOOF! SMOKIN'!* He wanted drooling tongues, turgid eggplants, and smiley faces with bulging hearts for eyes. Maybe enough cyber lust would give him the confidence to own his appearance without seeming conceited. What was wrong with being proud of his hotness? What was wrong with celebrating all his hard work? Vanity was a concept and term concocted by jealous people.

After an obligatory protest, he allowed himself to be convinced. Being photographed felt awkward at first. Vincent downed his drink and began to feel looser. He had another. With every few flashes, another layer of his inhibitions peeled away. Clothes were shed along with self-consciousness. He grew extremely aroused. This was a fantasy.

Unbutton.

Untuck.

Drop the shirt.

He did not need to be told twice. Vincent tightened his abs and pivoted his torso in the practiced way that made them pop.

Flash.

Unzip.

Roll your underwear down slowly. Look up, part your lips. Excellent. Flash. Ty grinned around his phone.

Show me your ass.

Vincent arched his back and lowered his briefs, revealing the dimples, then the crack. He slowly inched his underwear down, shifting his ass beneath, and gradually exposing each firm hairless globe. His butt had always been exceptional. With added workouts, it had become exquisite: full, hard, and heart-shaped. When Vincent turned, his erection was already pointing skyward, pulsing in synch with each camera click. He touched the head and brought a strand of ooze to his lips.

Flash.

He lowered the elastic and freed his balls.

Ty had never seen this side of his friend. His cock ached in his jeans. Ty stepped forward and looked at Vincent's cock. "It's as gorgeous as the rest of you." Ty wrapped a hand around its firmness. The erection twitched in his grip, simultaneously soft and rigid. Ty began to stroke its length. "Feel good?"

Vincent closed his eyes, "Yeah ... but ..."

"If it feels good let it happen. Let me help you forget Glenn." Ty took off his shirt and dropped to his knees. Vincent never knew he had tattoos. His ink was all symbols. Tribal.

The sight of Ty kneeling before him sparked something in Vincent. He commanded Ty to service him.

Spit on it.

Choke on it.

Take it all the way down.

Ty was good. Very good. The man knew how to give a good sloppy blowjob. Moments later, he grabbed the back of Ty's head and shoved his cock deeper into his mouth. He was nearing release.

Feeling the twitches on Vincent's thighs and hearing the catch in his breath, Ty increased the pace. He gagged with the explosion and the sudden flood in his throat. He greedily took every drop, sucking until Vincent took a step back and his softening prick slipped from Ty's lips. "That was quite a load."

Ty spat into his hand and finished himself off with a load that shot up and onto his stomach.

Vincent handed him a napkin. He was unsure what to say. This had been so unexpected. He didn't think of Ty that way. Vincent pulled up his briefs. "Thanks."

"My pleasure, we work well together."

Vincent ignored the statement and its connotations. Despite what just happened, he and Ty were nothing more than friends. The blowjob was an isolated incident. He wanted things with Ty to be as they were. Gay friends frequently crossed that line. Some folks called having oral sex "the gay handshake." The blowjob was simply something consensual that had happened after a couple of drinks.

When Ty asked to spend the night, Vincent reluctantly agreed. He was determined that this was going no further. Sex had only happened because of the booze and the photos, and the way Ty knelt there, wanting him so badly. What happened was not about Ty but about Ty's desire.

The two men crawled into bed. Vincent feigned drunken fatigue and turned his back when Ty tried to initiate a second round of sex. It was the simplest solution to an awkward situation.

7

Ty was too horny to sleep. After so long, he and Vincent had finally gotten together. Ty had longed for Vincent since he first saw the dark and handsome man on the couch at a party. Both had just turned 21. Vincent had recently moved to town. Ty was too shy to be direct, so he initiated a friendship.

That had been his mistake. Friendship had become a prison. Tonight, he had been freed. Tonight, they became something more. Many claim the best relationships begin as friendships. Vincent needed a man who supported and encouraged him.

Ty poured himself another glass of wine. He recalled Vincent saying how the flash and click had aroused him. He had seen how he responded. Ty pulled out his phone. *If being photographed turned him on, maybe he wants to take it a step further. Vincent is as hot as any of those studio models. If he can't see it, I'll prove it.*

Sporting a solid buzz and feeling sure of his plan, Ty read the rules of submission on the "Model Search" page of the Xclusiv Studio. He filled out the form with Vincent's info, attached the images, and hit submit.

"And, a star is born," he said into the bottom of his glass before climbing back into bed beside Vincent.

8

In the morning, Vincent made coffee. Neither man mentioned the night before until Ty was ready to leave. Instead of bringing up the blowjob, he nodded towards his phone and mentioned the pictures. How gorgeous the shots were. How sexy Vincent was. How well he photographed.

Vincent liked what Ty was saying, but the way he said it was making him uncomfortable. Was Ty trying to initiate something? Vincent almost told Ty to delete the images but stopped himself at the last moment.

Ty stumbled over his words for a moment before confessing that after Vincent had gone to bed, he had submitted the pictures to the "Model Search" portion of the Xclusiv website.

"That's not funny," Vinnie muttered.

"It's not a joke."

"Wait, so you did what?" Vincent's coffee cup clanked on the counter. Both men winced at the sound.

Ty bit his lower lip. "I know. But I was wasted, and I um, sent the shots to the Xclusiv site."

If this was true, Vincent was pissed. Ty had done this without his consent, but still, the thought of it was more than a little exciting. "Not funny."

"I didn't do it to be funny. I did it to show you how hot you really are."

"That was supposed to be between us."

"I know, I was drunk."

"Ty, how could you do something like that without asking?" But secretly, Vincent found it thrilling to think of his nudes in the studio inbox.

"I only did it because I knew you would never do it yourself. I can email them later and tell them to disregard the pictures."

"You don't have to do that. I'm sure they won't be interested."

Vincent wasn't fooling Ty. "Aren't you at least curious about what they'll say?"

"Well, I won't hold my breath." *But what if ...* he thought. He was curious how he measured up. Would they be interested in someone like him? Xclusiv Studio was home to the most desirable men in the business, men like Rex Reynolds, Dwayne Thorne, Peter Ray Thomas, and A.Z. Ambush. Only last week, on two different occasions, guys at the gym told him he should be a physique model. By the way they said it, Vincent knew they really meant nude XXX model. *Hard cock. Ass spread. Click. Click.*

Ty held up his phone and showed Vincent one of his nudes. "Look at that. You're beautiful. Tell the truth. You know damn well that you are hot enough to work for Xclusiv."

Vincent felt himself blush. Seeing the picture was a turn-on. He looked hot. Really hot.

Was Ty right?

Was he hot enough to work for Xclusiv?

If Xclusiv chose him, he would have proof of his appeal. Proof that he was desirable, that he had changed, and that he was far from boring. The thought of being a porn star excited him. Ty was right—he never would have submitted the pictures himself. Vincent was a pro at talking himself out of things he wanted to do.

If the opportunity to perform in a XXX movie arose, Vincent wondered if he would have the nerve to follow through. Before the break-up with Glenn, Vincent would have answered with an emphatic, *No.* Now he wasn't so sure. He may have the looks, the body, and the equipment for porn, but did he have the confidence, and the guts? There was one way to find out.

Let's hear what they have to say.

Let's see if they call at all.

"Let me know when they call you."

Vincent brushed Ty's comment aside, but the possibility filled him with excitement.

He asked Ty to forward him the pictures.

9

Two weeks later, Vincent was leaving the gym when he received a call from Ed Vittori. After introducing himself as the senior talent scout, promotional director, and "numbers guy" for Xclusiv Studio, Vittori said he had seen the photos and passed them on to the studio head, Woody Wilson. "Vincent, you should feel honored. We only call a small percentage of applicants. We recognize potential in your shots, but we need to see more. We need to see you in the flesh."

Vincent unlocked his car, tossed his gym bag in the back, and sat behind the wheel. "That's great. That's great." He could not believe this call was happening. "Thank you." Unsure of what to say, he aimed at being polite.

"At this point we're interested, but as I said, we need to see more. We would like to bring you out to L.A. to meet you in person. Have you ever been?"

"No. Well, just the airport." His thoughts were racing along with his heart. This was a dream come true.

Vittori said there was plenty more to see in L.A. than LAX. "Come experience WeHo and L.A. on our dime."

"When were you thinking?" Vincent could hear his heartbeat in his ears. This was really happening. Whenever they wanted to see him, he would make it work.

"How about this weekend?"

So soon.

Vincent said that sounded great.

"I'm sure I don't need to tell you that a lot of guys would kill for this chance. What have you got to lose? This could be the start of a lucrative career. At worst, it's a nice break from Chicago weather and a free trip to L.A."

Vincent considered his VISA bill. Lucrative was good. Additional income would be welcome. His recent splurge that included his sessions with Frank, spa services, and a mostly new wardrobe had been costly. He would be a fool to say no.

After minimal deliberation, Vincent agreed. A career in adult films was a big decision. Making porn was the sort of choice that could change a person's life. But he wasn't being asked to decide anything today. Right now, all he was being offered was a trip to L.A. Vincent could still change his mind, or Xclusiv might take a pass. This was the first step, but Vincent was taking it without hesitation. The new Vincent was eager for this adventure.

The following afternoon, Ed emailed the flight information.

10

That week Vincent almost called Ed Vittori a half dozen times and cancelled, but in the end, his desire for something more outweighed his fear of failure. Vincent knew an opportunity when he saw one. A face-to-face meeting with Xclusiv with the possibility of doing porn was the chance to do something exciting, something no one expected of him.

His biggest concern wasn't about the industry or the stigma of doing porn. He was mainly worried that he would go to L.A., meet the Xclusiv executives, and they would take a pass. Even if that happened, there was no harm done. He would be back to where he was now. No better. No worse.

Even if things didn't work out, an invitation from Xclusiv to audition was a huge compliment. If the studio was paying his way out there, they had to be somewhat interested. Didn't they?

Now was no time for self-doubt. He could do this. He would do this. Fear was just a pessimist's take on excitement. If he wanted a new life, if he wanted excitement, he needed to be willing to take some risks.

Since the day Glenn dumped him, Vincent had developed an aversion to being boring. That was Glenn's greatest criticism. He was too predictable, too conventional, and too blah. This trip was a way to lay all of that to rest once and for all.

Vincent was prepared to quit if he couldn't get his shifts covered at work. Server jobs were a dime a dozen.

"Then we'll see you at the office this Friday at 4:00." Ed gave Vincent the number of his direct line. "Just call if there is any change."

"Thanks Mr. Vittori."

"Call me Ed."

"Thanks Ed, I'll see you on Friday."

11

Xclusiv Studios was off Sunset Boulevard in West Hollywood. The outside of the three-story office building was box-like and unexceptional. He wasn't exactly arriving at the gates of MGM or Paramount.

Given the exterior, Vincent wasn't expecting anything quite so posh inside. He had all the typical preconceived notions about "the jizz biz." *Too many B movies and police shows.*

Through the double doors was a corridor lined with a dozen framed posters from some of Xclusiv's biggest hits, all of them signed by the stars of the films: *Donny By Candlelight, Fourth and Goal, Confessions of a Frat Boy, A Hole in One, Desert Getaway, The French Love Connection,* etc. Another set of glass doors opened onto a reception area, tastefully decorated in gray and slate. Soft instrumental music played on the sound system. An enormous tropical fish tank hummed and bubbled in a corner. The relaxed atmosphere was welcome. Vincent was extremely nervous.

He gave his name to the twink at the desk and said he had an appointment with Mr. Vittori and Mr. Wilson. After a quick confirmation, the slender blonde rose from the chrome desk and ushered him into the main office. The secretary looked familiar though Vincent could not place him.

Woody Wilson's office was large and sparsely furnished. More framed and signed posters of Xclusiv classics covered the walls; *Winter Heatwave, Sex Potion #9, Headhunter,* and *Full Service Body Repair.*

Woody Wilson was an imposing hunk of a man at his large glass desk. The head of the studio was muscular with a gray crew cut. A dark tan made his blue eyes sparkle. Two other attractive daddy types sat on upholstered chairs to either side of the desk. "Thank you, Kip."

The receptionist nodded and backed out the door. Vincent recognized the name. Kip Mason, the secretary, had been a big deal in the porn world four or five years ago, but then abruptly disappeared. No wonder he seemed familiar, though Kip Mason looked different off-screen.

Woody's voice was deep and resonant. "How was your flight, Vincent?"

"Very smooth." Vincent's voice wavered. He was standing before the head of the premiere gay porn studio, eager to discuss a possible future in the industry. Whose life was he living?

"Glad to hear it was turbulence free." Woody was ready to get down to business. "Let me introduce you to my colleagues. This is Ed Vittori. He wears a lot of hats at the studio. Ed is our promotions director, talent scout, and financial guru. I believe you two spoke on the phone."

Vincent nodded before moving to shake Ed's hand.

"Nice to meet you in the flesh, Vincent," Vittori said.

"Likewise." Vincent smiled. Ed had a shaven head, a brilliant smile, and the lean muscular frame of a runner or a yoga master.

"And this is Joe McCain, the visionary behind all of Xclusiv's high-quality still photography, sets, art-decoration; the entire Xclusiv look. Joe has an impeccable eye for recognizing what will work on camera, and what won't."

Vincent stepped forward. "Pleased to meet you, Mr. McCain." Given that sort of introduction, Vincent couldn't help but feel scrutinized. But, after all, having a keen eye for knowing what, and who, will or will not work on camera was the man's job.

Joe McCain was reasonably attractive, or at least he had been at one time. He was of indeterminate middle age. He was fit with reddened skin, a pronounced jaw, and convex eyes. The combination often indicated the use of some sort of steroids.

Woody grinned. "Tell us a little about yourself, Vincent, and why you are considering a career with Xclusiv."

Vincent took a deep breath and told the men that he needed a change. He said he wanted more out of life and explained that he was ready to shake things up with something exciting. "Then this opportunity landed in my lap." He talked about liking sex and admitted that he got off on the thought of guys watching him. "The thought of them getting off gets me off." Vincent added that he could always use the extra money. The three men nodded.

"Can you strip down for us Vince?"

He corrected the studio head. "Actually, it's Vincent."

Woody motioned with his finger. "Right, well then Vincent, can you strip down."

Vincent did as instructed. He wasn't sure if he was supposed to be businesslike or seductive while undressing. Was this a test or simply the means to an assessment? He needed to get out of his head.

"Show us your body. Flex your muscles. Good, very good. Maybe a little more weight training, cut down on the cardio, and bulk up a bit around the shoulders. Now show us your ass. *Very nice.* Now turn around again. Low-hanging balls. "Can you get hard for us?"

The request made perfect sense. Vincent assumed this would be part of the interview process. He just hadn't expected the "grow it and show it" bit during his initial interview. This was a test he needed to ace if he wanted to impress the triumvirate of the studio. Vincent was well aware of his strengths and how to use them to his advantage. Powerful men dig innocence and boyish charm.

Woody grinned. "You're blushing Vincent. I know it's strange, but it's all business. We need to know if getting an erection in front of people is going to be an issue, because if it is, you're in the wrong industry and there's no need in wasting anymore of anyone's time."

This was a make-or-break moment.

"I'm just nervous being here." Vincent hadn't come this far to go back home. "I can do it."

In under a minute, Vincent's cock was flush to his belly. A desire to work with Xclusiv eclipsed his nervousness. In the end, getting hard in front of the three men was a challenge as well as a turn-on. He made it into a game by bringing every sensation, every nuance of pleasure, to his face and body. With each stroke and manipulation, he imagined seducing the three men before him. *If you want to watch, I'll give you a performance.* He made frequent eye contact with all three, but mostly he made sure to eye-fuck Woody.

"Very nice," smiled Joe. "There's a freshness here. That Irish All-American/Boy Next Door look resonates with fans. We have Reed under contract, but he hasn't been able to pull off innocent for a couple of years. We don't really have any current talent on the roster that fits that type."

"Now Vincent, turn around all the way," Woody interjected, then adding. "Now show us your ass again."

Vittori said that Vincent was better than he had hoped. Then, looking to Woody, he added, "I agree with Joe. He has that fresh quality you don't often see in movies, at least not for long. Not fresh as in merely young, but fresh as in wholesome. Are you wholesome, Vincent?"

"I don't know. I mean, I guess so." There was no way to answer, and Vincent doubted it was really a question anyway. He suspected he wasn't being asked if he was wholesome, but if he could play wholesome.

Joe nodded to Woody. He was confident that Vincent's sex appeal would translate onto film. "Thank goodness for those boys from the Midwest. The camera is going to love you."

Woody bridged his fingers before him. "You need to tidy your pubic hair a bit as well. Otherwise, very nice." Maybe it was his imagination, but Vincent sensed something more than a purely professional interest from the studio head. Maybe Woody eyed all the models that way, but his scrutiny was helping Vinnie maintain his erection.

Woody exchanged a glance with Ed and then with Joe before speaking. "We all are in unanimous agreement that you have a marketable look, one that will be an asset to the Xclusiv roster of talent."

Vincent waited for Woody's word before he began getting dressed.

As Vincent shifted his erection and slipped on his pants, Woody explained that despite their enthusiasm, the real gauge would be his performance in front of the camera. "And ultimately, public response. Looking the part doesn't always translate into performance. We need to see how you work as a performer. Some models do more print work, others do movies, and some are great with personal appearances."

Woody elaborated further, but much of what he said didn't register with Vincent. His mind was racing. This was really happening. This secret fantasy was moving forward and coming into the light.

Woody leaned forward, "Vincent, we would like you to make a film with us, something to see how you photograph and show how you take direction? After that, we'll have a better idea of how you work with other models. We'll make it worth your while."

Boom! The offer.

Vincent didn't expect things to happen so quickly.

Don't overthink this; just accept it.

Hesitation had been his undoing before. Not this time. Vincent was not about to let this opportunity pass him by. "Yes. Definitely," he said with a wide grin. He reached out to shake Woody's hand but decided to tuck in his shirt and zip up his pants instead.

Woody chuckled at Vincent's awkwardness.

"Corn-fed cuteness," said Ed.

He was about to say something more when Kip appeared with several forms to sign. A photocopy of Vincent's driver's license and another form of I.D. were required.

Woody told Vincent a bit about Xclusiv Studio.

This must be my welcome to the studio speech.

Woody explained that he founded Xclusiv eight years ago after leaving Tandem Video. Although he had co-founded Tandem, he could not continue to stand behind the profitable, but inferior product they were producing. "My partner at Tandem, Corbin Kent, wasn't too pleased with me."

"He was furious," added Vittori.

"Especially when I left and took Joe and Ed here with me."

Woody said that he thought porn fans deserved better than what Tandem was churning out. Woody founded Xclusiv to make films that mirrored the style and substance of mainstream Hollywood, only with cock and ass and jizz. Woody made good on his promise by elevating production values and hiring the best. Xclusiv quickly emerged as a top-tier and award-winning company. "Despite the best efforts of our competitors," Woody added.

Vittori laughed. "He's not joking."

"They all wanted him to fail," added McCain.

Woody claimed that he liked all of his models to feel they were contributing to the Xclusiv legacy. "Because together we are making adult films of quality. I want them to take pride in being a part of this. I like all of my family to feel that way—the models, directors, and production crew. Over the past several years, Xclusiv has raised the bar for gay adult entertainment. We are making classics of the genre."

"Xclusiv is the best," added Vincent. "That's why I wanted to work here. I'm honored to be a part of that tradition." Though heavy on the flattery, Vincent meant 95% of what he said.

"And we have raised the bar even further because of talented and dedicated young men like yourself. Great to have you on board, Vincent."

Kip returned with the photocopied materials and nodded that everything was in order. Woody had the papers in one hand, a pen in the other. "There's just one thing left to do. You need a new name. Vincent, what's your middle name?"

"Sherman."

Ed pursed his lips. "Good God no."

McCain asked where he was raised.

"Akron."

Woody shook his head.

"But I've been in Chicago for a few years." Vincent explained.

"What's your father's name?"

"My dad is gone, but his name was Dean."

Joe turned to Woody, "That won't 's work. We just signed that big dicked kid from Texas, Dean Driver."

Ed looked up at the light and suggested Lux. "High school Latin," he joked.

"Vincent Lux."

"Vinnie D. Lux."

Woody shook his head and laughed. "Shit Ed, the D. Lux is too cheesy, even for porn. And *that* is saying something."

"Especially for a studio whose first bona fide star was Desi Lou." Joe added.

"How about just Lux?" Woody turned to Vincent and cradled his chin in his fingers. "Vinnie Lux has a ring to it ... Yes?" He asked Vinnie if he liked it. "We want you to be happy."

"I suppose." Vincent didn't care for the name, but he doubted he would feel an immediate connection to any pseudonym. *Be agreeable!* He was becoming the property of Xclusiv; it stood to reason that these men should name their product. This identity was not his own. To be a star he was happy to be whatever or whoever they wanted him to be. "Vinnie Lux, I like it," he added after a moment.

Woody took a seat on the corner of his desk. "Vinnie, I know this is happening quickly, but I speak for everyone here when I say we are excited to welcome you to the team. I'd like to schedule you for something next weekend if you're free."

Vinnie's eyes widened. "For what?"

"I would love to have you appear in a new Xclusiv movie. Not a starring vehicle, but something to introduce you, to ease you into the business and show you the ropes."

"Sure." Vinnie was not expecting to have something lined up that fast. Now that things were in order, he supposed there was no reason to delay. The more time Vinnie had, the more likely he was to talk himself out of it. "I'm ready."

"Great—now are you top, bottom, versatile ..."

Vinnie blushed again. Wholesome. Midwestern. The direct nature of the question embarrassed him. The new name required a new mindset. These questions were not prying; they were work-related. *This world has different boundaries.* "Versatile I guess."

Joe McCain said he liked his answer. "That doubles your chances for work, and it's always a plus when guys can flip-fuck. Lots of demand for that lately."

Ed tapped his pencil on the pad before him, "Any special skills we should know about?"

Joe smiled, "He means any special sexual skills; bondage, fisting, water sports, nipple play, ass work, no gag reflex ...."

Vinnie had no idea what to say. He wished they would just tell him who they wanted him to be. He was used to adapting to expectations. "I'm not into fisting or water sports. I mean, I've never done them, and not sure I want to try. I guess I'm pretty well rounded when it comes to regular sex. At least I haven't had any complaints."

"I bet you haven't," added Woody.

Vinnie shrugged. "When it comes to sex, I'm pretty standard I guess."

Woody pushed for clarification. "So do you consider yourself fairly vanilla?"

"I guess so." Vinnie didn't know how to answer. Best to start off with a little mystery. "Vanilla, but open to exploration." He was pleased with his answer; it sparked possibilities rather than problems.

Ed Vittori flashed that killer smile. "Great, this will help us figure out how to get the best performance out of you and what sort of scenes will make you the most comfortable. Then, if all goes well we can talk about expanding your repertoire a bit."

Woody winked. "You think you're ready?"

Vinnie was upbeat. *Be confident, not cocky.* He nodded. He thought he was ready. Maybe having sex on camera was the sort of thing you didn't know you were capable of doing until you were actually doing it, like making a tight parallel park.

"You'll do fine. You look camera ready." Vinnie's basket was still swollen. Woody nodded towards his crotch. "Save that load for the money shot. You'll want your first one to be good. Fans eat that up, or want to anyway." Woody scribbled a sum on a slip of paper and shoved it across the desk. "This would be your payment for the shoot and enough for incidentals until then. We have your number, we'll be in touch about your flight back to L.A. next weekend."

So, this is how it happens.

The sum on the paper wasn't an enormous amount, but Vinnie would have done it for far less. The new direction his life was taking was more a matter of principle than capital. Performing in a gay adult film was giving the finger to Glenn and Robert and all the guys who looked through him, or over his shoulder to the next guy. But, unlike Vincent, Vinnie didn't intend to wait his turn to have the things he wanted.

His turn was now!

Woody handed him $200. "Vinnie, get yourself a spray tan and a hair trim. A manicure and pedicure might be a good too. So, I guess we are set."

Vinnie nodded. "You don't know how ready I am."

Woody laughed. "Next weekend be ready to bottom. That's best for your first scene to safeguard against performance anxiety. There will be enemas on set and someone to help with all that. Not sure I need to tell you this, but eat lightly, always wise before bottoming."

He was not that green.

Ed told Vinnie to keep his cock under lock and key. "Minimal sex this week. If you do fool around a day or two before, try not to cum. You'll want your money shot to be its best, Vinnie Lux."

12

The following weekend, Vinnie Lux made his XXX film debut in the Xclusiv Studios production *Mancandy 2,* directed by former porn model Van Wendt. The threadbare plot involved the goings-on at a confectioner's shop. Vinnie's scene was set in the candy warehouse. For the scene, Vinnie was paired with Josh Lawless. Ginger-haired, bearded, and balding, Josh was a hairy-chested daddy. His rugged appearance provided an interesting contrast to Vinnie's lean All-American appeal.

A veteran of the industry, Josh Lawless had been making porn for seven years. He joked to Vinnie that seven years was "approximately 70 years in non-porn world." He added, "Woody likes to pair me up with the newbies because I make them feel at ease."

Woody was smart. Josh's easygoing nature and relaxed masculinity helped make Vinnie's first scene a pleasure to film. The thought of the camera rolling and the crew watching didn't bother him or break his focus. Quite the opposite, the watchers turned him on.

He was a new man. Vincent was gone, and Vinnie was making up for lost time.

Parts of the shoot were challenging. The lights were hot, and getting penetrated on top of several cardboard boxes was not easy. Everything felt as though it might collapse beneath him at any moment. Having Van shout the sexual choreography took some getting used to as well. "Lift his left leg." "Spit on his cock." "Lick his balls." "Munch butt!" "Pinch his nipples."

High-class problems, to be sure.

Van Wendt called him a natural.

The stop-and-go nature of shooting porn also took getting used to.

Cut!

Focus Check!

Position Change!

Lights!

Mind that sweat!

Sex on camera was an endurance sport; the actual sex was somewhat secondary. Porn sex was more a performance of sex; it was posing and emoting and vocalizing sex more than actually having it. Van joked that shooting porn was more like "an exercise video with money shots."

From the start, Vinnie displayed an instinctual understanding of pornographic performance and what looked hot on camera. Josh told him that ability was a gift, and it was what separated the amateurs from the skin kings.

Vinnie had heard that sometimes it's tough to orgasm after a long day of filming. Five minutes after meeting Josh, Vinnie knew that was not going to be a problem. The bigger challenge for him would be not cumming too soon. He almost lost it a couple of times when Josh tongued his ass and when Josh banged him slowly and steadily in the longer fucking sequences. Given his excitement at doing this for the camera, and the thought of future viewers, the greater miracle was that Vinnie held back as long as he did.

When he finally blasted, Van was impressed. The first jet of semen arced over his chest and onto the bed. The second and third spurts followed closely. Josh reached orgasm a moment later. The two closed the scene kissing and rubbing the goo of their seed across one another's chest.

After yelling, "Cut," Van walked over wearing a wide grin. He looked down at the bulge in his khakis and told the pair that the scene had passed the Van Wendt test, "Sure got me going."

"Is that so?" Josh reached down to give the director's crotch a squeeze, but Van batted his hand away.

"Save it for filming. Better yet, save it for that sexy Canadian of yours." He turned to Vinnie. "That was incredible for your first time. If you haven't already realized it, I believe you have found your calling. Hope to work with you again soon and I have the feeling I will."

Woody showed up on set a moment later. After a brief talk with Van, Woody pulled Vinnie aside and told him that he had done Xclusiv proud. "Van called you a natural." Any doubts he once had about a porn career were gone. He was no longer conflicted over wanting to be a star.

Being called "a natural" was more than he had hoped for. Now Vinnie needed to prove today had not been a fluke and that Vinnie Lux was here to stay, at least until he felt like leaving. He had the looks, the drive, and apparently the skills. He was ready to take this adventure as far as he could.

Josh grabbed a Red Bull from the food table and told Vinnie it had been a pleasure working with him. He was heading home. "I have got to give my husband a little something after a shoot or he gets jealous."

"He must be very understanding."

"Ian sure is."

Ian was a lucky guy. Vinnie could understand wanting to hold on to a man like Josh.

After a swig of his energy drink, Josh added, "I know what you're thinking, but Ian and I are very committed. Our relationship is more honest than those couples claiming to be monogamous but who trick on the sly. We are connected. Ian knows me better than anybody. This career has been very good for me, but at the end of the day it's just work. Ian is my life."

Vinnie nodded.

"Listen to me going on."

After the day he'd had, Vinnie was feeling invincible. He wondered if he could change Josh's mind and make them into something more than costars. He put an end to the thought after only a second. Playing that game would make him as lowdown as Glenn and Robert.

After a quick shower, Josh pulled on his jeans. As he bent to lace up his boots, he told Vinnie for the fifth time that he did a great job. "Most importantly, the boss loved it. Woody doesn't visit the set often so for him to come down here was a big deal. And he sure seemed to like what he saw." Josh clapped a hand on Vinnie's shoulder. "Take care of yourself, kid. Things happen fast in this business, and sometimes it gets weird."

Vinnie wondered what or whom Josh was cautioning him about. "Everyone has been nice so far."

"Well, you haven't met everyone," Josh added that not all the boys in the business are as nice as they appear. "There are some snakes. Poisonous ones."

He refrained from naming names. "You're a clever kid; you'll figure it out. Remember, it is only porn. Don't let it mess with who you are. I've seen guys come out of the business better, richer, and smarter. I've seen porn turn guys into assholes, into zombies, and into corpses. There's always a fresher face, a better body, a bigger cock, or a hotter ass out there. Right now, the new thing is you." Josh caught himself. He said his husband always told him he went on when he was tired. "Especially when I'm talking to someone new to all this. As for talking your ear off, this Red Bull doesn't help."

Still riding his high from the shoot, Vinnie was too excited to process much of what Josh was saying. Vinnie had actually done it. He had shot a porn film and done exceptionally well. He had been applauded by industry veterans who called him a natural!

Vinnie Lux—a born performer!

Too excited to return to his hotel, Vinnie began walking. He took a seat on a bus bench. He wasn't waiting for a bus; he just wanted to feel the sun on his face. After a moment, he opened his eyes. Vinnie didn't recognize himself as the hot guy reflected in a shop window across the street. So much about his life was unrecognizable. He had just had sex in front of an entire film crew and got off doing it. Where had all that confidence come from? He was not the same "boring" guy who was dumped by his boyfriend a few months ago.

Glenn would be shocked to hear that he had spent the day getting fucked by Josh Lawless in a porno. Yeah, that's me sucking his cock. That's me riding him. Still think you know me, Glenn? Still worried I'll fence you inside a white picket prison yard? Is Robert hot enough to do what I'm doing? Does he have the balls?

Vinnie wanted Glenn to drop to his knees and beg forgiveness, mainly to have the satisfaction of stepping over him and walking away.

13

The next morning Vinnie caught an early flight to Chicago. It felt as though he had been gone a week, though he only missed two shifts at the restaurant. In the past, he had covered for every other server. Now they could pick up the slack. Alana, the Amethyst manager, always said, "Servers are a dime a dozen." If that were the case, then he wouldn't be missed, especially for a shift or two.

Hard to imagine three days could make such a difference, but in those seventy-two hours Vinnie's world had changed so dramatically that he found it easier to think of Vinnie Lux as someone he became once his clothes were shed. Vinnie Lux was a magical persona, a genie freed by the click of a camera or the call for *Action!*

Once Vinnie turned his phone off Airplane Mode, it began to vibrate. He had several new messages, but he received an incoming call before he could look at them.

Seeing the call was from Mother, he became Vincent again. Seeing her name on his phone made him doubt everything he had done in L.A.

Why postpone the inevitable. "Hello, Mother."

"Well, I finally reached you."

Mother had a way of always putting him on the defensive.

He and Mother exchanged small talk as he made his way through the terminal to the ground transport. When she asked where he was, he said he was heading for the train, which was the truth. She asked what was new. *Nothing much.* That was a lie, but what could he say? *Everything is new, Mother. I am a different person.* He had not mentioned to her that he was going to L.A. Telling her that he was coming home from the trip now would only lead to more questions and more lies. He was not ready to have that conversation. Best not to tell her anything. Avoidance and secrecy were the cornerstones of their relationship.

Three years ago, Vincent told her he was gay. Hearing the news, Mother cried and prayed and said she worried he would die of "the AIDS." If he had it to do again, he would never have told her. Coming out to Mother was more frustrating than the closet had ever been. The subject was still taboo. Mother said she loved him, but his sex life didn't concern her.

Vincent tried to explain to her that it wasn't just about sex. Being gay was the way he saw the world. Mother didn't understand; she didn't want to. Mother preferred being placated to being informed. As a result, she knew nothing that was going on with him. Mother never knew about Glenn or that her son was in love, or that they were moving in together, or that the breakup had devastated him. She knew none of it. His role as her son felt stranger than his role as Vinnie Lux.

Telling Mother the truth about his trip was inconceivable. She would think he'd been brainwashed, gone insane, or was on drugs. This exciting new chapter of his life would be about punishing her. Mother would never believe the industry was legit or that doing this was a privilege. Mother would ruin his dream by making it her nightmare.

14

Two weeks after he returned from his trip to L.A., Vinnie was getting ready for his shift at Amethyst when his phone buzzed.

It was Ed Vittori from Xclusiv.

"Vinnie, how have you been?"

Vinnie stopped getting ready and took a seat on his bed. "I've been good. And you?" Vinnie had a tough time making small talk when all he could think was, *why is Ed Vittori calling?*

"...You're probably wondering why I called."

Ed didn't give him an opportunity to respond.

"...Vinnie, the studio is casting for a new movie called *Backfield in Motion,* with Mykel Z. set to direct."

Vinnie knew his work. Mykel Z. was a known name in the business.

"The film is going to be a top Xclusiv production with a larger cast, bigger stars, superior production values, and a solid plot. This one is a premium project all the way and we'd love you to be a part of it."

"Thank you! Yes! That's incredible news! Yes, I'll do it!" Vinnie was no longer sitting on the bed. He was on his feet. He felt no hesitation about saying yes to Xclusiv this time.

"Vinnie, I have got to tell you, this sort of production has GAVYN and Grabbys written all over it. This is the sort of project that can easily elevate Vinnie Lux from hot new face to star. Do you have any plans at the end of this month?"

"If I did, I don't anymore."

Ed Vittori laughed. "Your excitement is refreshing."

Vinnie repeated that he was thrilled to be asked.

"Do you think I'm ready?"

"We wouldn't be asking if we didn't. You're perfect for the part."

"Wow, thank you. Yes." Vinnie was trembling. Another role in another Xclusiv film! Not just any film, a top-tier feature.

"Woody will be so pleased. He called you a natural. I bet your ears have been burning. After *Mancandy 2*, everyone around here has been referring to you as a hot commodity. Woody has big plans for you. Vinnie, are you ready for the big time?"

Vinnie took a deep breath. This was like a dream coming true. He almost said he was born ready but refrained. As a Midwestern boy he had a certain image to uphold. "Thank you all for this chance and for believing in me."

"All you're lacking is some experience and polish—those will come." Vittori continued, "We are already convinced you have what it takes. Now we just need to be sure that you're committed to your career."

Vinnie cut him off. "I can assure you I'm committed. I'm willing to do whatever it takes to make the most of this career.

"That's good to hear. *Backfield in Motion* will have a few pages of dialogue, so there's a nice opportunity to demonstrate your acting skills," said Vittori, quickly adding, 'Do you act?"

"No, but I think I can do it." Vinnie was pretty confident he could pull it off. He had spent years in the closet pretending to be someone he wasn't, so a few lines in a porno should be a piece of cake.

"Great. As I said, the exposure will be huge. This movie will give the public, rather than the execs, a better chance to decide if Vinnie Lux has what it takes. The guys buying and downloading are ultimately the ones who matter. They're the ones who will decide your appeal."

Harsh but true.

As in every field of entertainment, the porn world is fiercely competitive. He needed to get used to the fact. Vinnie knew that he would need to prove himself time and again. Some crumble under that sort of pressure. Others fail to fulfill their hype. Vinnie Lux will be different.

I will be a success in this industry, no matter the cost.

Vinnie was not here to play.

Vittori said he needed to take another call. He emailed Vinnie the contract two minutes later.

Money had not been discussed on the call. Vittori had only said, "I think you'll be pleased." The paycheck for *Backfield in Motion* was significantly larger than what he was paid for *Mancandy 2*. The extra cash would chip away a chunk of his VISA debt. Once he was free of that, who knows? Xclusiv was his ticket to better things.

Vinnie had hoped he would be offered another role. *Mancandy 2* had been a screen test. *Backfield in Motion* was the real deal. This film was his chance to prove that Vinnie Lux was Xclusiv material. XXX legends were born at this studio. Gods were made here. Vinnie hoped to be as big as any of them. He was willing to pay the price.

The email also included the shooting dates as well as his flight information. At the bottom of the email, Vittori had added, "We were hoping you would say yes. We have a great scene lined up for you with a guy you are going to love!"

A moment after reading the email, his phone chirped. Vinnie answered without checking caller ID. "Hey Vincent, what's going on?"

He did not have the time for Ty right now. Besides, he had little interest in anyone who still called him Vincent. He needed to start thinking of himself as Vinnie Lux.

He told Ty he had just spoken with Ed Vittori at Xclusiv. "They want me for another movie, a bigger production."

Ty said, "Oh, so this is going to be a thing then?"

Vinnie almost told Ty to go fuck himself. He had been the one who sent the pictures to Xclusiv in the first place, he could at least try to show some excitement or at least a little interest. This was the sort of negativity Vinnie did not need in his life.

"Maybe I should get a commission for discovering Vinnie Lux."

Vinnie knew he would eventually hear it. He appreciated Ty submitting the photos, but that was where it ended. In fact, Ty was part of the life Vinnie was eager to leave behind. He told Ty he was heading to L.A. at the end of the month.

"Did you know there is a half nude shot of you on the cover of *Chi Guyz* this month? I was at Changes when they were dropping off the new issue. The inside credit says, Vinnie Lux, photo by Joe McCain, Xclusiv Studios."

The image popped up on his phone.

Vinnie felt a flush of excitement at seeing the still from *Mancandy 2*.

They didn't waste any time.

Promotion was everything at this stage in his career. Getting his face and booty out there was essential. His image was no longer his own. He signed it away when he signed the studio contract. With his signature, a part of him had become the property of Xclusiv.

Glenn and Robert would see the *Chi Guyz* cover. That alone was apt compensation for ownership of his image. A couple of months ago he would have paid for something like this.

Vinnie asked Ty to grab him a copy when he got a chance.

"I already grabbed you three. I was hoping I could come by and give them to you tonight ... Maybe stay awhile. What are you doing?"

"Thanks, but I'm exhausted. Plus, I need to get some things in order. Pack. Go to the store." Vinnie wasn't sure where his excuses ended and where the lies began.

Ty's sigh was a hand grenade of passive-aggression.

Vinnie had no patience for this. He was not going to feel guilty for not wanting to hang out. Ty was being immature. Fearing he might say something he would later regret, Vinnie said he had to go and abruptly hung up.

15

Two weeks later, Vinnie was deplaning in L.A. What seemed a dream before was now thrilling and real. *Mancandy 2* had not even been released, and his torso was already on the cover of at least one magazine. Xclusiv had sold photo spreads to several skin magazines. Now he was shooting a film that Xclusiv was pushing as their blockbuster of the season.

This was no longer a fantasy. This was happening.

Any doubt he once had about a porn career was gone. He was no longer conflicted over wanting to be a star. Even as a husky teen, he had harbored dreams of fame, which were some of his deepest and most shameful secrets.

Husky boys shouldn't expect to be anything more.

Nice straight boys don't desire such things. Lusting after fame was an embarrassing fantasy.

But he wasn't straight, and over the past few months he had come to realize that being nice closed more doors than it opened.

Vinnie had been a fan of porn since discovering a shopping bag of DVDs in the dumpster behind his building. In the week that followed, Vinnie watched, and he learned. Once he discovered Xtube and Porn Hub, he was hooked. His porn habit was another secret, but he was tired of secrets and tired of being ashamed. Once those two things were removed from his thinking, his path was clear.

He had never dreamt he might find fame starring in XXX movies. He had been content to be a voyeur and a connoisseur. However, now, 'content' was another word he needed to abandon. His breakup with Glenn made that clear.

Having those pictures sent to Xclusiv was the hand of fate intervening. Vincent was destined for fame, but he had to become Vinnie Lux to do it.

16

After landing, Vinnie called the studio. Kip answered. Vinnie had enjoyed several of Kip's films, but then three years ago, his output stopped. Vinnie figured he had quit the business. Kip had been so fresh and handsome. He was still attractive, but the spark that had made Kip Mason such an appealing ingénue had been extinguished.

Vinnie asked to speak to someone about filming.

Kip had the shooting schedule and information at hand. After what sounded like a few strokes on the keyboard, Kip told Vinnie to be on set the following morning at 10:00. "Someone would have called, they probably just haven't got around to it yet. We're filming the scene at the studio."

He was on site the next morning at nine-forty-five, and had been waiting at a coffee shop nearby for a half an hour prior to that. He was overly eager.

Upon being buzzed into the building, Vinnie was about to take the lift upstairs when he was approached by a tall, lean man. "You're Vinnie Lux, right? I'm Mykel Z., the director."

Vinnie extended a hand. "Nice to meet you. I'm excited about the shoot."

"We're happy to have you working on it."

He was very relaxed. Vinnie liked him right away. They chatted a bit more as Mykel ushered him to set. Mykel explained that his scene still required some set-up. Filming was set to start around eleven.

His scene partner, Christian Sabre; the lean, raven-haired star, was still due on set. Vinnie had heard the name but didn't know much more. When

Christian showed up fifteen minutes later, Vinnie recognized him. He had watched two of Christian's scenes on Porn Hub.

Christian was relatively new to the business. He had been a top stripper at clubs across the country and was approached several times with movie offers. He had resisted until last year, but times had changed. Christian made a few shorts for some online companies, and then, six months ago, Xclusiv recruited him. "I'd seen porn guys dance at the clubs. Guys lined up to tip them because they had been in movies. If making a couple of movies would up my stripping fee and tips I figured, why not?"

Backfield in Motion was his third film.

At the time, only one of Christian's previous features was out on DVD and streaming. "Soon enough I'll be everywhere. At least that's what Ed Vittori tells me."

Mykel Z. came over and asked about enemas. Both men had prepared. "Good," said Mykel, already leading the two models to a tented corner of the set. The domain of Sue, the makeup and hair person,

Mykel gave her some instructions regarding the look and was off to the next thing.

Sue turned to the men and motioned to the makeup chair. "So, who is my first victim?"

The two men looked at each other and started laughing.

Vinnie was beginning to relax.

Ten minutes later, Mykel came to retrieve them from Sue. "Break a leg," she said, giving the two models a thumbs up.

Mykel said he liked the way they were bonding. "That's good. Your characters are teammates. He gave them an overview of their scene and offered an idea as to the blocking. Soon after, they were shooting.

For the most part, Mykel just let the action between Christian and Vinnie unfold. He knew better than to mess with chemistry. Filming stopped a couple of times, but only to adjust the lights or camera angle. In his GAVYN acceptance speech three years ago, Mykel had said, "When the heat is there, it's a matter of capturing the sex rather than orchestrating it."

In their scene, Vinnie and Christian played teammates bunking together the night before the big game. Both players were nervous. A win tomorrow would mean the team was in the playoffs. The teammates were having trouble sleeping. *We'll sleep better after we drop a load.* The action started with two buddies stroking. *That feels so good.* Eventually, one of them suggests lending one another a hand. *This isn't gay. This is just helping out a pal. How does that feel?* Both decide to get a bit bolder. *Put it in your mouth. This isn't as bad as I thought.* And finally, they fuck. The scene ended with them falling asleep in one another's arms.

After both models delivered on their money shots, Mykel called cut. "Now just the final snuggle. Christian, why don't you spoon Vinnie and kiss him on the neck as you both fall asleep."

Filming was exhausting, but despite his fatigue, and the fact that he had just climaxed, Vinnie was still horny as hell. He invited Christian back to his hotel. "Maybe you want to come hang out a bit if you don't have plans."

Christian said he was up for hanging out for a while.

Their pairing at the hotel was as intense as it had been before the camera. They began kissing the moment they were through the door. Vinnie unzipped Christian's jeans and yanked them to his lower thighs. No underwear. Vinnie kissed him on either hipbone before turning Christian around. His kisses and licks grew more insistent. *Harder.* Licking until Christian was riding his tongue. Vinnie was relentless. "That feels so fucking good!" Christian began to jack his dick, exploding in only a few moments. Vinnie said he didn't need any reciprocation. "I just really wanted to do that."

After Christian's breathing calmed, he collapsed onto the bed. "You sure have a full bag of tricks, Vinnie Lux." Christian said he didn't have anywhere to be. Vinnie found an old movie on TV. They ordered Buffalo wings and beer from room service and fell asleep in one another's arms, mirroring the scene they had filmed only hours before.

Vinnie awoke to the clank of Christian buckling his jeans. Was it morning already? Yesterday had been both exhilarating and draining. Vinnie's long yawn ended with a question. "Where are you going?"

Christian needed to head out.

Vinnie moved to the end of the bed and wiped the sleep from his eyes. "Will you be around later? Maybe we could grab dinner or something."

Christian leaned down and kissed him before slipping on his socks. He told Vinnie that he seemed like a decent guy, but he wasn't looking for anything or anyone. "Messing around after helps clear my head. You asked me back here, and I agreed. You needed me. I needed you. We needed more, or maybe we just needed something real. Yesterday was nice and last night was even nicer, but it won't mean that much tomorrow, and probably less the day after. Take it for what it was."

Christian was rejecting him with a hard pass. His calm and direct explanation somehow made it even worse.

"...We had fun, but you don't know where I'm from or if I have a dog or a cat or a husband or a wife. You don't even know my real name. It isn't Christian Sabre, that's for damn sure." Christian lifted his fingers to his lips. "Let's just say I'm from a good family of Fundamental Baptists."

Before closing the door, Christian added, "One thing I will tell you, Vinnie Lux, you are going places."

Vinnie thanked him, but he didn't need Christian to tell him something he already knew.

17

An hour later, Vinnie was awakened by the buzz of his cell phone. Woody was on the line. He was in a bind. "I need your help. I realize this is last minute, but can you possibly stay in L.A. for a few extra days? I'll make it worth your while."

Vinnie sat up straighter and cleared his throat. "Um, sure. Yes, of course. Whatever you need, Woody."

Woody gave an audible sigh. "Great. Come by the studio in a couple of hours. We can talk more then."

"Sure," Vinnie stared at himself in the wall mirror across from the bed. He might miss some shifts at work, but his life had become more about priorities and less about responsibilities.

"Vinnie, you have really helped me out here. I don't forget things like this."

Something about Woody's response made Vinnie wonder if this was a test of his commitment. Extending his stay would cause inconvenience at the restaurant. Alana would not be happy. She would play the victim. He could imagine it in great detail. But this wasn't about Alana. If she gave him an ultimatum, he would quit. He was not about to jeopardize his new career for a mediocre server job.

"I just need to shuffle some things at home."

"Nothing too important I hope."

"Nothing important at all." Vinnie wasn't lying. He could see how little his Chicago life mattered. Most of what remained there for him was a past he wished to escape.

Vinnie added that the other thing he wanted to get done in the next few days was to create Instagram and Twitter accounts for his new "persona." A social media presence was essential for a successful XXX career, and Vinnie wanted to be a success.

"You're right, a social media presence is essential in this business. I can have Ed Vittori set up the accounts. He handles all our public platforms and networks. He's a whiz at that sort of thing. He's helped performers before. He can get your new account started—post some pictures—link you with the studio—connect you with other models. That way, you'll have a stable of fans right out of the gate."

"That would be terrific." Vinnie was grateful, but at the moment, he was consumed with having his first cigarette of the day.

"You are good to me, and I am good to you . . ."

He slipped a smoke from the pack, opened the sliding door, and went onto a tiny platform overlooking a parking lot that the hotel had the audacity to call a "balcony." He lit up and took a drag. *Ahhhhhh.* Now he could focus.

"...Helping each other out is what Xclusiv is all about. We are a team." Before hanging up, Woody added. "See you in a couple of hours."

"I'll see you then." Vinnie finished his smoke and started the coffee pot just as he stepped into the shower. Ten minutes later, he poured a coffee into the cardboard cup. He grimaced at the first sip—weak and bitter at the same time.

Clearing the steam from the mirror above the sink, Vinnie took a long look at himself. There was no denying that he was a different person. He could see it and feel it. He was no longer Vincent—no longer the gay man most likely to live and die in a cul-de-sac. After the things he had done as Vinnie, he could never go back to being Vincent, not the Vincent he had been. That bridge had been burned, and the charred wood was miles downstream.

I am no longer Vincent.

I am no longer that person.

Vincent was a skin he needed to shed. He had outgrown that hide. People recreate themselves all the time. Most stars fabricate a life as well as a history. Vincent lacked star quality. But Vinnie Lux had it in spades.

You are on your way.

Vinnie dropped the towel and took a handful of caked coconut oil. Still watching himself in the mirror, he smoothed it over his chest and down his arms, and back across his nipples again. His dick began to plump and twitch. He took more of the hardened oil and greased either side of his neck and then down his torso, chest, nipples, stomach—then lower. He watched his face in the mirror as he began to pleasure himself.

Not now.

Stop!

Vinnie studied his reflection, noting his best angles, best sex face, pleasure face, orgasm face ... His natural expressions weren't quite right. They needed to be a bit bigger. What if his lips quivered a bit with his shoulders back and chin up? The right orgasm face was important. This was porn; it was only fake if it looked fake.

18

Two hours later, Vinnie walked through the doors at Xclusiv. Kip rose from his desk to greet him and asked if he would like something to drink. "Coffee? Sparkling water?" Vinnie declined, but being treated like a star suited him. He could get used to this.

Kip said that Woody was expecting him and ushered Vinnie into his office. Following Kip into the office, Vinnie noticed a pink and white marbling of the skin on the back of Kip's neck. Were those scars? The marks disappeared beneath the collar of his shirt. Whatever had happened to the former golden boy of porn, it had not been pretty.

Woody rose from his desk and approached Vinnie. "There's the man of the hour." Then, grinning, he clapped a hand on Vinnie's shoulder and motioned for him to have a seat.

"I've seen the rushes from yesterday and they look fantastic. Mykel is very pleased. We all are. Vinnie, from the look of things, this movie is going to put you on the map."

"I am so grateful. Thank you"

"Thank you for staying to shoot the second scene for *Backfield in Motion.* Two scenes will up your billing and name recognition, as well as your paycheck."

"It sounds like you're doing me the favor."

Woody held Vinnie's eyes. "Let's call it mutually beneficial. At Xclusiv, we like to take care of our favorites, our cooperative stars..."

Did he just call me a star?

After seeing rough cuts of your scenes, I'm going to up your billing to third and make you back cover model on the *Backfield* DVD."

"Oh my God, I don't know what to say."

"You're part of the Xclusiv family now."

Woody Wilson was one sexy man, and Vinnie wanted nothing more at that moment than for the hot silver daddy of the studio to bend him over that desk and fuck him. He wanted to feel the cool glass of the desk on his cheek and Woody's tan, muscled body upon him and feel the hair of his chest scratch his back.

"We also need more photos." Woody was already texting Vittori, who appeared at his office seconds later.

"Vinnie agreed," announced Woody, pushing back in his chair, and locking his hands behind his head.

Vittori turned to Vinnie, killer smile at full wattage. "Welcome aboard, and again, congratulations on the second scene. That's the sure sign of a future champ." With the top three buttons of his shirt undone, Vinnie had a nice view of Ed Vittori's sculpted chest. From what Vinnie could see, the publicity genius looked hot enough to step in front of the camera himself.

Being in the office with both men, Vinnie had a sudden craving for daddy types. He was starting to spin a little fantasy of how this meeting might evolve. They would be side by side. He would be on his knees.

"I was just telling Vinnie here that we need to do more stills. We need another photo shoot."

Vittori nodded. "I completely agree. Vinnie, we like to take care of our favorites. We are going to need lots of new pictures for content. Let's set aside a couple of days. Also, I've been working on your social media."

"Already?"

Vittori shrugged. "I can get a lot done in a morning."

"Ed is the best," interjected Woody. "He's done a day's work while I'm still having my coffee."

Ed rotated his laptop and showed the accounts he had set up for Vinnie on Instagram and Twitter. "I took the liberty of already posting a few things," he said.

@VinnieLux–Corn-fed Porn Stud. 8.5". Xclusiv Studio star. Versatile.

Vittori had already posted three "tastefully edited" stills from *Mancandy 2* as well as shots taken on the *Backfield in Motion* set. The Vinnie Lux account already had nearly one thousand followers on Instagram and 812 on Twitter.

"How can I have that many followers already? How is that even possible?"

Vittori gave him a quick smile, "Being an Xclusiv man has its perks. That is enough to gain you plenty of new followers every day, at least for a while."

The profile and account looked terrific. Vinnie wasn't used to having his needs be a priority.

"I told you he was the best," said Woody.

Vinnie nodded. "I know. Now this looks so good I don't want to mess it up."

"I can work with you for a while. We can both post and you can see what I do to boost traffic. Eventually, I'll fade away and you can take over. Sound good?" Ed handed Vinnie one of his business cards. On the back, Ed had included the passwords for each social media platform.

"Thank you so much."

Woody clapped his hands. "Now that is settled. Let's talk about the movie." He told Vinnie that he would be shooting his second scene the next day. "As the replacement for Reed Connors."

Reed Connors.

"I'm replacing Reed Connors," Vinnie wasn't sure he heard them correctly, "But he's such a big star."

Woody said they were all set to shoot with Reed, but he suddenly became unavailable.

Vittori looked up from his laptop. "You mean uncooperative. Why do we bother?"

"Reed has his fans." Woody pursed his lips. "He has hung on longer than I imagined he would, I'll give him that."

Ed conceded the point, though he was clearly not a member of the Reed Connors Fan Club. "His unprofessionalism has no place at Xclusiv, especially in a production of this size." His eyes went to Vinnie, "But it all worked out I suppose. Reed is being replaced by someone sexier."

Vinnie blushed. Accepting flattery gracefully would take time. He was better, but he still had a good ways to go.

Woody nodded. "Trouble with Reed means that we can give our fresh talent a break." He spun his chair towards the window.

Are we being dismissed?

Vinnie was about to ask if he should leave when Woody spun back to face Vittori. "Reed needs to be taught a lesson."

Ed was on board. "He's making you look like a chump."

Woody's irritation was apparent. "Vinnie, this is a lesson on how the business can become unpleasant when performers are uncooperative." Woody continued, "The majority of Xclusiv stars treat this as a business, which it is. If they do drugs, they do them on their own time. They keep fit. They keep healthy. They stay pretty. And above all, they honor their commitment to the studio." The late morning sun hit Woody's face. "After all I've given Reed, all the chances and the second chances, he holds out for more."

"He's a punk." Vittori was stoking the fire.

Vinnie wanted to disappear. Anger rose in Woody's voice. "Reed may have gotten away with this crap last year, but no more. I'm through." Woody's hand smacked the top of his desk.

Vittori was enjoying this. "We've put up with this kind of behavior from Reed long enough. Any other studio would have dropped him by now."

Vinnie felt invisible.

"Reed betrayed me as well as Xclusiv. When I found him, he was a lowlife and he's still one. I gave him a chance, and he gave me an ultimatum."

Turning to Vinnie, Woody's tone softened. "Vinnie let me assure you this is not the norm. For the most part, we are a happy family here."

Being addressed directly did not make Vinnie feel any less of an intruder in this room. He was ready to suggest waiting outside, but Woody kept talking. "It's good for you to hear this. You're part of the Xclusiv family now. Reed was too, that's why his behavior especially painful."

Vinnie nodded.

Vittori nodded.

But Woody wasn't finished. "Since Reed is done here, he'll go straight to the competition. Send an email to the studios we're on good terms with and let them know if they want things to remain good between us, it's in their best interests to have nothing to do with Reed Connors."

Ed added that some studio will probably pick him up to spite Woody.

Woody chuckled. "Then they deserve him. I want Reed to get minimal work."

Vittori nodded. "That shouldn't be tough. He might be 27, but he looks a decade older.

"No film work. No clubs. No publicity. No print work. I want Reed to see he is nothing without his Xclusiv family. Let him go back to being a nobody."

Vittori was lapping up every bit of it. Either he was thrilled to see Reed get his comeuppance, or he took great satisfaction in being the studio henchman. Maybe it was a bit of both.

Woody stood, then Vittori stood, and Vinnie rose. They all shook hands. Evidently, the meeting was over. "Ed, take Vinnie to your office and fill him in with the details about the additional scene and clarify any questions he may have about his social media for the studio."

Moments after Vinnie took a seat in Ed Vittori's office, Ed lowered his voice,

"Reed is more than a model holding out for extra money."

Vinnie suspected as much. Reed and Woody had been lovers. They had even lived together. Claiming he didn't like to gossip, Ed continued. "No one thought them moving in together was a good idea. Most people saw Reed for what he was, but that didn't matter to Woody. His mind was made up. When they were together Reed figured he could do anything he wanted to because he was fucking the boss."

"It sounds awful."

"It was. I just hope it's really over. Maybe it is this time. Rumor is that Reed has hooked himself an even bigger catch. Some sucker with a guitar and a juicy recording contract." Reed leaned closer and asked Vinnie if he watched the talent show, *National Icon*?

Vinnie had seen it once or twice.

Supposedly Reed had left Woody for Cash Cranston.

"Cash Cranston?" A person didn't need to watch the show to have heard of the breakout superstar of last season. Cash Cranston was a beefy country singer with a sexy Southern drawl and a rising new talent on the music scene. "I didn't know he was gay."

"Neither does 99% of the country. When Reed left Woody for Cash, I think Woody finally realized that he had been played. However, Woody is a businessman. Reed could have still had his career if he would have behaved professionally. Instead, he kept the same attitude as before, only he isn't fucking the boss anymore."

For someone who hated to gossip, Vittori was doing great.

Kip buzzed the office to tell Vittori his twelve-thiry appointment had arrived. The interruption brought Ed back to the business at hand. "Okay enough of all that. Vinnie, we can discuss the social media stuff at a later time, or just text me if you have any questions. For now, let's get you briefed on your second *Backfield in Motion* scene. Is this your first experience with group action?"

"Group action. As in orgy? I didn't know that." Vinnie had taken part in a couple of three ways in real life, but that was about the extent of his experience.

Ed planted his elbows and asked if that would be an issue.

"Not at all. I'm happy to do whatever it takes to succeed in this business." Vittori smiled. "Group scenes generally take longer to shoot, meaning more work for the crew and less for the individual performers. I'll show you where it's all going to happen." Ed led Vinnie down the hall, through security doors, and down another corridor to another part of the building. A row of double lockers lined a far wall with a low bench before them. "This is where we're shooting the locker room scene. It's after the big game and the team is in a very celebratory mood after winning the championship…"

A smile crossed Vinnie's lips. Anyone who has ever seen a XXX film had a pretty good idea where this scenario was headed.

19

Don't sit on the second bench or your ass will be royal blue.

The sign pointed to the locker room bench in the middle of the set. It was the first thing Vinnie noticed the next morning when he arrived for the shoot. Because of the orgy scene, the studio had two people doing body makeup.

Viagra was available for the asking. Taking performance enhancers was being a team player. Everyone did them. This was porn! No time for a limp dick at an orgy. Cocks needed to be bars of steel, limbs of endurance.

After a slight delay due to sound issues and the lighting set-up, Mykel called the performers over to discuss the various groupings for the orgy scene. Just as he began to speak, there was a rising commotion in the hallway.

Mykel's expression was transparent. *Another delay!* Filming had not even begun and they were already an hour behind schedule.

The shouts in the hall intensified. Vinnie heard a crash. Reed Connors had arrived on set, unkempt but still sexy in army fatigues and a tight black T-shirt.

The ginger-haired production assistant, Gert, entered two seconds later. "Sorry Mykel, he barged past me."

Reed flicked his cigarette and raised a flask in salute. "Hello bitches," he hollered at the top of his voice, "I'm here and ready to fuck."

Mykel asked Reed what he was doing here.

"I just told you. I'm here to work."

"Reed, you are no longer a part of this production."

Reed must have known he had been replaced. Vinnie's first impression of Reed was that this man did not turn tail and run. Reed was ready to play as dirty as necessary to get what he wanted. "Mykel, you know I'll make this movie great."

"But in the process, you make me, the crew, your cast mates, and the entire set miserable."

"Come on Mykel, I can fuck better than any of these ladies. Bring on the fluffer. Gert, get over here."

Gert blushed but didn't seem opposed to the idea.

Mykel threw down his clipboard. "Reed, what the fuck do you expect me to do? Do you actually think I would go rogue on something like this and stick my neck out, for you? Obviously, the casting change came from above."

"From Woody?"

Mykel nodded. "Did you really think there would be no repercussions for fucking Woody over?"

Reed lowered his voice. Vinnie heard him say something about certain people at Xclusiv being out to get him. "People are getting in Woody's ear and telling him things. They're making Woody hate me. I never..."

Mykel cut him off. "Not my issue. Never was my issue." He told Reed there was no one to blame but himself. "You have fucked yourself over this time. There's no one else to blame and you know it."

Reed told Mykel to call Woody.

"I don't take orders from you."

"Get Woody on the phone. If I can just talk to him, I can make him understand."

Mykel lifted his ball cap and smoothed back his hair. "Woody does understand, finally. That's why he canned you."

"But I..."

"Again, your problem, your issue. Not mine."

The gathered cast sat on the sidelines. Reed had been all but oblivious to his audience.

"Why don't you take your cellphone outside and call Woody. I can't solve your problem. You're wasting my time, and theirs," Mykel gestured towards the cast.

"Mykel, who are you kidding? You're no better than me."

"That was true at one time, but not anymore. I'm sober now. I stopped being an asshole—you might want to consider it before your career is completely over."

When Mykel refused to get involved, Reed smirked. "I've got secrets on you. You have told me things."

"I know Reed, and I know some things about you too. I don't have time for your crap. Do everyone a favor and go. I've still got *my* job and right now you are messing with it."

Reed turned to the performers on set. "So I've been replaced by some up-and-coming talent." His loose air quotes took a jab at Vinnie's up-and-coming status.

Mykel cut him off. "I am not your pal. I never was. I tolerated you because of Woody. We all tolerated you because of Woody. Well, Woody isn't protecting you anymore."

"Then fuck you."

"No fuck you! And now get your has-been ass off my set."

"This isn't over. I'll get back with him, Mykel. You know I will, and when I do, the only thing you'll be directing is a stream of piss into the toilet." Reed pushed him aside. Instead of leaving, he grabbed a handful of Chex Mix from the craft table and approached the couches where most of the cast was seated."

"Hey Lee."

Lee Botello nodded and turned away. Apparently, Lee didn't want trouble. He did his job, and he did it well. He had said earlier that he had a good thing going at the studio.

"A.Z. You know that I know things, right?"

A.Z. Ambush looked up from his dialogue sheet and glared in Reed's direction before turning his focus back to the script. He only had three lines at the start of the scene, but it was excuse enough to avoid getting drawn into all this drama.

The other models busied themselves. No one wanted to catch Reed's eye. From what Vinnie had heard, most guys on set resented Reed's hold on their boss. Woody and Reed had a stormy relationship. This time things seemed final, but things could change again. For now, befriending Reed was tantamount to treachery, not an Xclusiv family value.

Vinnie likened Reed to a downed live wire—thrashing, lashing, and tossing sparks into the air. He eyed each model on the couches before approaching Vinnie. "Vinnie Lux?"

Vinnie nodded.

"So you're the hayseed replacing me?" Reed looked him up and down. "How generic. No accounting for taste, or the lack of it." Reed took a swig from his flask and wiped his mouth with the back of his hand.

Vinnie half-expected something like this. For someone who was supposedly so proud, Reed had little shame. Vinnie tried to remain calm and keep his breathing in check. He refused to give Reed the satisfaction of seeing him upset.

"Vinnie Lux, you are a complete nobody."

Looking Reed in the eye, he replied. "But I am still the complete nobody who is replacing you." Vincent went through life avoiding confrontation, but apparently, Vinnie was wired differently.

Reed asked Vinnie if he was replacing him in Woody's bed as well.

Vinnie didn't answer, but the thought was thrilling.

Reed was getting in Vinnie's face. "What are you 22? 23?"

"I'm 25." Remembering that Vittori had brought up that Reed was 27, Vinnie told him he looked good for 35. Vinnie Lux could give as well as take.

Reed tipped back the contents of his flask. "I bet you are a good boy, both professional and cooperative. Good work ethic, full of team spirit, and always giving 110%. I've hated your type for years. Boring as fuck and judging everyone around you."

"That's not... "

"Vinnie Lux, you have no idea what you're getting into. *None*."

Vinnie was about to echo a similar sentiment when Mykel stepped forward. "That is it! Reed, get the fuck off my set."

Reed turned. "Or what?"

"Or I'll call some people. And you don't want that." Mykel stepped forward. "I know things about you too. Woody has been protecting you from some nasty people, but no more. You get out or I will take great pleasure in letting those people know your address. My phone is right here."

"Fuck you." Reed was trying to save face, so Mykel's threat must have resonated. "This isn't over," Reed flipped the entire room the bird as he walked away.

Mykel turned to the talent. "Now that the drama is over, can we please film the scene?" Everyone applauded. The cast was more than ready. "Okay, to start, A.Z. and Vinnie, I want you over there against the lockers. Lee, as Coach Matthews you come out of your office and catch your team captains making out. They are so into each other they don't notice you. You're about ready to blow your whistle, but instead you grope yourself through your shorts. Vinnie, you look over and see the Coach. He moves closer. He is still hesitant. Vinnie, you motion for him to join in the action. When he does, you drop to your knees. The rest of you are coming from the showers in singles and pairs. Gert will time the entrances. Everyone clear on groupings? Any questions?"

He took the lack of response as affirmative. "Okay, so A.Z., Vinnie, Lee, places please. And, action."

20

The phone rang as Vinnie was putting on his shoes.

"Hey stud, hope I didn't wake you."

"Nope I was heading out for coffee." Vinnie said he was an early riser. "No matter how hard I try or how late I go to bed, I cannot sleep in."

"That's not a bad habit to have." Woody said that he heard yesterday's shoot for *Backfield in Motion* ran late.

"Yes, it did." Vinnie's phone read 8:35AM. Filming the orgy scene had gone on and on; switching positions, shifting partners, make-up retouches, etc. Ten hours of it. By the end, Vinnie was sick of sex, even with that sexy stable of orgy mates. During the final hour of shooting, he wondered what more Mykel could possibly want or need.

"If it's any consolation, it was worth the effort. I asked Mykel to stay behind last night and put together something for me to see. He was here until dawn. "Vinnie Lux, you more than hold your own in an orgy of veterans. And Mykel has become your new biggest fan. And I had Ed upload some shots to your Twitter and Instagram."

He had gotten the alert. Vinnie said that was great.

All this, and it was only eight-thirty in the morning. People at this studio were exceptionally devoted. They seemed to work around the clock.

Mykel called you a wild man, a force of nature. Apparently, he's still working on a clip with you and Lee, but he tells me that portion is electric. Good work. I like being proud of my boys."

Vinnie said he liked Mykel. "I've always been a fan of his work. *Hazing Hank* and *Two in a Foxhole* are both classics.

Woody was impressed. "When it comes to porn, most people don't pay attention to who's behind the camera."

"Well, I guess I'm not most people."

Woody asked when he was heading back to Chicago.

"My flight isn't until ten this evening."

"Since you have the day free, I would like for you to drop by the studio. I have something important to discuss with you."

Vinnie didn't say that he had the day free. He was supposed to have lunch with his friend Ralph. "I have a little something, but I should have plenty of time to swing by there."

Vinnie knew coercion when he felt it.

Woody wasn't asking him to stop by. He was telling him.

"I'll cancel my other plans." Woody needed to hear that Xclusiv was his sole priority. And if that's what he wanted, that's what Vinnie would give him. He was not going to jeopardize his career to have lunch with an old friend. *I'll try* was not something Woody was accustomed to hearing.

He left a message for Ralph cancelling their lunch. Ralph would understand. If he didn't understand, so what? They had worked together at Amethyst, and then last year, Ralph moved out here. He heard Vinnie was in town and sent him a text. Ralph was a nice guy, but he wasn't important.

Before hopping in the shower, he checked his followers again.

Instagram 4620
Twitter 2213

21

When Vinnie came through the doors of Xclusiv an hour later, Kip rose to greet him. Kip wore a long-sleeved black turtleneck, concealing the marbled warzone of scars that Vinnie had glimpsed on his neck and shoulder days before. "Woody has been expecting you."

When Vinnie entered the room. Woody was on the telephone. He motioned for Vinnie to have a seat. "Maxwell, this isn't something we should be discussing right now. Not on the phone. I'll notify you as soon as they're in. Your patience will be rewarded. I will make sure of that. If there is a discrepancy, we can work out an arrangement. Yes ... Yes ... Okay, by the tenth at the latest."

Hanging up, Woody leaned back in his chair. His biceps looked like melons in that shirt. Vinnie glimpsed the edge of some salt and pepper pit hair. Another tuft of hair peeked from his collar. Woody's eyes revealed the focus that made him a good businessman, and probably an exceptional lover. Reed's accusation echoed in Vinnie's head. *Are you replacing me in Woody's bed as well?*

Woody thanked Vinnie for stopping by. He liked having his wishes promptly met. "I have something I want to ask you, something we rarely do at Xclusiv. This could have been done over the phone, but, for me, talking face to face is preferable, especially when it's good news."

Good news. Vinnie liked the sound of things so far.

"After seeing your work in *Mancandy 2* and *Backfield in Motion*, everyone here, myself included, is very excited about your future at the studio. You're the complete package; photogenic, a sex pig, handsome, nice cock, and an incredible butt..."

Vinnie began to blush.

"And you're smart with a solid work ethic and you seem like a genuinely nice young man."

"Thank you."

"Vinnie, I would like you to be part of our core Xclusiv family. I think it's time we discuss a long and profitable partnership between Vinnie Lux and Xclusiv."

Vinnie really liked the sound of this.

"I have a good sense about these things. Spotting and promoting talent is Ed Vittori's job, but recognizing talent with a future at Xclusiv is mine." Woody stood and took a seat on the corner of his desk.

Woody's eyes were crystal blue and hypnotic.

"Vinnie, I have been watching you since the first day you came into this office, and I have not been disappointed. This is all a roundabout way of asking how would you feel about becoming an Xclusiv Studio exclusive?"

He had heard certain performers at the studio referred to as exclusives: Josh Lawless. Reed Connors. A.Z. Ambush. It was an elite group. Vinnie never considered the possibility of his being in their league.

Is this some sort of mistake or maybe a prank?

The exclusives were the top studio performers. He'd gone to Woody's office with hopes of being contracted for another film. But he wasn't expecting this.

"Being an exclusive, you will be joining the ranks of Peter Ray Thomas, A.Z. Ambush, Josh Lawless, Dwayne Thorne, and even Desi Lou, the first Xclusiv exclusive." The photos of each superstar lined the walls between Woody and Vittori's offices.

Had others seen his promise all along?

He had noticed guys on the sets of *Mancandy 2* as well as *Backfield in Motion* sizing him up and seeing if he had what it takes. The industry fed on competitiveness, and no one was in it to be mediocre.

Vinnie's head was spinning.

Woody continued, "This would mean a salaried contract as well as filming bonuses, guaranteed press, a publicity tour with club appearances, costar input, free gym membership, use of one of our apartments, and several additional perks. We will make you a star. The contract is for two years. At that point if things haven't worked out, either of us can simply walk away."

Vinnie was in disbelief. "Am I interested? Is this a trick question? Woody, this is a dream come true."

Woody chuckled. "Should I take that as a yes?"

"Yes, A definite yes."

"I was hoping you would feel that way. After you left the office that first day, I told Ed and McCain, that kid has a future here, if he wants one."

Vinnie remembered his first time in this office. Vincent had walked in, but Vinnie had walked out.

"Really?"

"Over the years I've become a pro at predicting success in this business. If a model has the raw talent, success is a decision. Commitment to their career will seal the deal. But some guys, like Reed, are their own worst enemy. Desi Lou was the same way. Last I heard he had squandered everything. Drugs can take over, like with Peter Ray Thomas. Some stories end in tragedy, like with Carter Gaines. I am great spotting talent, but I can't predict what a person is going to do with it."

Vinnie wondered if Woody gave that speech to all his new stars. If he did, it worked. Vinnie was determined to be one of Xclusiv's great success stories.

Woody buzzed Kip and told him to bring the contract and a bottle of champagne. He told Kip he needed him to be a witness for the contract signing as well.

Kip appeared with the contract and showed Vinnie the highlighted lines requiring his signature. Vinnie knew he should read through it, but doing so would be awkward. He didn't necessarily trust Woody, but it was essential to pretend that he did. He printed on one page, put his initials on another, and signed twice on the final page. Kip added his name as a witness, and Woody signed and dated the contract.

Done.

He was an exclusive.

Woody asked Kip to fetch Ed Vittori for a meeting. "We have some things to discuss with our newest exclusive." Woody leaned back in his chair. At that moment few things seemed sexier to Vinnie than a powerful daddy, secure in his own world.

Vittori simultaneously knocked and entered, laptop beneath his arm. "I'm told congratulations are in order." The fit of Ed's yellow polo and jeans were perfection.

Woody asked Kip to pop the bottle of champagne. "And pour the three of us a glass, and one for yourself as well."

After pouring, the office phone rang. Kip returned to the reception desk with a champagne flute in hand.

The remaining men toasted Vinnie's future at the studio.

"I can do great things promoting you." said Vittori. "But you make my job easy. You are an easy sell." He asked if Vinnie had noticed his upticks on Instagram and Twitter?

Vinnie had checked his followers before coming to the studio, twice. "Yes. Thank you. You are so great with this stuff."

Woody asked Vittori to send out a press release announcing that Xclusiv Studio had signed three new exclusive talents; Vinnie Lux, Dean Driver, and Gio Santiago.

Three?

This was the first that Vinnie had heard about other new exclusives.

Woody told Vittori to include that all three models were discovered in-house and that Xclusiv head Woody Wilson had personally chosen each young man to represent the future of the company. "Quote me as saying I'm confident of their collective and individual success. Blah blah. Ed, you know the drill, give a mini bio for each."

Vinnie asked if they needed him to write anything.

"We'll take care of your past," said Woody. "We created a bio about you so fans could connect with you and get a sense of who you are."

Vinnie wondered if anyone else saw the irony in this. If this was the way it was done, he was on board.

"Wait until you read your story," Vittori added.

"You've already created my past?"

"That is exactly what we've done," replied Ed. "We know how to sell a product. It's all in your contract."

"Trust us," added Woody.

The entire thing was a little unsettling, but also a great relief. He should have known that a change of name wouldn't be enough. His history was part of the fantasy. They were taking it all away and changing everything. Vinnie Lux was a fabrication of the flesh, a fantasy created by Xclusiv.

Welcome to the dream factory.

Vinnie assumed his possible past would be something that lent itself to porn fantasy. Maybe he would be an auto mechanic discovered working on Woody's car, or a student paying off his college debt, or an actor fresh off the bus replying to an ad in the trades about modeling opportunities. He could be a divorced dad paying child support, a club-kid eager for fame, a personal trainer who decided to share his physique with the world, or a rebellious rancher's son who fled the homestead because his family couldn't accept his being gay. Maybe they would make him a straight guy whose girlfriend goaded him into making gay porn.

Woody lit a cigarette. He had quit for an entire week, but started again yesterday. "I know, this dirty disgusting habit is killing me, but what the fuck, something will eventually. I plan on quitting."

"Me too." Vinnie fished a pack from his windbreaker.

Woody grinned as he reached to light Vinnie's cigarette. "In addition to the bio, we need new stills to accompany the announcement." Woody asked Vittori how the McCain shots turned out.

"See for yourself." Ed put his laptop on his desk and spun it around. Woody flipped through the pictures before exhaling, "What does Joe think?"

"He was pleased."

Woody curled the ash off the tip of his smoke. "Pleased doesn't sound as enthusiastic as I would like. This needs to be done right. We are announcing our exclusives. These photos need to make blood rush straight to your cock." Woody buzzed Kip and had him dial McCain and put him on speaker. The call went straight to voicemail.

Vittori said it never hurt to have something fresh. Maintaining interest on social media and keeping the attention of the cyber-set meant an abundance of fresh content. "And we learned from experience that it always pays to have a surplus, remember Carter?"

Woody exhaled through his teeth.

Vittori continued, "Two films in the can and he was gone. We hardly had any still pictures of him to circulate."

Vinnie read about Carter while researching Xclusiv. The article popped up on a Google search. Trim, blonde, and boyish, Carter Gaines had made a splash with his debut movie and his follow-up film. Carter was set to start his third picture when he was killed in an automobile accident. Vinnie had reread the article the previous morning. The young porn star had not been alone in the car. Kip Mason had been driving. Vinnie suspected the crash was the source of Kip's scars.

"Saturation is my game plan," said Vittori. "I want images of the new exclusives to be everywhere. So yes, more pictures. Definitely."

Seizing the opportunity, Vinnie asked about the other exclusives.

Woody apologized for not explaining earlier. "I was so excited after you agreed that I got ahead of myself." He said the studio wanted to do something big. "So this year, instead of one exclusive, we have three." Woody asked if he had met Dean Driver and Gio Santiago.

Vinnie had not.

Woody turned to Vittori. "Ed, all three new exclusives are in town. We need to make a new photo shoot happen." Flipping open his appointment book, Woody caught Vinnie's eye, "Call me old fashioned, but I never could keep track of anything without writing it down on paper."

He buzzed Kip. "Kip, do I have anything lined up this week that I don't know about?"

Kip said he was mostly open.

Woody told Vinnie the studio needed him to stay a little longer. "Three or four more days, tops."

"Of course." Vinnie would make it work. Availability was key. He was not about to let Dean and Gio get the extra publicity. Alana might fire him, but he should have quit when he buried Vincent and became Vinnie. He had been postponing the inevitable. Alana was prickly on a good day. Hopefully, when he asked for another week off she would let him go. He was tempted to wait until after the restaurant closed to call—then leave a message.

Servers are a dime dozen.

"Yes, I will be here." Vinnie reiterated.

Kip buzzed the office. Joe McCain was on line one. Woody punched a button "Hello Joe, you're on speaker. I have Ed and our new exclusive, Vinnie Lux, in the room with me." After some small talk, he told McCain the plan. "How quickly can we make this photo shoot happen?"

"Let me check my calendar."

"Great. I will let you sort that out with Kip. Take care, Joe."

Turning to Vittori, Woody said he wanted another press release. "This one should include the basics announcing the three new exclusives, mini-bios, stats, etc. We can also use that to announce that these three studs will be starring in the upcoming production, *Prime Meat: The Best Cuts.*"

This was the first Vinnie had heard about it. Another movie meant more publicity, another credit, and moving a bit closer to fame. More photos. More fans. More followers. More likes. More of everything was fine with Vinnie.

"I'll have it good to go ASAP." Vittori nodded as he typed at the keyboard. "Papers, magazines, bloggers, podcasters, and sites. I'll get it out later today with some of the solo shots."

"And then next week follow up with an expanded piece that includes the new pictures," added Woody.

Woody leaned back in his chair. "I would also like you to draft another press release saying that Xclusiv has dissolved Reed Connors' contract after it was discovered the aging star was involved in *questionable activities.*" Woody's air quotes made the accusation seem even shadier. "I don't care. You can list a few if you want—forgery, identity theft, prostitution, drugs ... I'm sure he's done them all."

Ed said that he thought "the issue" had already been addressed. "Are you sure, Woody? Usually, we keep studio news upbeat. Something like this might be construed as defamatory. Reed could sue."

Woody lit another cigarette. "Who is going to bankroll his legal fees, his new beau? Do you think that Cash Cranston is going to want to get involved in a lawsuit involving a gay porn star and a XXX studio? That doesn't mix well with Cash's guns, God, and glory fan base. If Cranston does bankroll a lawsuit, I have no problem dragging his name into this."

"But it doesn't have to be Cranston. Woody, you have plenty of enemies in the business. Corbin Kent has been waiting eight years to get back at you for leaving Tandem. And I can easily name two or three other guys who would love to see you go down."

Woody refused to budge on the subject. "Sometimes the risk is worth it." Then he abruptly turned to Vinnie, "Don't you think that sometimes taking risks is worth it?"

Unsure if Woody was actually asking him or simply acknowledging his presence, Vinnie remained silent. Best not to get involved. At this point in his career, he didn't need enemies.

Woody turned back to Ed. "The lawsuit doesn't scare me. If we're backed into a corner, I suspect we would have no problem digging up a few guys who'll swear under oath that Reed forged, stole their identity, sold them drugs, or anything else we want them to say. There is always a pack of hungry boys willing to do whatever it takes to be in the movies."

Maybe they wanted to see how Vinnie responded. Maybe they were gauging his loyalty or if he could be trusted. Or perhaps they wanted to see if Vinnie Lux was one of those hungry boys. False accusations were a dirty business. Under oath, they are perjury.

So many were willing to do anything.

Sometimes there's a thin line between ambition and crime.

Vinnie wasn't being asked, and he was not about to volunteer. If things were different, what would he do? Would he lie about something like this if his career depended upon it?

"The Reed press release will go out later today as well."

"Good man." Woody tapped an edge of ash into his glass ashtray and added that he wanted to eyeball the press release before it went out.

Vittori nodded.

"Enough of that." Woody stood and topped the three flutes. "To more pleasant matters," Woody raised his glass in a toast. "To Vinnie Lux. Congratulations on being our newest exclusive, and on becoming an official member of the Xclusiv family."

The glasses met with a ping.

He buzzed Kip and told him to bring in a stack of gym passes, the tanning and teeth whitening coupons, and a key to the condo.

Kip entered and handed a folder of coupons to Vinnie before handing a key to Woody. He asked if there would be anything else. Woody told him that would be all.

Woody handed Vinnie the key. "We set you up in our WeHo flat. Great space. Great location. It's a four-bedroom place I bought years ago with some money I inherited. I rent it to Xclusiv and the studio rents it out to you at a reasonable rate. Sometimes out-of-town guys will use a spare room, but right now everyone at the condo is a fulltime resident. It will be a good way to get to know some of the guys. You'll be sharing the flat with the other two new exclusives, Gio Santiago and Dean Driver, as well as A.Z. Ambush."

Vinnie said he had met A.Z. on the *Backfield in Motion* shoot.

"Of course." Woody pointed to the highlighted line. "Sign here. This just says we'll just deduct the rent from your salary." Ed Vittori was the witness.

Putting the paperwork aside, Woody took a seat. "How about having lunch to celebrate? Just the two of us."

Taking his cue, Vittori said he needed to start on the press releases."

"And Ed, I want to see the item about Reed before it goes out."

"Got it." Vittori nodded to Vinnie. "Welcome aboard, Vinnie Lux."

He wondered if there was another reason that Vittori wasn't joining them. Maybe Woody was interested in more than lunch. Like most flirtatious men, Woody was tough to read. A little afternoon delight was fine by Vinnie. He would do Woody Wilson even if he didn't run the studio. The fact that he did, made it even more of a turn-on.

22

Woody drove a Lexus. "When my old car got totaled, I figured, why the fuck not. I deserve it!"

Vinnie replied that it was a beautiful ride.

Talk on the drive to the restaurant was mostly just chitchat: the benefits of living in L.A., the noting of a few landmarks, and minor work talk—nothing remotely flirtatious.

Lunch began on the same note, friendly and somewhat informal but still a business lunch. After being seated, Woody's phone buzzed nonstop for the first several minutes. "Suddenly I'm a popular guy." Finally, he shut off his phone, "Business can wait. Right now, I am having lunch with a gorgeous man. I'd be a fool not to savor the moment."

The man was a master of flattery, punctuated by that gorgeous smile. Motioning to the waiter, Woody ordered two glasses of the house red. "The studio can take care of itself for an hour or two. Vittori, McCain, and even Kip are all more than capable of answering most anything."

The server brought their wine.

Savoring the moment, Woody made a toast, "To Vinnie Lux, my new exclusive and a captivating young man." Afterwards, he leaned very close. He touched the rim of their glasses again, "Very captivating."

Suddenly, and definitely, flirtatious.

Woody had it all: power, looks, charm, and money. Vinnie wanted to fuck this guy, but he needed to be smart about it. He didn't want to appear overly eager, even though he was. "Does being an exclusive make me a trusted member of the Xclusiv family?"

"Not quite yet."

Was Woody teasing or testing?

"How do I become a trusted member? What's your advice?"

"Simple, you need to trust me—completely."

Trust was never easy for Vincent. He knew from experience that when people say they need to be trusted, there is often a good reason for suspicion. But that was then. This is now. That was Vincent; he was Vinnie.

"If you play by my rules; we're good. But if you betray me, or the studio, after we have made a significant investment in you; things become not so good."

"Fair enough."

"Real trust comes in time."

"Of course." Vinnie could accept that. At least Woody was being upfront about things.

"I didn't mean to sound so ominous." Woody tapped out a cigarette and offered one to Vinnie. "This is a members club; you can smoke here."

He accepted a smoke as well as a light.

Woody lit his cigarette and blew the smoke upward.

Smoking gave Vinnie a moment to think. "Woody. I am going to do my best for you and for Xclusiv."

"I believe you will." Woody reached across the table and touched the back of Vinnie's hand. "Your attitude pleases me, but I need to see that attitude in action."

"You will." Vinnie's heart was pounding. They sat quietly for a moment. Woody began stroking the hollow of Vinnie's thumb. The only sounds were muffled talk from neighboring tables and a symphony on the sound system. Vinnie didn't know where this was headed, but he certainly approved of the general direction. Woody didn't pull his hand away until the server approached with the salads.

23

After the waiter cleared their plates, Woody eyed his Rolex. "I need to get back to the office this afternoon. Key conference call. I'll drop you by the WeHo flat on the way and introduce you to the guys."

Vinnie said that he had to swing by his hotel and collect his things if he was moving in.

"I'll have Kip bring your things over."

"Kip doesn't need to ..."

"It will save you some trouble. I insist."

Vinnie was not pleased at the thought of his belongings being gathered and packed by a relative stranger, but Woody's words about trust and being family were still fresh in his mind. *Was this another test?* Vinnie took a breath and tried to not make a big deal out of it. "That would be great," he managed around his discomfort.

Less than five minutes from the restaurant, Woody made a U-turn and eased to the curb in front of a four-story apartment building.

The building seemed well maintained both inside and out. The lobby was sparse but tasteful. Entering the elevator, Woody pressed 4. Vinnie was nervous, but excited. The elevator door opened with a ping. 4E was to the left. Woody gave a quick rapping knock before unlocking the door.

He handed Vinnie the key. "Welcome to your new home."

The flat was spacious with a color scheme of brown and gold. The furnishings were modern—a sectional couch, sleek chairs, a glass coffee table, and a widescreen TV. The kitchen was at the end of the communal area. Vinnie could also see a deck through the sliding glass doors. A hallway ran on either side of the kitchen. Down each hallway, there were two bedrooms and one bathroom.

"I love it." Vinnie asked how old the building was.

"Late 1940s. The building was one of many that went up in the big housing boom in L.A. following WWII." Woody had bought the place from an aging sitcom starlet.

Once they entered the space, Vinnie heard the unmistakable sounds of sex coming from one of the rooms.

"That's A.Z.," laughed Woody. " ... His boyfriend is in town for a visit."

Vinnie's bedroom was just across the hall. The room was furnished with a queen-sized bed, a dresser, and decent-sized closet. "Sheets, pillows, pillowcases, and towels are in the linen closet beside the bathroom. Xclusiv provides all that. The housecleaner comes on Tuesdays." Woody pursed his lips. "Let's see. The laundry room is in the basement. No coins required."

The sounds of sex from A.Z.'s room were growing louder, more fevered.

"I love it. I can't thank you enough."

"I like to keep my boys happy so they can focus on their careers." Woody fished a ring with three additional keys from his pocket. "Outside door. Mailbox. Laundry room." He dangled the key ring in front of Vinnie before dropping it into his hand. "General rules. Respect your roommates and the premises. No hard drugs. No hustling out of the apartment. Smoking on the patio only. Basically, refrain from activities that will cause me any problems."

The rules seemed fair. Vinnie appreciated the honesty.

The moans of A.Z. and his boyfriend were growing louder. Escalating. Someone was ready to pop. A cry of "Fuck yes, I'm there, I'm there" broke the tension. Woody started laughing. "I need to get back to the office. Kip will drop off your things later."

When Woody kissed him goodbye, he kissed him on the mouth. Vinnie even felt a bit of tongue. He may have been surprised, but he returned the kiss with fervor. A kiss like that was a promise of things to come.

When Woody left a moment later, the bedroom door opened as if on cue. A.Z. Ambush emerged, heading for the bathroom with his waning erection leading the way. He cupped a hand on the head of his penis to catch any remaining droplets of cum. A.Z. was a porn legend. He'd been with Xclusiv for years. "Hey," he said, seeing Vinnie. "When did you get here?"

Vinnie said Woody dropped him off five minutes ago.

"He said you were moving in. Sweet." A.Z. closed the bathroom door.

Feeling awkward, Vinnie went onto the balcony and checked out the view. He was still having his smoke when A.Z. and a cute young brunette appeared. "Vinnie, sorry I didn't get a chance to properly welcome you to the place. I was ... otherwise engaged." He added with a smirk. "This is my boyfriend, Roy."

Roy rolled his finger to draw attention to the ring. "Don't forget we're engaged to be engaged."

A.Z. flashed his matching ring. "Yep, *Forever, Roy*, engraved right here."

"And *Forever, A.Z.*" Roy added.

"Good to meet you, Roy." Vinnie shook his hand and introduced himself.

"Pleased to make your acquaintance." Roy had a lazy drawl that made him sound like a boy who took his time.

"Roy is up from Texas. We had a nice visit, but he heads back tonight. That is if he gets his butt moving!" A.Z. slapped Roy on the rear. "You need to hop into the shower before you go to the airport." Without another word, Roy went back into the flat.

"He's cute." Vinnie asked how long they had been together.

"Six months. Things are going well." A.Z. said this time he might be in it for the long haul. "I'm awful attached to that guy. He makes me happy. And he loves this big dick," he added with a laugh.

Vinnie told A.Z. he had heard him on a recent podcast with Dorian Mikado. In the show, A.Z. described himself as easy going—at least for this business. "That's why I've lasted so long. I stay in shape, no needles, nothing up the nose, and I try to get along with people. Of course, there are exceptions." Dorian asked for details, but A.Z. refused to name names. He wouldn't even tell Dorian which costars he would kick out of bed.

A.Z. was in the first gay porn movie Vinnie had ever seen, *A Hole in One*. When they met on set, Vinnie had been too intimidated for more than a cursory introduction. Then *BAM*, they were doing a locker room scene together.

Nice to meet you—now let me suck your dick.

Nice to meet you as well—your ass tastes exquisite.

A.Z. was the most popular African-American model in adult films. For years he had been the Black King of Gay Porn. Vinnie couldn't believe he was standing here shooting the breeze with his new roommate, A.Z. Ambush.

"That was crazy with Reed coming on set yesterday, wasn't it?"

"That was nothing compared to some of the star trips I've seen," replied A.Z. "Sometimes this business makes guys crazy. Reed isn't nuts. With him it's all about the drama. He lives for that shit and knows he doesn't have to be likable. He has Woody."

Vinnie said it sounded like things were over between Woody and Reed. "He even had Ed Vittori do a press release."

"Did Woody want to read the press release over before Ed sent it out?"

Vinnie nodded.

A.Z. shook his head and laughed. "Woody and Reed play games. They have for years. That press release will never go out. I've seen relationships like theirs, but not to that degree. Those two are like the world's tallest rollercoaster, up, down, and all around for the thrills. It's exhausting. They like drawing others into their drama. You're a grown man who can make up his own mind, but my advice is to steer clear of all that."

"Why would I be part of their game?"

"On some level, you already are. Woody hired you to replace Reed who came gunning for you on set. Now Woody personally dropped you off here." A.Z. paused to consider his words. "From the outside it looks like you are already a part of their game whether you want to be or not."

Roy appeared with a towel slung low across his hips. He ran a hand across the happy trail beneath his navel. "Were you all talking about me?"

A.Z. shook his head. "This one thinks everything is about him."

Roy stepped closer. "Well, isn't it?"

A.Z. gave him a lingering kiss. "No it ain't. Now get some clothes on. We need to get you to the airport."

While Roy was getting dressed, Vinnie asked A.Z. how he got his stage name. "I'm still getting used to mine. A.Z. Ambush is a stage name, right?"

"Oh yes. That was a name made in Hollywood. I didn't like it at first, but it's grown on me. I'm from Phoenix, born and raised. I was still living there when I came here to make my first movie for Bonanza Pictures. When I was filling out the model release form, I put the state in the wrong line. Somebody at the studio paired it with Ambush and A.Z. Ambush was born. Looking back, it was a damn good name, especially when you start out in a triple-X western." He said that being rechristened with a XXX name took some getting used to,

"So has being in the industry been good?"

"I like the money and I love to fuck, so yes, it has been a good thing. The problem in this business isn't the business; it's the guys who can't handle it. Once porn starts swelling your ego instead of your dick, it messes with a man." A.Z. shouted for Roy to hurry. "We need to be out the door in 20 minutes." He turned back to Vinnie, "There's a lot about this business that you can't tell a person. Most need to find out for themselves."

Roy emerged from the bathroom in jeans and a T-shirt. "I am ready. And now you're the one who needs to get moving," he said to A.Z.

A.Z. took Roy by the hand. "Come here. I have something else I want to say to you." Moments later, Vinnie heard laughter coming from the bedroom. Ten minutes later, they rushed out of the bedroom and out the front door. "Nice meeting you," Roy called out over his shoulder.

24

"Amethyst."

Alana answered.

Fuck!

Vincent looked at the clock. It was the dinner rush in Chicago. The call probably bypassed the host desk and went directly to the office. "Hey, it's Vincent."

"We miss you here. How are things with your uncle?"

He had forgotten that he had said he needed to return to Los Angeles because his uncle was in poor health. "Not good."

"I'm sorry." He could hear Alana shuffling through the clutter on her desk.

Vinnie told her things were indefinite. "My aunt is overwhelmed. I need to stay here a while. In fact, it looks like I might be moving out here."

The paper shuffling paused. Alana had been a restaurant manager for eight years. She knew a line of bullshit when she heard one.

So what if Alana didn't believe him. Let her fire him. He had the chance to become somebody.

"If I come back to Chicago, I'm worried that I would just be hopping on another plane back here in a few days. This way I can be with her afterwards. I don't want her left alone." Even if Alana didn't believe him, Vinnie was daring her to call him on it. She didn't want to piss him off. Alana was married, but Vinnie had seen her blowing the salad boy, and she knew he saw them. The incident was never discussed, but afterwards, Vinnie was given the best sections and prime shifts. Alana would probably be relieved to see him leave.

"I see." Her response was cold.

Vinnie was expecting this.

"Can I send your final paycheck anywhere?"

Vinnie gave her the address of his apartment unit.

"Your aunt and uncle live in WeHo?"

Keep your eyes on the prize. He was almost through with this.

"Uh, yes."

"I'll send the check out when we do payroll. Oh, and by the way, Vincent. You looked great on the cover of *Chi Guyz.*" Of course, Alana knew he was bullshitting all along.

An insistent knocking at the door cut the conversation short. *Perfect.* Vinnie had said all he needed to say. "I need to go," Vinnie didn't wait for a response.

Vinnie had forgotten that Kip was delivering his things. "Your timing is impeccable," said Vinnie, opening the door. "I was just quitting my old job."

Kip's eyes widened. "I hate that sort of thing," he said, offering Vinnie the handle of his rolling suitcase. "This should be everything from the hotel."

"The hotel just let you collect my stuff?"

"Gave me the key without a word," Kip added that the manager knows Woody. "They know me. They know the studio, and they know why you're here. Woody recommended that hotel for a reason."

It made sense, but that didn't make it any less unsettling.

"News travels in this town, especially among certain circles." Kip added. "Hotel clerks in WeHo see everything, but say nothing, especially with a hefty tip."

Vinnie wheeled the suitcase into the bedroom. By the time he returned, Kip was sitting on the couch. "Can I get you something to drink?"

"Some water would be nice."

He handed Kip a bottle of non-sparkling. "I appreciate you bringing my things over, but it wasn't necessary. I told Woody I could do it myself, but he wouldn't hear of it."

"Woody will do anything for his favorites."

Was that true? Was he a favorite? Vinnie found the thought intoxicating. "A favorite? I don't even know Woody that well." Vinnie attempted to show a casual interest in the comment, though his genuine level of interest was anything but casual.

Kip took a deep drink of water. "I know Woody better than anyone. If you were not a favorite you would not be an exclusive, you wouldn't be living here, he would not have taken you to lunch, and he would not have had me fetch your things. He wants to know all about you."

Did that mean he had Kip look through his things?

Vinnie remembered his dildo and felt a tinge of embarrassment. He had also made a list on the motel stationery of his steps and goals for becoming a porn legend. He had underlined that he would do whatever it took to succeed. The exposure was humiliating. He was grateful Kip did not mention it.

"It's a good thing that he wants to find out about you." Kip looked down at his hands. "I was a favorite at one time. I was the golden boy before Reed. I envy where you are right now. Being a favorite is wonderful, but get ready. The man at the front of the line has a target on his back. Someone is always plotting to take his place."

"So, you were a favorite?"

Kip nodded. "Years ago."

Vinnie asked what had happened. "With you and Woody I mean."

"Things don't always go according to plan. Circumstances changed, but I adapted."

Was Kip referring to the car crash?

"Favorites come and go, but not me. I made myself necessary. He needs me. Woody relies on me. I take care of him. He cannot make it through a single day without me."

Vinnie said he was pleased that things hadn't soured between them the way they had with Woody and Reed.

"Why would you say that? We are nothing alike."

Vinnie nodded.

"I would never turn on Woody. Like I said, it was circumstances." Kip pulled down his collar to reveal the scarring along his neck. "My dermal scarring is extensive. I've caught you looking. It's hard to cover scars in L.A." Kip lowered his voice. "The burns go down my neck and cover half my back. There are more scars on my legs." Kip exhaled. "After the accident, I wasn't so golden anymore."

Though craving a smoke, Vinnie didn't want to interrupt. He wanted to hear the story.

"It happened three years ago," explained Kip. "There was a big party at Woody's place, I was living with him at the time. The party was way over the top. Everyone in the industry was there, drinking all day, partying, doing drugs. There was sex around the pool and fucking in the bedrooms. It was the wild sort of party I imagined when I first got into this business."

"Do you mind?" Vinnie held up a cigarette and suggested they relocate to the balcony.

When they relocated outside, Kip continued, "At the time I was Woody's number one. I was the twink he took to the big parties, the award shows. Once, somebody got us in the People's Choice Awards. We sat right behind Daryl Hannah. We were a perfect couple. Everybody said so." Kip took a swig of his water. "That night the party was going strong. We were ready to make a toast to thank everyone for coming. Woody said he had a big announcement to make about six p.m. Well, six p.m. came and went. No Woody. When I went upstairs to get an Advil for someone, Woody was coming out of the bathroom buckling his pants. Guilt flashed across his face. At the time, I was still fairly sober. A moment later, Reed came out of the john, looked me in the eye, and wiped the corner of his mouth, just in case I had any doubt about what had transpired."

Vinnie took a drag off his smoke and shook his head.

"I'm not a fool. Woody getting a blowjob was not why I was mad. He runs a porn studio. Monogamy was never going to work for us. I was pissed off because it was Reed, and he did it at our place, in the middle of our party. All our friends were there. I warned Woody about Reed. The week before Reed even told me to watch my back. He said I wouldn't be Woody's favorite forever." Kip reddened. "I told Woody, but he said Reed was all talk. He promised to say something to him."

"So, it wasn't just a blowjob."

"No, it was the betrayal." Kip continued, "I didn't need to say a word when it happened. Woody knew I was pissed. I wanted to pulverize Reed, but he wasn't worth it. Instead, I started drinking like a man dying of thirst. Lee Botello saw me and asked what was up. Lee told me Woody and Reed had hooked up plenty of times. A minute later when someone offered me a Xanax I figured, *why not?* I was beyond caring."

Vinnie knew that feeling of being a chump. He had experienced something similar with Glenn.

"I had to get out of there. Everywhere I turned at that party there was either Woody or Reed. I went on the balcony for some fresh air. Carter Gaines was there. He was a nice kid, gorgeous but naïve. He was 19, and from the snake handler parts of Missouri. Golden haired like an angel. Fans couldn't get enough. Carter had a future ahead of him. That night he was almost as messed up as me."

Vinnie remembered seeing a picture of Carter Gaines featured in the entryway at the studio. Carter was a stunning blue-eyed blonde with a freshness that resonated with viewers. Carter had been more than promising. After only a couple of films, it was apparent that he was a superstar in the making. He was the 'It Boy' of the season. His face and form were plastered on the back of half the skin magazines sold that year.

"So in about two minutes Carter was hanging on me and saying I was the only one he could trust. He needed to get out of there as well. Woody and Ed came outside. I expected Woody to beg me to stay, but his eyes were on Carter. Maybe he and Ed were worried that the way Carter was swaying he was going to fall off the balcony. When they started coming our way I kissed Carter hard and said, *Let's get out of here.* As we headed down the steps, Woody called for us to wait. I didn't want to hear anything he had to say. I was seeing red. I was going to show him. I was so dramatic. That's a luxury of being young and beautiful. The next thing I knew, we were driving down the hill. Carter was in the passenger seat. The oncoming headlights were so bright. I should have pulled over, but there was no shoulder. When Carter grabbed for the wheel, I pushed him away. When I looked again, there was the tree."

Kip was visibly shaking. "I swear, that tree appeared out of nowhere ... Woody and Ed arrived moments later. Woody pulled me from the road, or so I'm told. I don't recall much after the tree, but I remember every knot on the trunk. I heard the details of the crash later. The next thing I knew there were paramedics talking; they didn't think I would make it. Carter was pronounced dead at the scene."

Vinnie had no response. What do you say to a story like that?

"I see Carter's face all the time, I ... Woody visited me in the hospital. He paid my bills, but I knew he could never love me again. He used to kiss me from head to toe, but the scars ended that."

Kip explained that by the time he was out of the hospital, he had been replaced, both at the studio and in Woody's bed. "Now Reed was living with Woody and I had been relocated to a studio apartment on the other side of town. When I moved in there was a vase of flowers on the counter in the kitchenette. The card attached read, *Welcome to Your New Place.*" Kip suspected that Reed had written the card. "And he wasn't referring to the apartment, but to my new status at Xclusiv. Reed had a blast twisting the knife. Maybe he was pissed because Woody didn't discard me altogether. Woody swore I'd always have a job at Xclusiv, and he's been true to his word."

Vinnie asked if he had ever discussed this with a professional.

"After the accident Woody set me up with a doctor he knows." Kip said.

Dr. Qualen helped him piece everything together. "He uses different things. Hypnosis. Suggestion. Color Memory." Kip's grip of the balcony railing tightened. "Qualen helped me fill in the blanks. He calls it unlocking the door. Since talking to him, the details are slowly coming back."

"Talking about it probably helps."

"I suppose so." His hands loosened on the railing bar.

A car alarm on the street startled both men. Kip noticed the time. "I had no idea it was getting so late. I need to get back to the office. Woody will think I've fallen off the face of the earth."

25

Vinnie began unpacking. There was his "Becoming a Porn Legend" list. He cringed at the thought of Kip putting it in his bag. At the motel, he'd had clothes in the dresser, in the closet, and on the floor. His toiletries were in the bathroom. His pills were on the nightstand. Amongst his things was a book on seven keys to success. Vinnie reddened at the thought of his belongings being seen, much less reported to Woody.

He couldn't dwell on all that. Obsessing over crap like this could jeopardize his future. That was not going to happen.

Let it go.

Hanging the last of his clothes in the closet, Vinnie told himself that this was home now. WeHo was where he belonged. Unfortunately, he needed to return to Chicago to settle some matters. Most of what remained there were relics from a former life. Breaking his lease meant losing his security deposit, but his freedom was worth it.

Vinnie made the bed and stretched out. Comfortable mattress. The day had been exhausting. New place. New life. New position. Now he was an exclusive. An hour later, he was awakened by music.

In the living room, Gio Santiago was seated cross-legged on the floor. Vinnie saw why Gio had been named a new exclusive. He had seen photos of the dark shaggy-haired stud. Gio was also featured in *Backfield in Motion*, but they didn't have any scenes together.

Gio looked up when he heard Vinnie enter and turned down the music. "You must be Vinnie Lux, I'm Gio Santiago; at least that's what they are calling me." Gio offered Vinnie a fist bump. "We're exclusives now, man." Running a hand over his bare chest, he offered Vinnie a hit off the joint. The smoke felt good. Vinnie hadn't been stoned in weeks.

"I hear we're taking pictures together tomorrow."

"With Dean Driver. The Xclusiv exclusives."

Gio asked if he had met Dean. "You know he lives here too?"

Vinnie nodded. After another hit, he asked Gio where he was from.

"I'm a celestial vagabond."

Vinnie had no idea what the hell he was talking about.

Gio released a mammoth hit and explained that he was a stoner with aspirations. "Xclusiv can call me a star or an exclusive or whatever they like, as long as the cash keeps coming. This is just another adventure. Life as a celestial vagabond isn't cheap."

First impressions can be faulty, but Vinnie hoped he and Gio would be friends. Gio's easygoing nature was a welcome change in an industry that seemed characterized by ambition and theatrics. "How did you get into this business?"

Gio took a hit. "Fate I suppose. A few months ago, I met a guy in Venice. We hooked up a few times and in under a week we were a thing. He treated me right. Turns out, Mr. Nice Guy had connections. He told me I was wasting my talent; that I could make good money. I figured he was talking about hustling. And I told him, no thanks. I'd done that and gotten busted. It couldn't happen again. He said there were options and started talking about Xclusiv. He introduced me to Woody and things just happened."

After another hit, Vinnie told Gio his story about getting into XXX in the aftermath of a breakup. Maybe it was the pot, or maybe it was Gio, but Vinnie ended up sharing a great deal. He regretted mentioning Glenn. *Why?* He had a new past, courtesy of the studio, a new history without Glenn and without the breakup. Porn stars do not get dumped.

Now it was Gio's turn. He told Vinnie his parents were from Honduras. "Roman Catholics. They never understood the gay thing. At 16 my dad caught me messing around with a guy in the garage and kicked me out. I've been on my own ever since." Gio said he did what he had to in order to survive. He had worked construction, tended bar, danced, stripped, worked the docks, been a mover, farmed, hustled, done retail, washed dishes, waited tables, bused tables, and he had even been in a band. Porn star was another temporary career choice.

"What's your take on Dean Driver, the other new exclusive. I haven't met him."

Gio shrugged. "I don't really know. Dean lives here, but I've only seen him twice. I like to party, but that boy takes it to another level."

The two men were trying to order dinner when A.Z. returned from the airport. "Airport traffic was crazy." A.Z. sniffed the air. "Got any more of that?"

Gio pulled another joint from beneath his bandana, "Always."

By the time the pizza arrived, Gio had shared that he felt bad about being an exclusive. "I'm not looking for a long-term gig. I want to earn enough to bankroll my next adventure." He said he had fantasized about living in a monastery in Tibet.

A.Z. asked if the monks were celibate.

"Not all of them," said Gio, "Besides, sex is great, but non-sex is great too. It's all a state of mind."

A.Z. cocked a brow and looked down at his crotch, "Tell that to junior." Then, taking a drag, A.Z. said that porn was the best thing that ever happened to him, but his time was coming to an end. "I plan to get out of this business soon." A.Z. was about to say more when his watch chimed. "Shit, I have a date at seven o'clock."

When Vinnie asked about Roy, A.Z. looked at him, "Oh my, you are green. Someone is going to have to tell you some things." Then, A.Z. was off to the bedroom.

"A.Z. is talking about a client," explained Gio. "Sex dates can be very lucrative. The extra cash makes it easy to save money, especially living here rent free..."

Rent was not free; it was deducted.

"Lots of guys in the business do it." Gio worked for Trusted Talents as well. "I'm good at what I do, I leave the client with a smile on his face and for my service I am well compensated. The gentleman gets his. I get mine. Everybody is happy. No crime in that."

Vinnie had no problem with the ethics of hustling. After all, making porn was fucking for money. "It's ridiculous that sex work is illegal. But you said you never wanted to get busted. Aren't you worried?"

"That is the beauty of it. The agency protects us from all that. If you're interested, I can introduce you to some people. The movies make us hot commodities. Everybody wants to fuck a somebody."

"But Woody said ..."

Gio laughed. "Trust me, Woody is aware of what's going on even if he likes to pretend that he doesn't know. We don't bring tricks back here, we respect that rule, but Woody knows about Trusted Talents."

"Absolutely he knows." A.Z. had put on a pair of jeans and was threading his belt.

"The agency screens the clients. They handle the money. They make sure we don't get busted. Trusted Talents has never had an issue with the cops," added Gio.

"The owner knows some very powerful people," added A.Z.

"There is more money freelancing, but the risks aren't worth it." Gio said that after he got busted for soliciting a second time, he spent a month in jail. "Both A.Z. and I did, before we got wise."

"Our situations are different than yours. We need protection more than you white boys," added A.Z., slipping on his loafers before heading to the bathroom.

Gio stretched, arching his back against the couch. No doubt about it—Gio was a sensual creature built for pleasure.

I am an Xclusiv exclusive alongside him?

Vinnie stopped himself. To succeed in this industry, he needed to dump his doubt and self-criticism. He had to believe he was as sexy and desirable as any of his fellow models.

When A.Z. returned from primping, he shifted the conversation back to Trusted Talents. "The agency is the best I've worked with; as much work as you want. If you like money, or the toys it can buy, Trusted Talents might be a good fit for you."

"I hope you have some action left after Roy's visit," Gio teased.

"Oh, don't you worry. I've got a reserve tank for times like these." With a wink and a sexy grin, A.Z. was out the door.

"I need to get moving too." Gio was meeting friends at a club. "You want to come along?"

Vinnie took a rain check. "After pot and pizza I am primed for the couch."

At twelve forty-five, Vinnie was awakened by a ruckus outside. He had fallen asleep watching television. The front door opened with a burst of laughter. A lanky silhouette stood in the doorway with a shadowy figure closely behind.

"We've got company," said the shorter of the two, "And I know him."

In a moment, the two figures moved into the television glow. Vinnie recognized them. The studio had already been building up Vinnie's third roommate and the final exclusive that year, Dean Driver. His photos were popping up everywhere. Driver was a sexy cowboy with a square jaw, and a cleft in his chin that looked like it had stopped a bullet. He was hung like a horse, with a big juicy cock that made Vinnie's mouth water.

Alongside Dean was Reed Connors. Woody would be furious if he knew Reed was in the studio flat.

After all, the apartment was studio property.

Maybe Dean was unaware of the drama between Woody and Reed, or maybe he didn't care. Either way, if he wasn't careful, Dean's career might be over before it began.

Vinnie could have said something, but that seemed too awkward. Dean Driver was a big boy. His social life was none of Vinnie's business.

Reed stepped forward, "Let me take the liberty of introducing you two. Dean Driver, lying on your couch is none other than Vinnie Lux."

Dean nodded hello.

Vinnie returned the nod. "I hear you're a new exclusive too."

Reed chimed in. "It's getting tough to find someone who hasn't been named an exclusive."

Vinnie refused to take the bait.

"Vinnie and I met on set yesterday. He replaced me in *Backfield in Motion*." Reed turned to Dean.

Dean nodded. He said he needed to take a piss.

"And now anybody who makes a XXX movie is suddenly a porn star." Reed wasn't letting up. Clearly, he was trying to get a rise out of Vinnie.

Though Vinnie said nothing, he was clearly annoyed.

Reed threw an arm over Vinnie's shoulder. "Calm down golden boy. I was only saying that Woody used to have one exclusive a year."

Vinnie pushed his arm away. Reed was trying to flip this. The issue was not Vinnie being overly sensitive. This issue was Reed being an asshole. Vinnie knew from experience that bullies rarely take responsibility.

Despite being a prick, Reed was still sexy as hell and aware of the fact. His interactions were infused with a sexual undercurrent, so even when he was being an asshole it still felt like foreplay. Reed's crotch was inches from Vinnie's face. The bulge. *Right there.* Did he imagine a hint of man musk?

Reed caught him looking. His smirk returned.

Vinnie reddened.

Thankfully Dean sauntered back into the room.

Reed perched on the arm of the couch. "I was about to say I'm sorry I couldn't stay for the shoot yesterday. Did Mykel manage to stay sober? I was shocked that Woody gave him such a big project so soon after his episode. It really was one of those jail or rehab sort of situations."

"Mykel was great. Everything went well, *eventually.*" Vinnie paused. "There were some *petty* interruptions, but nothing of importance. And Reed, thank you for dropping out or being let go or whatever happened, I'm really grateful for the second scene."

Reed smirked and said he was thrilled to hear it. "Lord knows, Xclusiv needs a hit. You know how things are. Everything is online. The Internet is dissolving the studios. Production companies are the future. You boys best cash those Xclusiv checks ASAP. Woody is in debt up to his ears." Rising from the arm of the couch, Reed went to the kitchen and leaned on the island. "I bet you're nervous having me here, touching things," He ran a hand over the countertop. "You're afraid you're breaking the rules. Did Woody tell you to avoid me? Did he give you his stick-with-the-winners speech? I hope you aren't that gullible?" He paused to look at Vinnie. "Oh my, oh shit! You are that gullible."

Vinnie had already found umpteen reasons to avoid Reed Connors that had nothing to do with Woody or Xclusiv.

Reed put an arm over Dean's shoulder. "My man here doesn't let his employer dictate who he can or cannot have as a friend, do you Dean?"

"What?" Dean had little to no idea what was going on.

Reed grinned. "You'll have to excuse my pal. He's overly medicated. As for you, maybe you enjoy having your decisions made for you and being property of Xclusiv Studio."

Vinnie wasn't going to sit and listen to this bullshit. "I'm going to bed," he said, rising.

Reed said he needed to get going anyway. "But remember," he held up two fingers and rotated them either way. "Two sides to every story. One day I'll tell you my side, even though I still don't give a fuck whether you believe me or not." And so saying he abruptly kissed Vinnie on the mouth before deep kissing Dean goodbye. "I hear you boys are shooting stills tomorrow. Don't stay up too late, you'll have bags. Ciao bitches." With that, Reed was out the door.

"Whew, he can be a lot." Dean adjusted himself and plopped onto the couch. "But sometimes he's worth it." He told Vinnie that Reed was phenomenal sex.

Maybe Dean was unaware of everything going on with Woody and Reed. Vinnie thought he could stay out of it, but he felt obligated to say something. "I wouldn't mention to Woody that you're hanging out with Reed. Woody banned him from the studio, so I doubt he wants him on studio property, including this flat."

Dean nodded. Reed told him about a spat with Woody. "That's how some keep the fires burning." Dean grabbed the remote. "And what you and I think don't much matter. They have ended things before, and a week later jetted off to Aruba. Some folks are that way."

Vinnie told Dean he sounded like a philosopher.

Dean laughed. "Nope, just wasted."

26

The photoshoot with Joe McCain was scheduled for one o'clock, but Woody wanted to make sure the session started on time. Woody knew from experience the cost of running behind schedule and took precautions, especially when dealing with talent.

On the morning of the shoot, Kip called at noon to say he was five minutes away. Kip was given the task of picking up the trio and bringing them to the studio.

When Kip phoned, Dean had been awake for about five minutes. He had overslept. Glitter was still in his hair and on his skin.

"Oh shit," Gio was laughing.

When Vinnie mentioned the glitter, Dean said that at some point last night, glitter just happened. At some clubs, it was in the air. Vinnie imagined Dean's lungs sparkling with the stuff, the bottom of each air pouch looking like a club floor at closing time.

Dean took a gulp of coffee and headed for the shower.

Once he was out of the room, Gio lowered his voice. "Vinnie, I have to tell someone."

"What?"

"The man I hooked up with in Venice—the guy with connections in the porn world? The guy who told me not to squander my sexual prowess..."

Vinnie nodded.

"Anyway, it's Joe." Gio read the confusion on Vinnie's face and added, "Joe McCain."

His mentor, his trick with connections in the business, was McCain?

If McCain was responsible for getting Gio's contract in the first place, he probably had substantial sway in making sure Gio being chosen as an exclusive.

Gio said that he hoped today wouldn't be too awkward. He explained that things with Joe had gotten weird. "Joe is partnered, but I didn't know about that until the last time we hooked up. It didn't bother me, not really."

The shock must have registered on Vinnie's face.

"Oh my god, I'm not heartless. I thought, okay Joe has a boyfriend, but these guys live in WeHo. I figured they were open. I didn't expect them to be one of the two monogamous couples in town."

Joe McCain had known they were monogamous. As Gio spoke more of how he and Joe met and fell in love—Vinnie could not help but put himself into the scenario, as the wronged partner. The flip side of this love story Gio was telling was a tale of betrayal and humiliation.

Vinnie tried to keep an open mind. After all, he wasn't Vincent anymore. He was Vinnie Lux. This was a different world with different rules. If bedding a stud like Gio meant neglecting to mention the boyfriend, then you didn't. Men do that. Men in power do it more. He suspected that was the way the industry worked.

He needed to shake this resentment against McCain. None of the things he was starting to feel could show on camera. He needed to grow up. His past was his past. Being cheated on sucks, but that was also part of the change that brought him here. He needed to put it behind him and get beyond his provincial notions or this business would eat him alive.

"So, what do you think?"

Vinnie jumped when Gio asked him the question. "I'm sure Joe will be professional."

"His doing the shoot might mean he's being a professional, or it might mean he wants me back. He knows where I stand. I won't be his dirty little piece on the side. When his partner found out, he confronted me in a fucking CVS!"

Thank goodness Vinnie never went that far, but only because he never ran into Robert. Vinnie's eyes widened. "Seriously?"

"Oh yeah."

"What happened?"

"Let's just say it was not one of my proudest moments. I could have handled the situation better."

Vinnie felt for Gio, but this situation concerned him for another reason. If McCain still harbored feelings for Gio, he might favor him in the photo shoot. The lighting would be his. The colors would be his. The action would revolve around him. The camera would be McCain's eye upon his beloved, relegating Vinnie Lux and Dean Driver to the sidelines.

Gio had not seen Joe since the CVS incident. "I called Joe when I got home and told him we were done. I said things were getting crazy and I didn't need this drama in my life. He left messages, but I didn't respond. So I don't know what to expect."

The downstairs buzzer shattered further discussion.

Kip was on his way up.

Dean emerged from the bathroom, towel over his shoulders with his impressive appendage swinging between his legs. "All open in there."

Gio nodded down the other hallway. "We have two bathrooms, and you pick mine. All my shit is in there."

"You should have stopped me."

Gio muttered something beneath his breath as he padded down the hall.

Dean was in synch with his Xclusiv image. This stud was born to wear boots and jeans and two-day stubble—the type of tall Texan who was easy going—until someone crossed a line and needed an ass kicking. That sort of man is always up for a good time. Except for the being gay, Dean was a cowboy cliché. His cock! Big, thick, beautiful—the sort Vinnie wanted to wrap his lips around. Vinnie couldn't take his eyes off that piece of meat. It was something to behold.

Any one, or any combination of his three roommates were more than welcome in his bed. They might be roommates and coworkers, but they were also porn stars, and Vinnie was quickly learning that porn had its own rules. In the porn world, sex meant everything and nothing at the same time.

Vinnie checked his phone.

Instagram 5991
Twitter 3328

Gio had more followers. And Dean, and his eleven-inch dick, had the most fans.

For now.

27

As a newcomer in the business, Vinnie devoted a large part of his day to his career: still shots, grooming, working out, and networking. Vinnie was ambitious, and he was excited about being a star. If making porn ever became tedious, it was time to retire.

If he wanted career longevity, he needed to take lessons from those who had endured in an industry fueled by a fresh supply of faces. A.Z. had been a top name for years. Ditto for Josh Lawless and Lee Botello, and to some extent, Reed. Those four were exceptions. Most porn stars burn out, wear out, or flare out in a few months—a fraction last a year.

Earlier that morning, A.Z. emerged from his room when he smelled coffee brewing. He needed some caffeine. "I have a date in Malibu today."

Vinnie was impressed. "Fancy."

A.Z. said this guy's home was amazing. "Thank God his place was unscathed by the fires. This gentleman is an A List star and a big fan of my charms."

Vinnie asked if he had heard of him.

"Unless you've been living under a rock. He's been nominated for an Oscar, maybe even two. I think." A.Z. winked, "I have even licked his Golden Globes until he moaned."

"Wow, so how much would a guy like that pay to see you?" Vinnie suspected he had crossed a line as soon as he asked.

A.Z. avoided giving a specific dollar amount. "I'm a request and it is an overnight. He pays plenty, but the cost is peanuts to this guy. Truth is, that man is so lonely. He's built a prison for himself, first with his womanizing public image, and now with this dedicated family man persona. He lives in mortal fear that someone will find out and it will all be over. He knows 90% of his adoring fans would bail if they knew the truth. Of course, sex plays a major part of the day when we're together, but companionship is important to him too. He doesn't really have that. He can be himself with me."

Vinnie told A.Z. he sounded like a therapist.

A.Z. laughed, "They call me Dr. Love."

"I don't mean to keep prying, but I admire how you approach all this. You're smart about it."

"I've had to be."

"So, do you invest or save? What are you doing with all the money you've got rolling in? I know it seems personal, but I want to be smart about this—and you seem like a smart guy."

"I'm glad you picked up on that." A.Z. said he had been trying to save for the past few years. "Some investing. Both my banker and my stock guy started as tricks. We have an arrangement regarding their fees. Within a year I should have what I need to be able to retire. Nobody wants to still be tricking when the phone stops ringing. That happened with Desi Lou. That dude helped put Xclusiv on the map. He was in a goddamn Madonna video! When his time was up, he had nothing put aside. Last I heard he was working the boulevard and looking worse for wear. Most had no idea who he was."

Vinnie took a drink of coffee. *That will never be me.*

A.Z. got to his feet. "I've got to get going. My ride will be here any minute." He put his coffee cup on the kitchen counter. "Can't keep golden boy waiting. Stardom spoils you."

Gio emerged from the shower ruffling his hair, those dark curls, that sly smile. Muscle and sinew moved beneath his copper skin. Gio was a masterpiece of design, a god's wet dream of man. Vinnie had to remind himself that he deserved to be an exclusive alongside Gio and Dean. Gio may be more beautiful, and Dean might have that giant cock, but Vinnie had the drive. In the end, that was the most important thing

Kip checked the time and said they were running late. Dean called from his room that he'd be ready in a few minutes. Gio said he would be there soon. While they were still out of the room, Kip leaned forward, lowering his voice. "I want to make sure you know that everything I discussed with you yesterday was said in confidence."

"Of course."

His voice dropped to a whisper. "I'm serious. If I hear you have breathed a word of anything I told you, I will make your life hell."

Was that a threat?

At first, Vinnie thought Kip was joking, but the look in his eyes made it clear that he was deathly serious. "You don't need to threaten me. I won't say a thing."

Kip grabbed his arm. "Good. I started talking and just got carried away. I don't need that goddamn accident becoming a hot topic again. You know? Half of the people at the studio still see me and remember that night and that I was the one behind the wheel. I own that I was responsible for the death of Carter Gaines. Living with that is my punishment and these scars are my penance. I carry that with me every day. I don't need people talking as well."

Vinnie reiterated that he wouldn't say a word.

Dean was belting his pants when he emerged from the bathroom. Dean looked like he didn't have a care in the world—but that might change. Things would get ugly when Woody found out he was palling around with Reed. WeHo was a small town with a surplus of eyes and mouths. People talk. Someone was bound to mention seeing Dean on the town with Reed Connors. The question was not if Woody would find out—but when.

Vinnie was not going to get involved. He wasn't here to make enemies, but he wasn't here to make friends either.

The tight fit of Dean's blue jeans and western shirt bordered on being obscene. He looked like a walking fuck machine. His tall, muscled physique looked good in almost everything, especially this. There was no hiding that horse cock in a tight pair of worn 501s, not that Dean ever wanted to disguise his calling card.

Vinnie asked if anyone wanted more coffee. Before either man could answer, Gio emerged from his room with a cloud of smoke. He'd gotten stoned after his shower. On the way to the shoot, Vinnie offered him a stick of gum. He told Gio he had weed on his breath.

Gio passed on the gum. "This is porn, not high school algebra class. Pot relaxes me. Plus, smoking also makes me profoundly horny," he added with a squeeze of his crotch.

28

Xclusiv was another Hollywood success story. At a time when many XXX companies were shuttering, Xclusiv had managed to endure. In eight years, the studio had gone from being a modest storefront business on Santa Monica Boulevard to usurping the currency exchange to the left and a derelict Chinese restaurant to the right. Xclusiv acquired the final storefront two years later. A redesign and upgrade of the enormous space followed.

Woody borrowed heavily to finance the expansion. Some of the cash came from less than reputable sources, namely a man by the name of Novak who had no affiliation with the FDIC or the banking system. The only thing that mattered to Novak was that debts be repaid in a timely fashion, with interest, of course. Loans were a large part of the Lavender Outfit's business. Repaying Novak was a concern that kept Woody awake some nights. Even when he took something to knock him out, he would sometimes awake in a panic, especially if he was alone.

Each month making restitution to Novak was a struggle. Delinquency on a scheduled payment was never an option. Novak didn't want excuses; all he wanted was his cash and periodically a percentage of the profits.

In the expansion and remodeling, Woody had used the converted buildings wisely. Two rooms were designated for mail order and general offices. The currency exchange became a dressing room with a makeup station, wardrobe, props, lights, equipment, and additional storage. Parts of the conglomerate were converted into sets. Four of the smaller rooms that had been a row of booths in the Chinese restaurant were turned into video chat centers for Xclusiv's popular One-on-One online broadcasts. The One-on-One program helped Xclusiv keep up with the times. Several once-solid companies, titans of the industry, went extinct by taking a business-as-usual approach to things despite the changing face of porn. Woody's former partner, Corbin Kent, recently announced that Tandem Studio had filed for bankruptcy. Empire Pictures was gone. Night Ride Releasing was no more. Hardwired, Redline Studios, and Mercury Men had all vanished. Watching some of his biggest rivals crash and burn gave Woody some satisfaction. By being proactive in the face of changing trends, he had saved the studio. In business and in life, a willingness to adapt was synonymous with the will to survive.

The surge of Internet porn was a concern, but the truth was that online porn had only broadened the market. More people were watching more porn than ever before. Woody took that as an opportunity. He looked for ways to leverage that uptick to broaden his market rather than as a drain on his consumer base. So far, he was defying the odds. But he still owed Novak a considerable amount.

Xclusiv was still around because Woody was smart enough to embrace trends rather than fight them. Since online porn was the future, he opted to lead rather than follow. The studio created online content: thirty minutes, one scene, and decent production values.

The studio also developed the popular One-on-One series. Many studio hopefuls worked every week building their fan base with a daily "members-only" jack-off show. If the studio wasn't sure about a model, One-on-One was an audition. The newbie was often cast in a thirty-minute online content scene if a model clicked. If that went well, the model was often offered a part in a larger studio production. Several Xclusiv careers began with One-on-One appearances; Bobby Feral, Javier, and Chance Jaymes parlayed their online work into more. Carter Gaines started out that way. One-on-One turned a profit, allowing Novak to get his cut and Woody to keep his fingers.

Finding One-on-One models was never difficult. Plenty of talented young men dreamed of working with Xclusiv. Models arrived daily by the busload, looking for some Tinseltown magic. *Possibility. Escape. Discovery. Overnight success.* The names changed, but the stories overlapped time and again. Most were fleeing something, seeking excitement, and hoping fame would solve all their problems. For many, the means to stardom was secondary. Fame was fame. If you're young, "gifted," and gay (or open-minded), the fast track to a fan base was a solo-sex show away.

As a general rule, you need three of the four: Face, Body, Cock, and Ass.

Show me how you make the world want to fuck you.

Dean Driver arrived in L.A. by bus. Dean wasn't stupid but he discovered life was easier if people thought you were. His birth name was Gil. Born and raised in a small Texas town, he grew up eager to cross the state line. He wanted more from life than Agrippa had to offer. Gil knew he was gay from a young age and was terrified his secret would come out. He knew what happened to Cocksuckers and Sodomites. When he was ten, a fellow rumored to be that way was shot and killed just outside the town limits. The law called it a hunting accident. It was a hunt all right, but no accident. Folks said the fancy man had it coming. His naked body was dumped out along the highway like a bag of trash. No trial. They just put his belongings on the street. People took what they wanted. The rest got hauled to the dump.

To avoid suspicion, Gil started dating a girl in his class, and she got pregnant. They had her condition taken care of over in El Paso. Lynette expected that someday she would marry Gil. When the timing was right, they would have a baby for real. Gil had no intention of letting that happen. A week after graduation, he hopped on a Greyhound. So long, Agrippa.

A week out of town, he met a man from Phoenix. Gil lived with him for a while, but after a month, he was restless. He snuck away without a word—packed his things, plus a little something extra for his trouble, and hitchhiked to Denver.

Gil was working at a restaurant in the Mile High City when a man of means started making eyes his way. Gil quit his job the next day. Things were good between them for a couple of months. But then, the relationship had turned ugly. The man had tried to stop him when it came time to leave, so Gil used his fists. Getting that out of his system felt good.

By that time, Gil was aware he was gifted below the waist. His daddy hadn't given him much, but he did pass on his big Texas-sized dick. Some claimed it was the biggest they'd seen. He knew his cock was his ticket to a better life. Word got around. The way some of these men were looking at him, Gil knew they would pay to sample the goods. They tipped extra if he included the hayseed routine.

Gil took a Greyhound to L.A. He thought up a name along the way, and the minute his feet hit the pavement, he became Dean Driver. He had a good feeling about L.A. Word travels fast in some circles, and news of Dean's appendage and skills spread through WeHo like wildfire. He made the right connections, fucked the right people, and six months later, Dean Driver was an Xclusiv exclusive. He didn't even have to change his name. But Dean had bigger plans.

He wanted wealth and luxury and spent a fair amount of time trying to figure out the best way to make that happen.

29

The photoshoot for the three new exclusives took place in the part of the Xclusiv studio that had become the domain of Joe McCain. As the resident studio photographer and designer, McCain had the power to make or break careers. He made models into stars, and Joe McCain stars became legends. His exquisitely lit and composed photos were the envy of the XXX world. His images adorned Xclusiv DVD cases and were key factors in rentals, downloads, and sales.

Knowing the value of Joe McCain to Xclusiv, Woody made sure he was kept happy. Woody appeased Joe by putting Gio on the payroll and making him an exclusive and a star. While on the surface, this might not have seemed like a huge favor—it was. Sure, Gio had all the elements to be a star—a lean and sexy body, a handsome face, a healthy sex drive, charisma, and killer smile. But Gio didn't have citizenship papers. Lack of proper documentation was an automatic rejection for Xclusiv employment—however, this time, it meant Woody risked losing McCain. Joe got offers from other companies. Any one of those studios would be willing to take on Gio, especially if it meant stealing McCain from Xclusiv. That was not going to happen.

"I'll make Gio's citizenship happen." Woody tried to get Gio legally registered by using his connections, but his efforts were thwarted. There were complications. Gio had two previous arrests. In addition, the nation had grown decidedly xenophobic. Immigration had become a politically charged issue. Whistleblowers were in place. Woody made the choice to take Gio on regardless.

Kip ushered the models to set ten minutes early. Woody would be pleased. Making the boss happy was important. Kip didn't like to think where he would be without Woody, and without Xclusiv. He had been dancing at a club when Woody approached with a $100 bill wrapped around his business card. He asked if Kip had ever considered being in movies. By the end of the week, he signed a contract. The following week they were living together.

Kip asked the models if they all knew Sue. "All three of you have worked with her, right?"

The three exclusives nodded. Anyone who does any work before the camera at Xclusiv gets painted, powdered, and dabbed by Sue. She was the only female on the studio payroll. Sue was not an artist, but she was reliable and a lot of fun. Both essential qualities on set. Sue had done hair and make-up for Xclusiv from the start. Woody brought her from Tandem when he started the company.

One of the models on the *Mancandy 2* set whispered to Vinnie that he had heard Woody and Sue were high school sweethearts. Vinnie found that hard to believe. They seemed nowhere near the same age. At the same shoot, someone else told him Sue didn't have to work. "She is an heiress. Her family is loaded!"

Sue took a step back, an artist taking stock of her canvas. "Well, you all three look pretty good. Not like that kid they had in here last week with all the back acne. Sheesh. I pulled Mykel aside and said, 'Can't we just have him wear a cape or airbrush the hell out of him in post?' I shouldn't push it, airbrushing will put me in the unemployment line."

If she was an heiress, she was working to keep it a secret.

Gio put his head on her shoulder. "Woody would never get rid of you."

"Damn right he won't. And he's wise not to. I know where all the bodies are buried, and this studio is a veritable graveyard."

Although Sue was being flippant, Vinnie figured there must be some underlying truth to it. If she had been around that long, Sue knew her fair share of secrets. Her hair and make-up chair was a therapy couch. Sue had covered bruises and track marks, varicose veins and dark circles. Some models told Sue everything. With her open personality, it was easy to be drawn in.

Sue was getting on Vinnie's nerves. He wanted silence, not chatter about who was fucking who or Lee Botello's gambling spree or Desi Lou's arrest for vagrancy. He needed to focus on this photo shoot, and being Vinnie Lux.

Yet, Sue kept talking. "You all look good. Gio's got this gorgeous skin. He doesn't need much. Dean, let's just cover than scar on your shoulder. How did you get that anyway?" Sue didn't wait for an answer. Dean was oblivious. He was busy texting.

"Vinnie dear, you are starting to break out a bit. Nervous about today? Sue will take care of that." Moments later, she took a step back. "You're perfect, or even more perfect."

Vinnie thanked her.

"Don't thank me, thank your momma and daddy or whoever it was who gave you those genes..."

The thought of thanking his parents for the genetics to make it in gay porn almost made him laugh out loud.

"You are all just so damn beautiful. Sort of frustrating for a straight gal working with gorgeous gay guys all day."

"There's always Rex Reynolds," teased Gio, "He's straight."

Dean stopped his texting. "So he says. Reed told me ..." Dean caught himself. He may not have been the sharpest tool in the shed, but Dean was smart enough to know that bringing something up in front of Sue was not a good idea.

At the mention of Rex Reynolds, Sue opened her mouth as if to add something, but seemed to think better of it. "Doesn't matter to me one way or the other. Rex Reynolds won't give me the time of day. Guess a big busty blonde is not his type."

Dean continued texting. "We love you, darlin'."

Gio gave her a kiss on the cheek.

"Thanks, you are dolls." Sue giggled and took a cigarette from her pack. "I need to go back downstairs, but I'll be back later if you boys need retouching. You know the drill; water, juice, coffee and some snacks in the break room. Be careful eating, don't smudge. Use the damn straws!"

"It's not going to matter since we'll be sucking cocks!" laughed Gio.

His comment brought Vinnie back to the photoshoot fantasy about to unfold. He had already cum once in anticipation of today.

Yesterday afternoon after his run, Vinnie fell onto his bed. The heat and the sweat made him horny. He started thinking about the upcoming photoshoot and being told to do everything he had fantasized about doing to two of his roommates—eating Gio's ass and sucking Dean's cock. He stripped off his running shorts and tossed them aside. He brought his jockstrap to his nose and took a deep whiff of the pouch, of his own sweaty musk. The scent sparked fantasies about shoving the jock in Gio's mouth while he fucked his beautiful ass or wearing the jock while he spread his cheeks and rode Dean's tongue. His cock was aching. He ran a hand across his sweaty abs for lube and stroked himself in a way that made every nerve come alive. Tugging a nip and now another whiff. A harder grip. *Faster. Tighter. Shit.* Vinnie was at the point of no return. With another stroke and his legs locked in a tremor. He fought a scream as a white load shot across his belly. He wiped it up with the jock and tossed it aside before heading across the hall to shower.

Wearing robes and boxers, the three men took seats in the break room. The wall clock read 12:15. Dean and Gio were busy on their phones—typing texts, checking messages, and scrolling.

Vinnie was anxious. He got up and poured himself a glass of orange juice. He was curious about Joe McCain. He'd met him during his initial interview, but aside from that, they hadn't exchanged more than a few words. Vinnie held his work in high regard and was thrilled to be working with him. He had heard McCain was a force of nature. One of those men that people say yes to.

A moment later, McCain entered the room. He had an energy that Vinnie had not seen when he met him before. Photoshoots transformed him. He was a man in his element. Beside McCain was Gert, the production assistant.

McCain gave Gio a kiss. "Ready for today?" Gio affirmed that he was. McCain then asked if they were ready.

So, he and Dean were afterthoughts?

Joe turned to Dean, who was still looking at his cellphone. Dean offered a fist bump. "Hey Joe."

"And Vinnie." They shook hands.

"Pleasure to see you again Mr. McCain. I am a big admirer of your work." Vinnie's comment prompted a snicker from Dean.

"I appreciate it Vinnie. I hope you're still a fan after today. And call me Joe. Mr. McCain sounds like you're talking about my father." McCain brought levity to the shoot, but took his work seriously. He expected the same of the talent. "If you are a professional, I'm a pussycat." McCain needed to reset some lights. He had them wait in the break room. "Gert will get you when I'm ready. Oh, and Gert, get a mop. The floor needs cleaning. I don't know why I can't expect..." McCain's words trailed off as he left the room.

After ninety minutes, Gert came and collected them. Spread out on a folding table were three pairs of Speedos with hearts on the front and Xclusiv written on the ass.

Gio teased Dean that his manaconda might not fit.

"It'll be a tight squeeze."

Both men dropped their robes and boxers. Gio was as perfect as Vinnie remembered. His ass was high, and round, and his six-pack looked more like eight. Gio had been right about Dean; packing his manhood into his suit was a challenge. Dean asked Vinnie if he liked what he saw before giving his shaft a shake. Vinnie blushed to realize he was staring. "Don't worry, I'm used to it."

Vinnie was flustered. "It's just that I…"

Dean winked. "Maybe we can talk about that later."

Gert could not have returned at a more opportune time.

"Ready in a minute." Gio whispered to Dean that "the ginger kid" was gaga for him. "You, my friend, will be the fuck that Gert can talk about fifty years from now. Though you might tear him in half."

Dean said he imagined Gert could take quite a bit. "He's got that look about him." Dean cupped his Lycra-covered crotch. "When I see that look, I know what they want. I just come with the package."

Dean and Gio dropped to the floor and did some push-ups. Gio paused and told Vinnie it might benefit him to join in. "A quick pump is good for a shoot, gets the blood flowing and tightens things up." Taking his advice, Vinnie did twenty quick push-ups and a plank.

Gio winked. "Your muscles look yummier already."

When McCain entered, all three men were ready. McCain called to Gert to bring the oil. Gert grabbed a spray pump and began misting their bodies. Joe stopped him after a couple of pumps. "That's enough, I want them to glisten, not be ready to roll in batter."

Dean and Gio rubbed the oil across their pecs and biceps. Vinnie followed suit. On one side of the room were three blue platforms of varying heights. Joe positioned them on the pedestals. "Let's make a Vinnie sandwich." He placed Vinnie in the center with Gio and Dean on either side. "Let's start with some simple shots. All three of you, standing straight, eyes forward, chins to the light." After a few pictures and minor lighting adjustments, McCain told them to look into the camera. "Now sell the fact that you belong on a pedestal. Nice." After several more shots, McCain draped Gio's arm across Vinnie's shoulder.

He instructed Dean to do the same. "I want to see the promise of getting some." Vinnie's hand to Dean's stomach. Vinnie and Gio were so close they were almost kissing. Moments later, off the pedestals. "Now kneel and lean into one another. Touching—lots of skin in contact—cheeks together. Dean, hand on Vinnie's hipbone. Lower, almost below the waistband. Let your fingers go below. Now playing with each other, but sex with the camera. This is a show. Play to the voyeur."

Half an hour later, Dean needed a bathroom break. So, McCain told the models to take five. "And when you come back, lose the suits."

During the break, Dean asked Gio how late he thought the shoot would go. He knew not to ask Joe directly—a huge taboo on set. Gio asked Dean if he had a hot date later.

"Something like that."

Now fully naked. Dean's cock hung a good ten inches soft, and Gio's fat-free body was absolute perfection. Vinnie was already having a hard time controlling his response to both men. He hoped this was a "no limits" shoot.

While fiddling with the lights, McCain called to Gert, "I need some oil on those butts. And those cocks need to glisten." Gert spritzed Gio and Vinnie's hands so they could smooth the oil on themselves. Dean asked Gert if he could put the oil on for him. "I don't want to get my hands greasy."

Gert swallowed audibly as he put a thin layer of oil on his hand and gave Dean's cock a few strokes. Dean told him that he liked the way he applied oil. He looked him in the eye. "You have a nice touch." A few strokes later, he grabbed Gert's wrist. "That's enough." Gert turned a deep shade of red, mumbled about being needed in the other room, and ducked away. Gio told Dean he was terrible.

The remainder of the afternoon was spent with hard-on shots and provocative poses. No penetration, oral or anal. McCain didn't go for reality in his sex shots. His pictures were about illusion and suggestion. Real sex didn't read as well as simulated sex. In the poses, they appeared about to do it or just finished. Everything was implied.

Vinnie wanted more. If only McCain had ordered him to suck Dean until he exploded or rim Gio until he squirmed. But McCain said nothing. On this shoot, he kept things professional. Vinnie wondered if that was typical or because Gio was one of the models. He had heard plenty of stories about photoshoots getting out of control.

Not this time.

Though he never would have called himself a size queen, Vinnie was mesmerized by the girth and beauty of Dean's equipment. Long, thick, with an upward curve and a pretty pink head. A dick like that could hit all the right places and maybe some new ones. It was heavenly agony to have that masterpiece inches from his hand, his lips, and his ass.

Judging from the bulge in Gert's jeans, the production assistant felt the same.

Though Gio was handsome and sported a sizeable rod, Vinnie didn't typically go for uncircumcised guys. He'd had sex with uncut men, but he didn't belong to the fellowship of the hood or anything. But he could learn to love uncut dick if it belonged to a man like Gio.

After several hundred shots, McCain slowly lowered his camera. "I think that is it gentlemen. We got what we need. You were all terrific. Good work and enjoy the weekend."

The models stood and stretched. Dean and Gio immediately went to grab something to drink. The photo session had been exhausting—holding poses, tensing muscles, pumping up, and maintaining focus.

When Gert handed the men their robes, the bulge in his pants was still apparent. As Dean took the robe from him, he stared at Gert's bulge and winked. Gert got so flustered he knocked over a stool. The papers on top of it scattered.

Amid the ruckus, McCain pulled Gio aside. Vinnie could only hear a word here and there. Before McCain finished speaking, Gio was already shaking his head. Vinnie assumed McCain was asking Gio to get together. Maybe the shoot reminded Joe of what he had been missing. After Gio appeared to reply *No* a second time, McCain walked away.

The side effects of the erection enhancer left Vinnie congested with a case of blue balls and a nagging headache. Some fresh air would help. Opening the window, he saw Josh Lawless cross the street and enter the studio. Vinnie smiled. Josh gave a man something to be happy about. He was a solid, kind, furry, cuddly, nasty, and sexy as fuck guy with a mustache that highlighted his dimpled smile. Vinnie had a crush on Josh since *Mancandy 2*. Recalling the shoot, his erection revived.

Moments later, Josh came through the door. Weeks ago, he'd asked Vinnie for a signed photo. But Vinnie wanted to wait until his new ones were ready. He sent Josh two new signed ones last week. "Did you get the pictures?"

"They came in the mail Tuesday. Thank you." Josh had such attractive manners.

"I'm flattered you wanted one."

Kip offered a smile that wasn't much of a smile at all. "He asks everyone for a photo."

"He's right, what can I say, I am a collector and a fan of the business and have been for years."

"It's true." Added Kip before announcing he was driving back to the flat. Josh needed a ride. Kip said they could drop him on the way. "That's what is so nice about driving a van, there's always room for one more."

"Plenty of nice things about driving a van." Josh offered.

Dean came out of the bathroom and gave Josh a high-five.

When they left the building, McCain was having a smoke outside. Josh gave the photographer a rocking hug and asked how the shoot had gone. McCain said terrific. "We have got some real talent here."

"Seeing them starting out fresh makes an old heart like mine beat faster." Josh gave McCain a good-natured shove. "Must be nice not to have to grease up the camera lens like you do when you shoot dinosaurs like me."

Sometimes even porn legends fish for compliments.

"I'll be your grease boy, Josh," Gio joked.

McCain's eyes flashed at Gio. Clearly he was not amused by the comment. McCain had been scheduled to meet with Woody after the shoot. "He was eager to see samples from today, but he's stuck with investors in the Valley."

"You free?" Josh asked McCain if he wanted to grab a bite. When McCain waffled, Josh made a face. His husband, Ian, was visiting his folks in Vancouver. Josh liked the mom but said Ian's dad was a blatant racist. "He practically brags about being one. I don't know how Ian tolerates going home."

McCain was parked in the next block. "I'm glad we're doing this." He shot a look at Gio, "I don't have any plans, so we can make a night of it if you want."

McCain wanted to make Gio jealous.

Before the two men left, McCain said he needed to load the camera equipment. Josh offered to help. "Guess I won't be needing a ride in the van," he said to Kip.

Gio and Dean waved goodbye, then Josh shook Vinnie's hand. Vinnie felt something slip into his palm, a scrap of paper with Josh's number. Vinnie curled it in his palm and put it in his back pocket. Calling Josh was a sweet option, but Vinnie would probably take a pass, although the offer was tempting. Josh was already committed. He wasn't looking for more than a trick.

The timing was wrong. Vinnie was leaving for Chicago tomorrow. He expected getting things in order and wrapping up his life there would take about a week.

Dean looked up from his phone. His plans had changed. He was going out. His ride was meeting him at a coffee shop a couple of blocks away. Kip asked why he didn't pick him up there.

"Because we don't have donuts."

Vinnie suspected the real reason was that Dean was meeting Reed.

As he crossed the street, Dean turned to shout, "Fun working with you all today. I will probably be out late."

Vinnie opened the door to the company van and noticed a black town car in the tow zone by the front of the building. Vinnie saw a hulk of a man in the driver's seat and the silhouette of someone in the back. The license plate said NOVAK. When Vinnie asked about the car, Gio said, "Nothing to concern yourself about." Then abruptly changed the subject by asking Vinnie if he had any plans for the weekend.

"Heading to Chicago," Vinnie explained about having to take care of things there. He figured he would be gone about a week. Relocating to WeHo made sense.

When they arrived back at the flat, Gio headed towards the shower. "Big Friday ahead of me." Apparently, he had an appearance scheduled by the agency.

"An appearance?"

Gio slipped off his pants and paused on his way to the bathroom. "A personal appearance, a dance engagement, a date, a meeting, a one-on-one conference; it goes by a lot of different names. Anyway, so I'm off to the Valley for the evening."

"Aren't you exhausted?"

Gio shook his head. "Today's shoot made me horny. Are you kidding? All that play and no follow through, especially with you two studs."

"Okay, okay. Enjoy your shower. I'm exhausted." Vinnie stretched out on the couch. He may have dozed for a moment because the next thing he knew, A.Z. was at the door. He was on his way out. A car was picking him up in forty-five minutes to take him to the airport.

A.Z. said his "A-list star" was taking him to a resort in Mexico for a few days. "He'll be shooting a few scenes down there." A.Z. joked that Mr. Movie Star might be walking bowlegged on the set, but "he'll be wearing the big old smile that America fell in love with."

"I'm jealous. I love the ocean." Vinnie said he liked the power of it.

"Too much for me. I prefer a calm pool in a five-star hotel with a floating bar."

Vinnie said he was heading to Chicago. "Taking care of some things, before moving here for good. You have time for a beer before your car gets here?"

A.Z. made a face. "I never acquired a taste for beer, but I will take a Seven and Seven." A.Z. said he would get it. "You were at a shoot all day." A.Z. handed Vinnie a longneck before mixing his cocktail.

The cold beer tasted perfect. Finally, Vinnie's headache began to recede.

A.Z. asked how the shoot had gone. "Sometimes those days take more out of me than making a movie."

Vinnie agreed and added that McCain was not what he expected.

"How so?"

"More approachable I guess."

"How did things go with Gio and McCain?" Apparently, Gio had confided in A.Z. as well. Vinnie said that everything seemed to go smoothly.

"I think they are over. The flowers stopped coming anyway. McCain used to send him flowers every day. He has the money, but I think McCain's partner got wise." A.Z. told Vinnie that he heard the boyfriend had moved out.

"When did you hear that?"

"Maybe a couple of days ago."

"Really?"

"No one involved has said anything to me. That is only what I have heard." A.Z. continued. "If that is the case, Gio should consider it. Being partnered with McCain means security, and McCain adores him. Gio might not want to pass that by just to be a free spirit."

"A celestial traveler," corrected Vinnie.

"Whatever. To each his own I suppose, but if that was me." A.Z.'s phone buzzed. "My ride is here."

Vinnie raised his longneck to him. "Adios, have a good time in Mexico. See you in a week."

30

Following delays at both LAX and O'Hare, it was after midnight by the time Vinnie unlocked the door to his Chicago apartment. Stepping inside was like entering a tomb. The air was stale. Décor that once reflected him was now a collection of artifacts. These were the remains of another life. Little of this mattered. Vinnie planned to take some photos, his laptop, a few clothes, his father's ring, and little else. Purging would start tomorrow.

The next morning, while his coffee was brewing, Vinnie made a list of what needed to be done. First, he had to tell his landlord he was moving. Subletting would be more trouble than it was worth. He wanted to be free of this place. When he flew back to L.A., he wanted no reason to return.

He'd give his friends their pick of things. The rest he'd bring to a resale shop or put in the alley.

He needed garbage bags.

Socializing wasn't on his agenda, but inviting his friends over would be an easy way to clear some things and give Vinnie the chance to gloat. Of course, they all knew about his success. He was sure he was a hot topic.

Vinnie gave himself a week to get everything done but hoped he could accomplish it sooner. Most of what he had were clothes. His place was mostly IKEA furniture and resale shop accents—the flat of no one special. Everything wrong with his life was mirrored in these rooms.

He added *Call Mother* to his list.

After another cup of coffee, he checked his socials.

Instagram 4620
Twitter 2213

Fortified by caffeine, Vinnie dialed his apartment building's management group. The exchange was civil. A rep from the company would be by tomorrow to inspect for damage. He scribbled the appointment on his pad. After the call, Vinnie began to separate things into save, toss, and donate piles. DVDs, CDs, gone. Books, gone. The clothes he'd worn as Vincent, gone. He could buy anything he needed in L.A.

Midmorning, he phoned Ty, who was clearly excited to hear from him. After some small talk, Vinnie said he was clearing his flat. He asked Ty if he wanted to have the first pick of his things before he took them to the resale shop. "I'm calling Randy and Cort tomorrow."

"You're back, and clearing your apartment."

"Makes zero sense to have a place in Chicago and WeHo." Moving there was smart.

Silence.

"Besides, work is there," added Vinnie.

More silence.

Ty was pouting. Vinnie tried to keep the conversation buoyant, but the effort was draining. Leaving Chicago was not a sad occasion, and Vinnie refused to make it one.

"My boss is giving me the stink eye." Ty said he would come by around seven o'clock that evening.

Vinnie was having a smoke on the back porch when Ty arrived with a bottle of wine. Their hug was awkward; when Ty moved in for a kiss, Vinnie dodged him.

Ty raised the bottle, "Ready for a break? I hope you didn't pack the glasses."

By then, the giveaway pile was waist-high.

"You weren't kidding about purging."

"Nope." Vinnie retrieved two glasses and a corkscrew from the kitchen. "If you like these glasses, they're yours. They're part of a set."

Instead of answering, Ty said he could use a drink and poured them each a glass of wine before taking a seat on the floor.

Vinnie apologized for not keeping in touch. "The studio keeps me busy, and being an exclusive requires even more time. This isn't just about me, it's about image and studio standards."

Despite Vinnie's attempt to sound important, the explanation did not seem to impress Ty. It seemed to have almost the opposite effect. He had heard Vinnie was named an exclusive. "You sent me an email link to the press release. You cc'd me and a few dozen people."

"Easiest way to get word out."

Ty said he supposed it was.

Vinnie wanted to be sensitive to Ty, but he was also exhausted. They had been good friends. Why couldn't Ty just be happy for him? Friends support one another. This sulking was the last straw. It wasn't just Ty. Vinnie had been "sorry" so many times in his life for so many things. He was done apologizing. That was Vincent. Now that he felt more fully Vinnie, he was ready to stop feeling guilty about having ambitions. He was through with the false humility.

Vinnie took a swig of wine. "Being a porn star has been great so far. Lucrative. Side perks like a free apartment, free gym, and sex with guys I've dreamed about." Vinnie neglected to explain that his "free apartment" was deducted from his salary.

"And this started because you wanted Glenn to regret dumping you."

Was Ty trying to bring him down? That may have been true at one time, but not everything he had achieved was all about his ex? He had a natural talent. "Glenn stopped being my motivation quite a while ago. I am making something of myself. This is a real opportunity."

"For what?"

"I don't know, for something I don't have." What was this? Why should he have to justify himself to Ty?

"So the move to WeHo is the next step in your big plan."

Was that an intentional dig?

Yes, Ty was hurt, and Vinnie was sorry he didn't feel the same way. But Ty was being an ass by referring to his career as his "big plan." He was mocking him and trying to make this sound absurd. News flash! This was happening. He was making it happen. Wanting something this badly reminded him of why he was alive.

"How long are you in town?"

"No longer than I have to be." The comment came out harsher than Vinnie intended. Ty didn't deserve that. After all, he had been supportive up to a point. He had helped get him into the industry. "I need to thank you in part for emailing those pictures."

Ty swirled the wine in his glass. "If I had it to do again, I would have asked you. Given another chance, I might do a lot of things differently."

"We were both drunk."

There were tears in Ty's eyes.

The way Ty was feeling was regrettable, but get a grip for fuck's sake, it was a blowjob. Big deal. Some guys just don't understand gay sex.

Ty said Glenn and Robert were on the outs.

"Too bad, they deserve each other." As Vinnie made quite clear. He had moved on.

By then Vinnie was ready for this visit to end. "Look through the clothes. Take whatever you want. Most of this isn't WeHo friendly. The studio expects a certain look." Maybe he was embellishing, but being an erotic performer came with certain expectations. He couldn't walk around looking like just anybody. His wardrobe needed to let the world know that he was someone.

"I thought you were sexier when you didn't think about it, like some casually beautiful college guy."

He's just embarrassing himself.

Vinnie asked if he wanted his large screen TV. "I only got it last year."

Ty said he was there when Vinnie bought it.

"No, it was Glenn."

Ty stopped looking through the pile. "Not true, Glenn was complaining about your crappy TV, so we got you a new one. You worried Glenn would dump you if you didn't upgrade. That's what an asshole he was..."

How could he have forgotten?

"That TV was a surprise for him. We picked it out, brought it here, carried it upstairs, and hooked the damn thing up. That was not Glenn. It was me!"

Vinnie conceded. "I'm sorry, I forgot. Do you want the TV?"

Ty threw the clothes in his arms to the floor. "No Vinnie, I don't care about your hand-me-down shirts or your secondhand TV." Ty was inches away. "I want you." He fumbled for Vinnie's belt. "You are all I want. It doesn't have to mean anything."

After today one thing was clear, sex between them would be nothing but meaningless. Nothing was going to happen.

Ty was becoming incoherent, dissolving before his eyes. Words poured from him. "You're all I want. All. You don't, don't think of me—not me—like that," Ty slowed his breath. "It's always been you."

Vinnie was silent a moment. "You need someone to love you in the right way. One day you'll find them."

"I don't want someone, I want you."

Vinnie sighed. He was trying to be compassionate, but this was like beating his head against a brick wall. There was nothing more to say. When Ty left the room, Vinnie figured he was going to the john, until he heard the front door close.

Did Ty just leave?

Vinnie texted him. Nothing. No response.

Vinnie exhaled.

Passive-aggressive bullshit!

Vinnie had been harsher than he intended. He didn't want to hurt Ty, but Ty saying that he preferred him as Vincent was not being supportive. Vinnie didn't need someone questioning his decisions—or he might start to question them himself.

Ty was a nice guy and they had been friends. But Ty loved Vincent, the boring doormat. That wasn't who he was anymore. He was Vinnie Lux now—and he wasn't about to be dragged back to being the person he used to be—not for Ty, not for anyone.

Instead of divvying up his stuff for his friends, Vinnie called the AIDS charity thrift store. The donations coordinator marked him down for pick up in three days. By then, the management company would be finished with the inspection, and the utilities would be taken care of. He loaded the downstairs dumpster with a dozen trash bags. Alley scavengers took most of it.

31

The following night, Vinnie needed a break from his purge and cleaning. Grabbing a coat, he headed out the door. The evening breeze felt good. Up the street was a bar where he could plant his ass and have a drink or two.

Less than ten people were inside, including the metrosexual bartender. The long room was bathed mostly in the glow of neon, save for the pyramid of light above the pool table in the back. Shania Twain was on the jukebox. A muted Barbara Stanwyck was emoting on TV.

Vinnie was relieved the bar was quiet. There were couples at two of the tables and a few solo drinkers at the bar. Taking a seat, he noticed a few guys checking him out. They knew Vinnie Lux. Hungry looks.

The bartender gave him a generous second pour. Some bars make their drinks so weak his pals called them children's portions. Not this place. Vinnie was on his second Manhattan and getting looser by the sip when Glenn came through the door of the Silver Dollar.

Vinnie's body tightened.

Shit!

Glenn looked good—hair tousled by the wind and the perfect amount of unshaven. When Glenn appeared in public, he always looked good, but Vinnie looked better. Glenn ordered a beer. Waiting for his change, he spotted Vinnie and smiled.

Shit!

He nodded to the bartender. Had that guy told him he was here? A moment later, Glenn walked over. Of course he would—Glenn was shameless. Vinnie had become a person he would notice. Now he had value.

Was Glenn always so transparent?

"Heard you were in town." By the time Glenn finished the sentence, he was leaning on the bar beside Vinnie. Tipsy. He must have been somewhere before. He asked Vinnie how he had been, flashed his dimples, and expected things to be okay. It must have worked before because he seemed confident that it would again.

Apparently, they were going to pretend to be friends and ignore the fact that Glenn fucked him over. Pretending did not mean forgetting. Glenn had humiliated him. In a way, Vinnie was grateful. If Glenn had not been a jerk, there would be no Vinnie Lux.

Glenn lifted his beer. "Vincent, you look great."

Vinnie nodded. He knew he looked good. And he had learned how to accept a compliment.

Glenn leaned close. "Robert and I broke up." He wasn't conveying news as much as extending an invitation.

"Sorry to hear that."

"Yep, I'm flying solo." Glenn was coming on strong, moving closer, rocking his crotch closer to Vinnie. Looking down and making it clear his cock was Vinnie's for the asking. He looked Vinnie in the eye and said he moved into a place just around the corner. "You should see it."

Vinnie said nothing. Most guys would take the hint. Not Glenn. "This is my neighborhood bar."

"Is it?" Vinnie looked around the bar a bit, wanting Glenn to see he was only mildly interested in whatever he had to say.

Who's the boring one now?

Glenn asked how long he was in town. "Vincent, we should get together."

Having Glenn hit on him was gratifying. For months after the breakup, something like this would have been all he wanted. Now, this was too little, too late.

Vinnie rose from his barstool and slipped on his coat. "As far as you're concerned, I'm on my way to the airport. And by the way, my name is Vinnie."

He left without turning to see the expression on Glenn's face.

One thing remained on his to-do list, and it was nothing he was very eager to do.

He decided to wait and phone Mother when he got back to L.A. He needed to be in a certain headspace to talk to her. Distance and a slight buzz were optimal for that chat. Instead of calling Mother, Vinnie called the airline and switched to an earlier flight.

His final morning in Chicago, Vinnie walked the lakefront and bid farewell to the city. When he first moved here, he needed a city of size with a familiar feel. He called Chicago home for a while, but his new home was elsewhere. Vinnie took a breath and scanned the skyline. He would miss the city more than the people.

That afternoon he returned to L.A. with one personal item, a carry-on, and one checked bag.

32

The moment the plane landed, Vinnie took his phone off airplane mode. His phone pinged. A text from Woody: "Please call."

Vinnie figured Woody had an update on *Prime Meat: The Best Cuts.* Woody had given him a brief description of the production: great lighting, great models, hot action, little dialogue, and no storyline. Woody described it as, "Nothing but hot sex sandwiched by credits." The production was also set to feature two of the One-on-One guys. Woody still needed to iron out some scheduling issues and finalize the secondary cast. Production was pending.

Maybe that hot silver daddy was texting to discuss something of a more personal nature. The possibility was exciting. Whatever the reason for his text, it could wait until morning. Vinnie was exhausted.

Vinnie checked the other rooms. No Gio. No Dean. Nobody. And A.Z.'s door was locked. Maybe A.Z. had been ripped off before. Porn sometimes attracted disreputable characters. Although they were all roommates, cast mates, and members of the Xclusiv family, they were all relative strangers to one another. No one knew much at all about the others except what they had been told, and most of that was fiction.

Before drifting off to sleep, Vinnie checked his socials.

Instagram 6391
Twitter 3712

The next morning, Vinnie heard someone in the kitchen. Gio was on a stool at the counter peeling an orange. He looked exhausted.

"How are things? Did you have a personal appearance last night?"

Gio nodded. "A couple." He asked Vinnie if he had talked to Woody.

"He sent a text, but I got it last night after I landed. I figured it was too late to call. Is it about the *Prime Meat* movie? Has he decided on a shooting schedule?"

Gio shook his head. "No. You need to call him."

"It's six o'clock in the morning. I don't want to wake him up. Is everything okay?"

Gio paused from eating his orange. "Just call."

"Give me a hint—is it personal or professional?" Vinnie was not backing down.

"This should be coming from Woody." Gio said he didn't like doing this sort of thing.

"What sort of thing?"

Gio took a breath before blurting, "It's A.Z. He's dead. In Mexico, drowned. Woody phoned last night. I don't know anything more. Woody has more details."

Vinnie was gobsmacked by the news. "What?"

"A.Z., he drowned in Mexico."

"I heard you. I just can't believe it."

Gio absently popped a section of orange in his mouth. "Before he flew down there, I told A.Z. I thought I was in love with Joe. A.Z. told me that if I really had feelings for him, that I had to let McCain know... I never got the chance to tell A.Z. I took his advice."

Vinnie was still reeling. *A.Z. dead?*

"I called Joe and said I wanted us to have a future, but that I didn't want to be his boy. Joe said the boyfriend had already moved out." Gio sighed, "I owe it all to A.Z. He gave great advice and I'll miss him. I don't say that about many people." Gio hadn't been to bed. "I've been trying to get ahold of Dean. He went out with Ed Vittori and it keeps going to voicemail."

Dean and Ed Vittori?

"On a date?"

Gio shrugged. "I don't know. I can't even think. I'm waiting for this Ambien to kick in. Sorry you had to hear about A.Z. this way. When Dean shows up, tell him that he needs to call Woody as well." Gio was already shuffling down the hall towards his room.

With the closing of his door, the flat grew silent.

Vinnie could hear his heartbeat and feel each hair on the back of his neck. *A.Z. was dead.* A.Z. had been a porn legend, a roommate, and a new friend. He had been excited about his trip with his 'A' list star. Maybe finding out what happened would help Vinnie make some sense of this. He needed to call Woody but decided to wait until seven o'clock.

33

Woody picked up the moment his phone rang. Exhaustion was evident in the grit of his voice. Vinnie apologized for calling so early.

"I'm glad you called."

"I heard about A.Z. Gio told me."

"I am in utter disbelief," said Woody. "Losing anyone is rough, but losing A.Z. is devastating. He was a member of the Xclusiv family. Never any trouble. Always a professional. A.Z. was always willing to do whatever needed to be done."

"What happened?"

Vinnie heard Woody fumble for a smoke. "I guess he went there for some rest and relaxation. Apparently he had a few too many cocktails and decided to go swimming. Not a wise decision. The currents along the western coast of Mexico can be treacherous. Someone from the hotel discovered his body the next morning in a tide pool."

Vinnie poured more coffee. "A.Z. talked to me right before he left. He went down there on a date. Some 'A' list action star had hired him for the week."

Silence. Woody took a drag on his cigarette. When he spoke, there was a distance in his tone. "As a personal trainer?"

"As I understood it, A.Z. was hired through Trusted Talents, as an escort."

"You must be mistaken."

A.Z. and Gio had said Woody knew about Trusted Talents. Vinnie was sure he had the name of the agency right. Maybe Woody didn't want to discuss anything like that on the phone.

Smart.

"You might still be tired from the flight. The news about A.Z. has everyone in shock. Take something and go back to bed. There's nothing more to do right now. When you wake up I think you'll be less confused about things."

Vinnie wasn't confused, but Woody was making it clear there would be no more talk of Trusted Talents or escorting. He told Vinnie the police would probably want to talk with him.

"With me? I wasn't even in town. I only heard about this an hour ago."

"You were his roommate. Though A.Z.'s death was considered accidental, the cops have additional questions before the case can be officially closed. Best say as little as possible."

Vinnie understood the subtext of Woody's comment. *Keep quiet about anything to do with escorting.*

"Why tarnish his memory. What does it matter now?"

"You're right. None of that is important anymore." Vinnie knew enough to give the expected response, even if it wasn't true.

"His death was just a tragic mix of booze, bum luck, and bad currents. Why agitate people? Let's just put this behind us."

Vinnie had no intention of agitating people or making enemies. "I'm just trying to make sense of it."

"We all are, but it's best to let him rest in peace. An investigation will cause trouble for A.Z.'s loved ones, the studio, and all of us. Cops have some lousy preconceived notions about the industry. A.Z. was your roommate. He went to Mexico to get away, and there was an accident. Case closed."

Vinnie heard the tinkle of ice. Was Woody drinking? It was not even seven-fifteen in the morning. "Call if the cops come by the flat. I'll do the same for you. I'm sure they'll show up here as well."

"Have you talked to Roy, A.Z.'s partner?"

Woody said he had called him. "Roy is coming to town to collect A.Z.'s things. As you might expect, he is just in pieces. Kip is picking him up at the airport this evening and bringing him to the flat for a moment, but he's going to be staying here."

"Poor Roy. Poor A.Z."

"Try not to focus too much on A.Z.'s death. Let's remember him as the sweet, funny, savvy, and always horny guy we knew and loved. A.Z. would want it that way." Woody had another incoming call. "I need to get this."

"Sure. We'll talk soon."

Hanging up, Vinnie felt in a daze. A.Z.'s death had been a shock and Woody's response was troubling. Why the secrecy? Why the attempts to control the narrative of A.Z.'s death? Was he speaking for himself, the studio, or for "some people" when he cautioned Vinnie about bringing things up to the police?

Heading to the bathroom, Vinnie noticed that the door to A.Z.'s room was ajar. The door had been locked when he came home last night. *I tried to turn the knob.* He had not imagined that. Vinnie pushed open the door. The room was a shambles. The contents of the drawers were spilled on the floor. The bedding was tossed aside. The closet was a mess. A.Z. was not a slob. Vinnie had seen his room. The extent of the mess was a sock on the floor and a drinking glass on the nightstand. A.Z. would not leave his room looking this way.

A tremor ran through Vinnie when he saw his own running shorts and jockstrap among the jumble. It was the dirty jock that Vinnie had used last week as a cum-rag. Why was it in the middle of A.Z.'s ransacked room. Vinnie found one of his socks in another pile. Mixed up in the mess was a note that Vinnie had written on the back of an envelope. What was this? The police were going to wonder why his things were all over A.Z.'s room.

Vinnie wanted no involvement in this. He suspected that last night he had interrupted the ransacking. Maybe the vandal was in Vinnie's room going through his stuff when he came home from Chicago. Hearing his arrival, they had probably ducked into A.Z.'s room and locked the door. Did they watch the knob turn as he tried to enter? Vinnie did not want to consider what would have happened if the door had not been locked.

Or maybe his soiled clothes and personal items were in A.Z.'s room for another reason. Whatever the explanation, it was absurd to think this break-in wasn't linked to A.Z.'s death. Someone thought A.Z. had something, and whoever it was tore this room apart looking for it.

The front door, the windows, and the sliding door to the balcony were all locked. No signs of a forced entry. Whoever was behind it probably had a key, or access to a key.

34

Vinnie had a smoke on the balcony. The air was dry. Sporadic gusts of wind brought more grit than relief. Vinnie watched a dust devil moving down the sidewalk and thought about A.Z. He had never known someone to die unexpectedly. Vinnie's father and all four of his grandparents had died so slowly their deaths were a relief.

As he stubbed out his cigarette, a police car pulled into the lot. Two detectives emerged from the vehicle and looked up at him. A moment later, they announced themselves on the crackling intercom. Vinnie buzzed them in.

Hearing the exchange, Gio ran from his room in a panic. "Woody warned me that the cops might be coming by. I didn't expect them so early." Gio grabbed Vinnie by the shoulders to emphasize the gravity of his words. "I am not here, okay. I was never here. You don't know me. You never heard of me. Got it? You and Dean were A.Z.'s only roommates."

Vinnie nodded. Gio grabbed his backpack and was already opening the window. With one foot on the fire escape he turned back to add, "I'm not going back to Honduras or one of those fucking camps. *Ever.* Call me after they've gone." His final words trailed after him as he ran down the metal stairs.

Vinnie forgot the names of the cops as soon as they said them. Both detectives looked like they came from central casting. Their faces were even less memorable than their names. The first cop asked Vinnie's name. The second made a notation. The first detective asked Vinnie if he was aware of the death of his roommate, Thaddeus Mills, aka A.Z. Ambush.

"I heard about his death this morning." He said he only got back from Chicago last night.

They asked who else lived there.

Vinnie mentioned Dean.

"Would that be the other roommate who goes by the name of ..." The detective referred to his notes. "Dean Driver?"

Vinnie said he had not seen Dean since returning.

"Is that unusual?"

Vinnie considered his answer. He was unsure how to respond. "Not unusual. I guess. I haven't lived here long, and we're roommates more than friends. Not seeing him isn't unusual. Dean has a lot of friends. He likes to go out."

"Any idea where Mr. Driver is?"

Gio had told Vinnie that Dean had gone out with Ed Vittori. He couldn't tell the cops without explaining how he knew, especially if he just got back into town. He regretted saying that now was a good time. He should have told the detectives to come back—but that would have only prolonged the inevitable. "Dean spends the night with his boyfriend sometimes." Vinnie didn't know why he said that. "But I'm not sure where he is now."

When they asked for the boyfriend's name Vinnie said he didn't know it.

The second officer exhaled.

The first officer resumed. "Were you aware of any of the details regarding Mr. Mills' trip?"

Vinnie asked if he could smoke. When they told him to go ahead, he said they needed to go outside. Vinnie took his time with the light. Smoking gave him extra time to think. Best to choose his words wisely. He remembered what Woody had said, *Best to say as little as possible.* After a couple of draws, Vinnie said A.Z. was going to Mexico to unwind. "I don't know much more than that. I didn't know him well. Like I said, we were roommates more than friends."

"Did he mention a traveling companion or someone he planned on meeting?"

Vinnie pretended to consider the question. "No. He mainly just seemed excited about the trip."

"Why do you think that was?"

"Because he was going to Mexico." His retort was sharper than intended. Why were the cops asking these questions? Why did an accidental death in Mexico concern the LAPD? This made no sense. "A.Z. seemed like a nice guy, but I didn't know him well. I only moved in here a little over a week ago."

"And are you both employed as performers by," The officer paused to refer to his notes with the trace of a smirk. "Xclusiv Studio?"

Fuck them.

Woody had said to expect a shitty attitude from the cops. He was right. They were condescending and smug. He was done telling these two pricks anything. Vinnie had some questions of his own. He addressed the other officer, "What happened? I haven't heard anything except that he died."

The second officer shuffled some papers and read a report from the local authorities in Mexico. "The fully clothed body of the deceased was found early Tuesday morning in the waters near Colima, Mexico by a local fisherman. Dead approximately five hours. The night before he was seen consuming multiple beers at a beachfront pub before walking along the bay. He drowned in approximately three feet of water."

The first officer added. "Local officers suspect he decided to go swimming and was pulled under by the current or hit his head on the rocks. The report talked about a possible head injury, the rocky shallow shoreline, and an undertow. The coroner's report shows no significant cuts or abrasions." He held up the graphic. Nothing was marked on the body diagram.

When Vinnie asked what that meant, the officer said, "That coroner in Mexico is doing a half-assed job."

"This was likely a tragic accident, but if foul play was involved, these people aren't messing around. Some advice, be careful of the friends you choose."

And now they were trying to scare him.

"Get back to us if you remember anything more." The cop handed him his card.

After a quick look, Vinnie pocketed the card. They were not going to rattle him. "I wish I could help, but that's all I know."

"I thought it might be."

"If you'll excuse me, I am going to take an aspirin and lie down."

The officer repeated to call if he remembered anything more.

After seeing them out, Vinnie grabbed another cigarette and returned to the balcony. He blew a column of smoke into the thick morning air. He grabbed his phone. Woody answered on the first ring. Vinnie said the police had just been there and that they just missed another costar. Woody would know he was talking about Gio.

"Your guests didn't see anything did they?"

"We stayed in the living room."

He was planning to call Gio to let him know the coast was clear. Vinnie said they regretted missing Dean. "I haven't seen him since coming back. I confirmed his residency, but they knew that." Unable to think of a way to hint at the information, Vinnie added that the police found the coroner's report on A.Z. to be strange.

"How so?"

"More incomplete than anything. Specifically on the state of things."

"Things?"

"The body."

Woody asked if there were any witnesses.

"None were mentioned. I guess a couple of guys at the bar saw him drinking alone beforehand."

Woody appreciated the call. "Knowing I can trust someone is the quickest way to get on my good side. This is a tragedy, but tragedy brings a family together."

Hanging up, Vinnie wondered if he had passed the loyalty test. He hadn't disclosed everything. He didn't mention that A.Z.'s room had been ransacked and that his things had been included in the debris. He was worried the police would want to look at A.Z.'s room. TV cops would have gone through his things and probably come up with a lead. In the real world, the cops that showed up today didn't seem to care too much.

In addition to the searched room, so many things didn't add up. There was the incomplete coroner's report, the fact that A.Z. didn't like to swim in the ocean, and that A.Z. said he hated the taste of beer.

Did Woody suspect something? Asking about witnesses seemed an odd question for an innocent man. Vinnie figured Woody knew more than he was sharing. Did he know about A.Z.'s room? If so, he would expect Vinnie to mention it. If that became an issue, Vinnie would simply pretend not to have seen the disarray.

After his smoke, Vinnie phoned Gio and told him the coast was clear.

"Who is this?"

"I'm sorry. Is Gio there?"

"Vinnie?" He heard a familiar laugh. "Joe McCain. Thanks for covering for Gio this morning. We appreciate it."

"Gio just jumped in the shower." McCain covered the phone with his hand. Vinnie could hear them calling back and forth. Things sounded cozy over there. "Want me to get him?"

"Just let him know it's okay to come home."

"Well, he might be hanging out here for a while—but thanks for handling things." Joe added that it was dreadful about A.Z. "What a terrible accident."

"Terrible." Vinnie echoed, refraining from using the word accident.

He could hear Gio say something in the background.

"Listen Vinnie, I've got to go. Gio needs me to soap his back."

His phone pinged. While chatting with Joe, Vinnie received a voicemail from Ty. He had no desire to listen to that right now. That petty drama seemed even more trivial in the wake of A.Z.'s death. There was nothing to discuss. Vinnie was not in love with Ty. That was a fact, not a discussion.

35

Vinnie shuffled to the bathroom, washed his face, and studied himself in the mirror over the sink. He wore exhaustion like a mask. Thankfully he had no filming or shooting in the next few days.

In the medicine cabinet was a bottle of Xanax. The prescription was made out to A.Z. Vinnie downed a pill and moved the bottle to his dresser drawer. Eager to feel the fuzzy calm, he poured himself a drink. Booze made it kick in faster. He stripped down to his underwear and stretched out on the couch. He was asleep in a half hour.

Vinnie heard the front door open, but the Xanax haze was tough to shake. A silhouette was in the entry, backlit by the afternoon sun. Dean was home. Vinnie squinted at the time on his phone—it was already two in the afternoon. Dean was either coming off a bender or still on one. Thankfully he was alone.

Vinnie said he had tried calling him. Dean slurred that he'd left his phone at the flat. Dean stumbled as he bent to slip off his shoes and took a seat at the foot of the couch. He unbuttoned his shirt. He was wasted. Maybe it was not the best time to tell Dean about A.Z., though he might need to know in case the cops came back. "I have some bad news."

Dean tossed his shirt aside. "Is this about A.Z.? I heard. I was with Ed Vittori when he got the call. We raised a few cocktails in his memory. He drowned, right?"

Vinnie wanted to ask about his date with Ed but now was not the time.

Dean undid his belt and slid out of his pants. He wasn't wearing underwear. He leaned back on the couch beside Vinnie and reached down to scratch himself.

Vinnie was keenly aware of Dean's nearness and his nakedness. His thick member was lying flaccid but heavy upon his thigh. Dean claimed he didn't know A.Z. well, but that he seemed like a nice enough guy. Dean stunk of sweat and liquor and diner grease.

No sound but distant street noises.

Vinnie felt the sexual tension. He tried to ignore the heat between them, but it was impossible and to pretend that Dean's beautiful cock wasn't inches away.

"Welcome home from Chicago. I like having you back."

Dean sat smiling at him.

It took Vinnie a moment to realize he was coming on to him. Even if Dean was wasted, his behavior seemed strange. Dean was making a move on him without another word about A.Z. That was not a normal reaction, but Vinnie thought it might be Dean's way of coping with grief.

"What about A.Z.?"

Dean started to play with himself and said he had something better to think about. Dean seemed to think the world revolved around his dick. He leaned back on the couch, closer to Vinnie "I've seen the way you look at me sometimes." Dean began to knead the muscles at the nape of Vinnie's neck. "You feel good." Dean finger flicked one of Vinnie's nipples, capturing it between his forefinger and thumb. The nub hardened. He kissed Vinnie's neck. "You like that?"

He should put an end to this. A.Z. was dead, Dean was drunk, and they were roommates. There were multiple reasons for saying no, and one big one for saying yes.

Dean's fingers returned to Vinnie's nips. He kissed Vinnie's neck. His breath was hot and stale—a mouth of fever. Another kiss. He whispered, "I saw you the other day." The nipple-play was borderline painful.

"Yeah, well, I..." Vinnie moaned.

"Shhh. I know." Dean raised a finger to Vinnie's lips, and then slipped the digit between them. "I like being looked at that way, especially by a stud like you. I kept thinking about us doing something during yesterday's shoot."

Vinnie let the fantasy take him away.

Dean continued. "Better like this. No cameras around. Unless you like doing it for the camera, and being told what to do."

Vinnie started to suck Dean's finger and reached down to stroke and play with Dean's fat monster cock which began to thicken in his hands. Vinnie's erection pressed the cotton confines of his briefs.

"I've thought about what might happen between us." His hand moved to the side of Vinnie's neck. He pulled him into a kiss. Slow. Deep. Dean moved a hand to the top of Vinnie's head, and slowly started to push down—the international sign for "Suck me."

With pleasure!

Vinnie put his lips to Dean's chest, his rippling stomach. Lips moving closer, tongue trailing and tickling. Dean's cock rose off his thigh. His fingers were on Vinnie's scalp. Massaging.

Fuck he has strong hands.

Vinnie nuzzled Dean's cock and inhaled deeply. His scent was a potent musky mix of ball sweat and nightclub. Intoxicated with Dean's heady aroma, Vinnie kissed down his happy trail and around his heavy nuts. This was a toy that would never grow old. Vinnie paused a moment and looked up at Dean, "This might help us forget."

"Just suck it," Dean didn't need a reason to get blown.

Vinnie tongued the length of Dean's rod before taking the head in his mouth. Deeper. Easing his throat as he felt the shaft expand. His skills were being put to the test, but based on Dean's response Vinnie was acing this oral examination. A cock like that makes everything disappear.

Dean's breath was quickening—there was a change in the rise and fall of his stomach. His hips rose to meet Vinnie's lips. With a whisper of *Yes*, Dean's back arched and the antidote for overthinking splashed across Vinnie's tonsils. Dean grabbed his head. His long legs extended in a palsy of release. Vinnie felt another spurt hit the back of his throat. He wrapped an arm around Dean's ass and held him tight. *No pulling out now. I want every fucking drop of juice. Every bit of it.* By the time his cock fell from Vinnie's lips, it was spongy and drained.

Vinnie licked his lips. Damn, he needed that. He kept his head on Dean's thigh and periodically licked the crown of his cock. He smelled his saliva on the sleeping giant.

When they moved to Vinnie's room, Dean assumed sex would continue. Fucking was his forte, but that was not what Vinnie needed. He doubted he could take Dean's cock without a lot of preparation. It sounded corny, but he didn't need to get fucked; he needed to be held. Nothing more. Losing A.Z. was jarring. He was embarrassed to ask, but when he did, Dean said sure. He was moments from passing out anyway.

36

Vinnie awoke with Dean's arm and leg draped over him.

Someone was knocking at the door.

Once he got his bearings, he remembered that A.Z.'s lover, Roy, was coming into town. He untangled himself from Dean and rolled him onto his back, naked.

Vinnie had no idea what to say to Roy. *What could he say?* All he could really do was offer his condolences. Time alone heals something like this, and the circumstances were horrible.

When he opened the door, it wasn't Roy, it was Reed. *Doors have a peephole for a reason!*

"How did you get up here?"

"Be thankful I didn't let myself in." Reed sauntered inside. As he did, a naked Dean stumbled from Vinnie's room to the john.

Reed eyed Vinnie head to toe. "I guess you weren't expecting me. Forgive the interruption. Is there room for one more at the party?"

"No, we..." Vinnie felt himself blushing.

"Calm down." Reed took a seat on the couch. "That boy has a national treasure swinging between his legs. I like it, you like it, and from what I hear, Ed Vittori liked it as well."

"Why are you here?"

"I'm here to see Dean. But I'm fine talking to you until he's ready. Do you have any beer?"

"You know where it is."

Reed walked to the fridge. "We just got off on the wrong foot." He twisted off the top and sucked away some foam. "I suspect we're a lot alike. Coming to town with big plans. Dead set on making it happen. Takes one to know one. Our type always wants to fuck the boss."

Before Vinnie could respond, the bathroom door opened, and Dean walked naked into the living room. He reached over the counter and grabbed a banana from the fruit basket.

Reed leaned back on his elbows. "So, I bet with A.Z. dead and Gio temporarily underground, this place is real cozy for you two."

He was such an asshole. Despite owing Reed no explanation, Vinnie said that things just happened. "I was on the couch and Dean came in. We were upset about A.Z."

"So, grief drove you to fuck?"

Around a mouthful of banana, Dean explained. "No, he just sucked me off."

Reed turned to Vinnie. "So, the blowjob was grief-driven?"

"I don't need to..."

"I'm kidding. I said I don't blame you. That cock is a treasure. I would lay odds that Woody has a plastic mold of it in stores by the year's end."

Dean laughed from the kitchen.

Reed took pleasure in making others squirm. He thought he was clever, but mostly he was rude. One day Vinnie would take great pleasure in putting Reed in his place.

When Dean took a seat on the couch, Reed leaned over and gave him a deep kiss. Reed licked his lips. "Did you gargle or is that Vinnie's taste?"

Dean repeated that he didn't reciprocate. "I didn't blow him. He knelt right there and did me."

Discussing this was absurd. They were adults. Sex happens, especially in the porn world. For something that he claimed didn't matter, Reed was making an awful lot out of this.

"I'm just glad you two were able to work through your grief."

Dean laughed. He didn't seem to take much of what Reed said seriously.

"This place looks almost the same as when I lived here." Reed leaned back on the cushion. "Of course, I only left when I moved in with Woody. But this place was nice—spacious, balcony, prime location. Reed continued, "Granted, the furniture is a little more worn . . ."

Vinnie sensed where this was heading.

"With A.Z. gone you'll need a roommate? Is Woody taking care of that?"

This was a new low. Reed was disgusting. A.Z. had been dead for two days. *Two days.* Roy had not even collected his things, and Reed was maneuvering for his room.

Despite a desire to ignore him completely, Vinnie said that he doubted Woody would ever allow him to live there.

"I might be on the *Absolutely Not* list, for now. But I can be very persuasive. Woody can't stay angry with me. I know too much. I could tell you things about your precious Woody... "

"And I know a few things about you?"

A smile played across Reed's lips. "Do you, Golden Boy? And where did you get your information; Woody, Vittori, maybe Mykel Z? Have you been listening to Kip? None of them will tell you the truth. Everyone has an agenda, including me. Open your eyes."

Vinnie loathed his lies and condescension.

Reed pushed off the couch. "In this business loyalty follows money. The right side is the side signing checks. You've heard I'm rotten, but I bet everyone who says so is on the payroll. Towing the party line is part of what Woody means when he talks about being a team player. You'll be surprised at what the studio might ask. Or maybe you won't be surprised. Maybe you've already agreed."

Vinnie was through listening to this. "I'm exhausted, can this be summed up in a sentence or two?"

"You've heard enough for today. Though I do have some parting advice. Golden boys get tarnished fast in this town. My advice is to have a backup plan. Innocence only sells for so long. That's why there's a new golden boy every year. I was a golden boy once, but I thought ahead."

"That must have been a long time ago." Vinnie was done.

Reed let the dig slide. "Not so long ago. You think I'm a prick, but I'm being honest."

Rudeness confused with honesty.

"Everybody else has you believing you're unique. You're not—you're just next. There will be another after you. Best to decide what you want to be after you're golden, because that day comes fast."

"What about you?"

"I thought ahead. I turned my tarnished gold into a crown. I became a bad boy. We last longer. Bad boys can age into nasty daddy sex pigs."

Vinnie couldn't just walk away. "I don't need advice from you. I know what happened with Carter Gaines the night of the accident." The moment he said it, Vinnie remembered that Kip had told him the story in confidence.

Reed returned to the couch and leaned so close Vinnie thought he was going to kiss him, until his lips went to Vinnie's ear. "You know nothing about what happened that night. Nothing." After speaking, Reed licked the perimeter of his ear.

Vinnie wiped away the saliva. "Bastard!"

"Always," Reed replied, "Now come party with us I'll tell you all about it. Meet us at eleven at Vixen."

"Do me a favor, hold your breath until I get there."

Reed enjoyed getting a rise out of him.

"Don't you have somewhere to be?"

"Matter of fact, I do." Reed stood. "Sorry to dish and dash. I'll see you later, Dean?"

Dean said he would be there.

"And Vinnie, if you want to come grieve A.Z. with Dean and I at the club. There will be plenty of cocks to suck there too."

Vinnie bristled. "Thanks, but no thanks. Roy, A.Z.'s partner, is coming here tonight."

"Give him my condolences." At the door, Reed turned, "And just so you know, Kip was too drunk to remember anything about the accident or the events of that night. He's repeating what he's been told. They're the ones—" Reed paused. "Kip would feel differently if he knew the truth. I've tried telling him, but that goes nowhere. Come out, and I'll tell you everything."

Vinnie was curious, but he did not trust Reed. And he had no intention of socializing with him. Even if he liked Reed, hanging out with him might jeopardize his career. The decision was easy.

When he left, Vinnie turned to Dean. "What the hell was that about?"

Dean flipped on the TV. "That boy is his own worst enemy. Always fighting the world."

"I was there when Woody canned him. He wanted to banish him from the porn universe. And Woody's reasons are becoming clearer every day. He isn't going to let Reed move in here."

"I give it even odds." Dean was flipping channels so much that it was like watching a slide show. "Reed has been banned from the studio twice since I've been around. The crazy shit is foreplay for those two."

Vinnie had more questions. "I don't know why you and Woody put up with him."

"Reed knows all the best parties. He is on a first name basis with 90% of the doormen and bartenders in this town. Going out with him is very cheap."

More flipping channels.

"Why does Woody let Reed always have his way?"

Dean paused. "Maybe he has no choice."

"What do you mean?" Reed had said something similar.

"Not my business, or yours either. I am a different breed. I am content not knowing what I don't need to know." Dean handed him the remote. "I need to shower."

Despite the teasing by Reed, Vinnie almost offered to wash Dean's back.

He grabbed his smokes and went on the balcony. The warm and thick evening air held the grit and grime. He stretched out on a chaise and listened to the street sounds. He was on the brink of dozing when he heard a tap on the glass. Dean slid open the door and stuck his head out. His tossled hair balanced nicely with his square jaw. "I have to be someplace before I meet Reed." Vinnie figured that meant either a trick or his dealer. "Join us later if you want."

"Like I said, I'm waiting for Roy—but have fun."

"Suit yourself."

Vinnie heard the patio door slide shut. Lazy with the heat, he stretched and then melted into the lounge chair. He was on the edge of dozing once again when the wail of approaching sirens roused him. He held his breath a moment, relaxing when he heard the cop cars pass.

After another smoke he stood and stretched. He got a whiff of his pits. He needed a shower to wipe away his sweat and the soot of the city. He needed one after that annoying exchange with Reed. The man was toxic. Reed had it in for him right from the start. He probably saw him as a threat. Vinnie should be flattered.

Sometimes he thought about being a star and living like one—being number one at the studio and landing Woody as his lover. His life would be luxury and travel. However, the current arrangement barely covered the porn star essentials: tanning, training, grooming, and whitening.

Trusted Talents was an option. Gio offered to make an introduction. They would take Vinnie on. Plenty of guys will pay to fuck a porn star. Wanting to do it live with a guy you've jacked off to on film is a thing. Vinnie had reservations. Escorting was bound to be like waiting tables, only with intimacy and bodily fluids. He wasn't ready.

Maybe there was an easier way to get the finer things.

Woody was a powerful big-dicked daddy bear of business. Vinnie imagined them together. Vinnie's hand moved to his crotch. He slipped a hand beneath the elastic of his briefs. Closing his eyes he imagined the sight, the heft, the musk, and the taste of Woody's cock as he massaged his hardening shaft. Maybe he would call Woody in the morning and suggest another lunch. Maybe this time, the meal would include dessert.

With the sounds of the city around him, Vinnie slipped the elastic beneath his balls and began to stroke himself. The thought of someone watching from a neighboring building made his cock pulse and thicken.

37

The buzzer announced a visitor. Through the crackle of the intercom, Vinnie could hear Roy's drawl. Vinnie took a look around the flat before opening the door. Roy stood with a suitcase in hand. He looked dazed and exhausted. Vinnie gave him a hug and said how sorry he was, "Can I get you a drink?"

"Whiskey and water."

"Ice?"

Roy downed his highball in a single gulp. When Vinnie asked if he wanted another, Roy held out his glass. "I might need to finish the bottle before I go through A.Z.'s things."

"There's no rush. It can wait." Vinnie put the bottle beside him. He would tell him about the ransacked room when the time came. Vinnie was also worried that Roy might find something more of his amongst A.Z.'s belongings, something Vinnie had missed. "So, did Kip drop you off?"

"No, I know how to get here on my own. I came here to see A.Z. enough times." Roy took a long drink and toyed with the ring on his finger.

Forever, A.Z., as Vinnie recalled. Was this the end of forever?

Then suddenly tears filled Roy's eyes. "I can't believe he's gone. This was going to be our year. We were ending the long distance crap. He was going to retire from porn and hustling. He was going go be Ted again."

Maybe Ted was a nickname for Thaddeus.

"A.Z. mentioned his plan to retire," added Vinnie.

Roy said the sex never bothered A.Z. "It was the always being on that got to him. The fans. The stalkers. The gawkers. He was tired of the guys who stared and then looked away. There was other stuff too, stuff he didn't say too much about."

"Like what?"

Roy shrugged. "He thought it best I didn't know. Since he was leaving it behind, he said it didn't matter." Roy circled the ice in his glass. "We were planning on a new life in Santa Fe. We'd been looking at property online. When we saw a place that was over our budget, A.Z. flagged it anyway. He said money would be no problem."

Vinnie asked what he meant by that.

Roy shrugged. "No idea." After a long pause, Roy asked to see A.Z.'s room.

"Before you go in there, you need to know something."

Roy didn't wait for an answer. He was already down the hallway. He opened the door to A.Z.'s room. "What the hell?"

"I was in Chicago. When I got back, this was the state of things." Vinnie didn't mention the locked door or the fact that some of his belongings were in A.Z.'s room as well.

Roy retrieved some items from the floor and tossed them back in the dresser. "They've been here."

"Who?" Vinnie asked, but Roy said nothing. "What are you looking for?"

Instead of answering, Roy felt under the mattress. With mounting frustration, Roy ran a hand along the seam of the curtains and tried to lift the carpet in the corners. "Either they found it, or he moved it before he left."

"What are you talking about?" Vinnie saw one of his T-shirts tossed near the foot of A.Z.'s bed. He had forgotten to look beneath the bed.

Roy sat back on the floor. Vinnie took a spot beside him, near his T-shirt. He would take it when he left.

Vinnie wasn't sure if Roy trusted him or was too beaten to care. "A.Z. kept a personal diary. He claimed he had it all down in writing—secrets people would never want shared. Photos some would never want seen. He said people would pay good money for what he had."

"What are you talking about?"

Roy looked deep into his eyes. "I need to know I can trust you."

"Yes, of course you can trust me."

His word seemed to be enough.

Roy continued, "A.Z. showed me once, not the insides but the book itself. He called that blue spiral notebook our nest egg. I suspect that's what they were looking for. Maybe they even would kill to get their hands on it."

"What are you saying?"

"I think that someone either wanted to profit from the notebook, or wanted the notebook and pictures destroyed." Roy grabbed his hand. "Help me. You've got to help me."

Vinnie sat silently.

"Please," Roy added.

Vinnie couldn't ignore him. Trying to think of something that might be helpful to clarify. He asked Roy who A.Z. was meeting in Mexico?

"Dolph Worthington."

Vinnie had ideas over who the A-list star might be but hadn't considered Dolph Worthington. He had been a top box office draw for over a decade. His on-screen image was tough, and his off-screen image was decidedly heterosexual. Dolph Worthington had three kids with his current wife and had been married twice before. There was considerable money and power invested in a man like that.

"A.Z. liked Dolph. The way he spoke about him, I can't imagine Dolph being involved. He wasn't specific, but it sounded like there were plenty of others implicated in the notebook—people he didn't like, and a few he feared."

"Have you spoken to the police?"

Roy shook his head and laughed. The booze was starting to show. "I've told no one. No one but you. I wasn't sure A.Z.'s death was foul play until I saw the room."

"Are you going to talk to them now?"

"Why, so I can make this shitty experience that much shittier? What good would talking to the cops do? I have no evidence. What am I going to say? My boyfriend was murdered because he was planning to blackmail someone, but now the blackmail material is missing. They would arrest me or laugh me out of there. No thanks."

Vinnie was relieved that Roy wasn't going to the police. He wanted to go over A.Z.'s room again to make sure he hadn't missed anything else. He was involved in this whether he liked it or not.

"Did you like him?" Roy asked.

"A.Z.?"

Roy was looking at a picture.

"I hadn't lived here long, but A.Z. was always very nice to me." Vinnie replied, not sure where the conversation was heading.

Roy continued. "A.Z. deserves justice." Roy took his hand again. "I need someone."

More commitment. Vinnie had to fight the urge to pull away.

Roy tightened his grip. "Please say you believe me."

Vinnie nodded. "I believe you. This is all very strange." Given the state that Roy was in, Vinnie chose not to mention that A.Z. was supposedly drinking beer and swimming in the ocean. Two things A.Z. told him he did not like. And there was the incomplete coroner's report. Roy didn't need more fuel for his fire.

"This was no accident. Will you help me?"

"I don't . . ."

"Will you?" Roy was pleading. "Just, please."

Vinnie could not turn him down. Roy needed an ally, if only to feel not so alone. Vinnie knew how that felt. Never to this degree, but Vinnie knew how it felt to feel that you have no one. "I'm not sure how I can help, but I'm here."

Roy sighed. "Thank God. And don't say anything. This is between us. Swear to me you won't breathe a word."

Vinnie shook his head. "Agreed." He didn't need to be told. Who was he going to tell?

Roy asked for another drink. When they rose to relocate to the living room, Vinnie bunched the T-shirt in his hand and tossed it back in his room.

Roy didn't notice a thing. He was already in the kitchen pouring another drink. "Someone will pay for this."

Now that Vinnie was an ally of sorts, he could hopefully talk some sense into Roy, or at least convince him not to do anything rash. "Nothing is going to be solved tonight. You're still in shock. You need some time to think about things more clearly. You have to know that A.Z. would never want you to get hurt."

"Well, I see it a little differently. Danger doesn't much matter when you have so little to lose."

"You think that now, but ..."

"No, No." Roy was adamant. "I'm going to find whoever is responsible for fucking up our future, and then I am going to fuck up their future."

Realizing that there was no reasoning with Roy in this state, Vinnie decided to shift the conversation. He wondered aloud if A.Z. had the notebook with him in Mexico. "Maybe they'll send it to you with his things."

"A.Z. was not dumb. He would never travel with it. That was precious. That was our future."

Vinnie nodded. "I would ask if you wanted to stay here, in Gio's room. I'm sure it would be okay. But Woody said you were going to his guesthouse, the casita as they call it out here."

"Yes, I already told him I'd be there tonight. I just stopped off to see the place. I'm glad you were here. Thank you." Roy grabbed his hand again.

"No problem." Vinnie's response was almost the opposite of what he was feeling. This was a problem. This was a big fucking problem, and his gut was telling him not to get involved. Roy needed a friend, a confidant, someone on his side. Vinnie had agreed. "I will keep my eyes and ears open." The response might mean anything.

"I wanted to come by. I thought I was ready, but..." Roy admitted it was too early for him to go through A.Z.'s things. "I'll probably be back to pack his things in a day or two."

Vinnie advised him to be careful, especially if there was foul play involved. "Keep your suspicions to yourself."

"I've only told you."

"Yes I know you've only told me."

Roy had to straighten up. Heavy drinking, loss, and a mouthful of accusations made Roy a wild card. "Roy, you need to be more careful. If what you think is true, and someone did kill A.Z., they might not hesitate to kill again."

Vinnie wasn't sure if Roy was listening or just quiet. Vinnie texted him so they had each other's number. "Text if you need to talk, or just want to hang out. I have a good amount of free time right now."

38

Following his tragic death, A.Z. was the subject of several porn blogs. Most mentioned his dependability, his professionalism, and his good-natured approach to his work. Retired porn performer Dorian Mikado devoted an entire episode of his video blog, *Between the Sheets With Dorian,* to the life and legacy of A.Z. Ambush. Mikado's online show was *the* source for backstage gossip in the gay porn world.

Dorian first met A.Z. on the set of the BDSM classic, *Bound for Leather*. The following year they costarred in *Danny's Dilemma* and *All Hands on Dick!* On his tribute show, Dorian also shared that, only hours after his death, A.Z.'s residence had been burglarized. Mikado promised more details in his next post.

The news made Vinnie shake. This bombshell would obviously get back to Woody. Someone leaked the story. Had Reed or Dean seen the room? Did Gio know? Had Roy told anyone? Whatever the source, the news was out there now.

This was problematic. He should have told Woody, or Ed Vittori, or the cops, or someone—but his things had been scattered all over the room. There had been underwear with a load of his DNA in here. Now his smartest course was to claim complete ignorance.

Two days later Dean came home with the tabloid, *The National Tattler*. Reed had given him the issue. The Christian-owned supermarket rag had an expose on A.Z., *Sex Star Meets Tragic End*. Framing the piece was a pic of A.Z. in his prime, as well as a grainy shot of him stumbling out of a club. In the lower corner of the double-page spread was a shot of the tide pool, with an arrow pointing to where the body was discovered, as well as a photo of the resort where A.Z. had stayed. The article was pocked with sordid bits—A.Z.'s immersion into "the gay porn lifestyle," drug and alcohol abuse, and a tragic end at age 37. A "close pal" described A.Z.'s anguished descent into sex addiction.

The piece mentioned his mother having a vision of his death two weeks prior to his drowning. In a photo, she stood on the porch of her home. The "long-suffering" Christian woman reportedly "prayed for her son every day." Vinnie tossed the tabloid across the room.

The studio planned a "Celebration of Life" memorial for A.Z. at the end of the month. When he heard the news Vinnie texted Roy. He felt terrible for not contacting him earlier but wanted to give Roy his space. "Vinnie here. How are you doing?"

It took Roy a few moments to respond. "Trying to move on."

Vinnie suggested lunch. "I'd like to see you."

"Working. Temp job for me in the Valley doing data entry. Still at the casita."

"Over the weekend?"

"Depends."

Roy sounded odd. Granted, Vinnie did not know him well, and he was also in a deep state of grief. Still, he had not been to the condo since the night he arrived in town. "Will you be in town until the memorial?"

"Not sure. Need to move on."

"Thought any more about A.Z.'s things?" Vinnie texted.

End of conversation.

The text exchange was shocking. A.Z. was dead, but life goes on! Roy and A.Z. had seemed so committed to each other. Vinnie remembered how upset he had been when Glenn had dumped him—it hadn't been so easy to just 'move on.' But then, everyone reacts differently. If nothing else, the texts eased Vinnie's conscience. Maybe Roy had just been in shock when he stopped by the condo after receiving the devasting news. The love of his life was gone. Roy had been angry and drunk. Perhaps he said things he didn't mean, and now he seemed to be moving on.

Despite the tragic death of A.Z., the filming of *Prime Meat: The Best Cuts* was not delayed. Shooting was scheduled for the following week. Filming days came with a double bonus. Vinnie was grateful. He needed the cash. The deducted rent was not cheap.

Prime Meat was also becoming more of an A production than originally anticipated. Woody and Vittori were now pushing the film as a major studio release slated as a showcase for the three new Xclusiv exclusives. Now Josh Lawless and the studio's top star, Rex Reynolds, had been added to the cast.

Rex Reynolds was the king of supposedly gay-for-pay porn actors. Two years ago, Rex made his first film and had been the top studio star ever since. Fans ate up Rex's bio—a hunky college student, broke and in need of tuition answers an ad for models in a local paper and poses for some nudes to pay his rent. The next month he filmed a solo. A month later, he was getting a hand job. Next thing he knew, Rex had a career in porn. His trademark was a reluctant willingness to be serviced. *I can't believe I'm doing this with a guy!* In gay-for-pay speak, "doing this" meant being done.

The whole straight man having gay sex fantasy was lost on Vinnie. WeHo was full of gorgeous, oversexed queer boys who would jump at the chance to supplement their incomes and egos. Why deal with a straight guy?

Mikado made frequent mention of Rex Reynolds in his column, often questioning why this straight guy was still making gay porn. *Does he need more school supplies? Is he renting a tux for the spring formal?* Dorian had a bitchy edge, but that was his appeal. *Rex Darling, seduction and non-reciprocal sex grow stale with familiarity. Just suck a dick for chrissakes!*

In his recent opus, *Cabin Fever*, Rex had started to reluctantly reciprocate. In the film, Reynolds stroked his partner and allowed a kiss at the end of the scene. Xclusiv was attempting to extend Rex's career with this familiar slow tease. To Vinnie's knowledge, nothing reciprocal was planned for *Prime Meat*. Reynolds was scripted to get a blowjob before fucking his partner.

The most surprising addition to *Prime Meat: The Best Cuts* was Reed Connors. The scoop was announced on an episode of *Between the Sheets With Dorian*. Mikado added that *Prime Meat* would include a deleted scene that A.Z. Ambush filmed with Lee Botello for the scrapped Carter Gaines vehicle, *Capital Gaines*. The feature had gone into production days before Gaines' death.

Mikado added that *Prime Meat* was to be dedicated to A.Z.'s memory.

Adding the scrapped A.Z. scene to the new production and using A.Z.'s name in a closing credit dedication felt exploitative to Vinnie. A.Z.'s death had become a marketing ploy.

39

Two weeks later, filming began.

Aware that three-ways can produce anxiety, Mykel took the performers aside before filming. "Aim for balance but try and do what feels most natural." Mykel rubbed his hands and said he felt good about this. "Any issues can be remedied in post-production." Editing was always an easy fix for the truth.

When Mykel turned to discuss something with the soundman, Gio joked that this week was going to wear him out.

"What do you mean?" Vinnie asked. Dean was texting, but listening.

Gio pointed to the call sheet. "I'm doing a scene tomorrow."

Vinnie looked at the schedule. Josh Lawless and TBA. "That's you?"

"That's right, I'm TBA."

"Does it stand for *that bottom, again*?" Dean looked up from his phone with a grin.

Gio punched him on the arm. "Nope, it stands for *this boy's ass*."

Vinnie fought to keep his frustration hidden. He congratulated Gio. Vinnie assumed the TBA would be a new hire, not one of the exclusives. The extra scene made it seem like Gio was the top new exclusive. Gio had all the ingredients, but he didn't have the drive. Dean was unmotivated as well. Vinnie was the only one with all the goods—the discipline, and the determination to take this opportunity somewhere.

A third scene for *Prime Meat* was also on the roster for tomorrow. In the afternoon, Rex Reynolds was shooting with Reed. Not only had Woody taken Reed back into the fold, but he was also pairing him with the studio's top star.

Or maybe that was Reed's punishment—penance on his knees. Maybe the role came with a price tag. Most guys loathe working with gay-for-pay. The shoots were tense and sometimes a psychological minefield; major stress and double the work.

Reed had promised he would be back—both A.Z. and Dean had said that Woody would forgive him

Vinnie hoped Woody would visit the set. Vinnie had been on edge since Dorian Mikado announced on his show that A.Z.'s room had been searched. Vinnie didn't mention that fact to Woody when he called that day, or the next. Dorian had let the cat out of the bag.

Trust is a very important part of the Xclusiv family.

The truth was not an option. Vinnie's only recourse was to say the door to A.Z.'s room was closed, and he hadn't looked inside. He would convince Woody that he was telling the truth. He had to. His career might be riding on this.

The return of Reed Connors was another sort of mind fuck. What did Woody see in Reed anyway? Sure, he was sexy, but he was looking rough. The drama was probably the hook. Reed was exceptional in that respect. Or maybe it was something else. Maybe Reed wasn't joking when he boasted about knowing where the bodies were buried. Woody might not have a choice. Whatever the reason they were together—Vinnie still considered Woody fair game. Reed had done the same to Kip, and Vinnie had no problem delivering Reed's karmic comeuppance.

His thoughts were broken by a tense exchange. McCain was agitated at having to discuss a lighting set up with Mykel. From how he spoke, McCain made it clear he considered himself alpha on set.

Vinnie felt for Mykel. The situation had to be humbling. As McCain continued, he began giving Gert orders. The assistant was frantically working to keep up—moving lights, changing a filter, and shifting props.

Vinnie assumed this setup was happening to give Gio the best light. Vinnie could use a man like that in his corner, at least until he had that much power himself.

Due to the delays, Sue was called to reapply some of the makeup. She smelled a bit boozy. Sue apologized for being quieter than usual. "I may have still been drunk earlier. Now my hangover has officially landed. As long as I don't get the shakes working around your eyes. I'm joking," she said, slapping Vinnie on the knee. Sue was there on two hours of sleep. "Coffee is the only thing keeping me vertical."

"You know better than to go out on a school night," Gio teased.

"You would think," she muttered, smoothing some body powder smudges on Dean. "You've got some circles baby. I wasn't the only one who had a late night."

Dean nodded towards his lap. "What can I say? Got to keep junior happy. Not many guys look at my eyes anyway, right Vinnie?"

Vinnie turned beet red. Thankfully Gio was on his phone, and Sue was numb from the night before, so no one picked up on the clue. Vinnie noticed Ed Vittori beside the food spread at the far end of the room. Rocking on his feet, he was smiling and uncharacteristically calm. Was Ed Vittori wearing a "post Dean" glow? Given his dual roles at the studio as head of finances and publicity, Vittori was typically a bundle of nerves. Relaxed looked good on him. His fit, trim torso was made for khakis and a Polo.

Gio leaned over to Dean. "Are you responsible for that?"

Dean offered some wordless version of *aww shucks*.

"You dog." Gio gave him a high five.

"I heard you and Ed went out when I was gone." Vinnie was eager to hear all the details.

After some urging, Dean said they spent a couple of days driving the coast. "Went to San Diego and had a good old time at the Hotel del Coronado."

Gio leaned back into the conversation. "I know another reason Vittori might be happy. Joe told me that Woody finally made good on the owed back pay yesterday, with a hefty bonus for his patience during the payroll delay."

Sue interjected. "I can confirm that Woody made good on what we were owed, and then some." Sue guided Gio back to an upright position and brushed the shine from the bridge of his nose. "That's why I was out celebrating. I probably spent half of my bonus on tequila."

"You should have called me," said Gio, "I bet you are a wild one to party with."

"Don't remind me." Sue nudged him from the chair. "Okay, everybody looks beautiful. Now, if you boys will excuse me, my stomach needs something." By the time she finished speaking, Sue was already en route to the craft services table.

When Sue left, Gio told Vinnie and Dean that Joe McCain had promised to take him to Hawaii with his bonus after they finished shooting. "Woody was very generous."

Filming the three-way for *Prime Meat* took almost ten hours. The shoot was exhausting. When Mykel called, *Action*, Vinnie had no trouble performing. None of the exclusives did, at first. The challenge was to maintain their passion, and their erections, with the unending starts and stops demanded by McCain. Joe was obsessed. This man was a far cry from the easygoing guy who had done their photo shoot. When filming resumed after the stops, it was often McCain, and not Mykel, who shouted *Action*.

At one point during filming, Vinnie ate Gio's ass while Gio gave Dean head. Vinnie stopped for a moment and coughed. Vinnie's neck was cramping from rimming Gio at a photogenic but unnatural angle for what seemed an eternity. McCain barked to get back in place and keep going.

Vinnie did as he was told.

Deeper. Get your tongue in there. McCain, not Mykel, was directing the action—telling Vinnie to eat his lover's ass.

Nice. That's it.

Vinnie didn't need to be told how to eat a beautiful butt like Gio's. Maybe McCain was getting off on this, pretending he was commanding this sex show, starring his lover, for his pleasure.

Do it!

As filming continued, McCain grew increasingly irritable—cursing the periodic appearance of a shadow, needing to reset, shouting at Gert to angle the light box a bit differently. Eventually, McCain moved it himself.

Vinnie's fantasy about sex with his roommates was undone by the stress. All Vinnie could think was how much more enjoyable it would be to rim Gio without interruption. McCain did not allow any of them to get lost in the pleasure of eating ass or sucking cock or fucking—none of it. The three-way had so little natural flow that generating the proper level of porn passion was almost impossible. Maybe that could be added in post-production as well.

Near the end of the shoot, Vinnie and Dean took turns fucking Gio. Hopes for double-penetration fizzled. Even after the douching and rimming and toys, Dean was still too big, especially paired with Vinnie's sizable rod.

"I am not going to be split in two for a movie, though I always dreamed of dying this way," joked Gio.

Mykel suggested Vinnie fucking Dean and Dean fucking Gio, but Dean didn't bottom. Vinnie was waiting for someone to propose he bottom for Dean. He was unsure he could take it all, but willing to give it a try.

Gio had his orgasm an hour earlier while Dean was fucking him. Despite his effort to hold off, Gio raised his hips and came hard. He said he couldn't help it, "That magic wand you got hits me just right every time."

Dean probably heard that sort of thing all the time.

Coming too soon is usually an issue, especially when it occurs without warning. But instead of being angry, McCain brushed it aside. If he or Dean had done something like that, Vinnie suspected that the response would have been different.

Dean stroked himself close and nodded to Mykel. At the signal, Gio knelt and started sucking. Vinnie licked Dean's heavy-hanging ball sac from behind. After some head, Gio began to fast-jack Dean. Vinnie moved to kneel beside Gio. Dean stood above them, breath quickening—a cowboy on the edge. Head back in ecstasy, eyeing the heavens. Dean tightened his thighs and clenched his teeth. With a guttural cry, he sprayed their faces with a sticky rain.

With his eyes closed, Vinnie heard Dean's cry of release and felt the jizz on his cheeks. Gio began to play with Vinnie's nipples from behind. Vinnie came by his own hand in seconds. After milking out the last of his load he collapsed backwards onto Gio. Dean fell forward onto them and Gio began to tickle Vinnie's sides, and then Dean began to tickle Gio. The scene closed with all three of them laughing on the bed. For Vinnie, it was the most genuine moment of the shoot.

40

The bathroom on that floor was equipped with a shower. Gio called first use of the facilities to get cleaned up. He said that he was most in need of washing the remains of the day from his body.

Vinnie asked Dean how he thought it went.

"Good," he shrugged. He was busy texting again.

After his shower, Gio sauntered over to McCain, wrapped his arms around his neck, and gave him a deep kiss. Gio asked if he was almost ready. McCain rested a hand on the small of Gio's back. He'd be ready soon. When they left, Joe and Gio waved to Vinnie and Dean and told Mykel they would see him tomorrow.

Vinnie wondered if McCain was going to commandeer the shoot between Gio and Josh Lawless as well. The scene was filming from ten in the morning until two in the afternoon with little time for delays. The Rex and Reed scene was slated to start directly after. Woody wanted both scenes done by the end of the day.

After a quick shower, Dean said he was off to meet Reed.

"Wait, so Reed is clubbing the night before a shoot?" Vinnie knew it was none of his business, but that was ballsy, especially coming off a suspension.

"Sure is," laughed Dean. "The way that boy parties, he might not remember to show up for the shoot at two in the afternoon tomorrow." Dean asked Vinnie if he wanted to come along, but Vinnie just laughed. "I am so exhausted; I just want to go back to the flat."

After Vinnie finished up in the bathroom, Ed Vittori was standing outside the door. He had been on set for hours working on his laptop. He handed Vinnie a bottle of water. "You were great today."

"Thank you." Vinnie always thought Vittori was hot and Vinnie was suddenly very curious about why Ed was here. Dean had already left.

Vinnie spoke to fill the silence. "I hope the movie turns out well. It's hard to tell when you only have one scene, but it felt like a good one."

"It will be brilliant; Mykel and Joe are pros at putting it all together."

Vittori was lingering. There had to be a reason. By then, Gert was busy prepping for the shoot tomorrow, and Mykel was focused on his laptop in the corner.

Ed lowered his voice.

Vinnie knew the reason for Ed Vittori's being here was coming.

"Woody regrets not making it here today. He had a business meeting with clients just passing through town. They had something to discuss over drinks out by the airport."

"Woody doesn't owe me any explanation."

"He feels he does." Vittori paused when Gert came within earshot and continued a moment later. "Woody has taken an interest in you." Ed paused when Gert rounded the corner to grab the trash bin. "Woody wondered if you would like a late dinner at his place this evening."

Vinnie tossed the plastic water bottle into the recycling bin. The invitation must mean Woody wasn't angry over saying nothing about A.Z.'s room, or that he wanted to confront him about it over dinner. Either way, tonight was not the night. "Please tell Woody that I am exhausted, or I can text him. This was a long shoot." The invitation was strange. If Woody would like to see him for dinner, he needed to ask himself. Why didn't he just text?

Ed said he would let him know. "Woody will be disappointed, but happy you gave your all in the shoot. Congratulations again on today."

"Have a good night." Vinnie watched Vittori walk away and wondered if he was an idiot to turn down the invitation. Vinnie was too tired to obsess over it. He took the stairs to the street. No Kip. No car. There would have been a driver if he had accepted Woody's invitation. Vinnie walked a few blocks and hailed a taxi.

In the cab, he received a text from Roy.

"Call me".

Vinnie texted back, "What?"

Roy responded: "Rather talk."

"Ok. Heading home. Will call in a few."

The cab was loud, smelly, and expensive. After a day like today, he was eager for a cocktail and a smoke. Vinnie poured a drink and dialed Roy. The call went straight to voicemail. "Hey Roy. It's Vinnie. I'll be around all evening. Give me a call and we can talk."

Moments later, Roy responded. No small talk. His voice was low and shaking. He sounded desperate. "I have to tell someone, but not over the phone. You need to know something I found out today." He had already called a car and would be at the flat within the hour.

Vinnie nursed his drink and had a second smoke on the balcony. Another balmy evening in WeHo. He blew a column of smoke to the heavens and wondered what was so urgent. *Something he refused to discuss over the phone.* Vinnie needed to be patient. He would know soon enough.

Tomorrow he would phone Woody and apologize for declining his invitation. He hoped the chat would result in a fresh invite.

After another smoke, Vinnie checked the time on his phone. It had been over an hour. Fifteen minutes later, Vinnie got a text. "Something has come up. I'll call tomorrow."

Exhausted and annoyed he was still waiting, Vinnie stretched out on the couch. Although he was curious, the cancellation was more of a relief than anything.

41

Morning light flooded the living room. An infomercial was blaring on TV. The remote was under his thigh. Vinnie grabbed his phone from the coffee table. Nine-thirty. He had slept long and hard. He was sore from the shoot and from sleeping on the couch. His head ached; this was more than a Viagra hangover. Dehydration and a couple of drinks—it made sense. Vinnie checked his messages. The exchange with Roy had not been a dream. Two additional texts came around midnight. The first read *Dusty*—nonsense. The second simply read, "False alarm. Never mind."

He sent Roy a follow-up text. "All OK? Let me know."

Vinnie waited a moment. No response. Vinnie put his phone aside. That was fine. He wasn't feeling human just yet anyway. After washing his face, taking two Tylenol, eating Greek yogurt, smoking a cigarette, and drinking coffee, Vinnie felt much better. He was on his third cup of coffee when Mother called.

"Well, you're home." Her greeting was also an accusation, as though he had been up to something unseemly—which was actually pretty accurate.

"Hello Mother." *Sorry I didn't pick up yesterday, but I was busy shooting a three-way for a porn movie!*

Mother launched into complaints about the neighbors, the news, and the weather. Few people and things met Mother's standards. Complaining was her prison and her paradise. Being unhappy gave her joy.

Vinnie lit a cigarette and took a deep drag. Now was the time to clear the air. "I finally had enough winters in Chicago, so I moved to L.A."

The pause that followed was so long that he wondered if the call was dropped. Mother loathed surprises. "What?"

"I moved to Los Angeles."

"Good Lord. To do what?"

He expected this. Her lack of support was a tradition. "I needed a change."

The argument fell on deaf ears. Wanting something new or different was tough for Mother to understand. She gave up on such things before he was born. "And you're just telling me?"

Vinnie wasn't going to engage. "Yes, I'm telling you."

"Well, it's your life I suppose."

Vinnie almost snapped but knew the resulting guilt and regret would not be worth it. He gave her his new address and said he had two roommates. He said he was working at an upscale restaurant and served Donna Mills on his very first shift. Mother said Donna Mills didn't look like she ate a thing. Mother preferred a palatable lie to an unpleasant truth.

Vinnie had another call. He wanted to check if it was Roy, but Mother defied interruption. She was in the middle of an extended monologue on the hazards of Los Angeles—earthquakes, drugs, tsunamis, gangs, wildfires, skin cancer, cults, and being so far away.

As though distance was a bad thing.

The caller on the other line left a message.

When Mother realized that Vinnie wasn't going to engage, her tone softened. "Maybe I can come visit."

Vinnie said he would like that, though they both knew it would never happen. Mother was unhappy with her life, but was certain anything else would be far worse.

The call ended with a cordial goodbye.

Would the time ever be right to tell Mother about Glenn and the break-up and the real reason for his move? *Doubtful.* Mother would not want to hear about it. She would stop him before he finished.

The voicemail was from Roy. No message, only a recording of a few seconds with a loud and piercing background noise. *Butt dial?* Vinnie pressed the Call Back option. Direct to voicemail. Vinnie listened to the voicemail again. *What was that sound?*

He was considering another cup of coffee when Woody called.

"My spies tell me the shoot was superb." Woody sounded raspy and sexy, as though he had smoked too much the night before. Vinnie imagined him lying naked in a tangle of sheets.

Vinnie thanked him.

"I apologize for having Ed invite you to dinner. That was tacky. I wanted to see you, but got stuck in that business meeting. I sent a text and Ed misunderstood. Don't hold it against me."

"No need to apologize." Vinnie added that it wouldn't have worked out anyway. "I was exhausted. I slept longer than I have in years."

"That good kind of tired." Woody agreed that filming could be long. "Especially with a perfectionist like McCain on set."

Vinnie heard Woody light a cigarette, and soon after did the same.

"I am calling because if you are free, I would like you to come over for dinner tonight." His voice deepened, becoming more intimate. "I haven't stopped thinking about you since our lunch." Woody knew the right lines and just how to deliver them. "I like you, Vinnie. It's been a while since I've had a date over."

Not a business meeting. Not a friend thing. Not a party. Not a business gathering. *A date. Definitely not mad.*

"I would like that."

"Splendid, I'll swing by and pick you up around seven."

"See you then."

After hanging up, Vinnie fantasized a bit about his private dinner at the home of the head of the studio. His fantasy ended when he recalled the pocket dial from Roy. After those urgent texts last night, Vinnie wanted an explanation. His call went straight to voicemail. Roy hadn't responded to his text. If Vinnie didn't hear anything by tonight, he would check. After all, he would be right there. He could pop back to Woody's casita and make sure Roy was okay. If Woody had questions about it, Vinnie could say he wanted to know if Roy made any decisions about A.Z.'s belongings.

42

At six forty-five in the evening, Vinnie emerged from the bathroom in khakis and a thin sweater. His Midwestern modesty was almost a fetish in WeHo. He knew his appeal. Vinnie Lux was the neighbor who mowed your lawn, then fucked you in the tool shed. He was the kid who played basketball in the park, back from college and all grown up. All American is a perennial favorite in the porn world, and Vinnie's socials were reflecting that.

Instagram 6993
Twitter 4012

Vinnie was still in his room when he heard pounding at the front door.

A moment later, Reed burst inside. His energy was noxious. He was wound up and ticking. He was going off before Dean closed the door. "That prick will pay for this."

Vinnie moved into the hallway but kept his distance. He was curious about the drama but determined not to get drawn in.

Dean lowered the volume on the TV.

Reed seethed, "That asshole Rex Reynolds fucking tried to shame me on set. *Me.* I'm not some fucking newbie. I have won awards. *Plenty of Awards!* Two GAVYNs, a Grabby, and four XXX Review plaques. I've been doing this for a while, and I'm good at it or I wouldn't be where I am. I've made eighty movies and Rex has made four or whatever."

Vinnie assumed Reed's rage was chemically enhanced.

"On the set today Rex was talking shit, blaming me because he couldn't perform, saying it was tough to get aroused with men. I was like, *Bitch, please.* He heard me and went crying to Mykel."

Reed continued, "Ms. Reynolds was pissed because I called bro-shit on his act. Then he made Mykel bring in a monitor and play *straight* porn. Such a fucking fake. That queen is way out of line. He's had plenty of dicks down his throat and plenty more up his ass."

It didn't sound to Vinnie like Rex had chosen Reed to be his costar. Truth and rumor blended in this business. Everyone gossiped. Everyone had reliable sources. Everyone knows, enhances, spins, and repeats.

Dean asked Reed what he was drinking.

Reed said it didn't matter. "Something straight up."

Reed came directly from the shoot. "He was still on set when I left, doing an interview with Dorian about filming the scene and mouthing all that bull about being a straight man in gay porn. Well, Rex Reynolds picked the wrong faggot to mess with." Reed downed his drink in one gulp. The venting and the whiskey quieted him—a fussy baby who needed his bottle.

Reed threw an arm around Dean. "Some people are assholes, you know? Fuck, I hate that Reynolds asshole. Let's go forget our names. I need to party tonight."

With Reed, eavesdropping took minimal effort. Vinnie was still in the hall and trying to be the fly on the wall. If Reed didn't want his business to be known, he needed to keep it down. Vinnie closed his bedroom door to announce his presence before coming into the common room.

Reed had another drink in hand. He eyed Vinnie head to toe, "Headed to the Sears sportswear catalogue shoot?"

Dean told Reed to back off. "Vinnie is not who you are mad at."

"You're right." Reed lifted his glass in apology and offered him a hit off a joint in reparation. Reed asked where he was headed.

The directness of his question made it tough to answer. Vinnie was hesitant to say he was headed to Woody's for dinner. That was bound to prompt a reaction, an insult, a scene, a mind game, something. Vinnie had no interest in that. "I have a date."

Reed straightened on the couch. "Is this suitor someone we know? Is it someone the Xclusiv family would look upon with favor?"

"What the hell are you talking about?"

Dean told Reed once again to back off, but Reed refused to let it go.

Reed would find out soon enough. Woody was fair game. Besides, Vinnie was not here to make friends, especially with Reed. "I'm having dinner with Woody."

"Kip said Woody called you," offered Reed. "And I doubted it was about business. I put it together when I saw you looking like you were off to some fish fry."

"Fuck you."

Reed enjoyed taunting him. "I wondered how long it would take for you to tell me. Just remember, Woody likes his diversions, as do I. And that's all you are, a diversion. I'd hate for that dear innocent heart of yours to be broken."

Vinnie was through playing nice. "You seem awful worked up over something that means nothing."

"Reed, take it down and light another joint." Dean passed him the bottle. "Let's just have fun."

43

At five minutes after seven, Woody texted that he was a couple of blocks away. Vinnie called so long and headed for the elevator. The Lexus was at the curb. Woody got out and opened his door. Woody's tan was perfect. His jeans fit him like a glove. Woody kissed him hello. Closed mouth, but lingering.

Woody put a hand on Vinnie's knee and smiled. He slid it further up Vinnie's inner thigh. Woody was awfully sure of himself, and with good reason. His hand moved higher, stopping short of Vinnie's crotch.

"No need to rush. We've got all evening," said Vinnie.

"That we do." Woody grinned and put the car in gear. "Hope you don't have any dietary restrictions. We're having fish."

Smooth ride.

Woody took Vinnie's hand as the car climbed higher into the Hollywood Hills. Eventually, the Lexus turned onto a private drive. Vinnie could see the house now—three stories, modern, perched on the side of a bluff. The casita was visible from the drive—around the back, beside the pool.

The stairs of the main house rose to a deck. Woody entered the code. When they walked into the living room, the view took Vinnie's breath away. With windows on three sides, the City of Angels was spread to the horizons. Then, a squawk and a whistle brought Vinnie back.

"Orson." Woody nodded towards his parrot.

The vibrant bird was a contrast to the subdued room, but all was secondary to the view.

Woody ran a hand over his chin. "I have this theory about Orson. I think he is a dirty old man reincarnated. He cannot contain his excitement when a beautiful young man is around." Woody was suddenly so close. One hand was on Vinnie's lower back, holding him close. Woody kissed him on the lips, the neck, and at the nape in a way that tingled to his toes. He felt the rough stubble of Woody's beard and it excited him. Woody's lips lingered for a second, and then he pulled away. He asked Vinnie what he would like to drink.

Vinnie needed a moment to regain his composure. "Surprise me." He moved to the window while Woody mixed their cocktails. "I could stand here all day and look out this window."

He handed Vinnie his drink. "And do what?"

"I don't know."

"Yes, you do."

Vinnie offered only the slightest hesitation. He felt comfortable enough with Woody to share. "You're right. I would stand right here and look out and imagine that I was going to make this town mine."

"Yes!" Woody said it so loudly that Orson began to fuss. He lowered his voice. "The first time I saw this view I knew that if I woke up every day and saw L.A. at my feet, then one day it would come true. We think alike."

The blue of Woody's eyes—so vibrant. Vinnie was going to have a good time tonight. "And you do have the city at your feet."

"Some of it anyway," Woody added,

Vinnie took a sip of his drink. He wasn't quite sure what it was, something with tequila. Vinnie didn't want to be nosey, but he wondered how Woody could have possibly afforded a place like this before he was a success. Maybe he came from money. "So, have you had this place a while?'

Woody answered without hesitation. He said he had inherited the place from a lover who died in the 1990s. He didn't say, but Vinnie assumed it was AIDS. "He taught me a lot."

"Like what?"

Woody offered a sly smile. "I could tell you, but I'd rather we teach each other some things." Woody leaned in to kiss him again.

Sexy, powerful men turned Vinnie on. The fact that Woody was also the boss made him a genuine fantasy. This gorgeous daddy could fast-track his career. His hand ran the lip of Woody's belt and dipped below the leather before hastily unbuckling him and sliding his pants to his knees. Woody stepped free. Black jockstrap. Vinnie ran his hand over the cotton pouch.

Woody stiffened beneath his touch. Vinnie leaned close, "Has everything you visualized come to be?"

"I've gotten almost everything." His hands were on Vinnie's ass, pulling him firm against Woody's hardening cock. "Let's move to the couch." On the couch Woody began to kiss Vinnie's neck again.

Vinnie pushed him back a bit. Vinnie began to unbutton Woody's shirt. He ran a hand across the dense fur on this silver daddy's chest before moving lower and doing it with the next button.

Fuck! This man was supreme. Woody was built the way Vinnie had imagined.

Woody was still answering the question. "Not everything. The only thing that I really have left, is finding the right person to share it all with."

If Woody was just feeding him a line, that was fine. Vinnie had an agenda too. Right now, this man felt great, looked great, tasted great, and could further his career. Why wouldn't Vinnie want to believe every word? Each had plenty to offer the other. Maybe Woody was done with guys like Reed.

"You'll find someone." Vinnie held his gaze. The sun was setting. "I imagine this view is great at night, and superb in the morning."

Woody pulled him closer. "It will be dark soon enough, and dawn can come quickly." Woody raised his glass to Vinnie's. "To rooms with a view and the view in this room."

Orson began to squawk when Vinnie took off his shirt.

"I told you." Woody slipped a hood over the birdcage. "If I don't cover him now, there's no telling what he'll do when you take off your pants. Say goodnight, Orson." The bird quieted almost immediately.

Woody moved closer. Thighs touching, junk touching, chest to chest—one nipple even moving over another. Woody pulled him close while grinding. Kissing him gently, then with a mounting urgency. Apart long enough for Woody to find his nipples. Soft then hard as crotches continued to grind and swell. A tongue in his ear. Vinnie spit on his hand and reached down as Woody took his tit in his mouth. Sucking. Harder. Then tweaked. *Fuck! So damn sensitive.* Hands exploring. Vinnie yanked down Woody's jock. His cock was pretty. Those big balls were full of cum but not for long.

They moved to the rug in front of the couch—a faux pelt both soft and luxurious. Hands became mouths and then time for more. And for the big encore, a tube of lube appeared. Vinnie knelt, elbows on the couch. His lower back was arched. He was offering his ass to Woody. "Fuck me," he mouthed over his shoulder.

Woody entered with little preparation. Fucking started with a stab of pain. Too deep. Too fast. *Breath through it. Breath through.* One of those times where you can only hope the next time is better. In moments, Woody shook. Vinnie felt the throb and surge inside him, and then the weight of Woody upon him. A minute later, Vinnie finished himself off while Woody played with his nipples.

Maybe Woody had a long day or needed time to get to know a guy. Maybe when you're the guy signing the checks you don't need skills to get laid. Woody had a XXX empire. Wannabes lined up to service him. The lucky ones bedded him. When a man has looks, money, and influence, being a five-star lover is the partner's concern.

Woody rose from the rug and returned moments later in a robe. He had a damp washcloth. Vinnie said he'd prefer a quick shower instead.

"Sure." Woody led him to the master bath. "I'll get dinner ready. I hope you like it."

"The shower or dinner?"

"Both, but I'm more concerned about dinner." Woody confessed that he had ordered supper from a Zagat-rated restaurant. "Cooking is not my forte, so dinner is really only a matter of restaurants or reheating."

Vinnie laughed. "Technically reheating counts as cooking. It counts whenever an oven or microwave is used. I'm sure it will be great," he added with a grin before closing the bathroom door.

The rain shower was sublime. Pulsing jets relaxed his scalp and muscles. He had to limit himself to five glorious minutes.

By the time Vinnie had finished his shower and returned to the kitchen, Woody was naked beneath a chef's apron. His furry ass was on glorious display as he bent before the oven.

"How was the shower?"

"Amazing."

"Good." Woody adjusted the knobs on the stove. "I'm not meant to cook."

"Maybe, but you look so damn good doing it," said Vinnie, nuzzling him from behind and grinding a bit.

"Don't distract me," Woody laughed and pushed him away.

Vinnie moved to the window. The glittering grid of L.A. was spread before him. A different creature after dark, the setting sun awakened a being with a million eyes. *Let them all watch.* Once upon a time, he hated the thought of people watching him until he realized he could turn them into followers. He called over his shoulder. "You're right, the view is breathtaking."

Woody moved behind him, arms around his waist. "And so are you," he said in his ear.

Vinnie turned, "You feel good."

Woody broke from the embrace to check the oven. Another shot of that hairy muscle ass. Dinner smelled terrific. Woody said it was ready.

Vinnie loved the salmon and wild rice with broccoli that Woody had "cooked." Woody said the name of the dessert, but Vinnie forgot it immediately—something French, warm, and chocolate.

After some wine, Vinnie figured he might as well bring up the issue of his finances. Maybe there was more work at the studio. He told Woody he was appreciative for all he had done.

"Jesus," Woody put down his fork. "Are you dropping out of the business?"

"No, nothing like that."

Woody exhaled. "That's good. We have a lot invested in you."

That was good to hear. "I appreciate everything, but I'm ready for more. I need more money. My pay only covers the basics, I need more."

Woody understood.

"... And my Xclusiv contract has me over a barrel. I can't work for another studio."

"And why would you?'

"I just mean for money."

Woody asked if he had received any offers. "Who has approached you?"

"No, it's nothing like that. "

Woody calmed almost immediately. "That's good, because that would not be a smart move." The moment was awkward. "No one steals my boys, especially my exclusives. We are family."

"No, I am very happy at Xclusiv," Vinnie assured him. "I need to do something to earn more money. I'm willing to do other jobs, learn the business side of things, anything."

Woody lit a cigarette. He appeared to be weighing options. "Only boys with ambition are interested in the business side. Are you ambitious, Vinnie Lux?"

"I suppose."

"Relax, I like that." Woody asked if he could dance.

Vinnie was unsure how to answer. "*Technically*, yes."

Woody laughed. "Not a rousing self-recommendation, but I appreciate the honesty." Woody kissed him. "Truth is, it doesn't matter. You don't have to do much. If you can flirt and sign your name, you'll be great. After all, you're an exclusive. We'll coach you. It's easy money—showing up, smiling for pictures, signing your name, doing a sexy dance to a few songs."

Vinnie blushed. "The dancing part worries me."

Woody brushed Vinnie's worries aside. "I know for a fact that you have some sexy moves."

"It's not that," Vinnie asked for a cigarette.

Woody took one from the pack and lit it for him. "We can get you work in a couple of different clubs. Have you ever been a bartender or bar back?"

"I used to be a great waiter, at least an above average one."

Woody didn't have many contacts in the restaurant business. "Porn and food don't mix as well as porn and liquor. Experience isn't important. These guys know hiring a guy in the industry is good for business. Men appear when they hear so-and-so is behind the bar. They want to see you in the flesh, and maybe take you home at closing. Some clubs even pay the studio a 'finder's fee.'"

More service-work. Vinnie didn't want to cheapen his brand. He had become Vinnie to be someone new. He wasn't about to take a step backwards now by getting a regular job. "What about personal appearances?"

"Dancing and appearances bring the most cash."

"I'd rather do the appearances. That would grow my career."

Woody liked his answer. He poured them more wine. "Let me talk to Vittori. He'll have news in a week or so. But for now." Woody disappeared for a moment and returned with a checkbook ledger. "Something to tide you over."

"I couldn't ask Xclusiv to do that."

"Not Xclusiv. This is my personal account. This is how much I believe in you."

"I really can't, I..."

Woody opened the ledger anyway. "We can call it a loan if you want. Think of it as a friend helping a friend."

Vinnie could use the money.

When Woody opened the ledger the phone in his office rang, "The landline is business. It never ends. It's always business hours someplace." Woody rose with a sigh. "I'll try to keep it brief."

Vinnie heard Woody go into his office. The conversation was muffled, but it sounded tense. Vinnie picked up his wine and sloshed a bit on the table beside the checkbook. He grabbed a paper towel to wipe up the spill. Dabbing the corner of the ledger, he noticed something. Five days ago there was a cash deposit made to Woody's account for $50,000. Memo: investment return. Fifty thousand was a sizeable deposit. What sort of investment paid that kind of dividend—in cash? The fifty grand was probably the reason he was able to make good on back wages. Vinnie heard Woody hang up the phone and spun the checkbook back to its original place as Woody entered the room. Vinnie asked if everything was okay.

"Oh sure. Business. New investor jitters. So much of my job is hand-holding, reassuring folks that Xclusiv is a great investment opportunity. I push the investor perks. They seem to go for those."

Vinnie wondered what those perks might be.

Woody picked up the pen. "Enough about investors and business. We were talking about you. How much money do you need?"

Tough question. Vinnie didn't want to ask for too much or too little. He wanted Woody to suggest something.

"Is $1,000 enough?"

"Perfect. Thank you!"

Handing Vinnie the check, Woody said he would talk to Vittori about lining up personal appearances and dancing gigs. "Ed knows everyone. If you're worried about dancing, you can work with Kip. He's terrific."

"I didn't know Kip was a dancer."

Woody topped their wine. "When I hired Kip he was the best stripper on the West Coast, and that is not an easy title to get. That kid was born to dance."

Stripping was probably the last thing Kip wanted to do anymore. He never even wore short sleeves. It's likely that those scars ruined his life. How does a person bounce back after something like that?

Woody's arm was around Vinnie's shoulder. He was gently stroking his back. Vinnie leaned into his soothing touch. He felt so content beside this gorgeous man, with this view of the shining city before them, and a check for $1000 in front of him. He asked for another cigarette.

Woody looked around. "I must have left them in the office. Do me a favor—go get the pack and I'll open another bottle of wine. The office is past the bathroom, second door on your right."

The pack of smokes was beside the phone. Retrieving the pack, Vinnie saw Woody's appointment book open on the desk. A notation on the page caught his eye. Last Monday—the doodle of a dollar sign with *D.W. 7:00* beside it. The next day, the cash bank deposit of $50,000 was made to Woody's account. Was D.W. Dolph Worthington and the $50,000 blackmail? Vinnie flipped to the week before. The day after A.Z.'s death was circled in red. Vinnie grabbed the smokes.

Maybe Woody knew about the notebook. And, when he heard A.Z. was dead, Woody searched the room and found the journal. Vinnie suspected that the next thing he did was get in touch with Dolph Worthington. Blackmail didn't seem so nasty when the target made millions. He owed wages to his family. Xclusiv was everything to him. Vinnie didn't necessarily agree with it, but he understood it. Besides, this was America! Being a shady opportunist is not only acceptable, but often revered.

Roy had said the journal included incriminating photos that someone would pay good money to keep buried. *That diary will be our retirement, our nest egg. We'll never have to worry about money again.*

Fifty-thousand wasn't much of a nest egg—not given the supposed content of the pictures, but maybe this was one payment—the first of several. Even superstars have cash flow issues sometimes.

Vinnie caught himself. He was speculating without evidence on the crimes of the man who had given him a job, saw his promise, and just loaned him a thousand dollars.

No sign of forced entry on the flat the day A.Z.'s room was ransacked only meant that someone had a key, or was invited inside. Woody had a key, but countless others did as well. Kip had fished a set for Vinnie from an envelope in his desk. A key to that flat was given to every guy who lived there. Reed bragged about still having his key.

Woody must never know he saw the ledger or the engagement calendar. "I found the smokes. I was looking for matches." Vinnie gave Woody the pack.

"I've got the lighter here."

Was he suspicious?

Woody handed him his wine and pulled Vinnie close. "You were saying something about the view."

After another glass of wine and sitting quietly with Woody in his arms, Vinnie asked about his life before WeHo, before XXX, and before Xclusiv.

"I need another cigarette." Woody said he was from a shit town in Missouri. "Homophobic. Misogynist. Racist. Not a good place to be different. Every bit of hate was a mandate from God. Instead of loving neighbors as themselves, they loved neighbors like themselves."

"You still have family there?"

"Relatives, not family. Life there was tough. I kept quiet about things. Being a reader saved me. Books made me see the world was bigger than my little town. Folks back home don't want to change. They don't want anything new. The thought terrifies them. Their world is one change away from total collapse. Imagine being that fragile."

He continued. "People found out about me during my sophomore year. I got pummeled. Teased. That kind of thing. The only reason I wasn't run out of town was because my parents and grandparents were born and raised there. Folks there hated strangers more than queers, but if I stayed my life would be on their terms."

Vinnie remembered feeling the same way. He took Woody's hand. Vinnie felt so close to him at that moment. Woody was a Polaroid coming into focus.

"I refused to compromise. I wasn't going to tolerate that. I skipped town the night I got my high school diploma. I was off to see the world."

"And did you see it?"

"Not really." Woody was only in L.A. a few weeks when everything changed. "I went to a Perry O'Hara signing at A Different Light. I was a big fan. I had read his memoir *Land of the Forgotten*, the novel *The Measure of a Man*, and of course, his masterpiece, *Dark Waters*. Those books were my escape from that small town. They made me see possibilities with my life. I told him that when he signed my book. He smiled and invited me to stick around. We went out for drinks. Lord knows what I said, but he must have found it charming. That night he brought me back here and it's been home ever since."

"This was Perry O'Hara's house?" Vinnie said that *Dark Waters* changed his life. He had enjoyed it, but saying that it changed his life was a gross exaggeration.

"Perry built this place after selling movie rights to two of his books in the mid 1970s. The studio gave him four million—unheard of at the time. Perry was a negotiator who enjoyed brokering his own deals. The smartest man I ever knew. We were so different. I can't imagine being into bookkeeping and financials. I hand everything over to Vittori and forget about it."

This futuristic castle on the hill, with expansive views now had an added appeal. O'Hara was an out gay author starting in the 1960s. He wrote novels, memoirs, and history. He chronicled everything from early gay rights to the hippie scene to AIDS, the disease that eventually killed him.

"Perry was positive but asymptomatic when we met. He started to get sick a few years later. By then Corbin Kent and I had started Tandem Pictures. Perry bankrolled us at the start. By then Perry knew he'd seen his last Christmas. When he died that summer, he left me this place along with the rights to his work. His blood family took me to court over his estate. He had broken contact with them years ago. The family felt his books besmirched their good name, until they saw their worth. Then, they came to scoop up everything from the boyfriend. They didn't count on me. Perry had been brilliant. He took all the proper legal steps with his will to ensure it would hold up no matter what his family tried. Eventually they gave up. I paid them a lump sum under an oath to never contact me again. I've been here ever since. That's my pre-Xclusiv story. Sorry you asked?"

"Not at all." His story moved Vinnie.

Woody offered Vinnie a cigarette and lit another for himself.

"Your turn. What led you to Xclusiv?"

Hearing Woody's story, Vinnie would not feel right telling Woody anything but the truth. He talked about his devastation after Glenn left him for Robert, but how that rejection motivated him to hit the gym. "At first, I did it so Glenn would find me desirable. I wanted him to realize he made a mistake. I'm basically here because I got dumped."

Woody said he couldn't imagine anyone breaking up with him. "You're too sweet of a man. Glenn's loss—you're perfect husband material."

Had Woody just said that?

"Thank you. I'm actually grateful. Being dumped by Glenn had a greater impact than being with him ever did. When he left me I made up my mind to be the sort of guy that no one dumps."

Woody looked at him. "Everyone gets dumped at some point."

Vinnie held his gaze. "Yes. Now if I am not enough, they don't deserve me." Vinnie read something similar in one of his self-help books, or maybe in several of them.

Woody raised his glass. "To the men and things that have brought us to this moment." They clinked glasses and drank. "Let me add that this moment makes me very happy. You're the sort of man I've been waiting for."

Was Woody on the level?

Vinnie had fantasized about Woody saying those words. But hearing it said sounded even better than he imagined.

Woody planted a trail of kisses across Vinnie's chest, teasing each nipple with his teeth, hard enough to make him gasp, relentless enough to curl his toes. Lips moved lower. Vinnie arching, undoing the sash of his robe and inviting further exploration. Cock responding. Hard wired to his nips. Lips moving lower. Taking Vinnie in his mouth. Suction, tongue action, and lips supreme. The man could blow. *Fuck! This man was good!* Vinnie dug his fingers into Woody's hair.

He pulled Woody back, looked him the eye and allowed him to resume.

Maybe he wanted to be spit upon. Maybe another time. Vinnie flipped him over and dove for Woody's ass. He parted those furry muscle globes and went to town—loosening him with his tongue. Then a finger to the knuckle. Then two. Taking his time. Vinnie wanted him to beg and grind. He wanted to hear Woody's sigh of gratitude as he slid his cock inside.

44

The men lay in each other's arms. Their second go-around was incredible. They were still in the living room, but the action propelled them from the couch to halfway across the floor. Both men were exhaustion wrapped in a smile.

Woody sighed. "That was extraordinary." Erotic exertion lingered in his voice. Woody's elbows, knees, and back had been branded by the carpet.

Vinnie kissed him. "I can't believe I'm here in your home." He admitted having a crush on Woody since he first walked into his office.

"On me, or on the head of Xclusiv?"

The directness made it a tough question to answer while still sounding sincere. "Both, I suppose. Your position got my interest, I was physically attracted, and your personality sealed the deal."

"Well said." Woody squeezed his thigh. "Glad you feel that way."

"I can't imagine being in your position. You must take on a lot."

"You have no idea." Woody lit a smoke. "Most guys need nothing from me. Some guys are misguided or they are looking for a father figure. Some need a kick in the ass. Some of them arrive already damaged. We take a hard pass on guys waving any red flags, regardless of good looks and a big dick. We don't need any of that at Xclusiv."

A few slipped through.

Reed Connors was a prime example. Sociopaths are geniuses at manipulation. Vinnie would lay money Reed hooked Woody by making him think he could be reformed. Powerful men love to be saviors.

"Most are like kid brothers to me. That's why I call us family. Some are more than that." Woody took his hand and kissed it. "You're something more."

"I am."

"You know you are."

Vinnie could not believe this was happening. "I know you think of everyone as family, so A.Z.'s death must be really tough for you."

Woody agreed that it had been.

"And with losing Carter Gaines a couple of years ago."

"Carter Gaines." Woody was visibly surprised to hear the name.

Vinnie said he read about him online. Not entirely a lie.

Woody didn't try to avoid the question. "Losing Carter was tough. He was twenty-two and such goofy kid really. Having him gone so suddenly was terrible. Losing Carter was tougher than losing Perry."

"So tragic." He asked if Woody had any thoughts about A.Z.'s death. "Was it officially declared accidental?"

Woody said he had no idea. "But I did hear about his room being vandalized."

If Woody was pissed at him for not mentioning the searched room, he was doing an excellent job at hiding it.

Even with the room search, Woody called A.Z.'s death a tragic accident. "The longer I live the more philosophical I become. Sometimes fate throws a curveball. Carter and A.Z. were horrible losses."

"How has Roy been holding up? Is he still in the casita?"

Woody said he assumed that Roy was fine. "Last I heard anyway. Roy left here a few days ago. Evidently, he had somewhere he needed to be."

Vinnie tried to mask his surprise. Why had Roy, after his urgent messages, left so suddenly without even a goodbye? "Did he leave an address or say anything about A.Z.'s things?"

"Roy left a note." Woody said he wasn't at home when Roy left. "When I came home and there was a piece of paper under the door thanking me and saying he had business to take care of."

"What about his job in the Valley."

"That ended Friday." Woody paused a moment before adding, "You two must have really hit it off."

"Not really. Just surface stuff." When Roy called last night and said he would be at the flat in a few minutes, Vinnie assumed he was still staying in Woody's casita. He must still be in town.

Woody said that Roy probably just needed some space. "As someone who has grieved the loss of a lover I can tell you, expect to be crazy for at least a year." A moment later, Woody asked if they could move to the bedroom. "If I fall asleep on the floor, I'll feel it tomorrow."

45

Though prone to insomnia in a strange bed, Vinnie slept soundly until he was awakened by a kiss from Woody. Vinnie stretched beneath the tangle of sheets.

"Did you want to sleep for a while? I need to get moving. Trainer at seven-thirty." Woody disappeared into the bathroom—Vinnie checked the clock. It read 6:00AM. Woody was brushing his teeth. Staying in this glorious bed sounded so good.

On Woody's return, Vinnie declared he was up—revealing his erection. Woody tackled Vinnie back onto the blankets. They wrestled until Woody had Vinnie's erection firmly in hand. "Do you always wake up ready for action?"

"Usually." Vinnie nodded, his breath catching at the feel of Woody's firm grip. He spat into his palm and began to stroke him. "I want to start my day seeing you cum."

The two men moved to the bathroom. "Come on," said Woody from the shower/steam/sauna. "I'll get you clean as a whistle."

'Be there in a minute." Vinnie still had to pee and that was never easy with a hard cock.

After he managed to piss. Vinnie stepped into the shower. The pulse of the rain jets relaxed him. Woody's cock throbbed against his thigh. Each man lathered the other. When Vinnie reached for Woody's erection, he grabbed his wrist. "I need my fluids, or my workout will suffer." Dwayne, my trainer, always says, "Never before, always after."

Woody moved behind him. Reaching around with a soapy hand, he began stroking Vinnie. One hand went across his chest at the shoulders, holding him while the other stroked him—firm, twisting, firmer, tight, tighter, faster. The hand across his chest was working a nipple. Woody held him tighter. Locked in the grip of this power bear, Vinnie was seconds from popping. The sensation of soap, the pulsing jets, and having his back pressed against Woody's hairy muscled chest made Vinnie come so hard that his knees buckled.

Drying off, Woody kissed him again and said there were extra toothbrushes under the sink.

Vinnie laughed, "Oh really?"

"For houseguests."

"That's what I mean." When Vinnie opened the cabinet beneath the sink, there were at least a dozen extra toothbrushes.

Woody kissed him on the cheek and said that if he hurried, he had a surprise for him. Two minutes later, Vinnie came out of the bathroom to the smell of breakfast. Woody was standing at the stove. Sometimes there is nothing sexier than a man with a skillet. "Last night I was overly humble about my cooking skills. Breakfast is my specialty. I make a mean French toast. Do me a favor and take the hood off Orson's cage."

"Sure thing." When Vinnie uncovered the cage, Orson began to squawk. "He's saying good morning."

Vinnie was looking out at the haze of the city and not thinking about much of anything. But then, he suddenly realized that Orson was the background noise on the "butt dial" from Roy yesterday. That made no sense. If Orson was on the voicemail that Roy had left yesterday, that meant he hadn't left when Woody said he did. Roy had been here, in the main house, as late as yesterday.

Woody was asking something. Vinnie was oblivious. Woody cleared his throat. "Not a morning person, huh? I was asking if you wanted syrup."

Orson's squawking gave Vinnie a moment to think, "Yes to syrup. If it's thick and sticky, I want some."

Woody kissed the side of his neck. "That's what I like about you. Are you ready?

Vinnie pulled a stool before the plate of French toast, dusted with powdered sugar. Sausage links too. Woody poured a generous amount of maple syrup on top.

Juice?"

"Yes."

"Coffee?"

"Always. This looks so good."

"Tastes even better." While Vinnie ate, Woody ducked into the bedroom. He emerged in a T-shirt and shorts moments later, just as Vinnie was putting the final forkful of French toast into his mouth. Vinnie declared it the best he had ever tasted."

Lighting his first smoke of the day, Woody leaned back against the counter. The bulge in his shorts looked as appetizing as breakfast.

"Dwayne works me to the bone. Dwayne Thorne is my trainer. He used to be with the studio."

Vinnie knew him. Dwayne Thorne had brought British bad boy sexiness to Xclusiv studio for a several films almost a decade ago. Actually, Dwayne was from Scotland—Inverness. He's the guy who made flipping his kilt and flashing his junk at circuit parties a thing. Dwayne retired from the business three years ago.

After coffee, Woody grabbed a pitcher from the fridge and poured a greenish smoothie.

Vinnie grimaced. "That looks horrible."

"Because it is." He tipped the glass in Vinnie's direction. "This is breakfast until I get rid of the middle age spread."

"I like your body." A muscle-daddy with some meat on his bones was perfection to Vinnie. "I like men who look like they have a life outside a gym.

"Says the man with five percent body fat."

"Hardly," laughed Vinnie.

"Then close. All I want is to get rid of these extra pounds before they become an issue." He kissed the nape of Vinnie's neck. "I hope last night was just the first of many cozy evenings." Downing the last of his smoothie, Woody grabbed his gym bag and pocketed his keys and wallet. "Feel free to hang out. There's a pool and joints in the cookie jar. When you leave, call an Uber and bill the studio account."

"Thank you. I had a great time. Last night was wonderful." Vinnie was trying to think of something to say to appear natural in the wake of recognizing Orson's screeching.

At the doorway Woody turned and grinned. "I could get used to you Vinnie Lux."

Vinnie smiled. "Have a good workout." Vinnie watched Woody pass by on the deck before taking the stairs down to the car.

Shit! Vinnie had no idea what to think. He rinsed his plate and fork and put them in the dishwasher. More coffee. He moved to the window. The house was still, except for Orson. A clock ticked in the hall. When Vinnie saw Woody's Lexus wind down the drive, he grabbed his phone. He scrolled to Roy's message and listened to it again. The noise sounded like a tropical bird, possibly a parrot. That didn't mean it was Orson. This was L.A—plenty of people here liked to keep exotic things in cages.

Vinnie wandered into Woody's office. He wanted to find something to soothe his concerns. something that would exonerate Woody rather than incriminate him. The desktop had been rearranged. The appointment book was gone. Vinnie shuffled through the remaining papers—notations on scraps, receipts, a letter, and an invitation. Not a shred of evidence, nothing to hint at a clandestine meeting or to clarify the source of the hefty fifty grand deposit. Desk drawers locked. File cabinet secure.

Vinnie scanned for anything he may have overlooked. His heart stopped when he noticed the small red light and surveillance camera in the corner above the window. *Shit! Shit! Shit!*

He jumped when Orson screeched in the other room.

The placement of the camera offered a panoramic view of the room. He should have expected visual security. He had probably been recorded last night too. No masking the footage, He just hoped like hell that whoever was in charge didn't review the footage unless there was an incident. He imagined what he looked like flipping through the appointment book last night. This morning would look worse. He had entered the office with clear intent and shuffled through Woody's personal papers. He tested locked drawers and tried to open a file cabinet. No denying his actions. *Fuck!*

Suddenly, Vinnie heard a noise. Someone was entering the code in the security system pad—four digits in rapid succession—he felt his pulse in his temples. Kip passed the office window on the wrap-around balcony. Vinnie didn't think Kip noticed him, but he couldn't be sure. The sunlight may have turned the office window into a mirror. Kip tended to avoid those.

Vinnie rushed to the living room by the time the glass doors off the kitchen opened with a *whoosh*. A rush of warm air entered before Kip closed the door. Orson began to screech.

"Morning Orson." Kip spoke and saw Vinnie at the same time. Woody neglected to mention that Kip was stopping by. Maybe Kip was another tool of surveillance. He didn't seem surprised to see Vinnie. Maybe overnight guests were the norm. Vinnie offered him coffee.

"I prefer this," Kip took a glass from a high shelf, opened the refrigerator, and poured some sun tea. Kip was marking his territory, making it clear he didn't need Vinnie acting like a host. Kip added two ice cubes to his glass, "I usually come by and water the plants, clean Orson's cage, see if Woody has dry cleaning, mail, all that stuff. Once a week, I even clean the pool. I do everything for Woody. He needs me to keep his life on track and make sure the road is smooth."

"I'm sure he appreciates it."

Kip took a long drink of tea. "He does. We look out for each other. I'm one of the few people Woody trusts."

"He just went to meet with his trainer."

Kip pulled a watering can from beneath the sink. "Dwayne Thorne at seven-thirty. Who do you think organizes his schedule?" If Kip knew Woody's schedule, maybe he knew about the DW meeting. If Vinnie wanted to learn anything, he needed to defuse things. Vinnie asked how he had been.

Kip eyed him as if gauging his sincerity. "No complaints." Kip slapped off the tap. The watering can was full. "How long are you staying, Vinnie?"

"Not long, but Woody invited me to stay as long as I wanted."

"He says that a lot."

Vinnie let the dig slide. Even before Kip had arrived, Vinnie had not intended on staying. Men like Woody Wilson enjoy pursuing their mates. The surveillance camera made him anxious to leave. He couldn't think with Kip around. He needed an excuse or a plan to get out. Kip was refilling the watering can when Vinnie answered that he wasn't staying long.

"I can give you a ride when I'm finished. This will take another fifteen minutes, tops."

"A ride would be terrific."

After watering the plants in the living room, Kip opened the door to Orson's cage and gathered the soiled newspaper sheets. Kip raised his voice over the screeching parrot. "Half the time when I come over here, I run into someone." Kip spread a fresh layer of paper in Orson's cage. "Sometimes a somebody, and sometimes a nobody."

Vinnie could not let another shady comment slide. "Yes, it's exciting to be a star."

Kip nodded. "I know. I used to be an exclusive."

"That's right. I'd forgotten." Although Vinnie didn't want to start anything, Kip needed to know that if he took a jab, he was going to get one back.

Kip filled Orson's water. "He calls sleeping with the stars test driving."

Vinnie bit his tongue. He wasn't engaging in this. "Kip. I care about Woody, but you need to know I am determined to make a name for myself at this studio. So if you have a problem with me, I suggest you resolve it—because I am not going anywhere."

Kip turned. There was a smile on his face. "Well, for the first time since we met I feel like I might be getting to know the real Vinnie Lux. I admire your ambition."

Unsure of how to respond, Vinnie said, "Thank you."

Kip lowered the door to the birdcage. Orson squawked in protest. "He always hopes that this time I'll let him out, but I never do." Kip went to the bedroom. When he returned he was sending a text while juggling an armful of clothes. Kip tossed the heap on the counter. "Dry cleaning." He left and returned a moment later. "No mail. Woody leaves his outgoing mail on his desk." He caught Vinnie's eye as he scooped up the clothes. "You didn't see any mail in the office, did you?"

"No."

"Oh, I thought I saw you in there earlier."

Orson screeched in the silence.

Vinnie calmed himself. "I was exploring. I had to look around every square foot of this gorgeous home! I can't believe this was Perry O'Hara's place." He had no idea if Kip believed him.

Ten minutes later, Vinnie clicked his seatbelt in place as Kip pulled the car out of the driveway. Skyway Drive was a steep blacktop that led down to the city. The curving road was equipped with few guardrails. On one side was a stone wall—on the other the pavement fell away into the mountainside.

Kip's hands tightened on the wheel. In a few hundred feet, he pulled to the side. Like much of Skyway Drive, this stretch had a minimal shoulder before a sheer drop of thirty feet to underbrush and thicket. A car coming from behind might not see them. "Is stopping here safe?"

"Nothing is entirely safe."

"Moderately safe is okay," Vinnie added with a nervous laugh.

Kip nodded to the tree by the passenger door. "That's where we crashed that night. That tree saved my life and destroyed my world. When we hit the trunk, I was thrown from the car. Carter went over the edge still buckled in, like you are now. He probably never even knew what happened."

"Then was he unconscious?"

Kip paused. "Yes, he was." He turned to Vinnie. "He was. I had forgotten that. He was slumped forward, and I reached to push him back. His head thudded against the window. When I turned back to the road, the tree was there."

Vinnie wanted to hear what Kip was saying, but not there, not with the very real threat of being rear-ended down a mountainside. "Let's move down the road a bit?"

Kip was entranced by his memories. "The car went over the edge and exploded at the bottom of the ravine. Carter was still strapped inside. Every time I pass this tree, I think of him." Kip ran a hand over the pink interplay of scars at the back of his neck. "Sometimes I remember more. Today I recalled the second before we hit, and pushing Carter back in his seat and then seeing the bark of that tree so clearly and then nothing." Kip stared at the bark a long moment.

"Can we go? I need to get back to the flat?" He hoped Kip wasn't offended, but sitting here was just plain crazy. Vinnie did not have a death wish.

Kip didn't hear him. "Someday I'll remember it all. Right now, it still feels like I'm seeing it all happen from the bottom of a pool—just shadows, sound, and vibrations—like I'm coming to the surface and can almost see it. And then it's gone."

Vinnie needed to think of something, fast. "Sometimes it's best not to rehash painful memories." Vinnie tried to open the door. The safety lock was on. He was captive. Trapped. He turned to Kip. "Move the car! Unlock this door or move the goddamn car."

"People say not remembering is probably a blessing, but they don't know. I suffer from not remembering it every day."

Vinnie looked to the side-view mirror. No oncoming traffic, for now.

Kip turned to him, "He was sitting right where you are. I wanted you to know that about me."

"Goddamn it, move this car!"

"Ok, let's get you home." Turning back to the road, Kip shifted gears and continued down Skyway Drive.

What the fuck?

Now Kip seemed perfectly normal, or at least back to his usual self. Vinnie tried to be calm. What had just happened? Was Kip haunted by demons? Batshit crazy? Or was it something else? Sitting there had felt like a threat.

They rode in silence for a while before Vinnie could think of anything to say. "Seeing that tree must be tough for Woody too. I know he and Carter were close."

"Woody takes a lot of new stars under his wing. He cares about them all, but some are users. Protecting him is part of my job." Kip looked at Vinnie. "You understand?"

A chill ran through Vinnie.

46

Being back at the flat was a relief. Vinnie had a smoke on the balcony. He needed a moment to relax after the drive home. And then he began to think more about Roy. He claimed to have proof. Whatever it was that Roy had discovered was too risky to mention over the phone. He said, *I'll be right there.* Then nothing. Vinnie tried Roy's number. Straight to voicemail. He'd already left several messages. If something had happened to Roy, the person responsible might have his phone. Vinnie tried to recall the messages he had left on Roy's phone. One was after some wine and weed, but there were other voicemails too. Vinnie tried to recall if he mentioned foul play, the notebook, or Roy's suspicions? Anyone listening to those messages might think Vinnie knew more than he did. He may be in danger.

Vinnie resented his involvement in this. Someone had scattered his things in A.Z.'s ransacked room. Someone wanted him involved and now Vinnie was up to his neck in all this whether he wanted to be or not.

He needed to think things through. Exertion, heat, and sweat often gave him clarity. A jog would be a good detox. If he was going to hit the pavement he had better do it soon. Today was already looking to be a scorcher and the air would only thin as the day wore on.

After changing and some stretching, Vinnie grabbed his phone, slipped in his earbuds, and closed his bedroom door. He slipped the key into the pocket of his shorts. Exiting the building, he turned up the music. Running in L.A. benefits from a great soundtrack. On previous runs, he had passed The Abby and Pump; Chateau Marmont, where Belushi overdosed; the Pacific Design Center, and the Rocky and Bullwinkle statue. He had taken a run down the Sunset Strip. What a trip! He ran passed plaques from the history of filmmaking, and blocks bearing the stars of many forgotten stars. Countless movies and TV shows were shot here. On these streets, déjà vu was around every corner.

Jogging was also great people-watching. Grandiose to grotesque—the Hollywood population was more characters than people. As a porn star, Vinnie was part of the circus, living the dream of stardom. Some of those he passed still clung to the hull of their capsized dreams, caricatures of their golden selves. When it started to get to him, he focused on his music and his footfalls.

That will never be me.

Never me.

Never me.

He had already achieved more than most. He had starred in three movies. Promos for his first two films were all over the gay rags. He looked good. One press sheet for *Backfield in Motion* had him photographed from behind, helmet under one arm, looking over his shoulder, wearing a smirk and eye black. *Vinnie Lux, Backfield in Motion. Coming Your Way Soon!* Vittori planted a couple of *Get to Know Him* pieces in different porn rags. *Vinnie Lux, Get a Taste of Him in Mancandy 2. StarBoyz* did a quick interview *Putting the D in Vinnie Lux!* His social media numbers were climbing. Fame was starting to happen.

Vinnie jogged past another homeless person—a pile of rags with a shopping cart, legs scaled and scabbed, skin like raw meat. Another person with dreams, now little more than a corpse with a pulse.

Never Me.

Never Me.

Vinnie ran until his eyes stung from sweat, sunscreen, and smog. After another block, he slowed to a walk. He felt every smoke he'd had over the past week. He moved to the shade beside a CVS parking lot. His breathing was returning to normal. As he shook out his legs, a car cruised by before pulling up beside him. A businessman was at the wheel. Suit. Tie. Expensive watch. The passenger window rolled down. His crew cut caught the sun. Vinnie felt a blast of cool from the car interior.

"Don't I know you?"

Vinnie shook his head. "I don't think so."

The man grinned. "You're Vinnie Lux. I've seen you in magazines. Dorian Mikado did a segment about you." The Dorian piece, *Lux Gets Physical* was posted at the end of last week. Vinnie had never been recognized on the street before.

Another homeless person was camped on a cardboard flat at the corner of the lot.

Never me.

The man in the air-conditioned car told Vinnie he was one of the sexiest men he'd ever seen. "I liked what I saw in those pictures. You look very talented. Now here you are, in the flesh." His name was John, and he was in town on business. "If you are free for a while to hang out I'm staying just up the street."

John was in his late forties. Well-groomed. Well dressed. Cleft chin. Brown eyes. Broad shoulders. Thin brown hair that was graying. Brown mustache. John was probably handsome once. He probably played high school football forty pounds ago. John fished a wallet from his breast pocket. "I'll make it worth your time."

The rental car smelled like melon air freshener. Hopping in the car of a random fan wasn't smart, but Vinnie didn't care. He needed to be desired. John didn't look like a psycho or vice. He looked like someone who could afford some fun. Woody's check for a thousand would only go so far.

John eased into the late morning traffic. Before they reached the corner, John admitted that his real name was Noah. "Like the guy with the ark." On the ride to his hotel, Noah said, more than once, that he couldn't believe he was sitting next to Vinnie Lux. "I met a star."

The situation was strange but starring in the wet dream of some stranger for cash got his dick hard. No fee had been discussed. Noah stopped at an ATM. Unsure of what to charge, Vinnie decided to see what Noah offered. He seemed to have a good idea what this type of thing might cost.

Noah's hand was on Vinnie's crotch. "I've only seen the goods in Dorian's column and in *Throbb*. I think it was *Throbb*. Didn't you do a spread in *Throbb*?"

Vinnie wasn't sure. Vittori had farmed out the photos. His image was no longer his own. Vinnie could be on anything from billboards to butt plugs. His face was scheduled to be on the three-ounce size of Sapphire Lube.

"Whatever magazine it was, I'm looking forward to seeing the real deal. I haven't seen you in any movies."

"I've been in *Mancandy 2* and *Backfield in Motion*. Both are due out in the next few weeks." Vinnie added that he had just finished filming his third movie and was named one of Xclusiv's exclusives.

"Dorian mentioned that."

Giving Noah a list of his credits was embarrassing. Vinnie had to get it through his head that he had nothing to prove.

Noah was oblivious. His hand was on the waistband of Vinnie's shorts, and then his jock. The venting of the pouch released the heavy scent of ball sweat. Noah moved his hand down the shaft to the head. Vinnie moaned. A bit dramatic, but being a sex god came with some expectations.

Noah took his hand away and smelled his fingers. "Lucky me, I like it a little rank." In the shadow of the Hollywood sign, Noah pulled into the hotel garage. Fifth floor. Noah led Vinnie down the hall. Room five-seventeen.

Inside the door, Noah asked if he wanted a drink.

"Just some water." Gamey from his run in the L.A. heat, Vinnie asked to use the shower.

Noah was on the edge of the bed. "If you must, but leave your jockstrap with me."

Vinnie slipped out of his jock and was about to toss it over when Noah said. Once again, "I can't believe I'm here with Vinnie Lux."

Believe it! Thought Vinnie. *Fuck it!* If Noah wanted Vinnie Lux, he would get Vinnie Lux. Instead of tossing his jock, Vinnie took the jock in his hand and walked over to Noah. He pushed the rank pouch in front of Noah's nose. "Smell it. Yeah, like that. Deeper. I like a man who knows what he likes." Vinnie took Noah's hand and lifted it so he was holding Vinnie's jock in place. "Now be a good boy and busy yourself while you wait for the real thing."

Minutes later, Vinnie emerged from the bathroom with a towel hung low about his waist. Noah was ready. His hands were on Vinnie's chest. Had he mentioned his nipples in any of the interviews? Vinnie's towel unfurled to the floor. Noah took his mouth from his tit and dropped to his knees. He buried his face in Vinnie's crotch, kissing Vinnie's thighs and balls.

"Big fucking porn star cock," Noah was no stranger to XXX dialogue.

Sex with Noah was a checklist—oral, rimming, missionary, doggie, cat, cowboy, reverse cowboy, etc. Impressing Vinnie seemed more important than enjoying himself. The performance ended with Noah rubbing Vinnie's load over his paunch. All that was missing was a camera crew.

After a moment Noah asked how he rated. "On a scale of one to ten." He wanted to be compared, critiqued, and advised. What was his best move? What needed improvement? What curled Vinnie's toes? He wanted everything but a score for his dismount. "You've probably been with thousands of guys."

Thousands!

"How do I compare with the porn stars you have sex with?"

Vinnie gave him a nine because ten sounded like bullshit. An eight or lower prompted more discussion. "I know you were good because I can't recall specifics, just the overall experience."

Noah said he had been with several guys who told him that he was their best and that if he was younger, he could do porn. That made sense. Noah had sex like it was being filmed—as if emoting passion for a hidden camera.

Noah was still talking. "Even if I got in shape, I could never do what you do. Not that you do anything wrong. You do you. But I was raised in a good home. I wasn't brought up to do something like porn."

Vinnie stood. "I have an appointment soon."

"I didn't insult you did I, it's just that I could never ..."

"I'm not insulted, just late. You still owe me."

Noah handed him a wad of bills. Vinnie shoved the money into the pocket of his running shorts.

He was halfway out the door when Noah said he would never forget today. "Can we take a selfie? I won't post it. I can't really show anyone who knows me. This is just for me, and a couple of friends. Otherwise, they won't believe me."

"Sure," said Vinnie. After all, Noah was a fan.

47

Returning home, Vinnie found his worries just where he had left them. He needed to call Woody and at least thank him for the wonderful evening, but the thought of calling him gave Vinnie crippling anxiety. What if he knew about the snooping? Vinnie was terrified that his career might be over. And he worried about Roy and the voice messages and that some shady people might think he knows too much. He felt like his head was about to explode. Tossing his keys on the kitchen counter, he heard laughter. Reed and Dean were in Dean's room.

Vinnie leaned against the doorframe. "What's up?"

Both men looked up and burst into laughter. They were glassy-eyed. A haze hung in the air. A tray with traces of white powder sat on the nightstand. Dean offered Vinnie a hit off the joint. "Go on Reed, you can tell Vinnie. He's cool."

"Are you cool Vinnie?" The way Reed asked the question made it sound like a challenge. Vinnie took a hit.

Reed nodded for him to take another. "We've been smoking all morning."

"After partying all night," Dean high-fived Reed.

Vinnie asked what was up.

Reed seethed, "That motherfucker's time, that's what is up."

Vinnie had no idea what Reed was talking about. Dean swung the laptop around. Stepping over some clothes, Vinnie got a clearer view of the screen. Rex Reynolds was bent over a bed. His hands grasped the sheet and his face was contorted in pain and ecstasy. Rex was on the receiving end of a brutal ass fucking.

Reed added, "It's not what's up, it's who's up—Rex's butt."

In the clip Rex squealed and moaned. "Yeah man, give it to me. I love your cock inside me. Fuck me. *Fuck me harder.*" The tight frame of the shot hid the face of the active partner. The room was seedy. Nondescript was the best description.

"I cannot wait until people see this. It will blow his straight boy act to smithereens. Payback is so good sometimes." Vinnie suddenly realized what was going on. Reed and Dean were uploading the Rex Reynolds footage onto Xtube and Pornhub.

Vinnie asked about the other guy who was in the clip.

"Just a buddy with a huge dick." Reed added that the guy was not in the business, "or on anyone's radar."

"With that amount of talent he should be in this business."

"He never wanted to, but he did always have a thing about fucking pretty muscle boys. When I asked if he wanted to fuck Rex Reynolds he jumped at the chance."

Dean laughed, "Here's where he says, *Fuck me harder. Split me in two.*"

Reed was grinning. "Fucked in the ass and shouting cheesy dialogue. Rex has never been more believable on screen." Reed took another hit. "I bet bubbles will be burst when this goes viral."

Vinnie didn't know what to say. The weed wasn't helping. He had heard rumors about Rex. Mostly that his gay-for-pay image was a gimmick concocted by the studio. This would ruin Rex's career, and damage the studio. "This is wrong." Vinnie wanted no part in this.

"He was wrong! Rex should not have pulled that crap in front of the crew. But, I was willing to give him a pass. Then, he trashed me on Dorian's show. He targeted my livelihood. I'm a decent guy, but don't cross me."

Believing he was a decent guy was probably something Reed needed to tell himself. There were differing opinions on the subject. Vinnie would be willing to argue the opposing point-of-view.

Dean replayed the clip.

Fuck me harder. Split me in two.

"Rex attacked me on Dorian's show—a professional attack."

Vinnie had no idea what to say. "But your fans are loyal."

"Are you serious? Oh, you should do standup. I can count my loyal fans on my cock and balls. Once you're no longer the fantasy, the loyalty goes. Rex will learn that soon enough. Rex told Dorian I was the worst lay that he'd ever had, that it wasn't easy to stay hard fucking the Holland tunnel. He thought he was being clever. He even insinuated that I was diseased."

"He said all that to Dorian?" Vinnie understood Reed being pissed.

"He told Dorian that sometimes the studio likes to pair their biggest star, meaning him, with a newcomer or someone whose career needed a boost."

"Could he have been misquoted?"

"It was on tape. Dorian and that boy toy assistant don't know how to edit much less splice something damning. But Dorian is on my shit list too. I thought we were good. Then he posted this piece without allowing me to defend myself. I wanted to kill Rex, but Dean came up with a more fitting form of justice."

"Dean?"

Dean said it was even easier than he figured it would be.

"Rex was talking on set about his gym in WeHo and his routine. A buddy of mine works there, and said Rex comes around late nights. He promised to text the next time Rex came to work out. When he texted last night I made sure my big dicked buddy was good to go. When Rex hit the showers, my buddy tagged along and gave Rex a peak at what he had to offer. Getting him to that motel room was easy as dangling bait. My pal ate his ass for fifteen seconds before Rex had his ankles in the air."

"And we were ready with the camera," added Dean.

"All we did was hid in a closet and pressed record."

Vinnie laughed at Reed's claim.

"I was not the one spreading lies, or my thighs." Reed nodded to the screen, "This is called ending the career of a gay-for-pay porn star." They watched the advance of the upload bar. "No one asked him to mention me in his interview."

"Rex is going to know you were behind it. He'll know you set him up."

"There's no evidence. The motel was a by-the-hour dive and the room was rented in cash under an alias. Nobody there remembers anything or anyone. It's a requirement for the job. And my buddy won't rat on me. Dean is cool. And you're not going to tell anyone, are you?"

"I won't." Vinnie hated being in this position—harboring another secret with the power to jeopardize his career. "But what about your friend who works at the gym. He is going to put two and two together. Are you sure about his silence?" Vinnie was trying to get them to reconsider and stop the upload. "Dean, how did you get involved?"

"Out of loyalty to my friend," Dean shrugged. "When someone attacks a pal, they attack me."

"That's why we get along so well," added Reed.

The upload bar continued to advance, moving in small bursts. Once the clip was uploaded, Rex Reynolds was over. Vinnie said what they were doing was wrong.

"It's none of your fucking business," replied Reed.

"Telling me about this made it my business."

"Dean *claimed* you were cool. I forgot you also worked as the official Xclusiv morality police."

"Sabotaging Rex is bad for the studio. Reed, don't you feel you owe Woody something after all he's done for you?"

Reed laughed. "Yes Vinnie, part of the reason I'm doing this is to repay Mr. Wilson for all the shit that he has done. One day you'll understand."

Vinnie took another hit when the joint came around. "I am starting to understand him pretty well. Last night he told me about growing up in Missouri."

"Missouri?" Reed shook his head. "Woody grew up in the valley, in Glendale."

"What reason would he have to lie?"

Reed laughed. "Why do you think, to get you to talk."

Was Reed telling the truth?

Reed said he fell for something similar once upon a time. "Tell Woody that if he wants you he needs new material. He probably used that hard luck story to hook Perry O'Hara. That's Perry's house by the way."

"He told me."

Reed wasn't finished. "Did Woody also tell you that Perry left him that house and the money to turn it into an LGBTQ writer museum in his name. Perry wanted that to be his legacy. Woody held that man's hand on his deathbed and swore to do just that, but once Perry died, Woody forgot his promise."

Vinnie had heard enough. "You will say absolutely anything."

197

"That's the tip of the iceberg. There's plenty you don't know about Woody. Someday when I hate you enough, I'll tell you everything."

Dean was rolling another joint.

The file upload had reached sixty-seven percent.

There was still time to stop this. "You realize that once that's done it can't be undone."

Reed laughed. "Well, rest assured, it is going up."

Dean called out that the upload had reached eighty-six percent. Almost the point of no return. Seconds later, the computer emitted an electronic chime. 'Done!" Dean shouted.

The bloodletting had begun. The clip was titled, *Rex Reynolds Gets Fucked*. Guys were already watching the clip. Responding. Downloading. Sharing.

Dean started the upload to Pornhub before heading to the bathroom.

Reed was still talking. "I'll fuck Woody and take the perks that come with that, but I don't follow him blindly. I'm not his accomplice. I won't go to prison for him—I'll tell you that much.

Prison? Accomplice? What the hell was Reed talking about?

"Plenty of guys are willing to be part of his shady schemes. You need to know what you are getting yourself into, Vinnie Lux. Sooner or later, Woody will put you in a position where you need to make a choice. He uses people, pits them against one another. This industry is all egos and agendas. Some guys see themselves as god's gift; others see themselves as a god."

The Pornhub upload was moving in leaps.

Dean asked if they wanted to order a pizza. "There is nothing but beer in the fridge." He brought Reed and Vinnie each a can.

Shady schemes. Prison. Reed needed to explain, but when Vinnie asked, Reed assured him that he didn't want to know.

"Try me. Unless there is nothing to tell." Challenging the word of a guy like Reed got results.

Reed laughed. "The man is ruthless. Woody fucked over Corbin Kent at Tandem. Screwed him out of the rights to their film library and used the money to start Xclusiv. He's dicked over plenty of talent. Ask about Desi Lou. Ask about the accident with Carter."

"Kip told me..."

Reed took a swig of beer and stifled a belch. "About the accident?"

Vinnie nodded.

"Kip *knows* what he's been told and that's it. Things did not happen the way they claim. Carter was conveniently incinerated. No body. No autopsy. No family. Nothing. And then there is Novak..."

An ambulance screamed by, breaking Reed's momentum. In the wake of the siren, Reed's tone changed. He seemed fearful that he had said too much. He tried to play it off as a joke. "I'm fucking with you. This town is full of liars; myself included. You're so gullible."

"What were you going to say about Novak?"

"Drop it." Reed was suddenly agitated and restless.

What was he so afraid of?

The computer flashed—upload complete.

Dean was ordering pizza. "And add a six pack of beer. Bottles."

Reed emptied his beer and grabbed his backpack. He told Vinnie he had someplace he needed to be. Dean came in the room a moment later. "I was on the phone with the pizza guy. Did Reed really just leave? He said he was paying."

Vinnie peeled two twenties off the wad from his rendezvous with Noah. "My treat." He could go for pizza and beer.

48

Dean was having the last slice of pizza, and Vinnie was on his third beer when Gio came through the door. His positive energy was a welcome reprieve from the last few hours. "Hey bitches." Gio saw they were stoned and asked if they had any more. "I brought goodies," he added. He had a 12-pack in the bag he was carrying.

Dean handed him the roach. "Did McCain get sick of you?"

Based on Gio's smile, things looked like they were going very well. He was back at the flat to pick up the last of his belongings. "Mostly clothes, though lately I haven't really needed those."

"Whore," Dean joked.

"Jealous?" Unable to contain his excitement any longer, Gio shared that in the morning, he and Joe were off to Hawaii. "We're getting married." Gio said he didn't hesitate when McCain asked. "Now I will be legal as well."

Vinnie offered congratulations. This marriage meant that either Gio was going to be a superstar, or that he was retiring.

Dean shook his hand, "Well done, buddy. You roped yourself a big one."

"Will you be working at the studio?" Vinnie tried to make the comment sound casual.

Gio had an idea as to what Vinnie was really asking. "One condition for our marriage was that I retire from the XXX business. He doesn't want to share me."

"What will you do?" Vinnie didn't know if he could give this up and walk away from his career just like that, even if he was in love.

"I guess I'll be a man of leisure." Gio fished another roach from the ashtray. "Joe said he wanted me to be his own exclusive." The cornball line, combined with the weed, brought giggles from Vinnie and Dean. "No more escorting either," added Gio. McCain talked to Novak yesterday. "I am off all the call sheets."

"That means it's official," added Dean.

"I really appreciated Joe doing that for me." Gio said. "He and Novak had a falling out years ago. Joe makes a habit of avoiding him, but he made an exception for me." Gio grabbed a beer from the fridge. "Joe is picking me up in a couple of hours. He had proofs to show Woody and he was also going to take the opportunity to break the news to Woody about my retirement, though Novak may have already given him a heads up." Gio took a swig of his beer. "I'm glad Joe is breaking the news to Woody. I would hate to have that conversation. Woody will take the news differently from Joe."

"You don't want to be in the line of fire," added Dean.

Gio said he didn't wish one of Woody's rages on anyone.

Vinnie asked what he meant.

"Let's just say his physique isn't natural for a man of his age."

Were they talking about 'roid rage? Vinnie had heard that juicing shrinks a guy's balls, but you sure couldn't prove that by Woody. That man had a big set of low hangers. Maybe it wasn't steroids. Perhaps anger was a byproduct of the pressure from running a successful porn studio. "I've only seen him go off on a tirade about Reed."

Dean shook his head. "Those two have stadium sized drama! You should hear the shit Reed says."

"Joe told me their crazy dynamic has been that way for years," Gio said it went as far back as the accident with Carter Gaines.

When Vinnie asked for details, Gio called it ancient history.

Dean needed a shower. He was meeting Reed. Once the shower spray started, Gio lowered his voice. "Joe told me that things are heating up between you and Woody. I didn't want to say anything in front of Dean, but Joe said Woody was issued a court ordered therapist. I figured you should know."

Vinnie was curious, but did not want to engage in all this.

"God's truth. Woody was court ordered to get therapy. Joe said when Peter Ray Thomas announced his retirement Woody went berserk. He punched a wall, yanked a framed poster of a Peter Ray Thomas movie from the wall and threw it through his office window. It smashed the windshield of a car parked below. Scary shit. Joe said a cop saw it come flying out the window. With Woody's connections he avoided charges, but the incident still resulted in mandatory counseling. He's better now. He's a different man without the juice, but his anger is still legendary. I didn't want to tell him I was retiring."

Vinnie understood Gio's reluctance; he also had confrontation issues. "I bet Woody will shake Joe's hand, offer congratulations, and wish you both well." Woody was too savvy a businessman to risk alienating McCain. Besides, with Gio off the payroll, Woody was no longer breaking the law. Gio's retirement would be a big relief. Woody was no longer employing him illegally.

"I feel like a jerk retiring after this big build up. Now I'll be Xclusiv by marriage. Once I know he's cool with everything, I will make a vow to Woody to send Joe McCain to work every morning with a smile on his face."

Wearing only a towel and still damp from his shower, Dean plopped down beside them on the couch. He shook Gio's hand. "Congratulations. I envy you. Meeting a nice guy and never having to worry about money sounds like heaven." When his time as an exclusive was up, Dean said he wanted to meet a nice guy and retire. "Nice and rich that is."

Gio nodded at Dean's crotch. "With your credentials I bet it's no time before some deep green queen snatches you off the market. We can be trophy hubbies together! *Real Househusbands of WeHo.*"

Dean laughed. "How about it, Vinnie? Do you want to be a trophy husband too?"

"I'm good for now." Vinnie made it clear he had no plans of retiring anytime soon.

Instagram 16K
Twitter 10.4K

Numbers don't lie. He had thousands of followers—men watching him, wanting him, worshipping him. Gio and Dean wanted creature comforts, nice things, and security. Vinnie needed more.

Gio asked if he had heard from Roy. "Is he still in town?"

Vinnie shared only that he hadn't heard from Roy in a couple of days. "A.Z.'s stuff is still in his room."

"Oh shit, I forgot." Dean grabbed for his phone. "I got a text from Roy last night." He showed them the screen:

2:45 a.m.

Don't need anything of A.Z.'s. Going through his stuff is too much. Take what you want and give the rest to Goodwill.

XOX,

Roy

After telling Vinnie he was the only one he could trust and making Vinnie swear he had his back, Roy went and texted Dean? To Vinnie's knowledge, Roy had not seen or heard from Dean since before A.Z.'s death. Roy texting Dean made no sense. "He texted you?"

Dean offered his phone. "That's his number. No one else would text that," he said.

Vinnie took Dean's phone and returned the call. Ringing. No answer. No voicemail. It was still ringing when Vinnie handed the phone back to Dean.

Dean hopped off the couch and returned a moment later in sweats. "If Roy is headed back to Texas. He might not want a lot of reminders of the past."

"Did he say he was going back to Texas?"

"All I got was this text. I just figured that's where he was going since that was where he's from."

It seemed Gio and Dean didn't have a problem believing this, but they didn't know everything that Vinnie knew. They didn't know about the notebook or the inconsistencies with A.Z.'s drowning, or Roy's vow to get justice for his dead lover. This version of what was happening made no sense, but Vinnie knew enough to keep his doubts to himself.

"Roy probably has things back home." Gio stood and shook his legs. "I don't know about you two, but I love a free shopping spree. If Roy wants us to have his things, I am happy to oblige."

"I was thinking the same thing." Dean added that he hoped they were the same shoe size.

The three men paused on the threshold before pushing open the door to A.Z.'s room. Gio said he didn't realize A.Z. was such a slob. "I thought my room got bad."

Dean didn't mention the mess and instead walked straight to the closet. Gio went to the dresser and was already checking the size of a pair of green jeans.

Vinnie lingered in the doorway. This felt like looting a tomb, even though Roy supposedly wanted them to have this.

"Suit yourself," shrugged Dean.

"Roy wants us to do this." Gio was admiring the pants in the mirror. "If the tables were turned, I would want my stuff to go to use. Maybe for Roy this is a way to keep a part of A.Z. alive."

"Yes! We wear the same size shoe." Dean grabbed two pairs of sneakers from A.Z's closet. "The man knew shoes."

Gio had the green jeans, some cargo shorts, and three shirts over his arm. "Didn't A.Z. have a laptop? Mine is ancient. I don't see it."

Dean shrugged. "Maybe he had it in Mexico.

The computer had slipped Vinnie's mind. He didn't notice if A.Z. had his laptop when he left for the airport. If A.Z. left his laptop computer behind, it was likely stolen during the break-in. A.Z. wasn't stupid or careless—of course he would have a digital copy of everything—the notebook, incriminating photos, and all pertinent emails. A.Z. would have taken precautions, especially since it was his 'retirement plan.'

Gio grabbed a duffle bag from the closet. In addition to the clothes he was carrying, he began to fill the bag with a belt, more shirts, and a large medallion. He pulled A.Z.'s black leather jacket from the closet. "Can you imagine the action this jacket has seen?"

Dean rushed by with half a dozen pairs of shoes in his arms. When he returned, he pointed to a pile of clothes. "Those are mine too."

Gio turned to Vinnie. "Whatever is left is going to charity. No homeless person needs an Italian belt or the shoes from Madrid." Gio had a point, but grabbing things right and left seemed wrong.

"Come on, Vinnie. What is the big deal?" Gio had stopped looking through the dresser. "You're making me feel bad."

Carrying an armful of clothes, Dean moved around Vinnie who was still standing in the doorway. "If you're not going to join in, then could you go disapprove elsewhere?"

Disapproving. Judgmental. He had been told he came across that way before. People had thought that about him since junior high school. Vinnie didn't feel like that, but he hated having his behavior interpreted that way. Besides, that was more a Vincent attribute. Now that he was Vinnie Lux, he didn't want to give people the same impression. Gio was right, at the end of the day, what did it matter? Vinnie moved into the room and took A.Z.'s denim jacket from the back of the desk chair. And as long as he was picking things out, A.Z. had a gray-cable pullover that would look great on him. "Maybe just a couple of things."

Gio laughed. "See, what did I tell you? Free shopping is fun."

"True," said Vinnie, trying on a Swatch. Gio was right, free shopping was fun, but it felt even better to fit in. Looking through the desk, Vinnie also took a fancy fountain pen, two T-shirts, the gray-cable pullover, and A.Z.'s Swiss Army knife.

Gio started laughing. "Shit, I am so high. I came here to get my stuff together, not to get more things to move. You guys should be going through my stuff."

Five minutes later, they were all finished going through A.Z.'s things.

Although he felt more a part of things, Vinnie still felt guilty, and even a little dirty being in A.Z.'s room and going through his things—but he only took enough to fit in.

He tossed the pen, the Swatch, and the Swiss Army knife onto his desk and Vinnie hung A.Z.'s denim jacket in his closet. Opening the bottom drawer of the dresser to put away his two new T-shirts, Vinnie saw a manila envelope. The flap was closed but unsealed. Vinnie reached inside and pulled out a notebook. *Fuck!* In seconds Vinnie realized what he had found—what had been placed in his dresser drawer. Why was A.Z.'s notebook in his room? Vinnie wasn't sure when he last looked in that drawer. He was sure the envelope had not been there the day before yesterday.

None of this made sense.

Vinnie almost leapt to the ceiling when Gio shouted, "Where is everyone?" Gio was in the hallway just outside his door. "Come out roommates, it's time for my goodbyes."

Vinnie slid the notebook back into the envelope, closed the bottom dresser drawer, and came into the hallway.

Gio was talking to Dean. "I don't have too much." Gio was taking two suitcases, a duffle bag, another bag, and a box. "You guys are welcome to whatever is left."

"Maybe later," Dean was headed out to dinner.

"You just had pizza." Vinnie called him a bottomless pit.

"I'm a growing boy. Besides, dinner is with Ed Vittori and that beats pizza in a cardboard box any time."

"He wants more of what he got at the Hotel del Coronado," teased Gio.

Dean gave a roguish wink. "If he offers me another side trip, I'll be back in a few days."

Vinnie wished Gio the best. "Congratulations on everything. I wish you all the happiness in the world. And for the record, I have smoked way too much weed today."

"Never too much," laughed Dean.

49

Since finding the notebook in the bottom drawer of his dresser, Vinnie had been unable to focus on anything else. The drawer had been empty two days before, at least he thought. Maybe he just didn't notice. For all he knew, A.Z. could have hidden the journal there before he left for Mexico. If it wasn't A.Z., then someone had hidden the notebook in Vinnie's room.

After Dean and Gio were both out of the flat, Vinnie grabbed a beer and returned to his room. He slipped the notebook from the envelope. This was not the original. Taped inside were photocopied pages. On the first page was a brief paragraph in ink.

> *This notebook covers the main points in my journal that I am in danger for knowing. I must take precautions—especially with the way people have been acting.*

The photocopied pages began:

> *The accident with Kip Mason and Carter Gaines was no accident. Carter was dead before the car went off the road. The reason was complicated.*
>
> *Woody invited Peter Ray Thomas to that party—but it wasn't to make amends. Peter left the studio a couple of months before, and Woody was still furious. He was acting nice because he was still on probation for smashing that windshield, which he blamed on Peter. The only thing Woody hates more than looking like a fool is being abandoned. Woody had invited Peter to a dinner party the previous week. He wanted to make sure everyone believed the falling-out he had with Peter was history.*

Woody hadn't forgotten. He had bigger plans.

Peter had a serious drug problem. For a couple of years, he'd been a junkie. Everybody had seen his tracks. Even at its worst, people bent over backwards because he was a huge star. Drugs were taking a serious toll. In films, Sue used extra makeup, and McCain lit him carefully to hide the marks.

Woody's plan for Peter was simple. He wanted him dead. On the night of the party, Ed Vittori was instructed by Woody to wait until Peter was wasted. Then, he was to offer him a doctored syringe, something pure enough to send Peter riding the beast into the hereafter.

Things did not go as planned. Apparently, Carter found the stash with the syringe. Carter was a sweet kid but always trying to act tougher than he was. In the end, he was a fool. Carter shot up the dose and died on the shag carpet in Woody's bedroom.

I was outside the door, so I overheard the exchange between Woody and Vittori when they found the body. Woody said he couldn't have that kid OD at his house. Xclusiv didn't need that sort of publicity. Woody said he had an idea. I heard the sliding glass door in his bedroom open.

When it closed, I opened the bedroom door. In the path light, I could see Ed and Woody walking Carter like he had too much to drink. It looked believable, unless you knew the truth. The car light went on. They put Carter in the passenger seat. Woody slapped his pockets and looked back to the house. It was close, but I doubt he saw me. He forgot the keys.

Woody headed back upstairs and left Vittori standing by the car.

His keys were on the dresser beside me.

I moved to the bathroom and watched from there.

Outside, Sue staggered over towards the car, and Ed moved to intercept her. She was drunk. Vittori led her back toward the party, away from the car.

Woody was in the bedroom next door getting the keys. He tried the bathroom door. Thank God I had locked it.

I looked out the window again. Kip had staggered from the shadows. He was a mess after catching Woody and Reed together. Kip started down the drive towards Woody's car. He and Woody were together at the time, so Kip must have had his own key because he just got in and sped off. When they heard the squeal of wheels, Woody and Vittori scrambled to Ed's car and sped after them.

An hour later, a few guys at the party, myself included, got a message. There was an accident. Carter Gaines was dead. Some thought it was a joke. Some guys looked around the party, saying they just saw Carter a couple of minutes ago. Time can be weird at parties.

Later we learned the car hit a tree. Kip was thrown from the vehicle before the car veered into the ravine and exploded with Carter inside. His body was burned beyond recognition.

Kip was in ICU.

Carter's overdose in Woody's bedroom had become something else entirely. The obituary all but wrote itself. Carter Gaines became another tragic story of another young porn star, another cautionary tale, and another tragic cliché. Everything worked out perfectly, except for me being outside the bedroom door. That worries me. Woody's glance back at the house worries me.

I wonder if Peter knows how lucky he was.

Far as I know, Kip knows nothing. He was in a blackout before he hopped into that car. As far as I know, I'm the only person who knows what really happened that night, except for Woody and Ed Vittori.

I worry about Woody checking the bathroom door and finding it locked.

Did he wonder who was inside and how long they had been there? There were cameras everywhere in his house though I imagine he would want all the footage destroyed. Maybe he had them turned off because of the party.

I worry that maybe Woody did see me. Maybe I was the reason he headed back upstairs. Maybe he knew who was in the bathroom.

I can't tell anyone because telling them would put them in danger. This is the best way.

The floor in the hallway creaked just outside Vinnie's door. The silence following was long and deliberate. Slowly and quietly, Vinnie closed the notebook and slipped it under the mattress.

Dean opened the door. "I'm taking off."

"I thought you already left."

"No, I was just helping Gio carry his stuff down to the car. Hey look. I'm wearing a new pair of A.Z.'s shoes."

Vinnie offered a thumbs up. The approving gesture meant nothing. Vinnie was still in shock from reading the photocopied pages. He hoped Dean didn't think he was acting strange. But they were both still high, so Vinnie figured he was safe.

"Ed is picking me up in fifteen minutes."

After what Vinnie had just read, he struggled to refrain from warning Dean. *Saying something would only put them in danger.*

Sure, Vinnie did not think much of Dean Driver. His behavior in A.Z.'s room and with the Rex Reynolds upload had been callous and malicious. Vinnie's desire to warn him had nothing to do with Dean. Vinnie would feel responsible if anything happened to him. Maybe a warped sense of duty, and all the guilt that came along with it, was another part of Vincent that Vinnie could leave behind. Starting now.

Saying something would only put them in danger—which meant that Vinnie was now in peril as well.

When the front door closed, Vinnie slid the chain into place and continued reading the pages.

I met Dolph Worthington at one of Novak's "mixers." I shouldn't say I met him. I met a guy who procured dates for him. The next day a representative called Novak to hire that "black guy with the big dick who makes porn." The money was extremely good.

I knew this was major. I was picked up at such and such a spot by an unmarked town car and driven to an enormous beach house in Malibu. Guard station—that kind of money. Still not knowing who I was about to entertain, I waited in this oceanfront living room for a half an hour.

Dolph appeared. His name was never mentioned. Ruggedly handsome in person—this was going to be a pleasure. I remembered him mainly from Prison Siege *and* Maximum Glory. *He was smaller than I expected, but muscular. A hot little fireplug.*

Mr. W. wasted no time with small talk. He walked up, dropped his robe, and we were off to the races. That was our first afternoon. He was impressed by my performance and recuperative powers. I tested both to the limit that day. He got his money's worth. I stayed at his Malibu beach house for two days that time. The money was pocket change to him. God knows what Novak was charging him for my services. My fees were already set, but Dolph was an extravagant tipper, so whenever he called, I cleared my schedule.

I saw a lot of his beach house that summer. Dolph began to trust me more. We swam together and in time he kept his security at bay.

Maybe A.Z. did swim in the ocean on occasion. Maybe he had been exaggerating when he told Vinnie that he hated it. Vinnie took the notebook of photocopied pages to the balcony. He brought his cigarettes. He would need them.

Dolph Worthington told me he was a fan. I got a kick out of that and returned the compliment. Dolph was rarely able to be himself. People always wanted something from him. He never knew if they were genuine. I think he appreciated that I was transparent. I was there for a set amount of money. Dolph said knowing that about me made him feel safer with me than with most people.

We fucked and talked a lot.

He said more than once that he loved me. He said if his career ended tomorrow, he would run off with me. I figured that was so much bullshit. How many top box office attractions run off with gay porn stars? TMZ would implode.

When he said things like that, I wondered if he understood our relationship. Dolph was sweet, but it was business. This was why I was a top escort. It's not all fucking.

I gave Dolph the fantasy—but I love Roy. He is my priority. And my future with Roy will be much cushier with money from Dolph. He makes ten million a movie, plus a percentage. He pocketed two million for a car commercial in Japan. He has a private jet. Private staff. Chauffer, butler, dog trainer, personal trainer, handyman, gardener, gardener's assistant, maid, housekeeper, chef, stylist, business manager, masseur, personal assistant, and secretary. He needs a team to manage his team. I would just be one more on the payroll. My valuable service would be keeping my mouth shut. I'm not proud of this. He trusted me, but he is a big boy with a fat bank account. He'll survive. I won't feel bad for using what I have to get what I need. I won't ask for more than that. I would never ask for more than Roy and I need.

Dolph was the one who wanted to take the pictures. He wrote me the gushy notes. I only collected what he offered and saved some random pubes as DNA backup for my story.

I'm coming clean. I am not the villain in this story.

Novak would kill me if he heard about this. Trusted Talents takes pride in protecting clients from such things. Novak assures his patrons that their experience would be safe and discreet. Novak had no high-minded principles. He knew that scandal or blackmail would ruin his business. Money is Novak's obsession. If he suspects me of damaging his reputation and business he would kill me.

All I want is to be comfortable with my partner. Dolph can slip me a check every month or do it in one payment. He never needs to hear from me again. If he agrees, he gets the letters and Polaroids. I'll even throw in the pubes.

I'm looking out for my own. Nothing more than that.

Every day I still struggle with the thought of doing this. I am not typically that sort of man. But I have been around long enough to know that aging porn stars without a nest egg do not fare well. I have no plans to be another Desi Lou, homeless and left for dead. Seeing the way he became human garbage in the course of six months made me want to strategize. Nothing wrong with getting my fair share—that's why this is the land of opportunity.

50

Vinnie fanned through the journal and the photocopied pages. Nothing was tucked inside. No photos. The hard evidence, so to speak, was probably with the original notebook, not the backup.

> *Not sure who to trust anymore. Almost certain someone found this journal. When I came home from a shoot, it was on my nightstand. I'm 90% sure that I had put it away.*
>
> *I shouldn't have mentioned to Woody that this was my last year at Xclusiv. I said five years from now no one will want to see my saggy ass and wrinkled face on screen—especially me. Woody was nice about it. He understood. At least he said he did. He's been weird ever since.*
>
> *Sometimes I think someone is keeping tabs on me. This new kid, Vinnie Lux, arrived out of nowhere. Supposedly he emailed his pictures, and a week later he is in a movie. Those One-on-One guys were PISSED when they heard they'd all been leapfrogged! Something is not right with Vinnie Lux. That kid is awful uptight for someone in this business, like he's hiding something.*

Vinnie's heart raced as he read about himself. If A.Z. didn't even trust him, why was A.Z.'s notebook in Vinnie's room? Vinnie wondered why he was involved in any of this. Someone had scattered his things in A.Z.'s room. Had the same person hid a manila envelope with a notebook of photocopied pages from A.Z.'s journal in Vinnie's dresser? And to what end—to involve him, to implicate him?

Vinnie might be a plant by Woody or Novak. Either of them may know about the journal. And both have plenty to hide.

Last week I saw Dolph again in Malibu. He is the only one who hasn't been acting strange lately, but he's an actor, though critics tend to call him a movie star. During my overnight, Dolph asked if my passport was in order.

P.S. A copy was necessary. This is my insurance policy.

Vinnie was shaking. There was no doubt in Vinnie's mind that the notebook was the reason A.Z. was murdered. If anyone other than A.Z. knew this copy existed and that Vinnie had read it, they would probably kill him. Someone had consciously put him in this position. After reading the journal, he doubted A.Z. would have stored the pages in his room. A.Z. didn't trust Vinnie. Vinnie shoved the notebook into the manila envelope and slid the works between his mattress and box springs. The notebook belonged in a safety deposit box.

Unnerved by what he had read, Vinnie sent Roy a text. *Hey Roy. Back in Texas?*

The message bounced back.

The account had been closed.

51

A text from Gio, "Joe just told me Woody has a new roommate for you two. Kip!"

Vinnie read the message and replied, "What?"

Gio answered, "True. Woody told Joe"

"SHIT! Call me."

Gio rang him a moment later.

"Gio, what am I going to do. Kip is crazy."

"But he's loyal as well."

"But I mean he is crazy as in he is unstable."

"I know, but sometimes loyalty trumps sanity around here."

Thank God it isn't just me.

"I guess Kip asked for a raise and Vittori couldn't make the numbers work, so Woody offered him free rent."

"Or at least reasonable rent." Kip probably jumped at the chance.

Gio empathized. "Maybe someone else will balance it. Woody is probably making plans for my room too."

Heat continued to grip L.A. Wildfires were raging. The breeze felt like bus exhaust. Pouring himself a vodka and pineapple, Vinnie returned to the balcony. The cocktail gave little relief from the heat, but at least it looked refreshing. Sweat trickled down the back of his legs. One smoke and then back to the AC.

His phone buzzed. Dumb with the heat, Vinnie answered without checking caller ID. It was Mother. She rarely phoned in the evening. "Vincent?"

"Mother!" They volleyed weather talk. Both places needed rain. A pause. Something was on her mind. "I got an envelope in the mail the other day and inside were some ... some pornographic pictures of you and a note that said, I thought you should know."

Who would fucking do that? Had Vinnie inadvertently listed his mother as his emergency contact on his Xclusiv paperwork? Jesus. Who had access to that information? Was this someone just fucking with him, or was this a threat—a hint about what was to come if he didn't watch himself.

He had to say something, "Mother I..."

She started to cry. Vinnie could kill whoever did this. Mother coughed and managed to clear her throat. "I just don't know what this all means. Is this a joke?"

"Mother, I make money taking off my clothes. I'm not being stupid about it. I'm investing." He hated that Mother found out this way, but coming clean was a relief. Vinnie knew this day would inevitably come, but he was not prepared for that day to be today. Well, if someone pulled this crap thinking they were going to ruin him, they had better think again. "Since coming to L.A. I've been modeling."

Mother said someone was at the door. "Mother please, I ..."

Dial tone.

He hated hearing her cry. Someone intentionally hurt her to hurt him.

That someone had collected the images, found Mother's mailing address, and even wrote a note disguising their malicious intent. *I thought you should know?* Who would do something like that?

Vinnie wondered if Mother would ask her prayer group to offer up petitions for his salvation, or was this a dirty little secret she would keep even from God.

When his phone rang, Vinnie thought Mother was calling back. It was Woody. He was driving through the Hollywood Hills with the top down. "I wanted to call and say I enjoyed last night." He had Vinnie on speakerphone.

"I had a great time too."

"Thanks to you ... Going through the day with a smile on my face." The wind sliced his words, The mountains were notorious for poor reception.

Woody said Gio was leaving Xclusiv. "If I'm going to lose one of my boys at least I'm happy it's to Joe McCain." The call went mute. The connection crackled. Woody spoke of "a fire that needed to be put out."

Did he mean the Rex Reynolds incident?

More lost words.

Woody asked Vinnie how long he had stayed at his place that morning.

"This morning?"

"Yes. Did you stay long? Did you take a swim at my place?"

"No, I didn't stay too long. I got a ride back here from Kip," said Vinnie. "He showed up about a half an hour after you left."

"This isn't usually Kip's day. Maybe he got confused."

Vinnie didn't answer for a moment. It was inconceivable that Kip, who knew Woody's schedule better than Woody did, got the days mixed up. Nope. Kip had known about their date and showed up on purpose. "He came by to change the paper in Orson's cage, and to pick up your dry cleaning." Kip showed up because his jealousy made it impossible for him to stay away.

Reception worsened. "Never mentioned it... Usually waits until Friday ... Orson." The flip of a Zippo. A first cough of inhalation. Woody told him Kip was going to be his roommate. "Sometime next week. The lease at his sublet...Found anything he likes...A.Z.'s old room."

A bad connection made it easier to feign excitement. "Looking forward to it." He mentioned that Dean heard from Roy. "Told us to take whatever we want of A.Z.'s."

Call waiting interrupted. Vinnie asked Woody if he needed to get that. The call turned intimate. "No, I want to talk to you." Lost words. Static. Call dropped. Woody redialed. "Better get this out while I can. Are you free?" He wanted to swing by.

"I want to see you." His voice dropped an octave. "There's something I want you to help me with."

"Oh really?" Vinnie thought of what he had read about Woody in the notebook. He needed to proceed with caution. Woody must not suspect that he knows a thing.

"I thought we could... a little wine and talk some...know you like the view." Woody had been thinking about him all day.

The connection sucked, but the invitation was clear. Woody must know nothing about the snooping. Vinnie was still in his good graces.

"I'll see you in a little over an hour?"

"See you soon." Vinnie started coffee and had another smoke before heading for the shower. His cock began to thicken under the spray. He thought about plowing the furry ass of a dangerous man. Vinnie knew it was wrong to think this way, but the air of menace made the thought of fucking Woody even hotter. More fantasy. Vinnie's dick was throbbing. Things felt a little too good. Almost. He turned the spray to cold. His cock needed to be at full capacity tonight.

52

While Woody mixed their drinks, Vinnie stared into the distance—deep in thought. After reading the contents of the notebook, conversation with Woody was difficult—but Woody didn't seem to notice his awkwardness. Vinnie needed to relax. "Did you get a chance to mention to Ed that I'm interested in personal appearances and club gigs?"

Woody looked up and grinned. "Of course, I did. I like boys who are aggressive about their careers. I like to encourage that sort of behavior."

Vinnie took a breath. Woody must not suspect a thing. Woody needs to believe that everything is as it was between them. Sex is always the best disguise. Vinnie approached him. "So, you like boys that are aggressive about their careers. You encourage that sort of thing. What else do you like your boys to be aggressive about?" He gave Woody a deep kiss.

Woody said that Vinnie's club dates were pending. "Ed is hammering out the booking details."

Vinnie unbuttoned Woody's shirt and ran his hands across his chest. He curled his fingers into the salt and pepper fur.

Woody lifted Vinnie's chin and kissed him. Vinnie returned the kiss, surprising himself at this hunger. Vinnie was doing what he had to do, and he was doing it well.

Woody put an arm around his waist and led him to the couch. "Ed is negotiating your fee. That sort of thing is in his blood. His old man was a top divorce attorney in L.A.—friends with the Governor, mansion in Malibu, the whole deal. The old guy was pissed when Ed dropped out of law school in his second year, came out, and started working for me in gay porn."

Vinnie asked how long Woody and Ed had known each other.

An enormous screech erupted from Orson.

"Ed and me?" Woody began to knead Vinnie's thigh. Moving higher. "We've been pals for years. We're blood brothers. This industry can be nasty—people turn on you. Ed has always had my back."

Blood brothers? Was Woody referring to the plan to murder Peter Ray Thomas, faking Carter's cause of death, or gas lighting Kip? Based on those three examples, blood brothers was a suitable description. Though "partners in crime" might have been even more appropriate—maybe they had even bigger secrets. "Friends that support you are important," added Vinnie eventually.

Woody lit a cigarette and offered one. "Devotion is the most important attribute in an employee, in a friend, in a lover ..."

"Devotion reminds me of religion."

"If that's what you want, you can make it that as well." Abruptly changing the subject, Woody asked if he wanted to go for a swim.

"I don't have a suit."

"We don't need them." Woody leaned in to kiss him and began to unbutton Vinnie's shirt. Vinnie knew he should flinch at this man's touch, but his doubts about Woody only fuelled his desire. Sometimes it felt right to fuck the wrong guy. Fear can sometimes add to foreplay. They undressed one another. Woody kissed him against the doorframe. One flight down from the deck was the pool, the pool house, and the casita. The temperature outside was stifling.

"This is going to feel so good."

Woody tossed him a towel from the outdoor cabinet, but Vinnie never had the chance to wrap it around himself. Arms encircled Vinnie from behind. Having Woody hold him this way felt both safe and threatening. Woody kissed the nape of his neck, the hollow below his jaw, the rim of his ear, and lower to the lobe. Woody's coarse chest hair scratched his back. Holding him so close, reaching around for a few strokes. Turning to face one another. Cocks touching. Woody moved his hips back and forth. His cock was already dripping. Vinnie felt ribbons of Woody's pre-cum on his thighs. Woody wrapped a hand firmly around both their shafts and stroked them together. Pre-cum makes the best lube. Bodies pressed together. No hands necessary—only sweat and dick juice to grease them. Cocks flush to bellies. Bodies moving with delicious friction. Building sensations. Woody's cock was still dripping. Pressed tight with the sweat and their slick excitement giving pleasure in the slightest movement. Vinnie broke away with his cock pulsing, his heart pounding, and his breath catching in his throat. "Let's take it inside."

In response, Woody stepped back towards him and spat on his palm. His hand wrapped around Vinnie's cock. "You're not going anywhere, not yet. I want you to cum right here. Cum for me, boy. I want to feel you quiver. I want you to lean into me when you to shoot your load into my hand. When you rise up on your toes ready to pop, like now. Like now! Do it for me, boy."

The words alone almost made him cum. Vinnie shot his load into Woody's hand. Holding his eyes, Woody lifted his palm and licked up every drop of Vinnie's load. "That's my good boy," Woody said.

Woody was freshening their drinks when his phone began to vibrate. An incoming message flashed. Identical to two previous messages sent in rapid succession.

Call Ed.

Call Ed.

Call Ed.

Woody handed Vinnie his drink. "I should have checked my messages earlier."

"I need to rinse off anyway." Vinnie took his cocktail into the bathroom. The rain shower could not mask Woody's cursing. By the time Vinnie was finished with his shower, Woody sounded calmer, but his phone conversation was still very tense. Woody was pacing. "Why am I only hearing about this now? I hope it was worth it. I hope he knows that he wasn't the only one getting fucked."

Woody was just hearing about the Rex Reynolds' upload now. What had he been doing all day? Vinnie assumed the Rex ordeal was the fire that needed tending from earlier.

A vase smashed against the wall.

Orson screeched.

Vinnie wanted to be anywhere but there. Although Vinnie had done nothing wrong, his silence still implicated him. He had witnessed the upload, knew the responsible parties, and did nothing. Said nothing. Came over here and had sex with Woody and didn't say a word. Woody had expectations. A team player would have called Woody as it was happening or destroyed the computer mid-upload. A team player would have at least said something. There was no way to salvage the scenario. Woody must never find out he was involved.

Woody ran a hand through his hair. He looked like an angry god with the lights of the city framing his naked torso. Vinnie wanted to drop to his knees to beg, to worship, to serve that raging beast. He wanted to drain Woody's wrath. Instead, he stood in the shadows and listened.

"Ed, we don't need this right now."

Another Orson shriek.

Woody threw the cover over the cage. "I don't give a shit. Rex is through. *Through!*" Woody paused. "I don't care what his contract says and by the time I'm through with him, neither will he. Rip it up. You heard me. *Rip. It. Up.* He violated the terms." Woody ran a hand down his torso and absently touched himself. "How can we make this work?"

He was in agreement with whatever Ed was saying.

Woody listened intently, but then, he had another idea. "How about we download and package the clip? The shaky-cam guerilla style scene could work, if it's showcased correctly."

Woody was not pleased with Vittori's input ... something about rights.

"I don't want to hear it. Why should we fret over a lawsuit? Rex has an exclusive contract. In order to sue us, the weasel behind this will have to show their face. When they do, we will countersue to negate their copyright."

Woody nodded towards his pack of smokes on the table. Vinnie lit one and walked it over to Woody before sitting on the couch and lighting one for himself.

"Ed, I don't know the answer. This needs to be made right." Woody threw his phone into the couch cushions. "Shit! Fuck!" He turned to Vinnie and nodded towards the couch. "It's the least expensive place to throw the phone when I'm pissed." Woody ran a hand down his face.

"What happened?"

Woody measured his words. "Someone uploaded a clip of Rex Reynolds getting fucked onto Xtube, Pornhub, and Tube8. Now the footage is everywhere. Thousands of views, who knows how many downloads."

Vinnie didn't know what to say.

"Not the end of the world, but the end of Rex. That commodity just lost 90% of its value. I hate losing money." Woody said that when he found out who was responsible for this—it was not going to be pretty.

"Do you have any idea?" Given that Rex's comments about Reed aired on Dorian's show two days before, Vinnie found it tough to believe that Woody didn't know or at least assume that it was Reed. He knew how vengeful Reed could be. Maybe Woody wanted proof, or maybe the entire Rex incident was another move in their ongoing game.

Woody suspected a rival studio. "Bill Lieder at FreshFilms has been jealous of Xclusiv since day one. Maybe Bareback Alley. Those brothers are involved in some shady dealings. Corbin Kent still has it out for me, eight years after Tandem." Woody confessed, "You don't get to the top by playing nice. I'm number one. Some folks wake up in the morning thinking of ways to take me down. So far none have succeeded."

"You need to relax. Let me make you feel better." Woody hadn't cum earlier. Vinnie knelt and took him in his mouth. Woody's cock stiffened. Vinnie maneuvered him onto the arm of the couch. Vinnie suspected Woody liked the feel of the couch arm between his thighs, lifting his big balls—full and heavy, not 'roid nuts at all. Legs spread and fabric on his bare ass. Vinnie began to suck him deep and fast until he felt the nearness of a load building. In seconds, the spray hit the back of his throat.

After Vinnie drained him, Woody moved from the arm of the couch to the cushions. "I was not anticipating that."

"That's why I did it. You looked like you needed to relax."

"I did." Vinnie nestled his head in Woody's lap. Woody finger-combed Vinnie's hair, kissed him, and told him he'd done well.

They had a few quiet moments until Woody's phone buzzed. He fished it from the cushions. "Figures. It's Rex." Woody hit DECLINE. "Our 'straight boy' was stupid. When you're on top someone is always looking to take you down. Rex got taken down."

Woody was right. Rex should have known better. Only a fool would provoke someone like Reed and then let his guard down. His career was over. Some guys just don't have the smarts to be on top, much less stay there.

Vinnie was getting wiser by the day.

Woody leaned down and kissed him. "I need to call you a car. I have to deal with this issue and you would be too tempting of a distraction to have about."

He might well be a criminal, but Woody sure knew how to give a guest the boot in style.

53

For days, Vinnie heard nothing from Woody except for two brief text messages—and one of those was an emoji. Woody didn't phone and he didn't return any of Vinnie's calls. Vinnie left messages on his personal voicemail. When he called the studio, Woody seemed to have just stepped away, or was with clients, or on an important call. The business was an excuse. Woody was always busy. Woody's job was the same. Woody was busy before, but still had made time to call.

The last time they were together, they had parted on excellent terms. Something had reshaped Woody's opinion of him. This might have nothing to do with him. It stood to reason he would be distracted by all this Rex business. Not hearing from Woody came with some very real concerns. Had he learned about the surveillance footage or the truth about the Rex tape? Vinnie wondered if Woody suspected he had a copy of A.Z's notebook?

Professionally everything seemed fine. In the studio news earlier in the week, it was announced that Xclusiv was moving forward with the Vinnie Lux film, *On the Strip*. Vinnie was thrilled with the announcement, but given his relationship with Woody, he wondered why Woody hadn't told him about the movie personally. He thought they had something. The news of his first starring vehicle should have come from Woody. Instead, Vinnie read about it along with everyone else. Last week Woody would have arrived on his doorstep and taken him to dinner—or sent flowers. Something.

Over the week, Vinnie reread the notebook several times. If half the things in those pages were true, he should be grateful Woody wasn't calling.

The contents were disturbing, but the most unsettling part was that he still had no idea who put the notebook in his room, why they put it there, or what he should do with it now. Vinnie couldn't turn it over to anyone. Telling anyone he had it might prove dangerous. Someone already knew it was in his possession—the person who put it there.

Later in the week, he got a call from Kip. "Hey Vinnie, guess who?"

Caller I.D. answered for him.

Kip asked if A.Z.'s room was clear. "Or my room now, I guess."

"Goodwill took the last of A.Z.'s things yesterday. Back to bare-bones—bed, dresser, night table, and desk."

Kip had scheduled to use his neighbor's truck. "I'll be there later today with my things. Woody told you I was moving in, didn't he? You two haven't been in touch, have you?"

Kip knew he hadn't talked to Woody. Vinnie had left plenty of messages. Kip knew exactly how long it had been since Vinnie had been worked into Woody's schedule. "How has Woody been?" Vinnie kicked himself for asking.

Kip said Woody had been so thrown by the Rex Reynolds incident. "That was such a strange thing."

"Yes, so unfortunate." Vinnie tried to sound casual.

Kip said Rex showed up at the studio acting crazy. "He pleaded to see Woody, but Woody refused. So, Rex went outside and put a note under Woody's wiper blade. When Woody found it, he tore it up without bothering to read it. Rex watched him do it and confronted Woody on the street. Rex said he had no idea how the video got leaked, claimed he was set up, begged for another chance, and blubbered about his termination. Woody said he was wasting his time. He offered Rex $200 for a bus ticket home. Rex refused. Despite crying and carrying on in the street, he said he had some dignity left."

"That sounds terrible." Vinnie imagined Reed's glee when he heard the story.

"But the upload worked out well for you, didn't it?" Kip added.

"What do you mean?" Vinnie was taken aback. He studied Kip but couldn't determine if that was just an offhand comment or if Kip was insinuating something.

"No offense—it's just a fact," Kip finally said. "I meant *On the Strip*. With Rex terminated, a gap opened in the production schedule, so the studio moved forward with your movie. Isn't that what you wanted?"

Vinnie had wanted his own starring vehicle, but not this way. Still—someone was going to benefit from this. Why not Vinnie? "Yes, having *On the Strip* moved up was a nice surprise."

The threadbare plot of the film involved the goings-on at a swinging L.A. apartment complex. Filming was slated to start in two weeks. It was announced that *On the Strip* would include the leaked Rex Reynolds upload. Vinnie didn't like the idea. A tagged-on, guerilla-shot fuck scene will look cheap beside the studio scenes. Vinnie did not want something like this dragging down the picture. This production was important to him.

Kip was still talking on the phone. "I would have mentioned something about moving in last week, but didn't know for sure, After my building was sold, they said we could all stay, but they increased my rent by 30%. When he heard about it, Woody suggested this place. I said I didn't know, but he wouldn't take no for an answer."

"That's great. Well, we are glad to have you." Vinnie felt like he had to say something. Woody wanted Kip here for a reason. Everything Kip witnessed would go straight to Woody. Every secret would be shared.

One secret was the Rex Reynolds clip. Though uploaded on a bogus account, Vinnie was concerned that it could be traced to Dean's laptop. The following day, when he lowered his voice and shared his concerns with Dean and Reed, they both turned to him and laughed.

"I can hardly hear you," said Reed.

Vinnie repeated that he hoped the activity couldn't be traced.

Dean shrugged.

Vinnie was dumbfounded by their lack of concern. Woody's vow to find the person or persons responsible for the Rex leak didn't seem to bother them. Vinnie kept his voice low. "I would not be surprised if this place was bugged. Woody has surveillance cameras at home and at the studio."

Reed zeroed in the comment. "So you pay attention to surveillance cameras?"

Vinnie had no idea what to say, but luckily Dean interjected. "But there aren't any cameras here. And why would this place be bugged?"

Reed told Vinnie that he was being paranoid.

Dean told him to calm down. "I doubt the flat is bugged."

Vinnie wanted to be like that and approach things like this with a shrug. Worry was more Vincent than Vinnie, but still seemed impossible to completely discard. Doubt works both ways. How could "doubting your home was bugged" ever calm someone or make them feel secure?

Reed seemed amused by the entire exchange.

"Woody wants revenge," Vinnie whispered.

Reed had heard enough. "Oh, Woody is upset! Well, I would be insulted if he wasn't upset." Reed smirked, "Listen, I hope your conscience doesn't cause you to make any foolish decisions," said Reed. "If you have any notions about coming clean over the Rex upload, you had better think again. Your silence makes you complicit, it's called guilt by association, darling."

Reed was right.

Lately, Reed had become even more insufferable. The *National Sing Off* tour was on hiatus, so Cash Cranston was in town. Cash recently closed on a place in the Hollywood Hills with his record advance. He may have placed second in the competition, but Cash was the fan favorite. Most believed he should have taken home the golden microphone.

"Cash is twenty-three, fresh off the farm, and horny 24/7," said Reed. "Last year he was living in the Tennessee Mountains and now he's in the Hollywood Hills." Reed told them about the money Cash was making from endorsements, his touring salary, and the advance on his recording contract. Cash was prepping for a press junket to promote his debut album, *Cold Hard Cash*. Reed said the disc was getting an A-rating from *Entertainment Weekly*. The first single, *Annie in the Morning*, was already climbing the charts. In the piece, they called Cash, the Newly Crowned Crooner of Country.

Dean offered Vinnie and Reed a joint. "You two need to smoke up or shut up or take it elsewhere. I am trying to watch this program."

Vinnie felt he had even more to worry about than usual, especially with Kip moving in. Reed's habit of overindulging and then oversharing was a concern. Kip would report everything to Woody.

Vinnie reminded them about Kip. "He's moving in this afternoon and just remember that if Kip hears it, Woody hears it." Vinnie dropped his voice to a whisper, "He must *never* know that you two uploaded that footage of Rex ..."

"Or that you watched it happen," Reed added.

Reed was an asshole. "Okay Reed," Vinnie dropped his voice again "I get it. I watched the upload. God, you're exhausting. That isn't what I'm talking about. The point is to watch what we say around Kip."

Dean nodded, but by then, he would have agreed to anything to continue watching *Game of Thrones.*

Vinnie had no idea if anything he said resonated. Kip was distracted and then up and off the couch. After a trip to the bathroom, he headed out the door. "Cash is expecting me."

Thank God that Reed would be gone when Kip arrived.

Vinnie was headed out as well. He told Dean he would be back around six o'clock in the evening. Vinnie had a meeting at the Blaze. In less than a week he was scheduled to make his official club debut as Vinnie Lux.

Two days earlier. Ed Vittori had phoned. Vinnie was still winded from a run when he accepted the call. "Hey, Ed. How are you doing?"

"You don't want to know." Ed was exhausted. "Trying to keep ahead of the Rex Reynolds fiasco. Plus two new releases and another going into production. Budgets. Books. Yes, I'm harried."

Vinnie asked how spinning the Rex story was coming. If that footage was going to be included in Vinnie's first starring film, he felt he had a right to know.

"The studio line is Rex was questioning his sexuality all along," Ed continued. "His career allowed him to come to terms with it in a safe environment. Blah. Blah. Basically, the studio was part of his coming out process. All BS, but pure PR."

"That's a gift to be able to take an ugly story like that and spin it into something borderline sweet."

"That's what I do. Listen Vinnie, the reason I am calling— Are you familiar with The Blaze?"

The Blaze was *THE* gay club in WeHo. All the hottest men went there— rich guys, movie stars—the A-gays, and the beautiful people. Despite a recent expansion that almost doubled the size of the club, there were still lines out the door most nights of the week.

"I heard about the Blaze even when I was still in Chicago."

"Good, because they are familiar with you. They are very eager to have you dance at the club."

News of his first dancing gig filled Vinnie with exhilaration and terror. He liked to dance, but dancing on a pedestal in front of a crowd was a different story.

"What will I be expected to do?"

"Dance a little. Sign some pictures. I'll send you with a box of promo cards." Ed promoted the hell out of appearances on social media. "The Blaze does heavy promotion too. This will really get your name out there. Your social media will explode."

Vinnie liked the sound of that.

Vittori continued, "The staff there have done this sort of thing dozens of times. Other than dancing and signing, they will probably want you to mingle, hand out drink tickets, and work the crowd. Keep the energy high. Make it the place to be."

"Isn't it already?"

Ed said successful gay clubs are constantly working to keep it fresh. "Things can change overnight. The gays can be mighty fickle." Ed Vittori told Vinnie he was texting Leon's contact info. "Leon is the manager. He's anxious to set up a time for you to come check out the club and discuss your music. Have four songs or so picked out ahead of time."

The gig sounded great, but Vinnie was riddled with anxiety. *What if he bombed? What if he made a fool of himself? What if he got up to dance on a pedestal and there were no watchers? What if started dancing and the watchers walked away?*

Vinnie feared being exposed as a phony, as not really a sex god—just as someone whose name used to be Vincent. And then the dream would end. He needed to keep those doubts at bay.

Vinnie went into the bathroom and splashed cold water on his face. He took two deep breaths, looked at himself in the mirror and gave a solid slap to one and then the other cheek. Confidence was sexy, not self-doubt. He slapped himself again. "I am Vinnie Lux. I am a success."

54

Leon answered on the first ring. He sounded pleasant but distracted. He told Vinnie to come by the club anytime. "Whatever works. I'm always here." They decided on the following day at three in the afternoon. "The doors don't open until five. That way I can explain what you'll be doing so there's no confusion."

"That sounds great." Knowing what to expect and what was expected of him made Vinnie less anxious.

"Don't be nervous. The crowd will love you. The only problem we ever have is with the performers." Leon said there have been issues. "Responsibility is key."

Vinnie told Leon he had nothing to worry about.

"I've heard that before."

Vinnie assured him. "No really. I am very responsible."

"Then we'll get along fine," Leon said.

Before hanging up, Vinnie said he was not much of a dancer.

Dancing skills were a plus, but not a requirement or even an expectation. As Leon said, "The crowd isn't coming to see you dance, they're coming to see you."

The Blaze was chilly during the day, but it warmed up as soon as the bodies started arriving.

When Vinnie entered, Leon got up from his barstool. Tall, lean, and north of forty, Leon had perfect posture and the carriage of a dancer. After a brief greeting, Leon gave him a quick tour of the club. From the back, Leon still looked in his twenties.

"You will be dancing on an island in the center of the large back room. Our headliner stage." Leon said he got his start here in 1994. "My first night of work was the night they opened. I was part of the first group Mr. Novak hired. This stage was where we used to put the best dancers—now it's where we put the porn stars."

Shady?

Leon wanted confirmation that the platform was okay. "It's six inches taller than the platform in the front room as specified in your contract."

"That wasn't necessary," Vinnie began.

"Yes, it was necessary. It was in your contract so it is part of the employment agreement."

"Of course." Leon was touchy, though in this instance Vinnie could hardly blame him. What an absurd demand! The pedestals were not even in the same room! Vinnie needed to have Ed change that request. Vinnie didn't want to come across like a diva.

"You have three sets of two songs each," Leon explained. "The guys are coming to see you, meet you, and maybe get a picture. Dancing is secondary to keeping the fans happy."

"Got it."

Leon ushered him into the dressing room. On the original floor plans of the Blaze, this room was probably designated as a double closet. The actual dimensions were difficult to determine since every inch of the walls and ceiling were covered with signed glossies of the porn stars that had danced here— Donovan, Desi Lou, Lon Flexx, Stryker, Eric Rhodes, Matt Gunther, Peter Ray Thomas, Stefano, Miklos, and dozens more. Most were full-body shots, signed to either Novak or Leon. One 8x10 caught Vinnie's eye. "Oh wow, A.Z. Ambush. He was my roommate."

The mention of A.Z. seemed to change Leon's attitude towards him. Leon turned towards Vinnie, put a hand on his forearm, and offered his condolences. "I was a big fan before he ever danced here. I saw him in *Five A.Z. Pieces* and thought, *now that is a man*. That's probably worth something, now that he's gone."

The handwriting on the glossy didn't look much like A.Z.'s, and Vinnie had spent hours reading and rereading that notebook. The photo was inscribed, *Best Wishes and Big Thanks to Leon and the Blaze, A.Z. Ambush.*

A glossy shot of Rex was just to the side. "Another of your Xclusiv buddies." Leon added that he wasn't shocked by the news. "It was going to happen sooner or later. When Rex was here, I caught him messing around with another dancer in the bathroom. I don't care. *Boys will be boys* and all that, but like I said, it was only a matter of time." Leon added that he didn't think any gay-for-pay boys he knew were actually straight. "Nobody is, but those boys. Troubled and confused, sure. Sometimes fluid or bisexual, but straight, nope."

Vinnie noted that Leon wasn't afraid to share his opinions. It was a little overbearing, but welcome after the earlier awkwardness between them. Leon nodded to the left. "You'll be signing and taking pictures with fans in there. Would you like to sit at a low table, or we can move one of the standing cocktail tables over."

"I don't care either way." Vinnie wanted no problems.

"Well your contract says that it is your decision."

Vinnie could feel Leon's fur start to rise. "The cocktail table. I'll stand. That way it will be easier to move from signing to posing for photos."

Having a preference and a reason for it seemed to satisfy Leon. The vibe between them returned to the better place.

Vinnie added that Ed Vittori was sending him with a box of photo cards.

"The pictures are always a big hit. Some guys collect them, like you are all stars at MGM or something. For the other picture requests—up to you whether you're going to charge or do it as a courtesy."

Vinnie knew what Leon wanted to hear. "I was planning to do it for free."

Leon actually smiled. "Some of the guys charge. That leaves a bad taste in my mouth. We want people to spend their money on cocktails."

Of course, you do.

Vinnie was anxious about this first interaction with fans. He had yet to experience the fan factor of porn stardom—not on this level. The Blaze gig was perfectly timed. *Mancandy 2* came out two weeks ago, and the autograph cards were advance promo items for *Backfield in Motion.* McCain's photos of the three exclusives started appearing in gay mags and on porn sites.

Today had been a success. Things with Leon ended on a positive note and Vinnie was just saying goodbye when the club door opened. A flood of light revealed three silhouettes. As they entered, the bald gentleman in the center stepped forward. Those flanking him looked like hired muscle.

Leon made a visor with his hand. "Mr. Novak, you're just in time to meet Vinnie Lux."

Novak stepped forward in very expensive shoes. He was impeccably groomed. He had an angular pockmarked face with sharp cheekbones and deep-set eyes. His lips were full. There was no disguising his aura of power. Based on his looks, Novak fancied himself a gentleman—but there was danger beneath the veneer. "I've heard good things." Novak said it was a pleasure, but said Vinnie would have to excuse them. Novak had business to discuss with Leon.

Instagram 18.3K
Twitter 14.5K

Kip was done unpacking by the time Vinnie got home. Kip only had two suitcases and a couple of boxes of odds and ends.

Vinnie was confused. "Didn't you say you needed to borrow a truck?"

"To get rid of things. I donated a lot of stuff to the Out of the Closet charity shop and gave away my bookcase and bed. I felt lighter almost immediately. Living in a furnished place makes me feel free. I can be gone in a cab ride."

Having Kip in A.Z.'s room would take time. It was jarring to see Kip's clothes in the closet, his things on the desk, and his books on the shelves. To mask his discomfort, Vinnie scanned the titles on Kip's bookshelf: *Dancer from the Dance, You Can Heal Your Life, Valley of the Dolls*, two Gordon Merrick titles, *How to Win Friends and Influence People*, and a Wayne Dyer book on cassette. His Grabby Award for *Most Promising Newcomer* served as a bookend. A photo of him accepting the award was on the wall.

Kip saw him eyeing the award. "That was one of the happiest nights of my life. That weekend Woody showed me Chicago. We stayed at the Drake, and went to terrific restaurants. We did Sidetrack, Man's Country, Big Chicks, Steamworks, all of it. We saw *Kinky Boots* before it went to Broadway. Woody couldn't take his eyes off of me." When Kip said he would like to get back there someday—Vinnie wondered if he was talking about more than Chicago.

Kip abruptly turned from the photo and congratulated Vinnie on his gig at the Blaze. "Ed wants me to tell you the promo cards are at the printers and will be ready by Thursday."

"Great, I'm getting a little nervous about it."

"They will love you," Kip told Vinnie that he used to dance at the Blaze back when he was still making movies. "Actually, I was shaking my ass there when Woody discovered me. He walked in and talked me up during my break—and that was it! I knew that night there would never be anyone else for me."

"Well, he..."

Kip wasn't listening.

Vinnie was unsure how to respond. He mentioned seeing Kip's photograph in the dressing room at the Blaze.

"... Woody fixed my teeth, cleaned me up. He recognized my raw talent." Kip said he liked dancing better than making moves. "I loved getting on stage—feeling the music and letting myself go. Pure therapy."

"If you miss it you should just go and enjoy yourself on the dance floor."

Kip dismissed his suggestion. "I don't miss dancing—I miss dancing on a pedestal with all those eyes on me. I miss the watchers."

55

A sea of admirers parted as Vinnie made his way to the island stage. The Vinnie Lux fans in the audience far outnumbered those who were indifferent. From the way ninety percent of the guys were eyeballing him, most hoped to get in his pants. The adoration sent blood straight to his dick. Not erect, but a full and ready state.

There were a few bitchy queens. That's just demographics. In any popular gay nightclub, that type is just part of the territory. Most haters slithered away once they saw that Vinnie was a decent dancer. By his second song, Vinnie was feeling the music. He understood what Kip had meant about dancing on a pedestal.

Between sets, Vinnie posed for photos and signed a few dozen promo cards. A couple of guys brought magazine spreads, and one drunken bear wanted him to sign his very hairy butt. Vinnie had a couple of cocktails to steady his nerves. He did a shot with the bartender, and another with a fan. Booze proved the perfect lubricant for his personality. By midnight Vinnie was drunk and exhausted. The gig was an enormous success.

Instagram 22K
Twitter 16.3K

Two days after his Blaze appearance, Vinnie set up an interview with Trusted Talents. After his personal appearance debut, Vinnie felt confident, but money was still an issue. He would be popular with the Trusted Talents clients. Stardom carried added cachet at the agency.

Gio said any Xclusiv star was a shoo-in at the agency and A.Z. had agreed. Unfortunately, neither was around to make a formal introduction. It was up to Vinnie to make it happen. Novak ran Trusted Talents, but approaching him directly was not the way things were done. Vinnie needed an introduction, and Leon seemed the easiest route.

When Vinnie phoned the club. Leon answered. Vinnie thanked him again. "I had a great time. I hope the club was happy." Leon said they were thrilled. Vinnie took on a confidential tone. "Have you heard of Trusted Talents? One of the other dancers was talking about it." Fortunately, Leon didn't ask whom. "I wanted to see about some freelance work. Do you have a contact?" He didn't mention Novak.

The Trusted Talents office capped a glass tower in downtown L.A. When the elevator pinged and the doors slid open, Vinnie stepped into a beautiful Art Deco-influenced reception area. Chopin softly played. Beige carpet hushed his footsteps as he approached the desk. He had an appointment.

The assistant nodded. "So you do," they said, rising to usher him to Novak's office.

Novak looked up from his desk. "Thank you, Jean."

As he stood, Vinnie caught a whiff of cologne. Self-made men rarely smell like the streets.

"Hello again, Mr. Lux." The men shook hands. Strong grip. Huge hands. Perfect manicure. A diamond pinkie ring. Rolex. The scent of a fine cigar hung in the room. Everything in this office, including Novak, reeked of wealth and power. He motioned for Vinnie to have a seat.

Beside his desk was a waterfall. Novak said the sound of running water kept him calm. Rather than the serenity of a tranquil Buddha, the calm that Novak exuded was more the stillness of a coiled snake. "So, Vinnie Lux, why you are interested in working for me?"

"Nothing mysterious. Trusted Talents is the best. This is the place and now is the time for me to make as much money as possible."

Novak eyed him intently. Men like Novak notice everything. His silent detachment made him even more intimidating.

"Mr. Lux, are you familiar with how we operate?"

"For the most part."

Novak clipped the tip from his cigar and leaned back in his chair. He paused a moment to light it, keeping his eyes fixed on Vinnie all the while. He took one puff, and then another, before he spoke. "Then why don't you tell me what we do?" Novak was menacing as hell and alpha as fuck—leaning back in his chair, knowing grin, cigar in hand. His thighs were parted wide, and a bulge beyond promising was on display. Novak seemed the sort of creature that would kill its mate.

Vinnie chose his words carefully. He wanted to impress Novak, but feared offending him. "Trusted Talents arranges intimate meetings for clients from a roster of eligible young men, like myself."

A perfect smoke ring emerged from those full lips. "Is that what I do?" Novak continued, "At Trusted Talents we arrange dates for patrons and make sure those dates are safe from the law and safe from extortion. The details of the date are not our concern. We handle the money, deduct the service fee of forty-five percent and turn the remainder over to you. No money changes hands between date and the client—ever. Not even tips. Gratuity is handled by the agency."

Vinnie figured Trusted Talents probably took a healthy percentage of the tip as well. Novak made it clear the rules were not up for negotiation.

Novak paused and stared at Vinnie for another long moment. "Availability is entirely up to you. Does that sound like something that would interest you? I can promise you we're the best game in town."

Vinnie nodded. "Yes."

"Because if you have any doubts," Novak said, "Now is a good time to walk away."

"No, I'm sure."

Novak leaned forward in his chair. "No drug use on dates. What you do on your personal time is none of my concern, but when you are working you are to have no drugs on your person without a prescription. Is that understood?"

Vinnie nodded. He refrained from asking if that rule also applied when the client offered the drugs.

"Follow my rules, and we can have a profitable partnership. Break them, and I can promise you—we will have a problem." Novak leaned forward and stubbed out his cigar before rising. The meeting was over. "You've made a wise choice with Trusted Talents, Mr. Lux."

Vinnie mentioned that he was unable to start work for two weeks. "I'm scheduled to make a ..."

Novak raised a hand to stop him. "Discuss any and all scheduling details with Jean." The slender assistant was already at the door, ready to usher Vinnie from the office.

As he was escorted from the office, Vinnie introduced himself. "Pleased to meet you, Jean."

The assistant nodded. "Nice to meet you, Mr. Lux." Jean said their preferred pronouns were they/them.

That evening Woody phoned to discuss *On the Strip*. Vinnie had not spoken to him in over a week. Woody told him he was on speaker. Ed Vittori was also in the office. Getting a "strictly business" call was almost worse than no phone call at all.

Friendly but formal, Woody gave Vinnie a quick recap of casting—a nice combination of experienced and fresh. Woody confirmed that the Rex Reynolds footage would be included. "We have veterans Lee Botello and Josh Lawless; the Hungarian duo of Christophe and Ivan "The Impaler"; and newcomers Hank London and Valentino Valdez. Both those new boys show lots of promise."

New competition.

Maybe one or both of those newbies was the reason for Woody's distance. The thought that Woody might bed all newcomers and that Vinnie was nothing special made him feel like a chump. Was their time together his usual routine? Vinnie had been so open with him, so gullible.

Although Vinnie had only been with Xclusiv for a few months, he was no longer considered a fresh face. However, he *was* an exclusive and his name was the one above the title. Promising or not, these newcomers were supporting players in a Vinnie Lux picture. *On the Strip* was his big chance. No one was going to take that from him.

Months ago, Woody probably called Vinnie a promising newcomer. He and Reed were set up to become adversaries. Woody played them off each other. He probably sang Vinnie's praises right before filming *Backfield in Motion*. Vinnie could see Reed walking out over something like that. Having Vinnie replace Reed only twisted the knife.

Competition was a reality of the industry. The business fed on fresh faces. Now was the time to prove he was one of those who would endure. Vinnie needed to get over his bruised ego and focus on the business of being, and remaining, a star.

Woody said there was one more thing. "I need you to share top billing."

Woody wasn't asking Vinnie, he was informing him. Vinnie had a costar. His opinion didn't matter. What he had been promised didn't matter. As the star of *On the Strip*—he'd been promised the cover, that his name would be fifty percent larger than the names of his costars. Not anymore. At Xclusiv, being a team player meant going along with whatever was decided. So boom, he had a costar.

The situation reminded him of getting dumped and being not quite enough—of never knowing when someone better was going to come along. Vinnie caught himself in the living room mirror. He needed to drop that Vincent crap. He was Vinnie Lux—and Vinnie Lux was nobody's victim. This business was tough, but he could take it.

"Guess who we landed as your costar?"

Thankfully, Woody didn't want him to actually guess.

"Peter Ray Thomas is coming out of retirement to join the cast."

"Wow," was all Vinnie could manage. Peter Ray Thomas had been a superstar, the recipient of every major gay adult video honor and award. At one point, he was the reigning poster boy of gay carnality. Everyone had a thing for the sexy bad boy of gay porn. He lived the role to the hilt.

"He's ready to come back. He's sober and eager to work. Looks good. He still owes us one more movie. I never thought we would get another one out of him." Vinnie was set for top horizontal billing, and Peter will be first vertically."

Peter Ray Thomas was a legend. He had legions of fans, but his name brought other things to mind for Vinnie. Peter Ray Thomas had been the intended recipient of the deadly syringe that killed Carter Gaines. Why would Woody hire someone he once wanted dead? Was it for the good of the studio—or was there another reason?

Kip said later that Woody was more determined than ever to find the party responsible for the uploaded Rex clip. He said Woody had sent a screen capture of the stunt cock to different people to ask around. Woody said that if Mr.

Stunt Cock has gotten a blowjob in this town, he would find out his name, and who put him up to bringing down Rex.

Vinnie hoped this would all blow over, but from the way Kip was talking, that wasn't going to happen anytime soon. This town could be so lonely. Vinnie didn't have anyone here he could talk to, anyone he could trust. He had that in Chicago—at least until Ty made it weird. Vinnie had postponed listening to Ty's voicemail. Now seemed as good a time as any.

"Vinnie, this is Ty. I'm sorry for the way things turned out. I told you how I felt, but you don't feel the same. I was mad—I said and did some things in the heat of anger. I'll survive, but I can't be your friend. Maybe that will change someday. If it does, I'll let you know. I hope things work out for you in California. Be well."

Then fuck Ty! Dealing with him was just another stressful situation. Obviously, Vinnie couldn't call him. He needed a confidant.

He regretted that things happened the way they did, but it was necessary. Ty could never see him as anything more than Vincent—and he was so much more than that.

Playing up a blowjob as anything more than what it was sparked Vinnie's irritation. Vinnie needed people who supported him. Meanwhile, Ty was still moping around being a victim. He was trying to guilt Vinnie into loving him. It was pathetic—and pity is the opposite of passion.

All that was a lifetime ago in a world of petty dramas.

These days the stakes were higher.

Twisting the cap off a beer, Vinnie headed to the balcony. Vinnie felt like getting buzzed tonight. He might even go clubbing. Maybe tonight, he would even join Reed and Dean.

His partners in crime.

56

Vinnie suffered behind dark glasses. He took two aspirin with a couple of glasses of water, and added A.Z.'s prescription bottle of Xanax to his gym bag.

The morning sun was brutal. The moment he stepped outside, the heat added to his hangover nausea. Soot from the hill fires stuck to his skin. He knew his mood would improve after sweating out some of the alcohol. Since *On the Strip* was set to shoot next week, hitting the gym was mandatory. He needed to look perfect.

Promising newcomers.

Working out would also help to clear some of the cobwebs from last night.

As clearly as Vinnie could recall, he was polishing off another beer when Reed and Dean came through the front door with a bottle of tequila.

Dean pulled out a pipe and a baggie. "Hash," he said, filling the pipe and passing it to Reed.

Vinnie was appreciative. It felt good to laugh. He was even getting along with Reed. But after his third tequila shot, Vinnie began to get messy. By the time Reed and Dean were up for the club, Vinnie was about to pass out. "I'm too wasted. I'm not used to this. You two go on."

Reed offered some chemical enhancement. Vinnie declined. Nothing up his nose or in a vein.

When they left, Vinnie grabbed a beer and returned to the balcony. He stretched out on the chaise and listened to the night sounds of the city. The next thing he knew, Kip was on the chair beside him.

Vinnie had no idea how long they talked. He recalled fragments of what he said, and what he remembered was worrisome. He told Kip about Chicago, his career aspirations, and feelings for Woody.

He had said a lot, but thankfully he didn't recall saying a word about Rex or the notebook. What he said was bad enough.

Kip would tell Woody everything. He might even twist his words, although he may not need to. Kip might even leak it to Dorian Mikado.

Vinnie was careless. All Kip needed to do was ask a leading question or two and then urge Vinnie to elaborate. *Vinnie had been a fool.* For all he knew, Kip had taken notes. Worry that he had let something slip was a legitimate concern, but Vinnie didn't know how concerned he should be. Of course, he imagined the worst-case scenario. He tried to tell himself this was Vincent thinking. This was not Vinnie Lux. Hitting the gym would help clear his head.

After a solid workout and steam at the gym, Vinnie took a Xanax and treated himself to a facial and massage. He needed pampering. He was a porn star. He deserved this. By the time he left the salon, he felt more like Vinnie Lux. He still had worries, but that raw panic he felt earlier was a memory. *Xanax is a miracle drug,* he thought with a smile. After the spa, he took another half tablet and waited for his concerns to blur even more.

When he got home Dean was dozing on the couch. Hearing the door close, Dean rolled over and handed Vinnie a piece of paper. *Call Ed.*

"Ed Vittori?"

Dean nodded. "Kip gave it to me on his way out."

Vinnie took a seat on the arm of the couch. He would call Ed in a few. He asked Dean how his lunch with Vittori had gone. "Did he want to rekindle things?"

Dean grinned. "There was a little of that, but I got the feeling that wasn't why we were having lunch."

"What do you mean?"

Dean asked if he really wanted to know—an invitation that was impossible to decline.

Vinnie nodded.

"He mainly wanted to know about you."

"Me?" Vinnie was grateful for the Xanax.

"Yeah," Dean's voice was rough from his nap. "He tried to slip things in, poke around for details, but I'm smarter than I look."

Vinnie knew that was true. On several occasions, Dean had surprised him with a comment or observation showing greater awareness than Vinnie expected. Dean was not some dumb horse-hung cowboy. He had more on the ball than most.

Muting the TV, Dean sat up on the couch "Ed wanted to know about you—what you like to do, if you call home, how close you were to A.Z. and to Roy. All sorts of things. Were things really like you said in Chicago?"

Vinnie cringed. Vittori needn't have bothered with the third degree, Vinnie probably answered most of those questions talking to Kip last night.

"I dodged the questions, which is easy because I don't know much. But all the while he was asking, I kept thinking, now why is Ed Vittori so curious about Vinnie Lux? And then I started thinking to myself, is that Vinnie Lux hiding some deep dark secret?"

Before Vinnie could respond, Kip came through the door and announced he would only be home for a few minutes. "I need to change my shirt." On his way through the living room, he paused to ask Vinnie how he was feeling.

Vinnie was grateful for the Xanax. "Sorry if I went on too much." He said the tequila went straight to his head. "Especially combined with heat."

As Kip started heading down the hall he turned and added, "I like when you're talkative."

Dean asked what that was about.

"Remember last night, I didn't go to the club with you guys because I was too wasted. Well, after you and Reed left I stretched out on the chaise and was having a smoke or two. When Kip got home, he came outside, and we talked."

"About what?"

Vinnie lowered his voice. "That's just it, I can't remember all of it."

Dean's eyebrows raised. In a moment he unmuted the TV.

His response sparked Vinnie's paranoia. Now this Vittori business as well. Vinnie needed to call him and find out what this was about. Opening the door to his room, Vinnie noticed something odd about the gold plate surrounding the knob. There were three long scratches—like the lock had been tampered with. Had the scrapes been there before, and he simply hadn't noticed? He took another half Xanax and stretched out on the bed. He picked up his phone.

Instagram 26K
Twitter 18.2K

The Xanax made it easy to postpone everything. By the time he phoned Ed Vittori an hour later, most of his worries had blurred. Ed picked up right away. He was on the freeway to Long Beach. He put Vinnie on speaker. Reception was choppy. Vinnie imagined Vittori tooling along the coast, windows wide, hot wind whipping up the sleeves and down the collar of his shirt, tenting the fabric from his tight body. Xanax made him horny as well. "Vinnie good to hear from you. Listen, I might lose you so I'll get right to the point. They loved you at the Blaze and want to showcase you again. We're working on some dates. Dorian Mikado wants to do a Q&A with you later this week for his video podcast. He's going to give me a time later today. If you haven't seen *Between the Sheets with Dorian*, the Q&A takes place on a prop bed. The show is great exposure."

Of course, he knew about Dorian Mikado's video podcast. Everyone knew about *Between the Sheets With Dorian*. The show was a sexy glimpse into the gay XXX industry, and often a silly playtime with the fantasy men of porn. Periodically a cringe-worthy episode would air—often when a guest showed up over-served. Sometimes personalities clashed. When that happened, the fluff interview went south fast. Dorian could be prickly. Vinnie thanked Ed for setting up the appearance. "I appreciate it. And I meant it when I said I am always okay with doing publicity." Vinnie heard the loll of Xanax in his voice.

Vittori praised Vinnie's attitude and enthusiasm. "Great, I ..." Words disappeared in a spark of crackles. "Dorian can be pain in the ass, but when it comes to exposure... hottest game in town. I'll let you know the... will be Wednesday." Dorian wanted to book you on his video podcast before the start of filming *On the Strip*. "By the time that movie premieres..." More crackles. Nothing. Crackles.

Filming an episode of *Between the Sheets with Dorian* was a rite of passage in the gay porn industry. If you were already big, Dorian helped you to stay big. The key to getting along with him was kissing his ass. Flattery did wonders. Having Dorian as an enemy could undo a future. Dorian did not ruin careers, but he held enough sway to make sure careers never happened. Heaven help the "dicklet," Dorian's word for gay male XXX starlets, who got on his shit list. They were RIP—ruined in porn. Dorian was essential. He connected stars to fans—and fans were the lifeblood of a porn star.

His club appearance had been superb for that, but personal appearances are limited to those at the club that night. Dorian's video podcast reached thousands. All of his previous episodes were archived and available on his high-traffic website. Clips from his shows were all over YouTube. Being the featured guest on Dorian's show had the potential for a huge payoff.

Vinnie had seen Dorian Mikado in half a dozen movies. One month after retiring from being a performer, Dorian began reporting on the gay XXX scene. After six months of work, he had a solid income from advertisements and endorsements. Since then, Dorian had turned his foothold into a bit of an empire. Dorian had become the key influencer in the industry. The fact that he had made a career for himself and achieved what he had was admirable. Vinnie heard that Dorian may come across as dizzy, but he knew exactly what he was doing."

Dorian put Vinnie at ease almost immediately. When Vinnie arrived for the taping, music was playing. The camera and recording apparatus were unobtrusive. The comforter on Dorian's big bed was hot pink. There were fuzzy pillows shaped like lips and dicks. Vibrant! Dorian explained how things would go. Dorian still had it—smooth skin, lean muscle, and beautiful eyes. Some tatted hunk was manning the lights and camera. Given the intimacy of the set, the nearness of Dorian and the half-naked camera guy, this felt more like an elaborate seduction than an interview.

After a final bit of make-up, Dorian and Vinnie climbed onto the hot pink bed. The assistant raised his hand for a countdown. That man had great pits. "In 5-4-3-2-1."

Dorian gave the camera a good eye fuck before he spoke. "Hi, I'm Dorian Mikado and welcome to *Between the Sheets with Dorian*."

After some initial questions about his career, the Xclusiv family, and some of his costars—Dorian's interview questions changed. The tone took a sudden shift. Dorian asked if he had seen the Rex Reynolds upload. Before Vinnie could respond, Dorian asked if he was aware that Rex had trashed Reed Connors in his podcast days before. The assistant ran the audio of Rex's rant.

"If I had known Rex was into dick, I would have made a move," joked Dorian. When he did, the assistant added a "boing" sound effect. Dorian abruptly turned back to Vinnie, "What's your take on Rex and Reed and all that?"

Unsure of how to respond, Vinnie laughed, but Dorian refused to let it go. Instead, Dorian pressed him further, asking Vinnie if he thought revenge might be a motive for the upload.

That was a tricky question to answer. "I suppose revenge could be a motive, but no one in the Xclusiv family would do something like that." Protecting himself meant protecting Reed.

"No one? Is that really true? How about Reed? Aren't you two pitted against one another? Is everyone out to be Woody Wilson's favorite?"

"You're being bad," Vinnie scolded. "Reed and I are good. Some rivalry, that comes with the territory—but nothing too bad, nothing juicy."

"And with Woody."

This interview was becoming very uncomfortable. Vinnie was unsure how to respond, eventually he spoke to say something. "I guess everybody does want to be Daddy's favorite." The moment he said it he wondered if the comment was a mistake. Was he saying too much? Was he responding correctly? Was he being a team player? Bringing up the topic of Rex and the rapid-fire questions had thrown him. Clearly that had been Dorian's intent. Dorian raised an index finger to his lips. "Between us."

"And your audience," Vinnie laughed.

"All joking aside, who is your biggest rival at Xclusiv? From what I've seen, there are a lot of stallions in Woody's stable." Dorian winked at the camera. "Maybe it wasn't revenge at all that took down Rex—but ambition."

Dorian turned the question to him. Vinnie acknowledged that it was another possibility.

"After Xclusiv dropped Rex, didn't your new film, *On the Strip*, move into Rex's old production slot."

Vinnie felt a rising along the back of his neck. The insinuation was vile. Being embarrassed or insulted would only encourage Dorian. Vinnie needed to take action. He needed to keep calm and do something. Dorian was attempting to link him with the uploaded footage on a video podcast. Action was the only answer. Vinnie's hand brushed across Dorian's leg, resting on his thigh. He smiled at Dorian and inched his hand higher, still out of the camera frame. "That is true. I am so excited about *On the Strip*. We start filming next week. Aren't you excited too?" Vinnie felt the heat coming from Mikado's crotch. He palmed his balls through the cotton. Hand moved higher, touching the side of the shaft and tracing his finger over the fabric to the tip and back again. Dorian's dick was thickening, then throbbing, leaping to meet Vinnie's touch. The head was tenting the elastic of his briefs. Now Vinnie was in control of the interview. He asked Dorian on camera if his video interviews ever turned pornographic. "I'm asking for a friend."

To the viewers, it looked like innocent flirting. Off-camera frame, the head of Mikado's cock had come into view.

"With the right interviewee." Dorian looked at the camera. "I'm afraid that's all we have time for today. Thank you, Vinnie Lux, for getting *Between the Sheets with Dorian.* Join me next week for more gay porn views, skews, and news." Dorian held his smile until the cameraman yelled cut. "My followers are going to lick that up. Did they or didn't they?"

"Oh, I think they'll know." Vinnie slipped the waistband of Dorian's BVDs below his balls. He licked his fingers and returned his hand to Mikado's shaft.

Dorian tossed a fuzzy pillow aside and sank back onto the bed. "How far we go is up to you."

The muscled cameraman cut the lights.

Dorian kissed Vinnie. "Do you have anywhere to be?" When Vinnie paused, Dorian added, "I promise the piece will be favorable."

Vinnie pinched a nipple until Dorian flinched. When his lips parted in pain, Vinnie deep kissed him. Hard. Pushing him away. Pulling him back. An even deeper kiss. Slapping Mikado's chest with an open palm. More heat between them. Working more on his nips. "I have all afternoon free."

After taking down the equipment, the cameraman stripped down. Very nice. Those perfect pits and the rest—more ink than pink skin. Camera dude shucked his pants. He was commando. His freed cock was half hard and had a wicked hook. His ass was a pristine oasis in the art covering most of his skin.

"This is Hector," said Dorian.

57

By the time filming began for *On the Strip,* Vinnie was fit, focused, and looking every inch a superstar. He hadn't smoked or drank in the last few days. No carbs. No sugar. Two workouts a day. Weights. Cardio. Yoga. His secret was discipline.

He had to be in top form to prove to the cast, crew, and Woody that this was a Vinnie Lux picture. He was the star despite two promising newcomers, despite the bootleg Rex Reynolds footage, and despite the return of his costar Peter Ray Thomas.

Mykel Z. was helming the picture. During the *Backfield in Motion* shoot Mykel had been bulldozed by McCain. The entire thing had been painful to witness. Vinnie intended to be respectful to Mykel, but at the same time—it was Vinnie's ass on the line. Vinnie Lux was the name above the title—at least *one* of the names. If he felt things were wrong. He would suggest changes. Vinnie needed to speak up for himself and that meant doing everything within his power to make sure his first starring vehicle was the best damn movie possible.

For the first time in Xclusiv's history, Joe McCain would not be in charge of photography and production design. Waiting for McCain to return from his Hawaiian honeymoon meant production delays. That was expensive. Woody didn't like to start a film with budget concerns. Kip said that Woody didn't feel guilty about replacing him. "He said that Joe gave him no choice and that business was business."

Woody replaced McCain with Aaron Fyre, an edgy young designer from New York recommended by an industry friend. Aaron was hired to "freshen up" the Xclusiv look. Porn had undergone massive changes since the studio began eight years ago. Porn aesthetics were different. Some saw McCain's style as dated. Whenever something is around long enough, it eventually needs to be rebooted, rejuvenated, or razed. There was talk that the McCain era had come to an end.

When Vinnie arrived on set, Mykel introduced him to Aaron Fyre. He offered a cursory smile but said nothing. Frye didn't need words. The look he gave Vinnie said it all.

Vinnie loathed gay snobs. He had served plenty of these smug fuckers as a waiter. Fyre was even worse—an arty gay snob. Thin and pale, layered in darkness, and self-importance, Fyre probably thought he was being edgy by working in porn. He mumbled that he needed to check on something—leaving before he even finished the sentence. Mykel called Fyre a perfectionist. "He really is very talented. He has already told me so, several times."

The two men started laughing.

When it was clear that McCain was out, Aaron Frye was already in place. "Woody demanded he be used." Mykel shrugged. "What do I care? He's the one putting up the money for this movie. I have a mortgage. Not really, but I have rent. I can't afford to mess with the guy who signs my check."

Fyre had an interesting style. His vision was a triptych of boldly painted rooms. The first was a seedy orange hotel room; the second was a dim raspberry barroom, and the third was the purple brick wall of a back alley. To contrast the set palette and unite the overall vision, each set featured several dilapidated props which had been painted white—a broken dresser, two three-legged chairs, a busted barstool, and two dented trashcans. Neon and dry ice were on hand to enhance the dreamy and artificial feel.

Fyre said his sets were, "Laying bare the artifice at the heart of the Strip."

Vinnie rolled his eyes. In the late 1980s and early 1990s, it was called stylized sleaze. The fever-dream visuals Frye had created were certainly interesting. Maybe this was a good thing. This was fresh. Fyre's vision would set *On the Strip* apart. Vinnie told Fyre that the sets looked terrific. Fyre smiled, revealing an odd jumble of teeth.

"Hope the Rex Reynolds footage isn't too harsh a contrast to the rest of the look."

Aaron nodded towards the orange hotel room. "The Rex Reynolds footage will be playing on loop on that battered black and white television." Woody wanted it like that—so that Rex Reynolds porn would be an actual relic."

A relic, Vinnie laughed to himself.

Lee Botello said McCain knew nothing about Aaron Fyre. "Woody said he got ahold of Joe, but when I talked to him on Monday—Joe had not heard a word from Woody."

Sue winced, "Joe McCain can be touchy. He won't appreciate not being told."

"I can't say I blame him." Lee said he wasn't about to say a word. "Longevity around here means minding your own business."

Vinnie found the comment ironic given the circumstances.

Lee continued, "Things will work out. Just sit back and watch Woody grease him up and go into action. Woody will say he didn't want to disturb Joe and deny any wrongdoing—all the while wearing a smile."

Sue gave Lee a playful slap. "He's done worse."

Vinnie was about to see if he could get more details when Mykel approached. By then, Sue was talking about her trip to Miami and blending bronzer to mask Lee's fatigue. "You look like you've been having fun."

Lee kissed Sue's hand. "You always make me beautiful, darling."

"Of course." Sue said she almost fell off her chair when she heard Peter Ray Thomas had joined the cast. "I hope I don't spend my time hiding track marks."

Lee said Peter was clean now.

"I am praying for him." Sue crossed herself and wished nothing but the best for him. "He's a nice guy, but such a tortured soul. We have always gotten along, but I've seen Peter get clean before."

Lee puckered into the lit mirror. "Apparently it stuck this time."

"Hallelujah," Sue handed him a mirror. "And you are finished."

Lee got up and kissed her on the cheek. "Gorgeous, as always. Thanks, Sue."

"If you need touch-ups. I'm downstairs studying." Sue had a test on Friday. Vinnie had no idea until then that she was working her way through law school.

Josh Lawless clapped Vinnie on the shoulder and pulled him in for a hug. Being in Josh's arms was like having the world disappear. Vinnie sighed and nestled for a moment. He needed this so badly. Sometimes being held by a man was better than sex. Actually, most times it was better than sex. Josh was a superb hugger. Ian was a lucky guy.

"Too bad we don't have a scene together." Josh was paired with "some guy Woody is keen on, Valentino Valdez." Josh hinted that Woody might be fucking Valentino. "After all, he is staying at La Casa de Woody Wilson."

Vinnie stood straighter to hear the news. He didn't know.

Josh nodded. "Staying in the casita. I've got the newbie again like I did with you not so long ago. Now look at you. Name above the title. You're a star. Lucky, I got my signed photo when I did."

"Stop."

"Well, when you get your new glossies send me a few."

"Sure thing." Vinnie was distracted. Hearing Woody was smitten with Valentino and that the kid was staying at the compound filled him with anxiety. *Was he no longer the favorite?* Vinnie took a measured breath and tried to exude confidence. Vinnie said Woody knew best, "It's great he paired you with Valentino. I can certainly vouch that you are primo in popping a guy's porn cherry."

"And about slipping you my number," Josh added. "I hope I didn't make you feel weird. That night I thought that with Ian gone it might be fun—but he's back home now."

"Okay. And to be clear, that was not rejection—that was a rain check." Vinnie was teasing but serious. Josh was always upfront. He never led anyone on. At every opportunity, Josh mentioned his husband. His devotion to Ian and to their relationship made him sexier.

Vinnie and Josh had calls all three days. Day One. Vinnie shot a scene as a hustler on the strip. After getting picked up by a john (Lee Botello), they return to his hotel room. The set captured the mood—a broken down brass bed with a bare ratted mattress, and a painting of fruit. The Rex Reynolds sex tape was looping on a three-legged TV.

Day Two. Reserved for any necessary backup footage and B-roll, though the story and dialogue for *On the Strip* were minimal. Also scheduled that day was the alley scene with Christophe and Ivan, "the Impaler." Vinnie had never met either one of them. Everyone called them the Hungary Boys—though without proper enunciation the joke often fell flat.

Day Three. His big scene with Peter Ray Thomas. Vinnie was nervous about filming with the porn legend. Once people heard he was filming with Peter Ray Thomas, everyone came forward with their own stories about the superstar. He sounded larger than life.

Peter Ray Thomas had been in rehab. He smashed a car, came to shoots bombed out of his mind, was caught shooting up in a broom closet, disappeared for weeks on end, went heavily in debt, and was detained at more than one border. Vinnie heard he had been jailed twice for drunk and disorderly. According to the notebook, when Peter tried to leave the studio, Woody had planned to kill him.

By the time the day of filming arrived, Vinnie had no idea what was true and what was hearsay. Most stories were secondhand, but if even a fraction of them were true, there could be problems. Vinnie told Josh he wanted a trouble-free shoot. "What if his coming back isn't a good idea? What if he's not okay?"

Josh said to give him a chance. "Coming back into all this can't be easy. He knows people are watching him, looking for gossip." Peter told Josh that he was worried that people will say he should have stayed away. "Don't be another one judging him."

Josh was right. He was being unfair. Vinnie was willing to give Peter the benefit of the doubt, but that did not mean he was giving him a free pass. His name was above the title as well. If Peter messes up, he will drag them both down. If he did *anything* to jeopardize *On the Strip*, Vinnie would say something. Josh assured him that most talk about Peter was hogwash. Even when he was using, he was more professional than a lot of guys who work for Xclusiv." Josh raised his water bottle to Vinnie's, "Here's to a smooth shoot." Josh was billed third after Vinnie and Peter Ray Thomas. In addition to being coupled with Valentino Valdez, Josh was also slated to do a scene with Hank London. "Whoever the fuck that bloke is."

Hank London was another promising new talent. "Woody paired you with both of the newcomers!" Vinnie said, "You'll be popping lots of porn cherry on this set."

"When duty calls," Josh shrugged.

Vinnie was grateful that Ed Vittori had been extremely supportive when Vinnie mentioned wanting to post his own shots on Instagram and Twitter. "Candids, onset shots, things like that. Hanging out with other porn stars. I think fans will eat it up."

Vittori agreed. "Tell that to some of your cast mates."

Now was a moment. Vinnie took two selfies with Josh and posted them on his socials. For the first shot they tweaked each other's nipples. *Nip play with buddy Josh Lawless on the set of* On the Strip, *coming from Xclusiv.* In the second selfie they were flashing pits. Vinnie had been inspired by those deep furry muscle pits of Hector the cameraman for Dorian. Vinnie leaned into Josh's pit and took a deep whiff. SNAP! *You want this! Thirst trap.*

Vinnie was reviewing filter options with Josh when Valentino Valdez approached him. "You mentioned my name earlier?"

Vinnie looked up from his phone. "That was Josh," Vinnie tilted his head to the left. "He just said you two have a scene together. I'm Vinnie Lux. This is Josh Lawless."

"Pleased to meet you." Valentino spoke in fractured English. He was actually Italian. "From Siena." He was stunning. Gorgeous face. Flawless skin. Open smile. Jet-black hair. Tight body. Vinnie couldn't blame Woody for being smitten.

Josh called him to come between them. "Come pose with us. Let's give fans a glimpse of this promising young star and make a Valentino sandwich. He tagged everyone, and added the hashtag, *#onthestrip* and posted the pic.

Vinnie took a selfie with Valentino as well.

Mykel called for Valentino. He had something for him to sign.

Josh reminded him to send a signed picture and gave Valentino a card with his address. When Valentino went to see what Mykel needed, Josh lowered his voice. "He is adorable. Bashful and beautiful gets me going. Add an accent and I'm in heaven." Josh squeezed his crotch. "Brings out my daddy side even more."

Vinnie expected to dislike Valentino. Instead, he felt almost protective of him. Valentino was a sweet, beautiful kid. Woody may be fucking him, but Valentino was no threat. He was gorgeous, but he had no spark.

While they were waiting for the lights, Vinnie took out his phone and read Valentino's bio on the Xclusiv site aloud, "Valentino Valdez was an ugly duckling that grew into a breathtaking 20 year old."

When Valentino realized Vinnie was reading his bio, he blushed and burst out that he was really 22. "This is all so quick."

Vinnie offered a friendly smile. "Don't worry, none of our bios are true. Everything in the business happens quickly, except setting lights for a shoot." Vinnie wasn't sure Valentino understood him, but he laughed at the joke. Valentino had the most beautiful way of smiling. He smiled fully, with his eyes as well as with his mouth. "Your English is very good. Did you learn it in school?"

Valentino said he mostly learned English from movies. "I love the movies and would dream of this place where movies are made. To be in Hollywood is a great thing."

"And now you are in the movies."

"I am," he said. And Valentino's gorgeous smile returned.

58

The first two days of the shoot were uninspired. There was nothing terrible about the dailies, but nothing particularly notable about them either. The porn classic Vinnie had hoped for simply was not happening, and all of it was beyond his control. Both cast and crew seemed to be sleepwalking through the shoot. For some, this might be just another movie. *On the Strip* meant considerably more to Vinnie. His name was above the title.

Vinnie was even part of the problem. His scene with Lee Botello lacked a spark. The passion felt forced. Although they had clicked on camera before—this time they did not. Part of the problem was the casting. Not Vinnie—but the role they gave him. He felt absurd as a tough street hustler. That wasn't his image. Besides, he was no actor. He needed to rehearse—but that took time and time meant money and the only thing worse than starring in a bad movie was being the reason that a movie went over budget. Vinnie needed time. He could do this. He kept thinking, *Stance. Gestures. Voice. Attitude.* Vinnie requested a second and third take to get the character right, but both retakes were worse than the original.

Mykel said it would come together in post-production, but Vinnie knew he was bullshitting him. Mykel was a top-quality director and intended to get this film in the can under budget. At some point it became clear Mykel did not have the patience, and the film was not budgeted for excessive retakes.

The second scene of the day, featuring Christophe and Ivan, was set in the purple alley. Christophe and Ivan both looked and fucked like beautiful machines. Their precision sex lacked hunger. For sex in an alley to send blood below your belt, the vibe should be "too fevered to get to a room." Sex is an alley says, "We need to fuck now!" Vinnie doubted the scene would hold anyone's interest a full twenty minutes.

SNAP! Vinnie posted a picture of the two men deep kissing on his social media. He tagged them both. *Deliveries in Rear! Some back alley action with*

Christophe and Ivan. Both men had a solid number of followers. The Hungary Boys were big in Europe. SNAP! Vinnie posted a second pic, a selfie with both men.

Based on what Vinnie saw, Valentino Valdez looked to be a major disappointment. No post-production magic could mask his awkwardness. He was breathtaking, but his beauty failed to animate. On film, Valentino came across as disengaged. Bland fantasy men have no place in porn. Nobody pounds one out to a do-me queen.

The Hungary Boys snickered.

Vinnie hoped Valentino couldn't hear them. Vinnie knew how that felt. He had heard others laughing so many times in his life. He hated the thought of Valentino going through that. Vinnie shot a look at the Hungary Bitches. Mykel gave Valentino his fair share of retakes—of starts and stops and pep talks. If a performer cannot respond to direction or come alive before a camera, there's really nothing to be done. Even with Josh as his scene partner, Valentino remained stiff—and not in a good way. Eventually, Mykel just kept the camera going. Watching Valentino filming the scene made it clear that porn is not for everyone. Even his climax was anti-climactic.

After Mykel called "Cut," Valentino fled to the shower. Valentino was humiliated. He knew he was awful. Vinnie took back every petty or jealous thought he had of Valentino Valdez, the promising newcomer. This was something Vinnie understood. He knew how it felt, hiding in the bathroom. He had hidden in bathrooms before, dreading the moment he would have to emerge and show his face. When Valentino eventually came out of the bathroom, Vinnie walked over and asked if they could take another selfie together. Vinnie kissed him on the cheek. SNAP! Vinnie offered and smiled, "I'll be able to say I knew you when."

Valentino offered that brilliant smile in return. He was stunning. That profile. Those lips. Those lashes. And above all, so soft and vulnerable. After a few selfies, Valentino had tears in his eyes. He knew Vinnie was trying to cheer him up. Valentino kissed him on the cheek. Vinnie snapped one last selfie to capture the moment. SNAP! The picture became his top post of the week on Instagram.

59

Two minutes before call time, there were footsteps on the stairs. The door whooshed open. Peter Ray Thomas stood there in the flesh. The creases in his skin were deeper. He looked weathered and rough but still sexy as fuck. The bad boy had tarnished into a nasty man. He wore the look of experience well.

"My ride got stuck in traffic," Peter had the voice of a man who had closed too many smoky bars. Thomas unfolded a sheet of paper and handed it to Mykel. "I need it signed. I have to be accountable for my day. Showing up. Sponsor crap."

Mykel unfolded the sheet. "Imagine, both of us, sober."

"I know. I don't think I've ever come to a set without a little something in my system."

"Understood." Mykel looked down at the sheet. "My sponsor can be a pain in the ass as well."

Peter ran a hand through his hair. "Nobody trusts me, and that's good because half the time I don't trust me."

"So, then you agree that it's okay if I sign this *after* you do what I am saying you are accountable for."

"Fair enough—and touché bitch!" Peter tossed an arm around Mykel. "I've missed you. We had so much fun, until it wasn't fun anymore. Sorry if I messed stuff up for you."

"Don't fret. I did fine messing up all on my own."

"But I did mess things up, didn't I?"

"Like nobody else," Mykel offered.

After how badly he screwed up, Peter admitted he was surprised when Woody called and offered him a role.

"He knows the business," said Mykel. "A lot of people are eager to see you back in a movie."

Peter shrugged. "Or to see me fail."

Mykel told him he couldn't think like that. "Woody is giving you a chance. He never hated you, he hated the drugs."

Vinnie knew otherwise. Woody had hated Peter Ray Thomas enough to plan his murder.

"And this," Mykel took a step back, "is your scene partner, Vinnie Lux."

"Nice to meet you, man."

"Likewise."

Peter offered a fist bump. "Hope I'm not too rusty, it's been a while."

Josh approached. "You remember Josh Lawless, right?"

"Hell yes!"

Josh grinned. "We go way back."

The two men bumped fists, elbows, and then hips.

Peter asked if there was coffee. When Gert brought him a cup, Peter asked where he could smoke.

Gert said there was smoking on the balcony.

Mykel started laughing, "Balcony? You know that's a fire escape, right?"

Vinnie liked Peter from the start. He was a good guy who made some bad choices. He was more than just the bad boy of XXX, and he wasn't even that bad anymore. The earnestness, humor, and intelligence that made Peter Ray Thomas a star were still evident. He oozed charisma. His fans and costars had wanted to save him. After arrests for possession and car theft, he was jailed for six months. Drugs hijacked his life until his options dwindled to overdose, prison, or recovery.

He chose to get straight.

When Peter went for a smoke, Josh whispered that Peter looked good.

Vinnie didn't expect to feel this attracted to his scene partner. Sure, he'd seen Thomas on screen, but meeting him in the flesh was an entirely different experience. Vinnie found himself *very* eager for filming to begin.

Before they started shooting, Peter told Vinnie he never thought he would make another movie. "Now I'm back."

The chemistry between Peter and Vinnie was electric—full of passion, energy, and spontaneity. Vinnie didn't feel much need to act. All the performing he had an urge to do felt very real. Mykel agreed and was wise enough to capture and not orchestrate their sexual dance. Peter and Vinnie laughed, wrestled, teased, and blazed until the crew and set faded, and then disappeared.

Afterwards, Mykel was effusive in his praise. He called the scene award-worthy and "a dick-dripping scorcher." Woody is going to be extremely pleased."

Hearing Mykel's praise felt great, but Vinnie didn't need to be told the scene was gold. *He knew.* He was in a different place when he heard Mykel yelling, "Cut!"

Mykel told Peter that he was better than ever. "No one is going to say you should have stayed away. You did it. Even better than when you started." Mykel leaned closer to him. "You did it straight, and you were better than ever."

"Thanks man, hearing that means a lot."

"Come here," said Mykel. The two men hugged. Breaking the embrace, Peter clapped him on the back. "We did it, buddy, you and me."

After the two men had their moment, Vinnie grabbed Gert. He asked the assistant to take a few pictures of him with Peter. Although Peter was initially hesitant, he eventually agreed.

Gert photographed them laughing, pretending to choke one another. In the second photo, Vinnie was licking Peter's ear. In the final shot, the two men stood facing one another, foreheads touching. Cropped at the rise of each man's ass, it was clear both were nude, dicks touching.

Before Vinnie could suggest another pose, Peter slapped Vinnie on the butt. "Great working with you Vinnie Lux. And thanks for making a day, which could have been tough, a lot easier. Much appreciated." Peter checked his phone. Two messages from Karl T. Vinnie suspected Karl T. was his sponsor or someone in NA. After that fuck session, Vinnie wanted to know everything about Peter Ray Thomas.

Josh looked at Vinnie and chuckled, "Oh, you're one of those."

"What?"

"Oh, you have been dickmatized by Peter Ray Thomas." Josh said that was why Peter remains a star. "He makes you believe it."

Vinnie hated to admit it, but Josh was right. Peter brought himself to the scene. Most performers bring their image.

But what if Peter wasn't just making me believe it? What if it was real?

Josh continued, "His eyes have that spark again. Drugs deadened them." Josh told Vinnie if he had designs on Peter, he needed to be patient. "Peter told me one of his sponsor's rules was no dating for a few more months. Apparently, relationships are a big trigger for him."

Life is a trigger.

Vinnie pinched Josh's butt. "My designs are none of your business. I hope that mark shows on camera."

Vinnie posted two pictures with Peter Ray Thomas with the hashtags: *#onthestrip*, *#xclusiv*, *#pornlegend*, *#peterraythomas*, and *#pornlegends*. The response to Vinnie's on-set pictures was terrific. He gained quite a few new fans by tagging his costars. By the time Vinnie was done posting, Peter had finished his call.

Vinnie asked if he wanted to grab a bite.

Peter declined. No explanation, just a simple, "No, but thank you."

After Mykel signed his accountability sheet, Peter took a quick shower. "Somebody is picking me up." Vinnie figured that whoever was picking him up was taking them both to a meeting.

"Great seeing everyone." Peter fist-bumped Josh and raised a hand to Gert and Sue before hugging Mykel, Josh, and Vinnie. Maybe it was his imagination, but Vinnie felt Peter held their hug the longest.

The final pairing for *On the Strip* was between Hank London and Josh Lawless. They had been on the couch talking all morning. Usually, Josh busied himself on a film set by flirting with everyone. Today it looked like Josh was focused on making Hank feel comfortable, though Hank already seemed at ease.

Vinnie took three candid shots of the two men. Then he took a shot of Mykel giving direction. Before posting, Vinnie cropped the picture to comply with community standards and tagged it, *#onthestrip*.

Josh and Hank's scene was set in the raspberry barroom. Hank was a patron, and Josh the bartender—and its closing time. "Let me just lock up."

The set-up was nothing original. Once the sex began, Hank went from somewhat quiet and reserved, to a sexual dynamo at the call for, *Action*. After taking turns with oral, Hank dove for Josh's ass. He pushed Josh's legs up to expose his ass and dove in, face first—licking, tonguing, tickling, and tapping with his fingers until Josh's eyes rolled back in his head. His cock was rock hard. Twitching. *Oh fuck!* Josh couldn't help himself. Before he knew it, his dick began to twitch. His load shot across his belly.

Mykel called "Cut."

Josh was red-faced. "Shit, I didn't mean to lose control like that, sorry."

"Nothing to apologize for." Mykel said that so far, the scene was a sizzler. "You think you can pop another load?"

Hank smiled and said that Josh would come again. The two men stepped closer and held eyes. Josh nodded in agreement. "A second load should be no problem."

Their wild fuck scene was still in progress when Vinnie left the studio. The three-day shoot had been exhausting. For two days, *On the Strip* looked as though it was destined to be nothing special. On the third day, everything turned around—Peter and Vinnie, now Josh and Hank. With these two additions, *On the Strip* had become something special—he didn't want to jinx it all by calling it a classic. Both of today's scenes were hotter than any of Vinnie's previous filming experiences.

Awaiting his Uber, Vinnie sent a text to Lee Botello. "Hey. Hope all is well. Film shoot went great today. Hey, do you have Peter Ray Thomas' phone number?"

The three dots of awaiting reply appeared a couple of minutes later. Lee responded with Peter's contact information along with the comment, "You got Peter fever? LOL."

After two cigarettes and a cocktail on the balcony, Vinnie sent Peter a text, "Hey, Vinnie Lux here. Got your number from Lee Botello. I had a great time filming today. Wondered if you want to hang out sometime?"

Vinnie worried it sounded too desperate—then stopped himself. He was thinking like Vincent—not like Vinnie. He was a porn star. He was Vinnie Lux—the text was eager and aggressive, not desperate. He was a sexual being. He didn't need to justify his desire. He had nine and a half reasons for wanting to stay in touch with Peter Ray Thomas.

60

After waiting for Peter to call, Vinnie took a Valium and went to his room. There were things to celebrate. Today was big. His scene with Peter Ray Thomas was going to be a classic. *Fingers-crossed.* His career was on track. A second Valium altered gravity. Vinnie became both heavy and light. Pure relaxation. Nestling into his pillows, he tried to keep positive thoughts in mind as he drifted off to sleep.

Vinnie slept ten hours and awoke groggy. Not hung over, just not awake. The buzz of his phone cut through his fog.

Ed Vittori congratulated Vinnie on the shoot. "Everyone is talking about the heat between you and Peter." Done with his praise, Ed got to his reason for calling. "We need a favor."

"By we you mean ..."

"Woody and the studio. We would like you to appear with one of your costars?"

Vinnie was confused. "Appear? Like another scene or another movie?"

"Nothing like that," Ed assured him. "We would like you to date one of your costars."

Vinnie didn't know what to say.

"This came right from Woody. I know he would be very appreciative."

"Sure, whatever the studio needs." Vinnie wasn't daft. This was no request. Vittori wasn't asking—he was giving Vinnie an order in the form of a question.

With a sigh, Ed Vittori continued. "Valentino Valdez felt very comfortable with you on the set. You remember how it was being new to it all—needing to get your name out there. Well, Valentino needs publicity. Woody said it would be a personal favor to him."

Maybe this favor would put him back in Woody's good graces.

Vittori said the studio would pick up the tab for everything.

Vinnie liked Valentino. The kid probably needed additional cheering up after his disastrous debut. Vinnie was planning to call him anyway to see if he wanted to have coffee. Now they could have a night out on the town—and on the studio's dime. This was a welcome favor.

"Response to the two of you together really registered." Ed cited the spiking numbers on Vinnie's account. 'This will help both of you as well as *On the Strip*. We'll be sure you two are seen and photographed." Vittori added that the onset pics were terrific. "There's buzz about this movie, and we just entered post-production."

"Whatever you need from me, just ask." Vinnie wanted to be sure his complete willingness was reported to Woody.

"That's why we thought of you, Vinnie. We know you're a team player."

"Absolutely!" Vinnie was excited about this. Vinnie was game for anything that meant more publicity and followers. They were his power. A studio date was really just a different sort of photo shoot. He and Valentino were friends pretending to be more. They were creating a narrative. Reality on social media had different parameters—and different rules. The way things appeared was more important than the way they were.

Vinnie assumed the date was also a form of damage control. Vinnie was certain that word got back to Woody about Valentino's crash and burn on camera. Xclusiv had investors and people to answer to. Studio backers might frown upon Woody signing the kid and flying him here. Especially when the results were mediocre at best. Profits were down. Bad time to make a bad investment. Woody could not afford to have Valentino turn out to be a disaster.

A fabricated affair with an established star accompanied by photos to showcase his beauty would help. Online popularity might save him. Vittori urged Valentino to consider sexing-up his Instagram and Twitter feeds. If porn didn't make him a star, social media might. Social media was a mighty beast.

Ed was still discussing an orchestrated build up. "We'll link your Instagram and Twitter accounts. Maybe a status change to—*It's Complicated*. Strategic leaks. The best publicity you can get is when people start talking. And we will make sure that they talk."

"That sounds great." As Vittori continued discussing the PR campaign, Vinnie realized that this phony romance might be a means to rebranding his persona. No more boy next door. That was Vinnie Lux, Act 1. The curtain was rising on Act 2. He saw the impact of romance on his feeds, but that sort of thing levels off in a bit. Instead, his plan was to become Vinnie Lux, Heartbreaker—eternal bachelor, ever available but unobtainable. Most guys have a thing for sexy studs that refuse to be penned.

This romance was going to be terrific publicity. It was simply a matter of making it believable. Everyone in this town used everyone else. Vinnie and Valentino were using each other, and the studio was using them both. That's how life played out in the business.

61

Two hours later, Vittori called back. He was agitated. No small talk this time. He needed another favor. "I have an eleventh hour job opportunity; can you help me out?"

"When is it?"

"This weekend."

"This weekend?"

"Trust me, last minute scrambling is not the way I like to do business." He said his ulcer hated it even more. "It's a good gig. Christian Sabre was supposed to work it, but he quit the business the day before yesterday."

"What?" Vinnie was surprised that Christian was so irresponsible. "Is everything okay?"

"I think so." Ed said that was how it usually happened.

"What?"

"Leaving the business. That's how guys usually leave the business—unless the business drops them first. Most quit out of the blue. One day they wake up and realize it's getting old or they're getting old. For whatever reason it all starts getting to them. Maybe the thrill is gone. *Whatever.* If that's how they feel, I'm happy they are moving on—but half the time that decision leaves me scrambling to put out a fire."

Vinnie had no idea. "I can't imagine doing that."

"Neither could most of them if you asked a month before," added Ed. "They can't imagine doing it, until they are in the middle of doing it."

Vinnie asked about the gig.

"Studio party in Palm Springs. Lots of fun and easy money."

Getting out of the city for a day or two sounded fabulous. Vinnie asked if he had heard anything more about Christian.

"He said the traveling and the pace were getting to him. He's ready for a simpler life. Doesn't even want to dance at clubs. Like I said, same old story." Ed understood, "As I said, I'm just not thrilled with the lack of notice. But thanks to you, that is solved."

Vinnie thought that Christian was being impulsive—no more movies, no more appearances, no more followers—no more dancing on a pedestal. Vinnie was sure Christian would eventually regret his decision.

Vinnie could not imagine returning to a quiet life. This Xclusiv world was complicated and potentially treacherous, but the payoff was worth it. Vinnie liked being somebody. There was no feeling like it.

Ed explained the gig. "For the past few years, Xclusiv had been a presence at the White Party in Palm Springs, sponsoring a pool party/tea dance and an A-list fundraiser. This year's charity recipient was the AIDS Alternative Wellness Foundation. The event was great exposure. Mostly you'll be standing at the entrance to the party and applying the temporary admission tattoos," Vittori laughed, "They love the porn boys, and like I said, that crowd tips."

Ed quoted the handsome appearance fee. Vittori was well aware that Vinnie was looking for work. On top of it, he had three times the number of social media followers as Christian, so why was he only being approached now? As an exclusive, Vinnie felt he should have been a top choice. Not a last-minute replacement for Christian. He would discuss this with Vittori after the event.

Vinnie and Dean got up at four o'clock in the morning to get there on time. Both men slept the entire way. The driver startled both of them when he announced they were there. After dropping off their things in the room as well as a wake-up shower, the two porn stars slipped on their Xclusiv speedos and went to the studio's display.

It was not hard to find. An enormous balloon cluster bearing the company logo formed an arch over the entrance to the studio's pool party and tea dance. The walls on either side were adorned with the posters of recent studio releases, including *Backfield in Motion* and *Mancandy 2*. Also on the wall were two full-body shots of Vinnie and Dean with an IN PERSON banner crossing their chests.

By eleven o'clock, Vinnie and Dean were standing on either side of the entrance, glazed in glitter and wearing wet white speedos. Vinnie took a selfie of the two of them and posted it on his socials with the hashtags: *#speedoheat*, *#palmspringsheat*, and *#xclusivpalmsprings*.

He used the same hashtags when posting a second and a third photo from the event. Vinnie was proud of his Instagram feed. His life looked so exciting— beautiful, sexy, and full of sparkle. He tagged the studio and Dean.

Vinnie and Dean's primary duty of the day was to apply the temporary tattoos for party admittance. Moments into the job, Vinnie realized the size of the tip was proportional to the sexiness of his tattoo application. The upper thigh was a popular application spot.

On his private account, Vinnie posted a shot of Dean's erection wedged into his tiny transparent suit. That squeeze was something to see. Those Speedo seams were put to the test. Dean said he liked it when guys eyed his crotch. This party was a solid sea of pumped-up shirtless watchers—muscled, moneyed, and hungry.

Vinnie and Dean received a dozen invitations to private parties. There were offers of personal services and party favors. During a break in the line, Dean turned to Vinnie. "While we're here, why not hit a private party, or two—for a fee. Plenty of money to be had here, especially for guys with a following." Dean said it was safer to work together. "In case things get weird."

Dean offered him some molly. Vinnie put the tablet on his tongue. After a half hour, Vinnie told Dean that picking up some extra cash was a great idea. "And these guys are all so nice." Call it molly, ecstasy, or MDMA—it was the miracle drug for social anxiety. "I love feeling like this," Vinnie said.

Dean laughed. "I'll see if I can negotiate an invitation. We are going to have a very profitable weekend."

After their duties as temporary studio tattooists were finished for the day, Dean and Vinnie ducked into their suite. Vinnie wanted a quick shower. "Out in two minutes."

Dean slipped off his speedo and began swinging his hips from side to side in front of the mirror. His cock slapped either thigh, pumping it up, and bringing more blood to that sweet slab of meat. Dean grabbed a jock from his backpack. "No shower for me. I'm just going to slip this on and go." Dean said being a little funky usually worked in his favor.

The shower was amazing, especially with the molly. Vinnie felt each of the sixteen water jets hit his skin. He felt the weight of his damp hair and knew the trail of every rivulet of water coursing down his frame. Glitter still twinkled on his skin. The shampoo smelled incredible. The soap was so soft. Distraction came easily.

After ten minutes, Dean reached around the bathroom door and flipped the overhead light on and off. "Vinnie Lux, we need to go." Dean was texting with a couple of guys. "Bidding war," he said, nodding to his phone.

By the time Vinnie was ready, Dean said they were expected ASAP at a bungalow on the compound. Dean had negotiated a hefty fee for them to be at this orgy.

When Dean told him the amount, Vinnie's eyes widened at the sum. "Each?"

Dean referred to the Palm Springs White Party working boy paradise. "Lots of money, lots of drugs, lots of flash and one-upmanship. And to our benefit there are also plenty of daddies with something to prove—and plenty of money to prove it with."

As Vinnie dried himself, Dean explained that it was some guy's fiftieth birthday. "A bunch of his friends are throwing him an orgy, with us as the guests of honor."

"A birthday orgy with friends?" Vinnie found it difficult to imagine.

"To each his own." Dean took Vinnie's speedo off the floor and took a deep whiff. Eyes closed. Another sniff. Deeper. Dean seemed a connoisseur. Chest swelling. Eyes still closed. Hand moving down, adjusting his junk. "You have got some pungent junk Vinnie Lux—you could bottle this stuff." Dean gave his cock a squeeze. "We should make candles with a musky junk smell." Dean was high. He tossed Vinnie his speedo before slipping into his black jockstrap. "We good to go?"

On the way to the bungalow, Vinnie stopped and abruptly said, "I think I saw ball scented candles at a place on Santa Monica."

Dean asked what the hell he was talking about.

"Ball scented candles. I think I saw them at a shop on Santa Monica."

"You're high," Dean laughed, "follow me." Dean led them down a path, beyond the pool, and around the back. A man of sixty or so with a deep tan and a saggy ass answered the door. He smelled of Old Spice and skin tags. He gave a name that Vinnie forgot almost immediately. He handed them each the agreed-on sum before taking Dean's jock and Vinnie's speedo.

"Can you hold on to the money until we leave?" asked Dean. "We're naked."

"Yeah, of course," the man rolled his eyes. "What was I thinking?"

A group of other older men were in the sunken living room. One of them finally shouted over, "Oh my god Reggie, this is an orgy. Quit behaving like you're Emily Post. Hello guys, pleased to meet you. Come meet the gang."

The music was loud, and the host was drunk. These men had been partying a while. There were five of them. They seemed like great guys—but molly loves everyone. Lots of dilated pupils in the crowd. Their looks of lust were undisguised. Someone nodded to the dresser. "Help yourself. There's plenty to drink. We have everything."

Even naked, these guys looked rich. Maybe it was the gold chains or the veneers or the butt implants or facial fillers or how they carried themselves. The men were watching Dean and Vinnie in *Prime Meat* and stroking their cocks. As they joined the group, the men looked from Vinnie and Dean to the TV and back. Eventually, someone began stroking Dean's cock. Once the first move was made, a wave of bronze and gray converged upon them.

Most of them were intent on impressing Vinnie and Dean— performing for them as well as on them. That often happens when a guy wants to fuck a porn star. And there were five of them. They wanted Dean and Vinnie to squeal and beg and come in buckets. They were relentless. *Sucking. Munching. Jacking. Tweaking. Kissing. Tongue trails. Nipple play. Filth talk. Fingering. Fucking.*

The orgy was no holds barred, until the paramedics were called. In the middle of giving Dean's balls a tongue bath, the birthday boy stood. He was sweating profusely and looking as pale as a deeply tanned man possibly can. His cronies thought he was having a heart attack.

Medical personnel were nearby. Twenty minutes earlier, there was a potential overdose at a PnP party at a bungalow across the pool. Birthday boy was luckier than the other guy. Birthday Boy had simply overindulged.

Dean had scheduled something for them later as well. Vinnie was exhausted, but Dean gave him another pill. "You just need to recharge. We don't have to go for another hour. Want to suck my cock until then."

Instead, Vinnie curled into him on the sofa. He needed a warm body beside him that had nothing to do with hard cocks or achieving orgasm. He just wanted to synchronize his breathing with someone. Surprisingly, Dean seemed intuit what he needed. They were on the couch the entire hour, listening to the outside sounds, and saying nothing.

62

By the time they returned to WeHo on Monday, Dean and Vinnie were zombies. The weekend in Palm Springs had been long, decadent, and extremely profitable. Vinnie had known that Dean's bumpkin bit was an act, but he had no idea that Dean was such a skilled negotiator.

Dean had the driver drop off Vinnie first.

Vinnie turned to him, "Aren't you coming up?"

Dean had somewhere he needed to be.

A weekend of sex, drugs, and booze in the desert had left Vinnie feeling as though he had been beaten and forced to eat sand—but the money and the bump in followers made it all worthwhile.

Entering their flat, Vinnie took a couple of aspirin and went straight to bed. His head ached. His eyes ached. He needed sleep.

A couple of hours later he awoke in a daze. He stumbled to the bathroom to take a leak. When the blower for the central air paused, Vinnie was struck by the silence of the apartment. Dean's door was open. He must still be out doing whatever it was that he needed to do. No sign of Kip either. Vinnie drank three glasses of water and started coffee. He sat in the shade of the back fire escape and smoked a cigarette.

Being home felt good despite Vinnie's concerns over having Kip as a roommate. So far, Kip hadn't been around the apartment much at all. And whenever Kip was home, it seemed he was usually on his way somewhere else in a moment. Kip kept his bedroom door closed. When he left the flat, he tended to lock it.

Vinnie poured a cup of coffee. On the way back to his room, he knocked on Kip's door. *No answer.* He turned the knob. *Unlocked.* Vinnie looked inside. Kip's room was very tidy. The only thing even slightly unusual were some papers on the dresser beneath a pocketful of change. The pages were face down. Vinnie slid the coins off the papers just as the central air kicked in. Through the hum, he heard the faint jingle of keys at the lock. Sliding the coins back as best he could, Vinnie backed into the hall and gently closed the door.

"How was the weekend?"

Vinnie raised his coffee mug to Kip. "Exhausting."

Kip passed him in the hall and opened his bedroom door. His eyes went to the papers on the dresser. He walked over and looked down at the coins. Kip slid the change into his hand and put it in his front pocket. He then folded the papers and put them in his back pocket. "You must have made that coffee strong—I can even smell it in here."

Moments later, Vinnie was at the kitchen counter when Kip announced that he needed to get back to the studio. Before leaving, Kip checked that his bedroom door was locked.

After another cigarette on the fire escape, Vinnie brought his coffee cup back to the kitchen. He grabbed his phone from the counter. Although his mind was still cloudy, Vinnie could have sworn he had left it in his bedroom.

Vinnie checked his messages. He had not heard back from Peter Ray Thomas. Vinnie respected his recovery—but Peter also lived in WeHo. Only a straight sponsor would equate hookups with being in a relationship. Abstinence is not the opposite of a relationship—Grindr is. Vinnie wasn't looking for a ring from Peter Ray Thomas, just a repeat performance.

Ed Vittori had texted him and asked how things went in Palm Springs. Vinnie responded, "Great."

Moments after Vinnie sent the message, Vittori phoned. "So it went well?"

"Dean and I had a great time." Vittori did not need to know about the side money. "The crowd loved the Xclusiv party. Everyone was talking about it."

"And they loved you and Dean as well." Vittori added.

Vinnie was pleased that Vittori had heard positive reports, but there was something about the way Ed said it that made Vinnie uneasy. Being watched seemed the same as being under surveillance.

Vittori said Vinnie's uptick in followers was impressive. "And this weekend people were tagging you right and left."

Of course, Vinnie knew about his social media numbers. He checked them several times a day. He had learned what posts brought the most traffic to his page and which brought the most follows. His fans used likes and comments to tell him what they wanted his world to be. They wanted muscles, sweat, parties, revelry, desire, and skin.

"According to the numbers," added Ed, "Everyone wants to see what is happening in the fabulous daily life of a gorgeous porn star."

"My daily life is not that fabulous."

Ed laughed. "True, but this isn't life, it's social media."

Vittori was also calling to discuss Vinnie's date with Valentino Valdez.

Vinnie had forgotten that was tomorrow

"The driver has been scheduled. Dinner reservations have been made."

Vinnie had not heard of the restaurant.

"Then afterwards a couple of hotspots."

Vinnie grabbed his cigarettes and headed for the balcony.

"This date is about being seen and photographed," added Vittori.

Vinnie was looking forward to seeing Valentino. They had some common interests, and Vinnie had enjoyed his company. The icing on the cake was that seeing Valentino would also mean a bump in likes and follows.

Vittori added that he had arranged for several bloggers to "leak" photos. "We control the narrative. We control the optics. Leaking the story makes it exciting. Press releases are obsolete in this day and age." Vittori told Vinnie to pick Valentino up at Woody's compound at seven.

"Got it."

Ed added that he had seen Vinnie on *Between the Sheets with Dorian.* "That was an interesting episode."

Vinnie took a drag off his smoke. "What made it so interesting?" After their playtime with Hector, Dorian had guaranteed Vinnie that he would be pleased with the final cut of the episode.

"It was just interesting to hear your take on things."

Vinnie had no idea what Vittori was talking about. *What had he said on the show?* He recalled Dorian asking about the Rex Reynolds upload. "I guess I'm not the best at live chats."

"You did fine, but you're at a different level now. You're an exclusive. The bigger you get, the louder your voice becomes. At Xclusiv, we don't speak of competition or rivalry within the studio family. Don't worry, it's not a big deal."

Yet it was significant enough to discuss.

Vinnie stubbed out his smoke and lit another. If Vittori was bringing this up to him that probably meant that Woody was pissed. Dorian had claimed that he had Vinnie's back. *If you can't trust a porn industry gossip columnist, whom can you trust?* Vinnie could kick himself. He was such a fool sometimes.

"You just need coaching on what to say and not to say. No matter, it's done now." Vittori reiterated the details of the date. Vinnie was not surprised when Ed said he would be at the restaurant to make sure everything went smoothly.

After hanging up, Vinnie recalled that he was also supposed to start at Trusted Talents tomorrow evening. *Fuck!* He couldn't call Vittori back now and tell him to change everything. Instead, Vinnie phoned the agency.

"Hello Mr. Lux. This is Jean." The voice was neutral, sexy, and smoky.

"Jean, I'm to speak to you regarding scheduling issues?"

"That is correct," they replied.

"I have an engagement tomorrow and I won't be able to socialize." Vinnie opted to call it socializing, at least on the telephone.

"No need for the call. Mr. Novak is aware of the date with Mr. Valdez. It's on your schedule. You are to pick up Mr. Valdez on Skyway Drive tomorrow at seven. Good luck on your first appointment."

"Okay, thank you." Vinnie stammered. He was so shocked he couldn't think of anything else to say. *What the fuck? His date with Valentino Valdez had been scheduled through Trusted Talents?*

"Will there be anything else, Mr. Lux. May I be of any further service?"

By then Vinnie was trying to breathe through his anxiety. "No Jean, you've been very helpful." The conversation upset Vinnie more than he cared to admit.

63

The moment he stepped from the car in Woody's driveway, Vinnie felt he was being watched. Glare on the upper windows in the main house made it impossible to see anything too clearly, but for a split second, Vinnie thought he spied a silhouette in the office window. Probably Kip—watering plants, or cleaning the pool, or delivering dry cleaning, or picking up parrot shit. Maybe tonight, Kip had watchdog duty. Vinnie looked to the window. The glass mirrored a hazy sky.

Vittori texted Vinnie to let him know the reservation at the restaurant had been pushed back an hour. Ed and Woody were still at the studio with the rough cut of *On the Strip*. Vittori sent an accompanying text that the driver would wait for them.

Vinnie crossed to the casita. As far as he knew, Roy was the last person to stay there before Valentino. Still no word from Roy. He had all but disappeared after voicing suspicions about A.Z.'s death. He even went so far as to make Vinnie swear to silence. Days later, Roy made the urgent call to Vinnie about something too sensitive to discuss on the phone. Then, when he finally texted, it was two simple words—"never" and "mind." Butt dials. The parrot. And then, Roy texted Dean, whom he barely knows, to divide A.Z.'s things amongst them. Then Roy left town. No goodbye. No call. No forwarding address. He even discontinued use of this phone. Roy had either gone missing, or he was in hiding. And no one else seemed to notice or care.

Vinnie saw Valentino through a downstairs window. The evening sun played upon his dark curls. His black lashes were so long and lush that they cast shadows. Valentino was even more beautiful than Vinnie had remembered.

Valentino smiled to see Vinnie at the door. Vinnie gave him a peck on the cheek and told him the reservation had moved back an hour.

Valentino asked if he wanted a drink, but admitted he wasn't much of a bartender. Vinnie went behind the bar and mixed them a couple of gin and tonics, ideal in the heat. He gave Valentino a heavy pour. Behind the bottles was a partial pack of smokes. Vinnie lifted the pack and asked if he could bum one. Valentino said they weren't his, but to go ahead. "Someone before me must have left them here, so I doubt it would matter."

Roy smoked, but did he smoke Marlboro reds?

Vinnie slipped the pack into his pocket as they took their drinks beside the pool. With the sun low in the sky, the air was finally beginning to cool. Vinnie leaned back and closed his eyes. He felt the breeze on his face and reminded Valentino of their discussion about old Hollywood. "I enjoyed talking about that with you."

"Yes, yes. I remember it well."

The two men spent the next half an hour in an animated conversation about movies and Hollywood. Valentino seemed the bigger film fan, but not by much.

Vinnie asked Valentino what he had seen since being in L.A.

"Very little," Valentino blushed. He said he was staying here and that made it difficult. He shared that mostly he hadn't seen anything because he did not want to go sightseeing alone.

Vinnie said he would be happy to see Hollywood with him.

Valentino's smile was dimpled and brilliant. He smiled with his eyes. "I would like that."

Valentino's accent was so sexy, and the conversation flowed effortlessly. Valentino was friendly and unguarded with an easy laugh. His lack of self-absorption was refreshing. Valentino seemed neither overly ambitious or desperate—nor was he vain or vapid. But L.A. had a way of changing people.

Seeing the house reflected in Valentino's sunglasses, Vinnie recalled the feeling of being watched. He turned to Valentino. "Is anyone around today up at the house," he said with a head tilt.

Valentino said that he had seen no one. "I was here since the morning. I spent most of the day floating in the pool."

In a few moments, their drinks needed freshening.

Vinnie asked to see the rest of the casita.

Valentino said giving him a tour would be his pleasure. European graciousness was so refreshing in Southern California. Moving through the modest rooms, Vinnie saw nothing that might be Roy's. A partial pack of Marlboros meant little to nothing.

Vittori texted. "Photographer running late. Wait another half hour before leaving. The driver has been notified."

After informing Valentino of the additional delay, Vinnie said he had been at a pool party two months ago at Woody's and may have left a Swatch by one of the pool chairs. "Is there some sort of place for people who leave things here?"

"A lost and found? I have no idea." Valentino then gestured towards the low stucco structure to the far right of the pool. "Maybe in the pool house."

"Since we have a couple of minutes, do you mind if I go take a quick peek?"

It sounded plausible.

"Not at all," said Valentino, settling back into his chair.

The pool house was in the shade of several low trees. *Locked.* Vinnie located the key above the doorframe. When the door sputtered open, Vinnie was hit by a blast of stale air and heat, along with the overwhelming scent of pool chemicals. Slanted sunlight cut through the panes and shadows. Seasons of dust and cobwebs cloaked the room. No pool parties lately. Among the stored items and junk were old planters and a stack of wooden planks. There were two mostly deflated rafts, a filthy patio umbrella, discarded tools, and two foam noodles. Vinnie cleared the dust from a game of cornhole and chuckled. The artwork on each was a man's hairy ass and thighs. The six-inch opening on each angled board was an asshole. The beanbags were beside the boards—red and blue and shaped like dicks. On the far wall, a bicycle with a flat back tire was propped beside a door. The one clear path on the floor led in that direction. This door was locked as well. No key above the frame.

Vinnie's phone pinged. A text from Vittori. "Photographer arrived. Please head to the car." With one last look around the pool house, Vinnie closed and locked the door, and replaced the key. He met Valentino by the patio door.

"Did you find your Swatch?"

"Nope, it wasn't my favorite one anyway." Vinnie said they should leave.

Despite all the insanity, Vinnie felt himself smiling. He liked Valentino, and now they would be seeing the sights of Hollywood together. Vinnie had made no real friends since moving here. Even A.Z. and Gio were primarily roommates. And even though Vinnie had been in L.A. for several months, he had not seen many of the sights either. Most of what he saw was what he had passed on his jogs. Seeing Hollywood with Valentino would be a welcome reprieve from the more stressful areas of his life.

Around the upcoming curve was the site of the accident that allegedly took the life of Carter Gaines. Although Vinnie said nothing, as the car neared the spot, Valentino took his hand. By the time Vinnie started to feel anxious about passing the crash site, it was already in the rearview mirror.

As the car turned off Skyway Drive, Vinnie looked into Valentino's eyes. *Deep brown with flecks of gold—the color of warmth.* Vinnie put a hand on his thigh. Valentino covered Vinnie's hand with his own. Intertwining fingers and leaning in, Vinnie kissed him. The driver was watching. After the kiss, they went back to holding hands. Valentino tucked a tuft of hair behind Vinnie's ear. Tonight he was going to forget about Trusted Talents, A.Z. and Roy, and all about that fucking notebook.

Vinnie had forgotten how nice it felt to relax with someone. He had not felt this way since coming to Hollywood. He never relaxed around Woody. He didn't even relax much around Glenn. He was always trying to be what they wanted him to be.

At the restaurant, they smiled for pictures and took selfies with fans. Vinnie checked out the room. He recognized a couple of bloggers. Vittori was at the bar looking very pleased with himself. Except for the late start, all was going according to plan.

Vittori sent a text. "Big influencers are at the table to your right."

When Vinnie saw the message, he turned off his phone.

They were on the VIP list at Sound Revolution. As they entered the club, more guys approached them for selfies—being loud, drawing attention. Vinnie recognized one of the "fans" as a One-on-One guy. Vittori wanted to guarantee that they made an entrance. After a few drinks, they headed to the Blaze for a nightcap.

The bar was packed. The weekly drag revue had ended moments before, so everyone was clamoring for cocktails. Leon saw them come in and had their server comp their drinks. When their cocktails arrived, Vinnie and Valentino toasted Leon.

At the Blaze, music dominated all. Conversation of any sort was difficult to impossible. After a couple of dances, both men knew where this night would be ending. By the time they left the bar an hour later, Vinnie and Valentino just wanted to be alone. Vinnie sent a text to the driver.

Before heading to the casita, Vinnie asked the driver to stop at the studio flat. "I'll be a few." Vinnie needed to grab some things. Valentino asked if he could use the bathroom. As they got out of the car, the driver caught Vinnie's eye. Vinnie reiterated they would be back in a few minutes.

They kissed in the elevator. He played with Valentino's nipples through his dress shirt.

No one was home, but the place smelled like weed. Loosened by booze, Valentino gestured to the air. "So this is your place?"

"I live here. The studio owns it. I share it with Dean Driver and Kip Mason. Bathroom is right there." Vinnie put a few things in a backpack and was coming out of his bedroom as Valentino finished washing his hands.

They kissed on the elevator down. They would have done more, but an elderly gentleman got on. Vinnie and Valentino were back at the car in less than seven minutes.

The driver gave Vinnie a look that he didn't understand.

Did he think they weren't coming back?

On the way to the casita, backseat kisses became heavy petting. Nipple play. Vinnie's dick was so hard that it hurt. Valentino unzipped his fly and slipped Vinnie's pants to his knees. He hooked the waistband of Vinnie's briefs beneath his nuts. Valentino ran his tongue along the shaft before taking Vinnie's cock to the base. He massaged with his throat as his mouth rose in unison with his hand. The momentum continued. Vinnie ran his fingers through Valentino's hair. Holy fuck! Valentino knew what he was doing. The driver was watching in the rearview. Vinnie caught his eye. He was getting off on this. His cock was probably pressing against the bottom of the steering wheel, making some sweet friction on that hard plastic. Holding the driver's eye, Vinnie moved a hand from Valentino's curls, down his back and below the waistband of his briefs.

Valentino was riding two fingers and still sucking cock by the time the car came to a stop outside the casita. The driver watched as the men straightened themselves. "Have fun tonight," Vinnie said, sniffing his fingers as he closed the car door. He suspected the driver was hoping for an invitation—instead he got blue balls.

Once through the door of the casita, the two men shucked their shoes. Next came a trail of discarded socks. They undid their belts, unzipped their pants, and shed them at the bedroom door. Naked except for their unbuttoned shirts, both men fell onto the bed laughing.

Vinnie was stroking him and fucking him. Both faster. Then fucking slower. Valentino was rock hard. He was getting close. Vinnie felt Valentino stiffen and then warmth on his hand. A moment later, Vinnie came inside him. No money shot. This was a private moment. In the aftermath, they lay in silence until their breathing aligned.

Five minutes later, Vinnie needed to pee. After taking a leak, Vinnie checked his breath. Not great. Vinnie looked beneath the sink—toothbrushes still in the package. How many houseguests did Woody have?

Vinnie grabbed the toothpaste from the medicine cabinet. Behind the tube was a pill bottle made out to Roy Campbell—and it was far from empty. Wherever Roy went, Vinnie doubted he would leave behind a half-used bottle of HIV meds.

64

Vinnie slipped on his jeans and slid Roy's prescription bottle into his front pocket. He tapped a cig from the pack of Marlboro reds. Maybe they belonged to Roy, or maybe not. The prescription bottle was his—and something he would not leave behind. Vinnie sat by the pool and smoked. The main house was dark. He could smell Valentino on his skin.

By the time Vinnie was on his second cup of coffee, Valentino was stirring. He slid open the patio door. Valentino was naked and so damn gorgeous in the morning.

Valentino said he had a wonderful time last night. He kissed Vinnie and asked him if he wanted to stay by the pool all day. "It is going to be so hot."

Vinnie lied and said he had to get home for an interview. He needed time to think things through. The date with Valentino had been terrific—but so many things going on around Vinnie were not terrific, and they were becoming more puzzling every day.

Their kiss goodbye lasted until the Uber arrived.

On the way back to the flat, Vinnie received three Google alerts for new Vinnie Lux content on the Internet. News and photos from his date with Valentino were starting to surface.

Vinnie's phone chirped. Caller I.D. flashed Leon. Vinnie thought it was going to be something about his upcoming gig at the Blaze. "Hey, Leon."

"Vinnie, we have a problem."

Not even a hello.

"A problem?" Vinnie was confused.

"We thought you understood. We thought the rules were clear." When Vinnie failed to respond Leon elaborated. "Last night you brought a client to your home."

"Only for five minutes."

"Seven." Leon added that the rule was for his own safety.

Vinnie was blindsided by the overreaction to what happened. "I just needed to get a couple things and he needed to use the bathroom."

Leon started to sigh in the middle of Vinnie's explanation. Evidently, Vinnie's excuse was unacceptable. "Mr. Novak expects obedience."

The driver with blue balls had ratted on him. Vinnie wondered if all this would be happening if he had invited the driver inside. Novak had probably heard all about the backseat blowjob and the finger-fuck.

Leon continued. "As you were told before, never bring a client to your residence. If you don't like the rules, Mr. Novak suggests you try elsewhere."

This entire thing was ridiculous, but Vinnie also knew the best way to defuse this nonsense was to profusely apologize. "I'm sorry. I wasn't thinking."

"Then be more aware. We're only thinking of you," Leon added.

Vinnie doubted Trusted Talents gave a shit about his welfare. He had met Novak. Fancy clothes can't disguise a thug. The rule was about control. If the boys took dates home, it would be easy to make future appointments on their own. Novak's concern was for his cut.

Leon said he needed to go. "Jean will be with you in a minute."

Leon put him on hold without a goodbye.

"Mr. Lux?" Vinnie recognized Jean's voice. "You are to be here at eleven-thirty, two hours from now. Be sure you are prompt." Their voice was firm, and the message was punctuated by a dial tone.

Vinnie arrived at the Trusted Talents building at ten minutes after eleven.

Before leaving the flat, he took one of A.Z.'s Xanax.

When he arrived at the office, Jean nodded for him to take a seat.

At precisely eleven-thirty, Jean returned.

"You're lucky, Mr. Novak isn't usually so forgiving."

Jean ushered Vinnie to a conference room.

Loosened by the Xanax, and trying to mend the situation, Vinnie said he was grateful to have been forgiven. "I mean, you have to know this is the best game in town."

Jean did not respond.

Vinnie looked around the room and asked if Mr. Novak would be joining them.

"He will not." Jean took a seat at the far end of the table. "From now on you will be dealing with me in all Trusted Talents matters. Things regarding the Blaze you will discuss with Leon. Do you understand the difference? Is that clear?"

Vinnie nodded.

"Mr. Novak instructed me to be sure you understand everything, so I am going to read it aloud. And afterwards, you will need to sign and date this list. If you do not fully understand any rule, please stop me and I will give you a fuller explanation. Is that clear?"

This was humiliating. He was being treated like an idiot. Jean began to read the rules. Vinnie had seen the rules sheet clipped to his contract but didn't pay attention. Jean was making sure he paid attention now. After reading each rule, Jean paused to see if Vinnie understood before continuing to the next. Reading the fifth and final rule, Jean asked Vinnie if he had any questions. "No further transgressions from these rules will be tolerated." Jean slid something from the manila folder they were carrying. Vinnie turned it over. It was an 8x10 of Rex Reynolds. "Shame about Rex, don't you think?"

Vinnie nodded.

Jean told him to think carefully before answering, "Is there anything you need to tell me?"

Jean was trying to read him.

Thank God for Xanax.

"Mr. Novak considers anything less than complete cooperation to be treason."

Vinnie knew what he needed to say. "As he should." Vinnie repeated that he knew nothing about the uploaded video. "But if I hear of anything I'll let you know."

Jean was still watching him. "See that you do."

Vinnie was desperate for a smoke. Tapping out the last Marlboro, Vinnie was about to crumple the pack when he noticed a piece of paper inside. On one side was the number and address for Grundella Services, and on the other was the contact info for Paragon Optics.

He had no proof that the partial pack belonged to Roy, but to his knowledge, no one else had stayed at Woody's guesthouse recently other than Valentino, who doesn't smoke. However, this pack was not that old. The cigarettes were still fairly fresh.

Maybe Roy had job interviews at those places. There was only one way to find out. Lighting the last of the smokes, he telephoned each company. Neither number was in service. He searched the Internet. No trace of either business— none at all. *Ever.* The street number on San Vincente for Paragon Optics didn't even exist.

65

Reed and Dean were on the couch when Vinnie came through the door after another date with Valentino. Reed said something about the smile plastered across Vinnie's face. His wisecracks did not dampen Vinnie's glow.

Vinnie's second date with Valentino was on Friday. They had planned on sightseeing, but when Vinnie came to pick him up, they never made it out the door. Instead, they had sex and hung out by the pool. Both men got a little sunburned, but neither man got tan lines.

On date three, they met for breakfast. "If I come to your place, we'll never get out of the house." Vinnie was only half joking. Served by a waiter whose surliness gave them the giggles, the men planned their day of sightseeing over omelets and coffee. Their day of adventure was more fun than either imagined. Both were game for anything. Nothing was too touristy. They began by comparing hand and footprints at TLC Chinese Theater.

Valentino's hands were identical to those of Red Skelton.

Click!

Vinnie's feet were the size of Gable's.

Click!

At the Hollywood Wax Museum, they mugged for photos with Marilyn, Crawford, and Bogart.

Click. Click. Click.

Being silly was the perfect therapy—there was nothing like being silly with Valentino. They crouched on the sidewalk to pose with the inlaid stars of several celebrities on the Hollywood Walk of Fame. Tyrone Power. Mae West. Lucy. Bette. Liza.

Click. Click. Click. Click. Click.

Being with Valentino was so easy. He could relax. He didn't need to be Vinnie Lux. He could be a clown, a romantic, or a geek. He could act like an idiot with Valentino—because with Valentino, Vinnie never felt like an idiot. He could relax and act like himself. And that was no longer Vincent either.

They explored side streets and curio shops. Both bought music to remind them of the day. Vinnie posted pictures on Instagram. #bestdayever #pornlove

At some point Vinnie forgot about posting photos to social media. It was ten at night by the time they returned to the casita for a naked swim. Afterwards, they toweled off one another. Vinnie poured them both some wine before they headed to bed. Neither man was thinking about sleep.

Reed looked up when he saw Vinnie come through the door. "Hey stranger," Reed was beside Dean on the couch.

"I'm only here to shower and change."

"Oh, off again?" Reed wanted details and for once, Vinnie didn't mind giving them to him.

"Yes, I'm going to Hollywood Forever Cemetery—with Valentino." The excitement in Vinnie's voice was apparent.

"Oh my." Reed enjoyed practicing bitchcraft. "Things seem to be developing quickly between you and this Valentino character. Do we need to get you fitted for an IUD?"

"You just keep doing whatever you are doing Reed. And while you are busy doing that, I'll be looking at some final resting places of the stars."

Reed shook his head. It was impossible to get a rise from a love-struck boy. "You are such a dork."

"Yeah, I guess I am." Vinnie said, heading down the hallway to the bathroom.

Hopping into the shower, Vinnie began to soap himself. He recalled the blowjob Valentino had given him beside the pool. The sun had been in Vinnie's eyes. He closed them tight—a black screen with explosions of red and purple. Valentino on his knees. Vinnie face-fucking him gently, then harder.

His eyes opened. He wanted to watch.

Vinnie put his fingers in Valentino's hair. The sun made it shine. Vinnie threw back his head. The windows of the big house reflected the golden haze of the wildfires.

Vinnie pulled Valentino off his pulsing cock. He motioned for him to pause. Vinnie knelt beside him on the patio stone. The two men held each other tightly. They deep kissed and rolled onto the stone. Their sweat and suntan oil-slickened bodies glided repeatedly over one another. Their cocks pulsed, growing harder with the glorious friction, bringing them both to the edge. Such delicious pleasure and heat. Valentino on top, sliding over Vinnie. Sweat and weight and movement—so much precum. They blasted hard. The only way to stay on the earth was to hold the other tighter.

Vinnie was standing in the shower, rock hard. Lathering had become something more. He turned the water temp to cold for a few seconds until his erection subsided. Vinnie would rather share his load with Valentino.

Vinnie regretted that he was meeting Valentino at a pivotal point in his career. His head needed to be in the game—not in the clouds. In five years, he would be ready for a serious romance. By then Vinnie hoped to be managing his own career. Whatever this was with Valentino was still in the honeymoon phase. Vinnie knew how this ended, and he didn't want that for Valentino or himself. He needed to end this soon, but not today. He was eager to see this cemetery. He was already committed to doing it. Besides, there were graves he wanted to see—Jayne Mansfield, Estelle Getty, Mel Blanc, Cecil B. DeMille, Marion Davies, and even Valentino's namesake, Rudolph Valentino.

Today was not the day. It was wrong to break up with anyone in a cemetery. If that was not a superstition, Vinnie felt that it should be.

Vinnie and Valentino were a hit on social media. Romance is photogenic. They were a hashtag: *#Vinnitino*. People commented on their posts with heart emojis. Dozens of followers were coming by the hour. Vinnie knew that eventually, fans would grow bored with *#Vinnitino*. Once this romance began its inevitable downward turn, Vinnie would end it.

One afternoon he and Valentino lay naked across the bed. Vinnie had his laptop open. They were lying close, looking for a bed and breakfast. They chose one near Big Bear. They rented a car and a cabin. One morning they saw a wild American eagle. Valentino wanted a bonfire with marshmallows and s'mores, and Vinnie loved being there when he experienced it. Valentino also wanted to go horseback riding. Vinnie had never done that before.

The trip was two days of paradise.

They enjoyed being tourists—sharing experiences, and mixing fun with discovery. Both men shared a playful joy in exploration.

Their list said it all:

An underground haunted speakeasy.

A dollhouse museum.

A restaurant in an old train car.

The graves of two actresses they admired.

An Op-Art installation.

A taxidermy museum and boutique.

66

A week after their cabin getaway, after another evening with Valentino at the guesthouse, Reed accosted Vinnie two seconds after he came through the door.

There was trouble. Stunt Dick had named names. "Tweakers suck."

Reed saw Vinnie stiffen. "Sorry to pop your love bubble, but you can relax. Stunt Dick only knew about Dean and me. Nobody has pointed a finger at you, yet. But whatever they ask you, when they ask you, you don't know shit. Keep your mouth shut."

Vinnie asked what happened to the Stunt Dick.

Reed gave him a look. "I don't know. After he ratted on me, do you think I care?'

"You said he was your friend."

"Yeah, he was." Reed opened a beer. "A couple of the boys probably suggested that he leave town." Reed smiled. "And I bet he was well bruised by the time they tossed him on a bus bound for Buffalo."

Vinnie didn't want to hear one more word. All signs pointed to Reed. Everyone knew Reed did this anyway. This was all just more of his ridiculous game with Woody. By then Vinnie realized that was all he had been to Woody—just part of a game. "A game piece," was how Reed had described it.

Why had Vinnie expected anything of Reed?

Now Stunt Dick was just more collateral damage in all this.

Woody and Reed were into some sick manipulation shit.

Vinnie said, "Enough." He went to his room and closed the door. Vinnie opened his laptop to check his messages while his phone charged. What the fuck? On his desktop was a file labeled The Notebook. Someone was tormenting him. He had no idea what to do. He held the pillow against his chest and wished it were Valentino. Clearly, someone was aware that Vinnie knew quite a bit. A chill ran through Vinnie. What if they thought Valentino knew something? Vinnie would rather hurt himself than hurt Valentino.

Dorian Mikado repeated the claims of "Mr. Stunt Dick" the following day. No names, no direct accusations, but enough hinting and bitchy commentary to tease. Whetting the appetites of a thirsty crowd was Dorian's specialty. He was a pro at slinging sleaze while navigating the rocky coast of slander. Dorian wasn't about to let this story go.

Vinnie had missed his chance to come forward with what he knew. Woody had asked him directly. Jean had asked directly. Kip had asked him indirectly. He swore to them all that he knew nothing. By coming forward now he would implicate, not exonerate, himself.

Anything less than complete cooperation is considered treason.

67

In real life and the fan world, *#Vinnitino* was still going strong. Vinnie still planned on breaking up with Valentino sometime soon. Vinnie knew that by doing it, he would break Valentino's heart as well as his own. No need rushing to break things off. Things at the studio were slow anyway.

Why spoil a fabulous summer?

One weekend in July, they miscalculated a visit to Palm Springs. They had a blast despite the scorching temperatures. They posted pics from all around the desert playground, beside the Sonny Bono statue and with a backdrop of the mountains. They took photos along the Palm Springs Walk of Stars—Liberace, Bob and Dolores Hope, and Howard Keel. Valentino even tap-danced beside the plaque for Ruby Keeler. Nothing is more intimate than being silly with someone and growing used to the conspiratorial sound of your blended laughter.

Vinnie and Valentino spent countless hours exploring L.A. Valentino had an encyclopedic knowledge of all things Hollywood, and Vinnie knew a great deal as well. They spent hours in the casita, naked in bed, and watching old movies. They visited memorabilia stores as well as resale and oddity shops. At some point, they began to imagine furnishing their dream home.

Vinnie knew he was only making their eventual breakup even worse.

Valentino made Vinnie want to quit smoking.

Fans often spotted them. Being a couple made them more recognizable. Vinnie and Valentino were happy to pose with fans. Sometimes drunk fans could be disrespectful. Valentino had one call him *Vaselino*, thinking that was so funny.

At least two or three days a week, they spent at the casita, baking beside the pool. Valentino mentioned buying inflatable rafts the next time they were in town. Vinnie recalled the air mattresses in the pool house. "We will need to fill them, but I know you can blow."

The inside of the pool house was still filthy. The chemical scent that Vinnie had remembered from before still lingered. The inner door, which had been locked, was now ajar. The smaller room was empty—and the floor had been recently cleaned. Inside, the pungent smell was a bit stronger. Vinnie came back outside and tossed the two mostly deflated rafts at Valentino. "Time to blow."

They never made it into the pool that day.

Some evenings, they lounged on Vinnie's balcony, listening to the nighttime city sounds. They spent a lot of time in bed, but it was more than sex. They read to one another, listened to music, and sometimes just held each other. Those lazy days of doing nothing were the ones that Vinnie held the dearest.

On the final day of August, Vinnie and Valentino were lounging at the pool. The day was like the one before—a cloudless, windless day with temps pushing one hundred. Like most days, this one was spent floating on their pool rafts and holding hands. They dozed in the heat until it got so hot it was time to roll off the raft into the pool.

After lunch, Vinnie said he had a treat for him. "How would you like to see my diving skills?"

Valentino said there was no need to try and impress him

"But I want to try and impress you." Vinnie began with a back flip.

Valentino applauded as Vinnie climbed from the pool and headed to the board once again. The second time he executed a decent swan dive, cutting the water and going nine feet deep, all the way to the drain. The pressure squeezed his head.

The sky was rolling light above. He paused, fanning his hands to keep himself deep. He caught a glint of light near the drain. He moved closer. The back-and-forth movement of his hands was rocking something on top of the drain. It was a ring. Vinnie grabbed it and pushed off the bottom to the surface.

He wrapped an arm on the pool drain and inspected the ring more closely. Vinnie read the inscription on the inside band—*Forever, A.Z.* Roy's ring.

"What is it?" Valentino was floating in the shallow end and looking at Vinnie.

"I just scratched myself."

While Valentino's raft was turned away, Vinnie slipped the ring into the pocket of his suit. The less Valentino saw, the better.

Vinnie was roused by the whoosh of a sliding deck door. Kip waved from the balcony. From where he was standing, Kip had a bird's eye view of the pool. Vinnie took his hand away from his pocket and wondered how long Kip had been watching.

"Come join us," called Valentino. As far as Vinnie knew, Valentino knew nothing about Kip's scars.

Kip declined the offer. He said he needed to grab Woody's dry cleaning. Kip lingered a moment before going back inside. Vinnie took a deep breath when he heard the click of the sliding glass door. He felt the ring in his pocket. Something had happened to Roy. The ring was more evidence. Vinnie just hoped that Kip didn't see him find it.

68

In mid-September, rumors began to swirl that Xclusiv was hemorrhaging money. Previously, the company had been on a slight downward trajectory. However, in the first and second quarters, the business took a nosedive. For the studio to survive, cuts were necessary. Rumors circulated that the studio would be shuttered in three months if nothing changed.

The rumors were confirmed in a group email that began, *Dear Team.* In the letter, Woody and Vittori explained that during the rebudgeting, there would be an immediate production freeze. Cuts in the production schedule were forthcoming. Touring salaries were cut by forty percent, and marketing took a forty percent hit as well. In order to sidestep disaster, cuts were being made now. Salaried employees would receive a separate email or phone call. Some were furloughed.

Vittori telephoned Vinnie to tell him his salary was being cut by thirty percent. "Purely a financial decision," Vittori had said. Vinnie said he understood. *What was he supposed to say?*

Vinnie could hear the relief in Ed's voice. "That's why you are one of our favorites."

The pay cut hurt, but the production freeze and marketing cuts concerned Vinnie more. He wasn't in this business to become wealthy. He wanted fame. Being an exclusive was his chance to be somebody. He was not going to let that slip away.

The studio news was followed by a dip in morale. Dissatisfaction was rampant. People began considering their options and looking elsewhere. A few jumped ship. Vinnie knew four non-exclusives who took work at other studios. Woody interpreted such things as a betrayal. All four models knew they would never work for Xclusiv again. The studio was down to two One-on-One guys. Production maintained a bare-bones crew. Gert was gone.

Less work and more cuts had everyone on edge. Kip proved an exception. He was given more work, much more. Instead of a weekly cleaning crew at the studio, the task was simply added to Kip's duties. Kip didn't mind. He almost seemed grateful. Vinnie knew Kip wasn't motivated by money. Woody was his motivation, and this was an opportunity to prove his loyalty.

Eager to keep some career momentum, Vinnie did what he could to get more press. He checked his followers several times a day. When Vinnie wasn't seeing Valentino or working for Trusted Talents, he did promotional work for Xclusiv. He passed out lube at a trade show and signed photos at a bathhouse anniversary in Houston. Vinnie posed for selfies at street fairs and did any podcast that he was asked to do. He had learned what to say, what not to say, when to deflect, and when to say, *No comment.*

Vinnie asked Vittori what he thought of Valentino joining him at the gigs. "You know, two porn stars for the price of one." Vinnie's idea was met with a less than enthusiastic response. Despite their popularity as a social media couple, producers did not want Vinnie showing up with his boyfriend—and neither did his fans.

Ed sighed. "Social media is one thing, reality is another. The crowd at these events do not want to see you two on a date. These are gay men. They want to be teased. They want the chance to maybe get in your pants."

Given the financial restructuring of the studio, Xclusiv opted not to renew the six-month contract of Valentino Valdez. His work visa had lapsed. Given the political climate in the States, no one was eager to give him an extension. Cutting Valentino from the studio roster was a simple choice. Woody had Vittori do the dirty work. Valentino was in bed beside Vinnie when he got the call from Ed. He was direct. "Unfortunately, we have to terminate your work permit."

With budget cuts everywhere, the news of Valentino's firing didn't surprise Vinnie. He had been waiting for something like this to happen. He gripped Valentino's hand. "I am so sorry," he said.

Pain pooled in Valentino's eyes. He understood. Valentino had stopped caring about stardom long ago. Losing his contract and visa meant more than the end of his career. It meant leaving the country—and leaving Vinnie.

That night Vinnie held him until dawn. He kissed away his tears and whispered all the things he loved about him. He fucked away some of the sadness. Stroking Valentino's hair, Vinnie was grateful for this beautiful, unexpected interlude in his life, but nothing lasts forever. They had something wonderful, but destiny had intervened. Life goes on. This wasn't a bad thing.

Now they will both remember this with love. Now their time together would always be close to perfect.

Losing Valentino would be painful, but stardom meant sacrifice. Marriage would have solved the problem, but Valentino was too much of a romantic to turn a wedding into a solution. One of the things Vinnie loved most about Valentino was that he believed in love so completely. Valentino had pride. He would not accept a pity proposal. Vinnie said nothing. As deeply as he felt for Valentino, now was not the time. If his career were more established, things would be different.

Valentino had nowhere to go but home to Italy—back to life before, back to his old name, and maybe even back to whatever drove him away. He had hinted at something in his past, but Vinnie didn't pry. Whatever was haunting this beautiful boy ran deep. That unknown sadness was part of his beauty. So much about Valentino was still a mystery. Vinnie didn't even know his real name.

On the ride to the airport, Vinnie and Valentino shared few words. They held hands with a grip both tight and tender. Neither man could look at the other. Instead, each man looked out his own window. Vinnie tried to keep it together. No tears.

This is for the best, became his mantra.

The car angled to the drop-off area. The driver took Valentino's suitcases from the trunk. Tears welled in Vinnie's eyes as the last bag hit the pavement. Valentino was crying too. *This was it.* They hugged. On the brink of losing control of his emotions, Vinnie took a few breaths through his mouth. *No. Not here.*

He waved the driver on.

Both Vinnie and Valentino took a moment to breathe. Vinnie was grateful that LAX was bustling, but not overwhelming. They rolled Valentino's bag to the ticket counter. Two gay guys at the next window recognized them. One nudged the other. They turned. Turned back. Laughed. A moment later, Valentino's bag was checked, and his ticket was in his hand. Vinnie decided not to leave until the very last moment. Walking towards security, both men kept their eyes straight ahead. They had a conversation filled with vague promises and someday plans.

"I can visit Siena when things settle down."

Valentino smiled. "You would like it there." Still walking. Eyes still straight ahead. "Or I could come back here and visit."

The crackle of an overhead speaker put a slight pause in the back and forth.

"Or we could meet in New York."

"We can visit all the time."

"Let's make plans once you're settled."

Neither man took much stock in what was being said, but the bullshit buffered the inevitable moment to come. Pretending this was not the end made parting bearable. A few feet from security, the overhead speaker repeated a loop of indecipherable instructions. Ahead of them, a sizeable line of people zig-zagged between ropes. "Here we are."

Valentino put down his bag.

Vinnie felt his chest heaving. *Keep it together.* They hugged. They kissed. They hugged tighter and broke apart. Both men were keenly aware of sharing a private moment in a public place. Valentino reached into his carry-on and slipped a card into Vinnie's hand. They hugged one last time before he turned and walked away.

Valentino was already three deep in the line by the time Vinnie realized he had forgotten to get a picture of their parting. He waved to get Valentino's attention and remembered the envelope in his hand.

On the card inside was the word "Us." Enclosed was a picture of them at a beachfront diner. That day they had walked the Venice shore to the Santa Monica Pier holding hands. They stopped for a lunch of omelets at a place with plates in rainbow shades of knock-off Fiestaware. That day they explored the beachfront shops, swam, walked the outdoor graffiti art galleries, and sat on the sand watching the sunset.

Vinnie looked at the photo. So many colors were in the picture. Valentino had written on the back of the photograph—*The time I knew there was love.*

That had been a perfect day. One of many they shared.

Vinnie managed to get ahold of himself in the cab line.

This was all for the best!

He gave the driver the address and leaned back in the seat. Looking out the window, he felt depleted and tried to console himself.

What's done is done.

Nothing lasts forever.

If it were meant to be, this would not have happened.

ME

Not all relationships are meant to last.

But some are.

Vinnie stopped himself. He could not go there. Regrets were a waste of time. Vinnie pulled out his phone and went to his socials.

Instagram 61.2K
Twitter 49.2K

69

Despite bouts of longing for Valentino, Vinnie maintained that it was all for the best. He needed to believe that. He fought the urge to text Valentino, phone him, or to even send videos of things that Vinnie had seen around "their" city. Contacting Valentino after they had said their goodbyes would only reopen the wound. Their break was clean. Missing him would pass. There was no point in making things messy now.

Vinnie tried to keep busy. Although the studio had little for him to do, Vinnie did what he could to remain relevant. His followers were his power. He needed to keep them happy at all costs. They were proof he was still a force.

With his extra free time, Vinnie increased his availability with Trusted Talents. Some of his dates were good, some were rough, but the vast majority of them were forgettable. In his first few months at the agency Vinnie saw dozens of clients and developed a few regulars. Vinnie was dependable, punctual, and polite. He had become a model employee since bringing Valentino back to his place on his first appointment.

Jean was pleased. Novak was pleased. Even Leon seemed to have warmed a bit, or at least defrosted. The last time Vinnie performed at the Blaze, Leon had knocked on the dressing room door and apologized for disturbing him.

Leon had smiled. "You are on fire tonight!"

"Thanks." The room was so small that Vinnie was unsettled by Leon's presence. "I'm just taking a few moments before mingling." To get in the right headspace between a dance set or appearance, Vinnie typically required a cocktail and a cig, followed by five minutes of alone time.

Vinnie enjoyed chatting with fans, signing photos, and posing for selfies—especially when he had a slight buzz. Fans were wonderful—it was the watchers that he found unnerving. The watchers remained anonymous, staring from the shadows, never approaching, always watching—and always with the same hunger in their eyes.

Leon was lingering. His presence was making Vinnie feel claustrophobic. "I'll be out in about ten minutes or so."

"Do you want another drink?"

Vinnie said he was fine. "No, on second thought, I'll take another."

Anything to get him out of there.

Earlier in the evening Vinnie had heard that Jean had taken over the management of Trusted Talents. Apparently, Leon was out completely. Now he focused solely on the Blaze. Maybe the demotion had humbled him.

While flattening a stack of crumpled tips, one of the other dancers at the club told Vinnie that he heard the whole thing. "Novak told Leon he didn't want to spread him too thin," the dancer laughed, rolling a fist over the money roll.

Novak had made the right decision. Jean was a complete professional; logical, intelligent, and even-keeled—an ideal person to be in charge of an operation like Trusted Talents. Jean had a sort of power over people. Vinnie wanted Jean's approval. And Jean knew how much praise to give, and how much to withhold.

On Vinnie's first date he brought Valentino briefly back to the flat for a moment. Since that infraction, Vinnie had been a model employee at the agency, and that was due in a large part to not wanting to displease Jean. Vinnie only risked that happening once—and it had nothing to do with the rules. It was about the client.

The date was a request and it had been arranged for Vinnie to go to the client's suite at a luxury hotel in downtown L.A. Vinnie had been instructed to ask for Room 3428 at the front desk. There was an envelope with a note accompanying the keycard.

Come Upstairs. Let Yourself In!

When Vinnie looked up from the note, the hospitality clerk was smirking.

Vinnie returned the look. *Fuck off! Who cares what you think, you petty queen?*

A few months working for Trusted Talents had toughened him.

Inside suite 3428, the shower was running. At least the guy would be clean. Vinnie called, "Hello."

"Be there in a minute," came the muffled response.

A note was pinned to the terrycloth robe on the bed.

Make yourself comfortable and get undressed.

By the time Vinnie was in the hotel robe, the shower had stopped running. Over the whirr of a blow-dryer, Vinnie heard, "Out in a minute."

When the bathroom door opened, steam rose to the ceiling. Ty emerged from the fog with a towel about his waist.

Vinnie sat up on the bed and tightened the sash of his robe. "Ty, what is this? What are you doing?"

"Surprised?" Ty smelled of hotel toiletries.

This was not a surprise. This was an ambush.

Ty took a step closer, "We used to be friends, Vincent. We told each other everything."

What he was saying was true. Vinnie had trusted him. He had thought they were friends, but Ty had just wanted to sleep with him all along.

"We even talked about our past with one another." Vinnie paused for a moment. Something was coming together in his head. Vinnie's lips thinned in anger. "You're the one who sent that envelope of nudes to my mother."

"I said I got carried away..."

Vinnie cut him short. "You fucker—to do something like that and now show up here. All I can say is whatever you hoped to achieve with all this failed miserably. You are pitiful."

"Never call me that." Ty backed Vinnie against the bed—so close Vinnie felt his erection. Ty gave him a swift push backwards onto the bed. In seconds Ty was straddling him, pinning Vinnie's hands over his head. Ty was stronger than he looked. Pilates and insanity are a deadly combination.

In a few seconds, Vinnie managed to buck Ty off balance and push him to the floor. Grabbing his jeans from the chair, Vinnie hopped into one pant leg and then the other. By the time he slid them up his hips, Ty was up and blocking the door. "I paid for you, Vinnie Lux!"

"Well, this is a *No Sale* situation." Vinnie's chest was heaving. He slipped on his shoes. His polo shirt was slung over his shoulder. He needed to get out of here. "And now, I am leaving. You need to step aside."

In his rush to block the door, Ty's towel fell to the floor. He was no longer erect, but his dick hung heavy. "I'm not moving."

Vinnie was pissed, and although he had never used his fists in his life, he fought the urge to throw a punch. "Ty, step aside. I'm leaving you—again. And I am rejecting you—again. Now get out of my way, and get some goddamn therapy!" Vinnie wanted to hurt Ty. He had crossed a line.

He did not need Ty or his petty crap in his life. He was glad that he made him cry. *Fuck you, Ty!* How can a man have a plan like this and be surprised when it backfires?

Vinnie shoved Ty aside and went out the door. Ty grabbed the towel from the floor, wrapped it around his waist, and followed Vinnie into the hallway. "You're here because of me, don't you think you owe me a minute."

"I don't owe you shit," Vinnie seethed, slipping his shirt over his head as the elevator pinged arrival. Vinnie stabbed at the *Close Door* icon. As the steel doors came together, Vinnie saw Ty naked in the hallway, crying,

On the elevator ride down, Vinnie dialed Jean to get ahead of this incident. He asked Jean to line up another date. "This last guy was nuts. I walked out on him. He was a stalker from my past."

Sometime during his explanation, Vinnie realized that Jean didn't care. Not about the past, or Ty, or anything that Vinnie was talking about. Jean said the appointment was paid upon booking. "If the charges are contested, I will handle the situation. I will see that he doesn't become a problem for you again."

He should have known Jean would take care of everything.

Vinnie enjoyed working for Trusted Talents. Escorting was more improv acting than anything. Clients rented a fantasy, and each guy wanted his own fantasy version of Vinnie Lux. Some men liked him sullen with a hint of disdain. Most saw him as the boy next-door, back from college and suddenly sexy. He became the Vinnie they wanted him to be. Clients commented regularly on how "real" he seemed.

Working with Trusted Talents, Vinnie made a good amount of tax-free money. He invested some. Saved some. Blew a little. He was flown to London on a private jet and joined the mile-high club. He was taken to beach resorts and penthouse parties. He attended functions with celebrities.

Vinnie's life resembled the fantasies that he had once dreamt about. But the fabulousness wasn't half as satisfying as he supposed it would be. Experiencing great things, without someone he loved by his side, caused Vinnie to feel even lonelier.

70

Profits for Xclusiv Studio took another hit in the third quarter. Additional cutbacks were announced to take effect immediately for the remainder of the fiscal year. Woody acknowledged his past extravagances but in no way apologized for them. Woody maintained that in this business, you needed to spend money to make money. "I just have to take it easy for a while. Everything will be different once the books get squared away."

Vinnie was a team player and hard-wired to please, but blind allegiance to a troubled business was foolish. By then, Vinnie had come to realize that the loyalty demanded by the studio was not a two-way street.

This was about more than money. Vinnie more than covered the pay cut with his income from Trusted Talents. What Vinnie could not afford was having his career put on hold indefinitely. He needed a Plan B—just in case.

Woody had changed. In the past few months, he had grown so distant and distracted that he almost seemed like a different person. Vinnie feared the worst—that Woody had seen the footage in his office. Vinnie had shuffled through the papers on his desk, looked through his appointment book, and tried the locked drawers of the file cabinet. The footage would be unnerving for anyone to see, but especially someone with things to hide.

The following week, Woody sent a group email that began:

To the Xclusiv Family,

In the quest to build a solid foundation, the studio will be doing additional retrenching...

The email explained that Woody and Ed Vittori were working to streamline the studio's financial future and to determine "the optimal plan of action"— whatever that meant. Vinnie was willing to make the sacrifice for now, as long as his career got back on track once the financial crunch at the studio eased.

As time passed, Vinnie began to doubt that Woody had seen the footage. Something else was bothering him. Given everything that Vinnie knew, that could be a number of things. Whatever it was distracting Woody was causing him to keep things between himself and Vinnie strictly professional. Vinnie was fine with that, as long as he wasn't walking around with a target on his back. He figured that Woody would never intentionally harm a commodity.

The letter from Woody left everyone at the studio on edge.

Dean and Reed were on the couch when the email came through.

Reed read it out loud, followed by commentary. "This is a bunch of bullshit. The studio is making money hand over fist. Woody is starting to believe his job title—like he's the one making the calls at Xclusiv."

What the fuck was Reed talking about?

Dean gave Reed a look.

"What?" Vinnie repeated.

Reed scoffed. "Vinnie, you always have questions and want to hear about so many things, but are you willing to pay the price for knowing what you're told?"

Vinnie nodded.

Reed grinned and continued. He said that the reason for the budget woes was not because the company was doing poorly, but because Xclusiv was no longer privately owned. Xclusiv had become a holding for NCC Inc., which was Nova Canyon Commodities Incorporated. NCC Inc. was the legit branch of the Lavender Outfit on the West Coast. "Nova is Novak."

Vinnie never knew whether to believe Reed or not. "How do you know all this?"

"I make it my business to know things."

Vinnie believed him this time.

In some ways, the NCC Inc. takeover of the studio was good news. Whatever Woody thought about Vinnie wasn't so important anymore. Vinnie was a star at Xclusiv and a top moneymaker at Trusted Talents. Two Novak businesses stood to profit by keeping him in a good place—unless Novak discovered something or decided to update the product line.

71

Coming home from a date the following week, Vinnie ducked into a convenience store for smokes. Taking out his wallet to pay, Vinnie also pulled out the slip of paper from the cigarette pack. Both Grundella Services and Paragon-Kamden Optics had proven to be dead ends. As far as he could tell, those companies did not exist, or if they did, they had not been around for at least a decade.

As the vendor made change, Vinnie bent to light a smoke and noticed the headline of the *National Tattler*: *CRANSTON'S GAY LOVENEST!* Below the bold black words was a picture of Cash Cranston and Reed engaged in what looked to be oral sex beside a backyard pool. Black blocks covered their privates and mouths.

Witnesses confirm that National Sing Off *contestant Cash Cranston has been in a homosexual relationship with leading gay porno actor Reed Connors for several months.* A sidebar promised more pictures inside!

Vinnie tossed a copy of the tabloid on the counter. The clerk said this issue had just arrived.

Vinnie took a seat on a bus bench with his cigarettes and opened to the cover story. On closer examination of the pictures, it was clear the photographer was a professional. These shots did not look like some pictures a random birdwatcher snapped after they "happened upon" Cash and Reed having sex. The angle, the focus, and even the composition of the images made it clear that this was a professional job. The photographer had been positioned.

The piece did not bother Reed in the least. He was thrilled to have his name in print and especially pleased to be referred to as "a leading porno actor." He seemed either oblivious or unconcerned about what the article would mean for Cash's career. He asked Vinnie if he could keep the issue.

The scandal was covered extensively—TMZ, Perez Hilton, Dorian Mikado, and various other online sources for gossip. The repercussions on Cash's career were swift and severe. Sponsors backed out. Record sales skidded to a halt. Concerts were cancelled. His lucrative recording contract was terminated. Even his management abandoned ship. The Country Crooner had croaked. His career was over.

Although the *National Tattler* piece ruined Cash, it put a spotlight on Reed Connors and brought a boost to his career. Woody moved him into Gio's old room. By the end of the week, paparazzi were camped outside the WeHo building.

Reed gave interviews when asked and commented freely on any question he was asked. He was prone to saying outrageous things when quoted or on camera.

"I never fuck anyone who doesn't have a pool."

"If I spent all my time worrying about damnation, I'd never have the time to whore around the Hollywood Hills."

"I've had sex with three actors up for Emmys this year. In fact, I was naked in a hot tub with the *real* trophy of one of the nominees in my hand when the nominations were announced." Naturally, the comment opened a floodgate of speculation.

"The secret to my success? Some say length, some say girth."

"What would I call my memoirs? Probably something like, *Balls Deep.*"

Reed made great copy. He captured public interest and he was born for the tabloids. Knowing the press was watching, Reed made sure to keep things interesting. One evening at a yacht party, Reed fell overboard. He was tossed a life preserver, climbed back on deck, stripped down to his briefs, and ended up dancing until dawn. He returned home in just his underwear.

Two nights later, Reed got knee-walking drunk at a club and made out in an alley with an "up and coming" soap actor. The guy was going commando in sweats and was clearly aroused.

Reed's time had arrived. He hired a publicist.

Sometimes Vinnie stood smoking on the balcony and looked down onto the gathering of paparazzi. Seeing him, some would rush from the shadows, enormous cameras poised. Then, when they realized it wasn't Reed, the cameras lowered, and the tabloid press retreated back into the shade.

Vinnie was envious. All this attention that was being heaped upon Reed was so undeserved. Vinnie knew that the fame game was random, but this was ridiculous.

Two weeks later, Reed's popularity continued to crest. By then his social media numbers had tripled. He appeared on several radio programs, syndicated talk shows, and countless podcasts. His agent was working on getting him a cameo in the next *Sharknado* film.

Vinnie suspected there was more to the story from the start. He doubted this was all the result of a shocked amateur bird watcher. No "aghast birdwatcher" would have lingered and taken an entire roll of photos.

Vinnie suspected that Reed was behind the leaked photos, using Cash as a fast track to fame. Reed was capable of betraying Cash, or anyone else, for personal gain. All Reed had to do was to make sure the photographer was in place. Once they were ready, it was just a matter of getting Cash to take the action outside. Reed had used the same general setup to destroy Rex Reynolds—only this time Reed was in front of the camera instead of behind it.

Vinnie could imagine Reed convincing Cash to go out by the pool.

No one is in the woods. No one can see over the hedge.

Cash probably never knew what happened until the pictures hit the stands.

If Reed was behind it, Vinnie was impressed—disgusted and jealous, but still impressed.

In addition to the attention and the press, Reed nabbed a starring role in Xclusiv's first feature in months. After suspending production on Vinnie's new film indefinitely, Woody gave the green light to a new Reed Connors movie that was slated to begin filming ASAP.

The following day the studio announced the next Xclusiv Studio release would be *Inside Cash*, starring Reed Connors. Vinnie could have predicted a gimmicky title for Reed's movie. The hackneyed bank job concept was supposedly cranked out on a series of bar napkins.

In porn, as in life, timing was everything. A Reed Connors movie was money in the bank. Vinnie understood, but the news still hurt. Vinnie had been assured that production would start on his next film as soon as the financials were resolved. He had been told he was next in line. Yet, the money was there for *Inside Cash*.

For now, Vinnie needed to smile and be a team player. The broken promise made him realize that he needed to depend upon himself, and no one else, for his career. Even if Woody found the perfect Vinnie Lux vehicle, there was no guarantee Vinnie would star in it. Promising newcomers arrived in town every day.

The business became more cutthroat once a guy had something to lose. If Vinnie wanted a new Vinnie Lux picture, it was up to him to make it happen.

72

Lately, Josh Lawless was also making news in the porn gossip blogs. Earlier in the month, Josh shocked friends, family, and the gay porn world by announcing his separation from his husband, Ian. The couple had been together for fourteen years and wed on a Malibu beach two years ago.

Dorian Mikado spared none of the details when describing how Josh had dumped his longtime partner after falling boots over brains in love with U.K. newcomer Hank London. The two men had been inseparable since costarring in *On the Strip*.

Vinnie couldn't believe it. Josh had been so devoted to Ian.

Dean was surprised that Vinnie had no idea. "You were on the set. Didn't you notice their chemistry?"

"Yes, but," Vinnie shrugged. "I guess I didn't consider Josh and Hank as anything more than scene partners who clicked."

Dean turned back to the TV. "I thought Ian was the only one in town who didn't know about them."

During his podcast, Dorian also disclosed that Josh Lawless and Hank London were set to headline a still-untitled "couples" movie after *Inside Cash* wrapped.

Since Woody was still not taking his calls, Vinnie dialed Ed Vittori and voiced his concerns about the production schedule. Ed said he did not know all the details, but that Woody felt a Josh and Hank movie made sense right now. Vinnie said he would love to do a scene for either movie. "Fans keep asking about my next movie."

"We don't hear that as much on our end."

What was that supposed to mean?

Ed Vittori knew damn well that Vinnie was getting more followers every day. He struggled to sound unfazed. Vinnie needed to stay calm. "I really would love a part." Vinnie hated the tinge of begging in his voice. "I could do a 'guest star' or 'special appearance by' thing. I could do anything?"

Anything was such a desperate word.

Ed said Woody wouldn't go for it. "He'll say you're too special."

More excuses.

Vinnie thanked him and said to pass on word that both films sounded great. "And if it works, I would love to be in either one."

"Noted. And I will pass it on to Woody." Vittori said he had to go to jump on another call.

Now Vittori was giving him the brush off.

Vinnie needed a way to spark public interest, get some press, and convince Vittori, Woody, Novak, or anyone else calling the shots at the studio, that Vinnie Lux was still relevant, still a star, and still capable of attracting a sizeable audience.

Getting a Vinnie Lux film made would be easy if he were capable of blackmail. A.Z.'s notebook could ruin lives and reopen at least one investigation. Whoever put the notebook in his room knew that. They had mixed his things with those of a dead man and created a file called Notebook on his desktop.

He was being goaded. Vinnie had said he would do anything for his career—but it wasn't true. He was speaking about his determination, not his ethics. Someone thought his *anything* included blackmail. He would never use A.Z.'s notebook for profit or a career boost. Someone thought him capable of blackmail—someone who turn-by-turn put him in the middle of all this.

Going to the cops would just get him killed. The Lavender Outfit had no problem fitting a guy with a pair of cement heels or a rope boa. Turning the notebook over to the police would mean arrests. At best, Vinnie would survive testifying at a mob trial. Even then, he had no intention of going into the witness protection program.

No blackmail. No cops. He had to be smart about this. He needed a safety deposit box for the notebook, the ring, the prescription bottle, and the cigarette pack. He would include a letter addressed to law enforcement officials. Whoever was behind all this needed to know that the cops would find out everything he knew if anything happened to him. He also needed a duplicate of the notebook. Having a copy stowed in a safe spot could save his neck.

Vinnie slid the notebook into his gym bag. There was a place to make copies on the way to the gym. He needed a workout, but it was too damn hot for a run outside. And everywhere he ran reminded him of Valentino. The gym would be fine. Vinnie did some of his best thinking on a treadmill, and these days he had plenty to think about.

73

Making two copies of the pages took under five minutes at the FedEx on Santa Monica Boulevard. Vinnie felt relief as he stapled the still warm pages and slipped them into his gym bag.

His gym was the cruisiest place in WeHo.

Vinnie got on the treadmill and started to jog at a medium pace. He tried to focus on his footfalls. After ten minutes, Vinnie felt a flush of panic. He stopped the machine and rushed to the locker room. Inside his gym bag were the two stapled copies, but not the notebook. *Shit!* He left it in the copier at FedEx. Grabbing his bag, Vinnie broke into a sprint across the lot. He didn't slow until he reached FedEx.

Coming through the door, slick with sweat, Vinnie rushed to the machine and lifted the flap. *Shit!* He ran to the service desk. "I left something on a copier earlier. Did anyone turn anything in?"

"For Vinnie Lux?"

Vinnie nodded. "Yes, that's me."

The sales associate handed him the notebook. "Someone turned it in right after you left."

Vinnie's name was nowhere on the notebook. *How did they know his name?* "And you said they left it under my name?"

"That is indeed what I said," The clerk was eyeing the next person in line.

Vinnie asked what the person who returned the notebook looked like.

The clerk shrugged. "Like half the guys in WeHo—good looking, good build, sunglasses, ball cap. That's all I know and I'm not sure of that. I've had a line all morning. And I've got a line now."

Vinnie stepped out of the way and flipped through the pages. Nothing seemed to be missing. No note was left inside. He wondered why this "WeHo type" didn't just take the notebook—unless they didn't need to, unless they had the original.

Since his name wasn't on the notebook, the person who returned it must have watched Vinnie leave it there. He was a porn star, people noticed him. But this didn't sound like a fan. A fan would have scribbled a note, left their name and number or a Post-it on the inside cover—something. A fan would want to be acknowledged. This person wished to remain unknown. Very unusual.

If the WeHo clone had been following him before, maybe they were still trailing him—still watching. They knew Vinnie had made two copies. Maybe the watcher returned the notebook because they wanted everything. The perfect time to get all three would be when he had all the copies on him.

Like now.

Vinnie became hyperaware.

Leaving FedEx, Vinnie tried to see if he was being followed without being obvious. Plenty of men were on the street—hanging out, sitting in cars, and driving by. *So many eyes.* Typical WeHo cruising looked a lot like being tailed. Half the guys on Santa Monica seemed to be loitering with intent. The clerk was right. WeHo definitely had a type.

Vinnie took a roundabout route home. He hoped that might make it easier to tell if anyone was still following him.

In a couple blocks, Vinnie ducked into a coffee shop. There were still too many people about. If someone were following, they would have to give up, enter the coffee shop, or linger outside. Vinnie scanned the chalkboard menu and ordered a medium roast and a bran muffin. Waiting on his order, he spotted Peter Ray Thomas at one of the tables. Thomas was so immersed in the pages before him that he didn't notice Vinnie approach. He only looked up when Vinnie blocked his light. A spiral notebook was open before him. He grinned and stretched his arms overhead.

"Hey stranger." Vinnie was too embarrassed to bring up the voice messages he had left, or the fact that Peter had ignored them. No answer was answer enough. Vinnie asked what he was doing.

Peter nodded to his notebook. "Recovery stuff. Fourth step." Peter flipped the notebook closed and motioned for Vinnie to sit. Peter took a drink of his coffee. "So, what have you been up to?

"I've been working. My boyfriend, I guess you could call him, and I broke up?"

"That's rough." Peter took another swig of his coffee. "Where did you guys meet?"

"On the set of *On the Strip*."

"No way, who was your boyfriend?"

"Valentino Valdez." *Did Peter really not know?* The summer romance of Vinnie and Valentino was the talk of the porn world. They were the golden couple. He and Valentino were a goddamned hash tag—#*Vinnitino*! Didn't Peter follow the gay porn blogs?

"Not sure I know him."

"Gorgeous. Italian. *On the Strip* was his first, and last, movie."

Peter shook his head. "Then I doubt I met him. I showed up, did our scene, and left. You were about the only new person I met." The flash of light off a passing car crossed Peter's face.

Vinnie had forgotten to watch if anyone followed him inside. When he took a seat with Peter, he sat with his back to the door. Vinnie adjusted his chair slightly, so the entrance was in peripheral view. He nodded to the notebook. "So this is your fourth step?" Vinnie popped the last of his muffin in his mouth.

"Yep, all my secrets and defects."

Another notebook of interest.

Peter Ray Thomas had been the bad boy of the studio. He was part of the core family at Xclusiv. Peter had probably seen a lot of things. Maybe something he knew or had seen was the reason why Woody and Vittori had allegedly tried to kill him. Now he was writing all this shit down to tell his sponsor. Vinnie didn't want Peter to put himself, or anyone else, in danger. He pointed to Peter's coffee. "Is that cream or cream and sugar?"

"Lots of both." Peter's grin was wide. "Typical addict."

Vinnie got their refills. He tried to scope out the room. When he returned, he angled his chair more towards the door though he worried the clone might already be within listening range.

After thanking him for the coffee, Peter added. "I like you Vinnie, you're a good guy. And not just because of the coffee refill."

"Glad you realize that." The two men clinked mugs.

Cheers.

"I'm trying to be a better person, so I wanted to say that." Peter tapped a pen on his notebook.

"Does the notebook help?"

Peter signed, "This is to see my defects. Own my part in the past. All that"

Vinnie chose his words carefully. "Some things you probably wouldn't share, right? Like things you know would do more harm than good." Vinnie knew he had made a mistake as soon as he spoke.

Peter took offense, "With all due respect Vinnie Lux, please back the fuck off. It's my life and my program. This demands honesty. Sometimes that hurts people, but that is how you stay clean. They say there is no other way."

"Oh, of course. I didn't mean anything by it. I'm sorry, I was out of line."

"Yes, you were." Peter took a couple of slow breaths. "Thank you for apologizing, Vinnie."

"I really was just curious."

Convincing Peter was impossible without further explanation, but that would probably just put him in more danger. Vinnie backed off, saying the porn business was an easy place to make bad decisions.

"I can't blame porn. It shaped my life, but it didn't warp it." Peter stirred his coffee and continued, "I was a bruised fruit even before I stepped in front of a movie camera. Porn just … accelerated my speed of ripening." Peter grinned as a dark curl unfurled across his forehead. Vinnie had never found him more attractive.

Sensing Vinnie's attraction, Peter responded. "I'm not getting involved with anyone for a year. Relationships are one of my triggers."

"Of course," Vinnie said, resenting the accuracy of Peter's assumption.

Was he referring to anyone in particular?

Vinnie was curious. "The wrong people, what happened?"

"More than I care to remember, I'll tell you that much," Peter pointed to the notebook. "I've got a long record of bad choices, bad friends, and doing without thinking. The way this is going I am going to use up every page."

Peter had known, seen, or done something to make people want him dead. He might not even recall what it was. That didn't matter. Sobriety revives memories. And powerful men detest loose ends.

And now Peter was remembering more every day.

He made an easy target if someone wanted him dead. Addicts relapse all the time. No one bats an eye when a known junkie overdoses. It would be regrettable, a shame, and a cautionary tale. But the death of an addict is rarely suspicious, especially an addict who did porn. Peter would be a statistic before the rigor mortis kicked in.

Vinnie looked around the coffee shop. People were coming and going. Milling about waiting for orders. Moving chairs. There was no way to keep track of anyone. Maybe no one was following him. Lately, Vinnie had a hard time telling where legitimate fear ended and where irrational fear began.

Peter nodded to the barista that they would be right back. "They know me here."

"You should take your notebook."

"You're probably right," Peter slid it under his arm.

Vinnie followed Peter into the alley to share a smoke. They leaned against the brick and passed it between them. "Did you hear about Josh?"

Peter exhaled a column of smoke. "Nothing bad I hope."

If Peter didn't follow industry talk, he might not know a lot of things. Vinnie told him about Josh and Ian's breakup over Hank London. Peter said that was sad to hear. He stopped Vinnie from saying more. "Part of getting sober is minding my own business and keeping my side of the street clean."

What was he implying? Vinnie got defensive. "I wasn't gossiping. I was telling you the news in case you wanted to reach out as Josh's friend."

Peter apologized. "I told you I could be an asshole. Bet you're sorry you stopped and said hello. Little did you know you would be dealing with my crap." Peter stubbed his cigarette on the brick. He leaned close. Vinnie thought they were about to kiss. Instead, Peter offered a grin. "See you later, Vinnie Lux. Back to my character defects," he turned and waved the notebook over his head.

Vinnie adjusted himself and hoisted the gym bag higher on his shoulder. Exiting the alley, Vinnie looked either way. He saw no one suspicious.

With the recent lull at Xclusiv, Dean occupied the couch even more. When he called the studio, Dean was told the same thing Vinnie had been told. Woody would call when something "special" came along. Apparently, Dean wasn't right for parts in either of the new Xclusiv productions either.

Dean claimed that he didn't care. "I'm getting tired of all this."

Vinnie said nothing, but he had heard on Dorian's podcast that Xclusiv had recently signed Ajax Wood, a kid from the Dakotas with an even bigger dick than Dean. Dorian posed the question, "Was Xclusiv putting its reigning stud, Dean Driver, out to pasture?"

The studio was keeping Ajax Wood under tight wraps. That probably meant he was the latest tenant at Woody's guesthouse. Or maybe, with what Ajax was packing, he was staying in the big house. Maybe that monster cock was balls deep in Woody right now. Ajax might be doing him right there in the living room, up against the window. Woody's face pressed against the glass, hot breath fogging the view. And all of it, serenaded by squawks.

Vinnie felt for Dean. Things were tough at the studio, unless you were Reed Connors. Reed had bookings, invitations, offers, and no time for Dean. *That had to hurt.* Reed was not willing to share one sliver of the spotlight.

Maybe it was out of desperation, or spite, or a need to get his balls drained— but Dean eventually got off the couch. Within a week of going out, he started dating a "nice enough" pilot. Vinnie had never met the man. Dean said he flew the L.A. to Sydney route. "We only see each other once every few days, but when he comes home, he is ready, and so am I. Time apart works for us." Dean said the pilot loved his big juicy asset.

Vinnie assumed as much.

Within a month, the pilot promised Dean the world. Gifts. Travel.

"What are you going to do?"

"I've never had much stability in my life, might be worth giving it a try."

The pilot asked him to move to Long Beach.

By leaving town, Dean was all but abandoning his career. Vinnie couldn't fault him. He was saving face. Besides, Dean had always wanted a pampered life, and he said more than once that there wasn't room to breathe in L.A.

The air was fresher in Long Beach.

"The pilot will be good for me. We can live anywhere. Maybe we'll move to Australia. That would be something." Dean said that Woody took the news very well. "He even shook my hand and said, Good Luck."

Vinnie was sure that Woody's response had everything to do with having Ajax Wood on the payroll.

"I told him I could drive up when the studio needs me," added Dean.

Vinnie doubted that Woody or the studio would take Dean up on his offer, unless they needed him around to keep Ajax Wood in line.

74

When Dean moved out, the dynamics of the flat shifted. Dean had been a buffer between Kip and Reed. When Dean was around, they tended to be civil to one another. After he left, Reed and Kip mostly pretended the other one didn't exist. The tension was palpable. Vinnie hated living with that kind of negative energy in his home.

He missed Valentino. Vinnie missed having fun. All this other stuff didn't seem important when Valentino was around. Every part of Hollywood reminded Vinnie of days of sightseeing and adventure with Valentino. Vinnie didn't have days like that anymore.

Shortly after Dean moved to Long Beach, Ed Vittori called. Vinnie hoped it was about a movie role. Instead, Ed asked if Vinnie wanted to go on tour. "Get out of town for a while—connect with fans, little dance gigs. It will be a great opportunity for you. Some places you dance might not be quite as nice as the Blaze."

Vinnie tried to keep an open mind.

Vittori continued, "Maybe with an adult theater and a couple of bathhouses added."

In the past, Vinnie had resisted an extended tour. It was too easy to forget a man on the road. Vinnie felt he needed to stay where the action was. But nothing was happening at the studio—at least for him. The time had never been right before. Maybe now was the time. The entire city reminded him of Valentino. And connecting with fans was smart. If Vinnie could increase his social media numbers enough, perhaps Woody would make a new Vinnie Lux picture a priority. Things were getting very strange around town. The road might also be the safest place for him to be.

Vittori was eager to set dates. "Just give me the word. And if you are willing to drop your appearance fee for a cut of the cover charge, I can start lining up dates by the end of next week."

Vinnie told Ed he wanted a day to think about it.

"Well don't think too long."

When Vinnie hung up, Reed was behind him in the doorway. "Welcome to the downside of your career."

"What is that supposed to mean?" The thought of being hundreds of miles from Reed suddenly added to the appeal of an extended tour. Vinnie would not miss this sort of bullshit.

"If they want you on tour, it means they want you gone. It means Woody and Vittori are tired of you squawking about your next project and how it was promised to you."

"I haven't whined."

"You've put yourself forward about this with Woody and Ed more than once. They take that as telling them how to run the business. They want you away," Reed made sense, but he also made a pastime out of fucking with people.

"Those tours can be endless," Reed added. "More cities, more dates, and more clubs tagged on. Shitholes."

Vittori had even implied that.

Reed continued, "Touring is a loop that leads nowhere—Davenport, Albany, Tulsa—and before you know it, you're dancing on a Tuesday in Omaha and folks are asking themselves, 'So, if this Vinnie Lux is such a big star, why is he dancing here in the middle of the week?" Reed was taking pleasure in this.

"Fuck you."

Reed knew how to push Vinnie's buttons; but he swore he was telling the truth this time. "I wouldn't want to hear it either, but that's where you stand."

"This is to connect with fans."

Reed shook his head. "Listen to what you are being told. That means Woody and Vittori think you *need* to connect with fans. Vinnie, you're an exclusive. You've done movies and gotten press. Porn stars don't need to go looking for followers. That's why they're called followers. If your career were headed anywhere, you would have a solid following. You never see the truth in things. You were Woody's guy when you showed promise. But not so much these days, am I right?"

Vinnie fought the urge to slam the door, but he was curious what else Reed might have to say. When Reed was on a roll, his mouth tended to move faster than his brain.

"Sometimes a guy comes to town with the drive, the hunger, and the look—but he just doesn't click. Sound familiar? Don't beat yourself up. As for Woody, he likes the stars who click." Reed paused when Kip emerged from his room and headed to the bathroom. When the door closed, the conversation continued.

Reed lowered his voice. "Looking at your career, I can imagine that you're desperate, but don't do anything stupid. Just remember, you were complicit in the Rex Reynolds business. So don't get any big ideas about saving your career by trying to tank mine—people have tried before and it has *never* ended well for them."

"Is that a threat?"

Reed smirked. "I'm not going to threaten you. From where I'm standing, it looks like your set to self-destruct. You have enough to worry about on your own. Whatever you decide, have a nice day."

Reed was such an asshole, but Vinnie wasn't about to go on tour now. Touring was synonymous with running away. Vinnie refused to be written off so easily.

75

Gio and Joe McCain returned from their wedding and Hawaiian honeymoon looking tanned and relaxed. They bought a condo on Maui. Some figured Joe was retiring, and that was the real reason that Aaron Fyre was hired—some saw it the other way around.

Lee Botello had claimed that McCain didn't know *On the Strip* was in production until shooting was wrapped. "That's what he told me, that he didn't know a thing."

Despite the supposed financial issues at the studio, Woody wanted to throw an extravagant party to celebrate the union. Woody was very keen on the appearance of things. He had Kip plan the celebration the following week.

As with most Xclusiv gatherings, there were theatrics. That was to be expected—combine an open bar with most guests trying to "be someone" or to get noticed and the results might be anything.

The majority of guests at the party were in the industry—costars, exes, crewmembers, investors, etc. Only one blood relative attended, Gio's sister, Inez. Gio spoke to no other family member. He softened around Inez. She referred to Joe as her new brother.

Aaron Fyre was present. Although on the studio payroll, Aaron had never met Joe McCain or Gio. Seeing Fyre in attendance, Vinnie suspected Woody had an ulterior motive for the party. Woody wanted to make things right with McCain, especially since now people were talking about Fyre's "fresh look" with the sets for *On the Strip*.

McCain did not seem fazed in the least.

Vinnie would have found that surprising, but last week Reed had been very chatty. Vinnie suspected he was speeding. That night Reed told him he had heard that when McCain told Novak that Gio was leaving the agency, Novak agreed. But he asked for a favor in return. Supposedly Novak then gave McCain an envelope of cash. Novak said to have an extra long honeymoon in Hawaii.

Vinnie didn't understand.

"He was paid to stay away."

"Reed, how do you know this?"

"It doesn't matter how I know—I know." Reed said that McCain had accepted the offer. "Novak wanted him gone so his protégée Aaron Fyre could step in."

"Aaron Fyre is Novak's protégée?" When Vinnie scoffed, Reed swore it was the truth. "Novak always has some thin pale thing to put forward—a junkie painter, a junkie poet, and now a junkie designer. He likes creative boys with a habit, but Novak is such a sick fuck that getting rid of them once their time is up is probably his favorite part."

"What are you talking about?"

Reed showed no signs of stopping. "Novak is paying the salary for Fyre. Doesn't matter whether Woody approved or not. Novak was in charge. He does not make requests. Novak forced Woody to make the *right* decision."

At the celebration for Gio and Joe, the booze was flowing. Others had their own drug, or drugs, of choice.

If Aaron Fyre was Novak's protégé, it explained why Leon and Jean were in attendance. A boy with a habit needs watching.

No one was shocked when Dorian Mikado entered the room. Someone behind Vinnie whispered that Dorian was looking paunchy.

"Maybe he unhinged his jaw and swallowed someone whole," muttered one of the One-on-One guys. The comment was followed by laughter between the two.

Supposedly, Dorian was there to get an exclusive on the nuptials, including some pics and video clips. That was the story. But it seemed too wholesome for Dorian's audience. Vinnie suspected that the video blogger also hoped to uncover some dirt.

Dorian was trying to corner Josh Lawless. Last week Josh's affair with Hank London and his divorce from Ian took a turn. Hank London returned to the U.K.—alone. He was bored with his American affair. Josh was devastated. Leaving someone to be with someone who leaves you two weeks later is humiliating—especially when it happens publicly.

Vinnie was shocked that Josh had shown up at all.

Reed came late. His entrance was designed to upstage the guests of honor. This party was an opportunity for Reed to flaunt his newfound fame. He would not have missed it for the world. He arrived with an entourage, including a young filmmaker shooting "raw footage for a reality show."

Woody was watching Reed. There was no masking his desire. Woody looked eager to rekindle their twisted relationship.

Vinnie turned away. Reed had been right about Woody. He was turned on by public opinion. Vinnie was embarrassed that he ever found Woody attractive. *Those two deserve each other.*

Gio was standing behind Vinnie. "He can't let it go."

Vinnie turned, "You mean Reed?"

"Yes Reed, Can't say I miss his bullshit."

Vinnie told Gio that he missed having him around. "Even though you weren't home all that much. Reed is in your old room now. He's been unbearable since the story broke."

"You mean like trying to steal focus at my party? Like he is trying to do now."

Vinnie nodded. "Pretty much. At least with him in demand he isn't around that much, just long enough to get on my nerves. We're at your party. I don't want to talk about Reed. It looks like married life agrees with you."

"I can't complain." Gio flashed the ring. "Joe loves me, and the way he looks at me, I feel cherished."

Vinnie understood the appeal, but doubted that being cherished would be enough for him. Love had not been enough. He was in love with Valentino, and he let him go.

Gio asked how Dean was doing.

"Dean is gone." Vinnie assumed Gio had heard about Dean's semi-retirement, but Joe had said nothing. Vinnie had just started telling Gio about Dean and the pilot in Long Beach when Lee Botello staggered over. He threw an arm around each of them. Lee had a real fondness for any event with an open bar. His shirt was unbuttoned to the waist with his thick pelt on display. He was feeling no pain.

"You two men make working in this business a pleasure." Lee was slurring his words.

Gio mocked offense. "Are you hitting on me at my own reception!"

Lee gave a hearty laugh. Even shitfaced, he had a surplus of easygoing charm; Botello was a minor league Josh Lawless. Lee knew that—but didn't care. Lee wasn't out to be number one—he was out to have fun. Vinnie found that incredibly sexy.

"Where is Roy?" Liquor made Lee louder than usual.

Vinnie tried to shush him.

Lee said Roy had been staying with him. "He left Woody's and asked if he could stay with me. I didn't ask questions, I just said sure."

Lee was getting louder. He was starting to attract attention. "Roy was upset when he got there. I figured I would ask the details later. The next morning I had a meeting downtown and when I got back, Roy was gone—just like that."

Vinnie offered to get Lee some coffee.

"No, coffee is for coffee drinkers!" The suggestion made Lee even louder. "Roy left without so much as a word. Do you think that's right?"

Vinnie shook his head. This was not the time or the place.

Lee said it didn't seem right. "Especially with those Texas manners of his. I'm no expert on men, but I am an expert on Texans."

Lee was going to get himself killed if he didn't shut up. Seeing no other solution, Vinnie leaned back and gave him a hard, juicy kiss—a kiss wet enough to bring forgetfulness. When their lips separated, Lee was speechless.

Finally!

Everyone had a Lee Botello story. His longevity in porn was commendable. Lee had plenty of stories, going all the way back to growing up in Oklahoma. Lee was fond of talking about the benefits of a porn career. "Fuck films gave me opportunities to net some serious cash." Serious cash was necessary to maintain Lee's lifestyle. Lee wasn't extravagant—he just liked to gamble.

Every few months, Lee would disappear. He usually ended up in Reno on a drugs, sex, and craps binge. Once Lee returned from a casino up there with two naked chorus boys. Lee didn't gamble to win. He won to keep gambling. For Lee, winning big was usually more expensive than losing his shirt—at least in the long run.

"Whoa," said Gio, "Sue looks great."

Vinnie agreed. Sue rarely wore makeup or was "put together" for film shoots. She was meeting a guy at a club downtown. Vinnie didn't think of Sue that way. Few guys at the studio did. Sue was a pal. Vinnie heard that going to law school was just Sue's latest thing to do. Before that, she went to art school. Vinnie wondered if her supposedly prestigious family knew of her side job. Maybe keeping it a secret gave Sue a thrill.

For much of the celebration, Kip Mason and Ed Vittori were deep in conversation in a far corner of the room. Neither of the men mingled, and no one interrupted their talk. Vinnie wondered what they were so thick about.

Gio saw him staring. "Is *that* also something that happened while I was in Hawaii?"

"Those two?" Vinnie said he had not heard a word.

Gio laughed. "Well, it's happening right in front of you. Look how close they're standing. Trust me, those two are into each other."

Could that be true?

Seeing Kip and Vittori so thick made Vinnie anxious. Despite what Gio was saying, Vinnie did not believe those two were whispering sweet nothings to one another.

Gio waved to Joe across the room. Joe McCain raised his champagne flute before returning to his conversation with Dorian Mikado.

"Speaking of things happening right in front of you." Vinnie nodded to Mikado and McCain. Vinnie felt like an ass. It was a stupid comment to make to one of the grooms at a wedding celebration.

Gio didn't seem perturbed in the least. "Joe and Dorian have known each other for years. He calls Dorian his first husband, though they were never married." Gio said that it happened years ago. "Before Xclusiv. And then they went from lovers to friends."

Vinnie asked if that bothered him.

"If they want to have a roll in the hay for old time's sake—fine by me. If it's going to happen, it will happen. But I've got the ring. I'm the one Joe McCain married." Gio wiggled his ring finger, "Now excuse me, I need to mingle."

When Gio walked away, Vinnie looked around. Making small talk at parties filled Vinnie with dread. The best solution was another drink. Vinnie propped himself against a wall near the reception area. Through the doorway, he saw Josh Lawless slumped in a padded chair. His hair and clothes were a mess.

"Hey."

When Josh looked up, sadness ringed his eyes. Josh fingered the ice cubes in his drink. "Hey Vinnie."

"What's up?"

Josh said he was trying to hide.

Vinnie asked if he wanted to be alone.

"No, I'm not hiding from you. I'm mostly dodging Dorian. We used to be friends, but he wants dirt and right now I'm standing in a heap of it."

"Dorian is determined."

"He is relentless, and it's not just him. It's Sue. It's Mykel. It's ninety percent of the people at this party. They all saw how stupid I was."

Vinnie assured him that his friends and his fans still loved him.

"This is about my life, not that other crap. Everyone at the party wants to talk about my breakups. *Break Ups. Plural.* I fucked up big time." Josh finished his drink and handed Vinnie the glass. "Can you bring me another one? I can't go in there. If anyone asks if you've seen me, say that I left."

A few moments later, Vinnie handed Josh a fresh cocktail. He asked about any hope of reconciling with Ian.

Tears welled in Josh's eyes. "I hurt him so bad. He moved back home."

"To Vancouver?"

Josh nodded. "Ian loved me, not *Josh Lawless, the Fuck Machine.* He didn't like sharing me, but he did it because he loved me. He worried that one day some on-screen hookup would become more." Josh said he had assured Ian that would never happen. "If I had it all to do over, I would not give Hank London the time of day." He took a swig of his drink. "But there are no do-overs." He paused before adding. "All I want is Ian. If he came back, I would leave this all today."

"You need to talk to him. You can't give up."

Josh didn't want sympathy or to feel better. His pain was payback for the pain that he had caused. Josh covered his face with his hands. "I am such a fool."

The crowd in the other room sounded suddenly louder and looser, as though someone might walk into the reception area at any moment. The party would be up for grabs in under an hour—hookups, harsh words, and more.

Vinnie needed to get Josh out of there. If Dorian found him in this state, he would eat Josh alive. Being drunk and remorseful at an industry event was not a good look. Vinnie imagined the headline, *Lawless in Tears.*

Pity is the kiss of death for a porn star.

Vinnie convinced Josh it was wise to leave. "We need to get you home."

"I need to say goodbye." Josh tried to stand but fell back onto the couch.

Vinnie helped him up and steered him towards the outer door instead. "You can explain tomorrow. Joe and Gio will understand."

Josh seemed to consider the statement before leaning on Vinnie and heading to the elevators.

A cab was coming down the street.

Perfect timing.

Josh gave the driver his address. The taxi smelled new; usually, cabs reek of sweat, booze, perfume, or air freshener. On the ride, Josh continued to talk about Hank leaving him. "Ian makes me sad, but Hank pisses me off. He's back home saying, "Oh, what a jolly dalliance. But it ruined my life."

Vinnie hated seeing Josh this way.

Josh said that he still believed in love. "I came tonight because Joe and Gio have something special, and when people find each other, it's worth celebrating." But Josh said the party reminded him of what he had lost with Ian. "We had something special, and I turned it into shit."

Vinnie sometimes felt like that with Valentino. Turning from the window, Vinnie caught the driver's eye in the rearview mirror. Josh was still talking, and the driver seemed very attentive. Vinnie began to get nervous about this cab that didn't smell like a cab and that just happened to be passing the studio.

When Vinnie told Josh they would talk more at his place, the driver quickly turned his attention back to the road.

76

The taxi glided to a stop in front of a bungalow with a roof of terra cotta tile and a trellis along the walkway. The front lawn, vines, and shrubbery were dead from the heat.

While opening the door, Josh mumbled a drunken apology for the mess. The cottage was filthy. Inside it was sweltering. The air was stale and heavy. The bungalow smelled of cut wood despite the fact that Josh's living room was littered with beer cans, pizza boxes, fast food bags, and an ashtray—the artifacts of two breakups. Josh needed a cleaning service.

"Being where Ian and I lived, and then where I was with Hank. This place has a lot of memories."

"You should rearrange things," Vinnie said, cracking a window. "Or paint. But it smells like you've been working at something."

Josh said the only good thing to come out of all this was that it gave him time to focus on his pet project. "Want to see what I've been doing?"

"Of course." Vinnie wanted to encourage anything that got Josh out of his funk. Following a passion for anything seemed a step in the right direction.

Josh opened the door to the second bedroom and flipped on the light. The sawdust swirled. "Since Hank left, I've been working almost nonstop to convert the spare bedroom into a mini-museum." Josh said he was organizing and getting ready to display his shrine to the XXX gay business. "This is my therapy."

"Wow," was all that Vinnie could manage.

Surrounded by so much to see, Vinnie barely noticed Josh leave and come back with two beers. Framed gay porn movie posters adorned the walls. Multiple binders were on a Lucite table with signed photos of dozens of XXX stars. *Hundreds.* The boxes scattered about the room held more gay porn ephemera. Action figures. Promo items. Josh had a box of signed "star mold" dildos.

The shelves along the walls stood floor to ceiling.

Vinnie was trying to take it all in. "This is incredible."

Josh said he started saving things years ago. "Some called me crazy and some say its corny, but being a part of this industry has meant something to me."

Vinnie said he couldn't believe how much he had.

Josh said there was plenty more. "All the movies and magazines are in the garage."

Vinnie was already looking through some of the binders.

"Those are autographed photos and promotional one-page sheets." Josh pulled out a colossal plastic tub. "These are production notes, production invoices, and payroll." Vinnie crouched down and started looking through the plastic bin. Xclusiv invoices. When Josh went to pee, Vinnie pocketed a couple of them. He was replacing the plastic lid on the tub when Josh returned.

"I'm still unpacking stuff. There are half a dozen more boxes in the closet."

On display in the makeshift museum was a wrestling singlet worn by Rob Cryston and a pair of Peter Berlin's leather pants signed with a silver Sharpee. There was the glove of Daddy Zeus, two original signed Matt Sterling scripts, and a framed glory hole used in a Joe Gage opus. On a stand was a teased Chi Chi LaRue wig beside a signed photo with an additional binder of LaRue's production notes. Another notebook held photos and snapshots from industry parties and events. Vinnie flipped to a candid shot of Carter Gaines.

"That was taken at Woody's place on the night he died." Josh tapped the photo. "Only a couple of hours later, Carter was dead. This is probably the last picture of him."

Vinnie said that it had been tragic.

"None of us could believe it."

A display case held a pair of Fred Halsted's worn jeans beside the beloved pot pipe of Al Parker. There was a Casey Donovan's speedo, Joey Stefano's tighty-whities, and a signed copy of Bobby Blake's book *My Life in Porn*. There were pictures of porn stars at the Gaiety in New York, the Bijou and Man's Country in Chicago, and Nob Hill in San Francisco. A giant cut-out of Jeff Stryker was propped in a corner.

Josh's Grabby Award sat on a shelf, the centerpiece of several other industry plaques and accolades. They weren't all his. Josh purchased a few of the statuettes and certificates on eBay. Some colleagues needed cash more than mementos. "Some guys aren't sentimental at all about their time in the business." Josh added that several of the donations were posthumous.

Initially, Vinnie offered his blind support, but now that he had seen some of Josh's collection, he was sure this was the start of something important. I can see guys paying to tour this. I would pay to see this."

"Yep, porn saved me, and I am proud to have been a part of it."

Vinnie noticed a shot of himself in one of the binders. He felt good to be a part of all this. He had signed his first photo for Josh after filming *Backfield in Motion*. "I remember when you asked for this." Vinnie chuckled, "This may have even been my first autographed photo as Vinnie Lux. Now here it is, sheathed in plastic." He understood how Josh felt about being a part of a bigger history.

Vinnie turned the page.

"And here is something from an old friend of ours." It was a glossy photo of A.Z. in a clear plastic sleeve. "He was so handsome." On the back of the photo were a few lines about what a pleasure it was working with Josh. The word pleasure was underlined—twice. The inscription was signed A.Z. Ambush; beside his signature was a heart and arrow. Once more, the handwriting attributed to A.Z. in no way resembled the writing in the notebook. "A.Z. wrote this?"

Josh took offense that Vinnie might be questioning the signature's authenticity. "A.Z. was standing right beside me when he wrote it, close as I am standing to you." Josh gestured around the room. "I don't have fake stuff in my collection."

"I just wasn't sure." Vinnie was trying to backpedal as best he could.

"Lots of times the studio sends forged pictures," added Josh. "Part of Kip's job at Xclusiv is to reply to fan requests. There is none of that here. It is all the real deal. I can vouch for it."

If this were A.Z.'s signature, that could mean one of two things—either A.Z.'s handwriting had changed dramatically, or the notebook pages were forged. If the copied notebook pages were counterfeit, that begged a bigger question, *Why?*

77

Coming home to a quiet apartment, Vinnie was too anxious to sleep. After two hours of tossing and turning, he stopped trying. TV was no help. Nothing was distracting enough. He had so many questions. So much didn't make sense. At dawn, he smoked a cigarette on the balcony. The city flattened with the sharp contrast between light and shadow. Vinnie snubbed out his smoke. He retrieved A.Z.'s notebook from his room.

This was definitely the work of a different hand.

Vinnie reread the entries.

If the notebook was a fake, it was reasonable to assume the content was phony as well. Why else copy it—in longhand? Vinnie suspected this fake was planted to deceive him. *But why?* No practical joke was this impractical. Whoever was responsible knew the weight a dead man's words would hold. After the search, it was logical for Vinnie to assume it had been to find the notebook. They wanted him to take the journal pages as gospel.

But why include his things in the jumble of A.Z.'s room?

Vinnie was lying on his bed trying to make sense of things when he heard Reed trying to get his key in the front door. Seven-thirty in the morning and Reed was just getting in from last night. He came down the hall, pounding on doors. "Everybody up. Come on, Wannabe. Come on, Scarface."

Vinnie opened his door. "Kip isn't home. And calling him Scarface is just plain rude."

"True. It's inaccurate too. The scars are everywhere but his face. I'll call him Patches. Thank you for catching that and correcting me."

Reed prided himself on being unfiltered, but mostly he was just an asshole. "I just say what most people are thinking." Reed neglected to add that the reason for that was that most people over the age of five know better. His popularity continued—podcasts, cable TV, print interviews, and probably *Celebrity Rehab* in a season or two.

Reed was still talking. "No one cares about Kip anyway—except Ed Vittori apparently?"

Last night the two men had been inseparable. When Vinnie didn't find Kip at home this morning, he assumed they spent the night together.

"I have a film crew that was with me to shoot rough footage to pitch my reality show. Two networks have already shown interest."

"Yes." Reed had told Vinnie, twice, last night.

"I need Kip and Ed to sign release forms to include them in the background. My people had a release form to sign, but didn't want to disturb them. I need him to sign now." He raised his voice and once more called for Kip.

Dealing with a wasted Reed was maddening. "Like I said, Kip's not home."

"He's not?"

The thought that Reed was a criminal mastermind was hard to swallow. Vinnie did suspect that Reed orchestrated the Cash Cranston leak. Then last week, Lee Botello had told Vinnie some juicy gossip. He said he had heard that Reed was pissed because Dean Driver started fucking Cash Cranston too. Lee added. "Rumor is they had been hooking up ever since Reed introduced them. When Reed found out he swore to get even."

Vinnie pictured a romantic weekend in Cash's hillside home, just the two of them—and a well-placed photographer. Setting Cash up was probably like leading a lamb to slaughter. *Click! Click!* Cash was over, Reed was a media sensation, and Dean was left high and dry.

Lee didn't stop there. "He said he knew someone who knew a guy that Reed hired to do a background check on Dean Driver or whatever his original name was. Anyway, whatever that detective discovered was the *real* reason Dean retired to Long Beach."

Given the things Reed said and the threats he made during his routine rants, his response didn't shock Vinnie. The bigger bombshell was definitely the rumor that Dean was also having an affair with Cash.

Reed was still pacing the hallway. "Why isn't music ever playing in this flat? We need music. And we need alcohol. Let me text about that."

Reed was even more exhausting than usual. Dealing with him on no sleep was doing nothing to ease Vinnie's headache.

While Reed was texting, Vinnie asked who was coming over.

"A few guys from the club. One of my film crew is coming. The party is still going. Woody is coming and bringing that freak, Aaron Fyre. Other people too." Reed offered Vinnie some blow. "You need to catch up."

Despite his fatigue, Vinnie declined. Coke was the last thing he wanted.

"What kind of porn star are you? Turn in your card."

Vinnie asked if Gio and Joe were coming as well.

"Who?"

"Gio and Joe, the guests of honor."

"They bailed hours ago." Reed synched his playlist with the speakers. Techno throbbed, poking at Vinnie's headache. Reed was too wasted to dance, but drunk enough to think that he could. A loose turn and a half bottle of stale beer spilled across the kitchen counter, dripping onto the kitchen tile. This was already too much, and the guests hadn't even arrived.

78

Vinnie had too much on his mind to deal with this nonsense. He needed to leave. He threw some things in his backpack, including the notebook and one of the copies. He crept out of his bedroom when Reed was in the bathroom. The thump of synthesizers covered the opening and closing of the back door. The elevator was too risky. The stairwell zigzagged down to the plywood storage cages. Beyond that were some bikes and eventually a door that opened onto the alley.

Outside Vinnie heard the squeal of brakes and backed into the shadows. Two taxis pulled to the curb. In the front cab were Woody, Aaron, and Leon. Lee Botello and three young shirtless guys were in the second. One of the twinks was on the film crew. Thankfully, none of them had seen Vinnie. Stumbling from the cabs, the remaining partiers had become lead-footed nightlife zombies, not knowing what they hungered for, only knowing they craved more.

Taking the alley to the far side of the building, Vinnie spied a city bus at the corner and hopped on board. He rode for a while without a plan. Eventually, he grew impatient with the pace of the bus. He hopped off outside Best Brew coffee shop. No reason. It seemed as good a place as any to be.

The coffee was good. Vinnie sat for a full hour, trying to come up with a plan of action. One guy and then another looked his way. Porn stars in coffee shops draw attention. This wasn't smart if he was trying to disappear.

Today fame was not a pedestal but a cage. Exhaustion made it hard for him to focus. His brain felt shredded at the edges. Maybe there was something more in the notebook. The thought that someone might be watching made Vinnie too paranoid to look at the notebook here.

Across a weed-choked lot, he spotted a motel that looked like a good place to disappear for a while and maybe sleep. Vinnie needed time to get a handle on things. He needed a clear head. He had some cash, a couple of charge cards, his phone, and his charger. In his backpack was almost everything he would need. If not, there was a Walgreens on the corner. Vinnie returned to the counter and ordered a glazed, a powdered, and a large coffee to-go.

The orange neon tubes of the *Vacancy* sign buzzed, and the 'C' flickered off more than on. The place had no name as far as Vinnie could tell. Bells announced his arrival. The lobby smelled like an overcooked pancake. The clerk recognized Vinnie but said nothing. He didn't need to.

A woman was in the office watching a western on TV. She shouted something to the clerk.

Vinnie asked for a single room. The man needed his current license and a credit card. "The pool is closed," he added.

"No worries. I didn't want to swim." *Especially here*, he thought.

The clerk ran Vinnie's card before handing him the key to Room 217. Their eyes locked. The guy was making his interest known.

Definitely lock the door once I get in the room.

The woman in the back room yelled about a misplaced remote. Seeing an opportunity, Vinnie grabbed his room card, offered quick thanks, and made a hasty retreat.

The rooms were all outer entry with a cement walkway from the ground floor to the stairs. Room 217 was the first room to the right at the top. Vinnie was expecting dingy, so he wasn't surprised. When light from the open door spilled into the room, Vinnie saw things scatter into the shadows. He hoped it was just fatigue. Vinnie bolted and chained the door and turned on the ceiling fan. He opened the window but kept the shades down.

No one outside.

He sat at the desk and slid the notebook from his backpack. The powdered doughnut was a blast of sugar.

At least one person, whoever planted the notebook in his room, knew he had the pages. However, it was likely that person didn't realize that Vinnie suspected the notebook was a fake. Vinnie could use that to his advantage. Whoever was behind this didn't consider the handwriting, or imagine Vinnie would encounter verified samples of A.Z.'s writing. Both the 8 x 10 at the Blaze and the personalized shot in Josh's collection seemed to indicate that someone else had written the pages planted in Vinnie's room.

He began looking through the notebook. Then, on a separate sheet of paper, Vinnie started to list the incriminating things included and those accused of the wrongdoing. Vinnie wasn't sure what he was looking for, but there had to be something.

- Some money from Mr. Worthington would go a long way in securing our future.
- Novak would shit a brick, tie it to my feet, and toss me in the Pacific if he heard.
- Vittori was instructed to wait until Peter was good and wasted and give him an overdose from a doctored syringe.
- Woody couldn't have that kid discovered at his house. Xclusiv didn't need that sort of publicity.
- Woody said he had a plan.
- I heard Woody and Vittori carry the body out the back and watched from behind the window blinds as they loaded Carter in the car.
- Kip hopped in and took off. He was so messed up by that point he probably figured Carter was passed out instead of already dead.
- His body was burned beyond recognition. The most convenient thing for all involved.
- I am the only witness and the only one who knows what happened that night except for Woody and Vittori. Woody would probably kill me (or have me killed) if he knew.

The notebook even cast suspicion upon Vinnie.

The entries made accusations about Woody, Vittori, Novak, and Dolph Worthington. Based on the contents of these pages, any one of them had ample motive to want A.Z. dead. But if the notebook was a phony, it stood to reason that the forger would use it to cast suspicion elsewhere—exonerating themselves or even removing themselves from the story completely.

Vinnie rolled across the bowed motel bed. The spread held the subtle reek of something foul. Vinnie pulled the comforter from the bed. The sheet smelled just as bad.

Opening his backpack, Vinnie took out the three Xclusiv invoices he had swiped from Josh's collection last night. He felt a tinge of remorse. He'd been tipsy, but he planned on returning them. At the time he took them, he had been curious about salaries. Maybe if somebody has something on Woody, they might be getting something extra in their check. In the light of day, he saw how a blackmailer probably would be smarter than to leave that obvious of a paper trail. Seeing the sheets now, it didn't matter anyway. Talent was not broken down by individual performer, but by the totals of primary and secondary models. On the invoice, he noticed something else—*Paragon-Kamden Optics*. That was a company on the slip of paper in the empty cigarette pack, the company with no business listing at an address that didn't exist.

Grundella Services was on the invoice as well.

Bogus companies. Vinnie could think of only one reason for two bad companies to be on an invoice—embezzlement. Someone was padding the books and collecting a fat check. Ed Vittori was the likely candidate.

He's our numbers guy.

Vinnie wondered if he should keep the invoices. He took a photo instead. Did he even want proof? Coming forward had never been a part of this. No one wanted police involvement. The cops hated this world and everyone in it. Bringing the information to Woody was too risky. Someone had intentionally involved Vinnie in all this. There must be a reason. He was in far too deep not to want some answers.

The story seemed to start on the night of Carter's death. Josh had pictures from the evening. Vinnie had seen a couple of the photos last night. Something might be in those shots. Vinnie had started looking through them but got sidetracked by "the last photo" of Carter Gaines.

As tempting as a few hours of sleep sounded, he needed to see those photos now. He needed to go back to Josh's place. The truth was more important than sleep.

79

The bungalow looked more neglected in the light of day. Vinnie knocked. No response. He knocked louder. No doubt Josh was sleeping it off. Vinnie knocked a third time. Hard.

Movement inside.

Given the double break-up, the binge, and the probable size of his hangover, when Josh opened the door in his white briefs, he looked better than Vinnie expected. Josh shielded his eyes from the sun with a beefy forearm. He looked like a grizzly roused from hibernation, chest hair trailing down to a hefty cotton pouch. Josh scratched his head. "What time it is?" Without waiting for an answer, Josh shuffled down the hallway.

Vinnie followed him inside. He had rehearsed what he was going to say. "I stopped by to check on you."

"I'll live," Josh grunted.

"And I was eager to take a closer look at your memorabilia room. It is really something." Vinnie was ready to explain, but Josh didn't care.

"Knock yourself out," Josh was already heading back to bed. "Just be quiet."

"Do you mind if I make some coffee?"

Josh had slipped off his briefs and was sprawled on the bed with his beefy ass on display. He was already snoring.

Vinnie found a binder in the memorabilia room with a dozen photos from the night Carter Gaines died. The pictures featured the expected crowd: Woody, Vittori, Dorian Mikado, Kip, Josh, Lee Botello, Peter Ray Thomas, McCain, Sue, Christian Sabre, A.Z., and Reed, as well as some people that Vinnie didn't recognize. Most of the crowd looked like industry. Dwayne Thorne was there, looking hot in a signature kilt, flashing his ass at the camera. In the background of a couple of the shots, Vinnie saw Leon from the Blaze.

The last two pictures in the album were of Desi Lou, Xclusiv's first superstar. He looked bloated and ruddy. Two months later, he was living on the streets. Vinnie saw nothing to clarify the mystery of what happened that night.

Next, Vinnie began going through Josh's extensive 8 x 10 collection. If the forger was a performer, maybe they used the same writing to sign their glossy to Josh. There were several binders. Vinnie began flipping through the pages, eyes on the writing and the signatures. The plastic sleeves held signed pictures of such porn legends as Jack Wrangler, Joe Simmons, JD Slater, John Davenport, Blade Thompson, Diesel Washington, all three of the Rockland Brothers, Casey Donovan, Zak Spears, Lee Ryder, Gus Mattox, Jon Vincent, Rod Garetto, Kris Lord, JC Carter, Francois Sagat, Scott O'Hara, and more.

Vinnie found Woody's scrawl. Next to it was the signature of Lee Botello. The contract was only a signature, not enough to determine much of anything. The document was followed by an 8 x 10 of Lee with a note to Josh. Lee was not the forger.

Retrieving the notebook from his backpack, Vinnie looked at the writing. It was familiar. He had seen it somewhere else. He was sure of it. Vinnie opened another binder of glossies—Kip Noll, Lou Cass, Thom Katt. Tom Chase. Tristan York. Steve Cruz, Tyson Cane, Pierre Fitch. Another legal document.

Eyes crossing with fatigue, Vinnie remembered the coffee. On his way to pour himself a cup, Vinnie heard the deep creak of the bungalow. Maybe Josh was moving around in bed. Vinnie paused. Silence returned. Crossing the hallway, Vinnie noticed the front door was open.

What the fuck?

Vinnie tried to remember through a fog of exhaustion. Josh had let him in and went back to bed. Vinnie was the last one inside. Maybe he hadn't fully closed the door and a breeze blew it back open.

Creaking.

Every house has its peculiarities.

Vinnie closed the door. He heard the clock on the mantle. Josh's snoring had stopped. The house popped once more. Maybe it was expanding beneath the morning sun. Looking for the sugar, Vinnie heard something behind him. He caught a shadow from the corner of his eye and in the same instant he recalled where he had seen the writing.

The scrawl was on the Wall of Fame posters in the entryway at Xclusiv. The poster was for *The French Love Connection*—one of Kip Mason's biggest hits.

It was a full-body shot of Kip climbing out of a pool in a silver speedo. Kip had signed it with a red Sharpie:

> *Big thanks to everyone at Xclusive for making this movie possible. Thank you, Woody. Thank you, Ed. Thank you, Joe. Love you all more than you know. Xoxox, Kip Mason.*

Vinnie recalled the loop of the capital "L," the slant of the letters, and the squared commas. The handwriting was identical to the notebook.

"Hello," said Kip.

Vinnie gasped. "Oh Kip, you startled me. I just made coffee. Would you like some?"

Kip neared. "Aren't you going to ask why I'm here?"

Vinnie remained silent.

"Woody wanted me to swing by and check on Josh," said Kip. "His behavior last night had a lot of people concerned."

"I was checking on him too." Vinnie said he had brought Josh home last night and he was not in a good place. The coffee maker beeped. "I didn't hear you knock at all."

Kip produced a key ring from his pocket. "I came in the same way I come and go other places—passkeys. Woody was smart. He invested some of that Perry O'Hara money in real estate. Josh gets the same perks as you. This bungalow is also the property of Xclusiv."

"I didn't know."

"Now you do."

Something more was coming.

Kip continued. "I was so concerned about Josh, that I even drove over here last night too."

Vinnie felt his heart race.

"I heard you talking about A.Z.'s photo. I was standing in there," Kip pointed to the living room. "Eavesdropping wasn't hard, especially when Josh took offense after you questioned the *authenticity* of A.Z.'s photo. I stood listening to that and asked myself, why is Vinnie so interested in that—and now you're back."

Vinnie felt time slow to a standstill.

Kip took a switchblade from his pocket—the blade appeared with a click. "The notebook is what I mean. The pages. When I heard you question A.Z.'s writing, I figured you knew the notebook was a fake." Kip ran the blade over the countertop as he moved closer. "The writing was an oversight."

Vinnie claimed he didn't know anything. "Believe me, I don't understand any of this."

"Of course, you don't." Kip seemed happy to explain. And things were going along fine—until you got involved."

"I didn't get involved. You got me involved. And if things were going so great, why did A.Z. have to die?"

Kip's lips thinned. "Because A.Z. wanted to ruin things."

Vinnie's back was against the sink. The basin was empty, but four empty beer bottles were on the counter.

"If you're about to call for Josh, save your breath," Kip grinned. "I gave him an injection to knock him out."

Back still to the sink, Vinnie slid a step away. "You killed Carter, and A.Z."

"Yes, and no. I killed Carter and Roy. Technically I did not kill A.Z., but I did have a hand in it." Kip fished a phone from his pocket. "Roy's cell," he said, putting it on the counter. Kip played a voicemail Vinnie had left, then a second, and a third. In each message, Vinnie hinted at their suspicions over the death of A.Z.

"I can explain those."

Kip feigned attentiveness. "I was hoping you would."

"Well, I wanted to let..."

"I was being sarcastic," Kip sneered. "I know why you left the messages. I've had this phone since the day I slit Roy's throat. I even used this blade. I asked for his help in the pool house. There's a backroom there."

The locked door.

"Roy had moved in with Lee Botello and came back to get the last of his things from the casita. We had a drink and toasted A.Z. Roy didn't suspect a thing—not from me anyway. I asked if he had a minute to help me with something. He saw the blade a second too soon. He ran but didn't get far. I put something in his drink. Roy was stumbling when he fled the pool house. I tackled him on the cement. He fell hard. I expect that was when he lost the ring you found in the pool."

Kip had been watching.

"I dragged Roy back to the pool house. Flipped his limp body into that metal tub and slit his throat. He bled out like a pig. Hardly a drop got on the floor. Add boiling water and lye. I kept the temperature of the water well over two-hundred degrees. By the next morning, Roy was bones and fillings—dissolved by aquamation."

Lye was the stinging scent Vinnie had mistaken for pool chemicals. "Getting rid of Roy was a lot easier than getting rid of that smell. I packed what was left of him in a suitcase and tossed him into the Pacific—a little at a time. Driving along the coast and disposing of him was actually very relaxing."

Kip was sicker than Vinnie had ever imagined.

"I found the journal by accident," he said. "I was searching A.Z.'s room, not looking for anything in particular. The passkeys are a good way to make sure that nobody has any secrets that I don't know about. A.Z. had a doozy. He was careless. The notebook was in his bedside drawer. On the page I opened to, he wondered about the death of Carter and what he had seen from the bathroom that night. I had no choice. By putting it in that notebook, A.Z. had signed his own death warrant. We planned his murder that evening."

We?

"I found his notebook the night you came back early from Chicago."

In his eagerness to get out of Chicago, Vinnie had changed his flight.

"That time, A.Z. did a good job hiding the notebook. I trashed his room trying to find it." Kip shook his head. "And then you walked into the flat two days early. I didn't have time to put anything back, so I carried your stuff to A.Z.'s room and mixed it in the mess. I was behind the locked door that night."

The blade never wavered for a moment. Vinnie was praying for some sort of distraction.

"We burned the original notebook. We couldn't risk having it around. However, after A.Z.'s demise Novak, Woody, and Dolph Worthington were made aware of a notebook and that it had some interesting things to say. Nothing specific—only that it was the diary of A.Z. Ambush. Each of those men had plenty to hide, secrets A.Z. may or may not have known."

So much still made no sense to Vinnie. "Why the fake notebook for me?"

Kip smiled. "We needed to see how rough these boys were going to play with a blackmailer of course." Kip saw the dumbfounded look on Vinnie's face and explained. "You arrived like you were God's gift to porn and gave everyone your big speech about doing whatever it takes to succeed, blah blah blah. You were handed a ticket to the big time. We figured you would use it."

"I was never ambitious enough to resort to blackmail."

Kip nodded. "Yes, unfortunately. You didn't ask for money or use it for career leverage. Instead, when given the keys to the kingdom, Vinnie Lux decides to play Nancy Screw."

"Why did you kill Carter in the first place?"

"Carter had to go. Audiences were eating him up. Woody was eating him up. Carter was not smart—not stupid like you. He was just gullible. I handed him the syringe and dared him to enjoy the party like everyone else. He did it right there with no hesitation—as trusting as a kid brother." Kip shrugged. "No backwoods runaway was going to ruin my plans. The Peter Ray Thomas part of the notebook was pure fiction. No one got a syringe by mistake. That needle hit the bull's-eye. Carter did not deserve the attention. I did. No one remembers Carter Gaines today."

"Because you never gave him the chance."

"Exactly. Who knows though, if you die now, you may be remembered. People love tragedy. Maybe death will be your big break."

Vinnie ignored the jab. "So, what about your plan didn't work?"

Kip asked what he meant.

"Did you plan on the accident that ended your career?"

"That was unexpected. As we rounded the curve that night, Carter's body convulsed in a post-mortem spasm. I only looked away for a moment." Kip shook his head. "No, the scars were not part of the original plan."

"And instead you became Woody's servant?"

"Devotion and control may look similar, but the end game is very different. I'm Woody's eyes and ears." Kip grinned. "When Woody wants to know about something, I tell him. When he wants information, I give it to him. I control what he knows."

"So then you know about the $50,000 Woody got from Dolph?"

Kip said he had no idea what Vinnie was talking about.

"I saw the memo about the D.W. meeting followed by a cash deposit to the studio account."

"Oh, Vinnie. I am going to miss having you around," laughed Kip. "D.W. was not Dolph Worthington—it was a manuscript. A collector wanted to buy the working manuscript of Perry O'Hara's *Dark Waters*. Woody wanted cash to avoid a paper trail. That's always a mistake. Ask Ed Vittori."

Vinnie asked what he meant by that.

"Working the desk at Xclusiv, I have access to almost everything. In the first few weeks in that position I found out Vittori was cooking the books. He was sloppy. The ledger was fiction—inflated costs, bogus expenses, a separate account ..."

Grundella Services. Paragon-Kamden Optics.

"Skimming money from DVD sales, appearances, tours—everything. Vittori was playing with fire. Taking money from the studio meant taking money from Novak. Swindling the Lavender Outfit is bad. So, I talked about it with a friend of mine who had moved to town. He convinced me to copy some invoices and have a chat with Ed. Vittori has been my bitch ever since. For example, he will collaborate whatever story I concoct about today." A smile curled across Kip's lips before he lunged. The knife sliced the air. Vinnie grabbed the longneck from the counter. Kip swung the knife again. Vinnie deflected the blade with the bottle. Breaking it on counter, he wielded the jagged neck.

Kip had the blade inches from him. "Drop the bottle or the story ends here."

Seeing his odds as slim to none, Vinnie let the brown bottleneck fall to the linoleum.

Kip kicked it aside. "Since it has your prints on it I can say you attacked me."

Vinnie shook his head. "Why would I do that?"

"Drugs. Desperation. Jealousy. Guilt. Childhood demons. Career failure. Most feel signing you at the studio was a huge mistake—McCain, Vitttori. Even Sue joked that there was nothing special to highlight on your face."

Kip was lying.

"Woody gave you a chance, but he wanted nothing to do with you after he saw the footage of you searching his office. He's a businessman. Woody has things to hide. He wanted to fire you, but Vittori convinced him to keep you around."

"And why was that?"

"Because Vittori does as I say." Kip swung the blade and sliced Vinnie's thigh.

"You're crazy." Blood soaked through the gap in his jeans. "And how were you involved in A.Z.'s death?"

"I planned his murder, but as far as committing it—let's just say I had help from a friend."

"Who?"

Kip asked why he should tell him.

"Because otherwise I'll die thinking that you're a liar."

Kip considered Vinnie's comment before calling over his shoulder. "Hey baby, come out here. I need you to settle a bet with a dead man."

Footsteps approached in the hall. Dean leaned against the doorframe. Kip backed up to kiss him. *Open mouthed. Hungry.* "Dean here is brilliant, but shy."

Dean grabbed a fistful of Kip's hair. "We agreed you would take care of this."

Kip turned. "Vinnie thinks I killed A.Z. I told him otherwise." His hand moved to Dean's crotch.

Dean looked over. "Hey Vinnie. I was hoping the next time I saw you that you would be dead."

The comment landed like a punch.

"I thought you moved to Long Beach." Vinnie tried to ignore Dean's hardening cock.

"No pilot. No Long Beach. I lied." Dean smiled. "Most folks underestimate me. People talk when they think you're too slow or too stoned to notice. A.Z. figured me for a dumb, big-dicked Texan—but I'm not dumb and I'm not from Texas. A.Z. should've known better than to believe my studio bio. Killing A.Z. was strictly business."

Vittori had been Dean's alibi the weekend of A.Z.'s death, and vice versa. On the day of A.Z.'s drowning, Dean and Ed were supposedly having their lover's tryst at the Hotel del Coronado in San Diego.

"I drove to where A.Z. was staying. I watched and waited until he was alone. Then I sauntered up as the big dumb Texan. *What a coincidence!* A slap on the shoulder with the added jab of a needle full of something strong enough to bring down a bull. A simple drowning and A.Z. Ambush was gone. Now the notebook was mine."

Mine, not ours.

"You see, I want a lot out of life, but I hate to work."

Kip was nuts, but Dean was diabolical. If they were accruing a fortune together, Kip would be wise to watch his back. Dean did not seem the type who liked to share.

More footsteps in the hallway.

"Finally," said Kip. "I've been waiting for my witness."

Vittori entered, looking rattled. Ed turned to Dean, "We can't keep doing this. This is crazy."

"You have no say," said Dean.

Kip slid the blade up his sleeve.

"You don't want Novak to hear about Paragon-Kamden Optics," said Dean.

Vittori was shaking his head and backing away. "That won't work anymore. I'm done. Novak knows. On the way here, I stopped to see him. Novak is the one who sent me."

"Bullshit." Kip spit the word. "You came because we called."

Vittori was firm. "I told Novak about both of you, and what you're doing to his businesses."

"You're stealing from him too." Kip didn't believe him.

"I told him, and I told Novak that you wanted more. Paragon-Kamden Optics was pocket money. You had me add Grundella Services and Variety Tax and all that. Blackmail. I told him you're after his business."

"That's not true," said Kip.

Vittori stood firm. "It is true. Believe what you want," Vittori shrugged. "Novak asked me to deliver a message. He was feeling generous. He gave you both an option—leave the money, leave the pictures, and leave town immediately—not tonight, not tomorrow, now."

Dean said he would set Novak straight. "I don't know what you told him."

"I doubt you'll get close enough to open your mouth." Vittori removed the gun tucked in the back of his pants and aimed the barrel at Dean.

"Novak isn't God." Dean said they had options.

Vittori laughed. "The options are stay or go. If you stay, your options are up to Novak. He decides how much you suffer."

346

Kip slid the switchblade down from his sleeve and charged Vittori. Batting the gun aside, Kip plunged the blade into Vittori's stomach. The gun clattered to the floor. Kip yanked the blade free and stabbed him again in the neck. Blood pulsed from the throat wound. Vittori sank to his knees with a look of shock on his face and in a moment he slumped forward. Blood pooled on the linoleum around him.

Dean stepped back. "I'm not leaving the money. Pack your things and wait for me at the flat. I'll be an hour. Take the knife."

Kissing Dean, Kip ran down the hall and out the back door.

After the screen slammed, Dean stepped over Vittori's body. "I had Ed Vittori's balls in my pocket for those cooked books. He would do anything I asked—even deliver a fake message from Novak. Ed didn't realize it would be the last thing I asked him to do. He couldn't be trusted. I wanted him dead and I wanted Kip to do it." Dean picked up the pistol. "You see, no bullets in Vittori's gun."

"And you aren't going to the flat to pick up Kip."

Dean nodded. "Correct." He had already emptied the bogus accounts.

Vinnie needed to think of something—fast. "So, you're still a ways away from being home free." Vinnie continued. "Kip is a con man. It may take time, but he's going to put this together. He'll know as soon as you don't come to the flat."

Dean said he would be long gone by then.

"But you won't be free of him," Vinnie needed to talk fast. "Kip won't rest until he finds you."

Dean loaded the gun. "I'll deal with that problem when it arises."

"That might mean a lot of looking over your shoulder—but there is a solution."

"Which is?"

"Pin it on Kip. I will swear he killed Vittori, which is true. A witness is important. Otherwise, with both of you leaving town there will be questions. If you kill me, there is just your word as to what happened and from what I've heard your past might be an issue. I'll be a good witness. I'll be convincing and when the heat dies down, I'll disappear." Vinnie didn't mind leaving L.A. He had grown to hate the stink of this town.

"Why should I trust you?"

"Because I know what you're capable of doing." Vinnie repeated his idea. "Kip takes the blame. The cops are happy, you get the money, and I'm alive. You need to decide. If you kill me, you'll need to explain that too. Let me live and there is a chance for you to walk away with the money. That's what this is all about—right?"

Before Dean could answer, Josh stumbled into the kitchen, wiping the sleep from his eyes.

Dean tucked the gun beneath his belt.

Josh was clearly still under the influence of whatever shot Kip had given him. He shuffled to the refrigerator and took a swig from the milk carton. Josh felt something and looked down. There was blood between his toes. He saw the smashed bottles and then Vittori sprawled on the floor. He dropped the milk carton. "What the fuck!"

Dean said something terrible had just happened. "Vinnie was just calling the police."

80

The Case of the Porn Star Killer made headlines, mainly in the gay rags and local papers, before being picked up by a national news source. The lurid nature of the crime captured the public's fancy—at least that week.

Vinnie did what he needed to do to survive. Vinnie didn't like lying, and he didn't like feeling guilty—but he suspected he would like death even less. So he made good on his promise to be a star witness. He wasn't lying so much as omitting; Kip really did stab Ed Vittori to death, but the story of how it happened changed.

According to reports, Kip Mason came through the bungalow door bellowing for Ed Vittori. "Where are you, you thief?" Kip was raving about some pages that he claimed were proof of Vittori's embezzling. Lux and Driver were in the living room.

"We looked at each other a moment," added Dean. "Before going to see what was happening."

"It all happened so fast," added Vinnie.

"We were in the hallway when we heard Ed shout, 'Don't. Don't.'"

"We didn't know Kip had a knife."

Dean said when they got to the kitchen, they saw Vittori slump to the floor and heard the back door slam.

Asked if he thought Kip was on drugs, Vinnie paused. "Well, I, I shouldn't say. No, I can't really say." Lying to the cops is easy when you tell them what they want to hear.

Josh's confusion as a witness added gravity to the story.

"He slept through it all," said Vinnie. "We were going to brunch to try and cheer Josh up." Vinnie added that Lawless had been depressed over personal matters, primarily the aftermath of his break-ups.

Josh said he had forgotten the planned brunch though Vinnie and Dean maintained that they had all made plans the night before.

"That's how Kip knew Ed was here," added Dean.

During questioning by detectives, Josh admitted that most of the previous night had been a blur. No surprise. Josh still reeked of booze.

When Kip went to the flat, he grabbed his gun. He waited two hours for Dean and fled when he realized that something had gone wrong. He drove to a storage area the studio had near Venice Beach and parked on a side street.

For almost forty-eight hours, Kip Mason, aka James Vanderkirk, was a wanted man. His scars made him instantly recognizable. Kip knew it was only a matter of time, and he had a good idea of what was ahead. The following day he was roused by the sirens of more than one cop car. He loaded the gun. He was done fighting, but there was no way they were taking him alive. Kip considered a spin of Russian roulette, but in death, as in life, Kip always preferred a sure thing. He didn't leave a note—his confession was his brains splattered across the studio's DVD backlist.

The homicide/suicide scenario came together nicely for the detectives. The cops had the motive, witnesses, and the culprit in a body bag. Nice work. Case closed before the weekend.

The headlines destroyed the studio and devastated Woody. The depth of the betrayal shook him to the core. Vittori was embezzling, and Kip's devotion had resulted in murder. His rivals were pleased that Woody Wilson had finally gotten his comeuppance.

Just as interest in the case began to fade, a leading tabloid featured an interview with Josh Lawless. He claimed that in the aftermath of the murder, the bungalow was haunted. The tabloid ran a doctored shot of Vittori levitating above the kitchen sink. Josh moved out later that week, though Vinnie suspected he left because of another ghost—his memories of Ian.

Jean, Novak's assistant, told Vinnie that due to circumstances and the recent headlines, Trusted Talents needed to sever ties with him. Vinnie understood, and the news came as pure relief. With the studio in shambles, Vinnie was freed from his contact as well. He received several film offers. The Porn Star Killer Case had made him a hot property. The money was very good, but he declined.

The headlines also gave Vinnie a spike in followers. The tragedy was gold in that respect—but Vinnie didn't care about the increase. He hadn't cared about his numbers in a while. Followers used to mean something, but he had changed. Vinnie wasn't looking for the love of strangers anymore. The thought had lost its appeal. All Vinnie wanted was to look into the eyes of someone who mattered to him.

Suspending his Twitter and Instagram accounts was an easy decision to make.

They were only numbers.

81

The phone was ringing. And then, Valentino was on the line.

When Vinnie first heard his voice, he was unable to speak for a moment. "I'm sorry, you might not want to hear from me."

"Hello, Vinnie." Valentino took a breath. "I'm glad you called."

That simple sentence changed everything. Vinnie said he hated how things ended. "I was stupid—and afraid."

Valentino was in Siena. "It must be destined. This call would not even go through if I was at home on the farm." Valentino admitted that he had thought about Vinnie every day since coming home. "Still chasing your dream?"

"No, I woke up." Vinnie added that he was tired of L.A. and of being Vinnie Lux.

"Life is too short to be unhappy," replied Valentino. "Maybe the business taught you what you needed to learn."

"Or showed me where I needed to be."

Valentino had not heard about the Porn Star Killer Case. Vinnie told him the same story he told the police. Valentino cried when he heard what Vinnie had endured. "I'm so sorry for you."

Valentino asked Vinnie what he planned to do.

"That depends on you." Vinnie wanted a second chance.

Valentino told him to come to Italy. "You said you would when you had the time. Now you have the time. Life is different here."

After the events of the past several months, Vinnie craved anonymity once again. That was another thing he had been wrong about. Disappearing wasn't the opposite of being watched. The opposite of being watched was being seen.

Before hanging up, Valentino said his real name was Giovanni.

That evening Vinnie was bound for Florence. Valentino planned to take the train from Siena and meet him there. As the plane circled to land, Vinnie felt excited again and alive for the first time in ages.

All he had been looking for was a little happiness.

Once the plane landed, Vinnie dialed Jean's private line. During the flight, Vinnie had made up his mind that there was something he needed to do. He told Jean the truth about what Dean had done. "I know how Novak feels about thieves and blackmailers." When Vinnie finished, Jean was silent. Vinnie continued. "Keep that information to yourself or pass it on to Mr. Novak. Dean's fate is in your hands."

"I'll do as I see fit." Jean hung up the phone.

Vinnie was happy to toss Dean to that pack of wolves. They would give him the kind of justice he deserved. None of that was Vinnie's problem anymore.

Vinnie was ready to close that chapter and become someone new. As he walked through the terminal, he saw himself reflected in the windows. He was done being Vincent the doormat and done being Vinnie Lux the grasping super stud. Instead, perhaps it was time to blend the best parts of each together. Maybe in Italy, he would become Vincenzo.

Vincenzo and Giovanni.

He liked the sound of that.

EPILOGUE

In the village where they lived outside of Siena, Giovanni and Vincenzo needed to go to the coffee shop in town for Internet access. When Giovanni first told him about the lack of a signal, Vincenzo thought he would go out of his mind.

No Internet? And Siena was an hour away.

There was a period of adjustment. During his first week at the cottage, Vincenzo came into town every day to use the Internet. Sometimes he had to wait for an available computer. The dial-up service was slow, and the connection frequently dropped. As a result, his usage tapered off in the weeks following.

Cell phone reception was even worse. He had to stand in the middle of the town square to talk to Mother. The thought was unsettling to her. Mother did not understand why he had moved to Italy, living as "a farmer among foreigners." However, she was happy he was keeping his clothes on.

He mentioned his friend, Giovanni. Mother didn't ask anything more about Giovanni than his name. "Maybe next week," she said. For now, she was happy that he made her son happy. Vincenzo said he had to go. He told Mother he loved her.

For the first time in his life, Vincenzo felt he was where he should be.

Farming was a full-time job. Giovanni had inherited everything when his parents died just two months apart. Brain cancer. Breast cancer. His world was shattered. Giovanni told Vincenzo that he had needed more from life than a monastic existence on the farm. He fled to Rome for a month and hit the clubs. Someone gave him a business card. He did test shots. Woody called. "Then I was on my way to Hollywood, and I met you. And I stopped being lonely for the first time since losing my parents."

Giovanni said the farm was where he belonged. On the modest tract of land were a three-hundred-year-old stone cottage, a side building, and a house garden. The two men started raising chickens. They worked all day in the fields, fucked before dinner, then watched a movie from the closet full of tapes and DVDs. The selection reflected a love of Hollywood's Golden Era. Sometimes, after the movie, they would fuck again. Then, at dawn, it all started over again.

On Wednesdays and weekends, they loaded the vegetables and the eggs on the truck to sell in the village. Afterwards, Vincenzo bartered with another vendor for a bouquet of wildflowers that he gave Giovanni before they returned to the farm. Sometimes on the drive home, when the sun was low in the mountains, Giovanni would sigh at the beauty and say that this was his Hollywood ending.

Whenever he did, Vincenzo would agree.

ABOUT THE AUTHOR

Writer and historian Owen Keehnen is the author of fiction and non-fiction books including *Night Visitors, Dugan's Bistro and the Legend of the Bearded Lady*, and *Voices in Isolation: 4 LGBTQ Plays at a Social Distance*. He also recently published *Sex Tour in a Hearse: the Selected Queer Poetry of Owen Keehnen."*

Keehnen has collaborated with St Sukie de la Croix on three volumes of *Tell Me About It*—a queer studies series from Rattling Good Yarns Press in which an array of LGBTQ folks answer specific questions.

For several years, Keehnen has been committed to preserving the rich LGBTQ history of the Belmont Rocks—an organic queerspace from the early 1960s through the 2003 demolition of the site. In June 2022, the area was reopened as AIDS Garden Chicago.

Keehnen was inducted into the Chicago LGBTQ Hall of Fame in 2011 and lives in Chicago with his husband Carl and their dogs, Vince and Daisy.

Instagram: Owen Keehnen

ACKNOWLEDGEMENTS

Thank you to Rattling Good Yarns Press. Ian, thank you for your endless patience and for taking so much time to make sure Watch Me was the best that it could be. Working with you has made me a much better writer. I'm beyond appreciative.